Nice to Come

Home To

Nice to Come

Home To

REBECCA FLOWERS

Riverhead Books

a member of Penguin Group (USA) Inc.

New York   2008

RIVERHEAD BOOKS
Published by the Penguin Group
Penguin Group (USA) Inc., 375 Hudson Street, New York, New York 10014, USA •
Penguin Group (Canada), 90 Eglinton Avenue East, Suite 700, Toronto, Ontario M4P 2Y3,
Canada (a division of Pearson Penguin Canada Inc.) • Penguin Books Ltd, 80 Strand,
London WC2R 0RL, England • Penguin Ireland, 25 St Stephen's Green, Dublin 2,
Ireland (a division of Penguin Books Ltd) • Penguin Group (Australia), 250 Camberwell
Road, Camberwell, Victoria 3124, Australia (a division of Pearson Australia Group Pty Ltd)
• Penguin Books India Pvt Ltd, 11 Community Centre, Panchsheel Park, New Delhi–
110 017, India • Penguin Group (NZ), 67 Apollo Drive, Rosedale, North Shore 0632,
New Zealand (a division of Pearson New Zealand Ltd) • Penguin Books (South Africa)
(Pty) Ltd, 24 Sturdee Avenue, Rosebank, Johannesburg 2196, South Africa

Penguin Books Ltd, Registered Offices: 80 Strand, London WC2R 0RL, England

The author acknowledges permission to reprint lyrics from
"Thunder Road" by Bruce Springsteen. Copyright © 1975 Bruce Springsteen,
renewed © 2003 Bruce Springsteen (ASCAP). Reprinted by permission.
International copyright secured. All rights reserved.

Library of Congress Cataloging-in-Publication Data

Flowers, Rebecca.
Nice to come home to / Rebecca Flowers.
p.   cm.
ISBN 978-1-59448-961-7
1. Single women—Fiction.   2. Sisters—Fiction.   3. Family—Fiction.
4. Adams Morgan (Washington, D.C.)—Fiction.   I. Title.
PS3606.L686N53   2008   2007028922
813'.6—dc22

Printed in the United States of America
1   3   5   7   9   10   8   6   4   2

Book design by Meighan Cavanaugh

This is a work of fiction. Names, characters, places, and incidents either are the product of the author's imagination or are used fictitiously, and any resemblance to actual persons, living or dead, businesses, companies, events, or locales is entirely coincidental.

While the author has made every effort to provide accurate telephone numbers and Internet addresses at the time of publication, neither the publisher nor the author assumes any responsibility for errors, or for changes that occur after publication. Further, the publisher does not have any control over and does not assume any responsibility for author or third-party websites or their content.

For Andrew,

as in all things

Nice to Come Home To

O_{ne}

Prudence Whistler was at a conference at the Sheraton on Connecticut Avenue when she saw the woman she was supposed to be by now.

Pru was trying to persuade the executive director of an important nonprofit to give her a job. She'd followed him out of the Gerald R. Ford Room, where he'd been giving a talk called "Follow the Money!" The conference ("A Passion for Mission!") was for fund-raising professionals, and as if to compensate for the dullness of the proceedings, everything ended with an exclamation point.

As soon as he'd seen that an attractive woman wanted something from him, the executive director scooted right in close to Pru, one hand sliding along her back. He'd pushed a fleshy ear practically into her mouth, although the hallway was empty. Pru tried not to stiffen. She needed a job. She'd been without one for ten days now, the longest she could ever remember. Soon it would be two weeks. Two weeks, with no job. She took a deep breath. He was way inside her personal bubble. He was, in fact, looking down her personal bubble's shirt.

The executive director began fingering the back of her bra strap while Pru blathered on, hardly aware of what she was saying. She still wasn't used to the game. She had hoped that the nonprofit world would be a decent place, full of well-meaning people working shoulder to shoulder for a noble cause. Like how she had first envisioned a Communist society: men and women working together as equals, in matching unisex jumpsuits and caps. She'd had a lot of illusions like that when she'd gotten her first nonprofit job, more than ten years ago, after graduate school. But she'd found that this world, too, had its share of huge egos, inflated salaries, and horrendous working conditions. And also little power games, like this one.

"Prudence," he said, interrupting her spiel. He bent to squint at the small, neat print on the name tag pinned to her chest. "Is that your handwriting? Am I supposed to be able to read that?"

She was barely able to refrain from sighing audibly. She looked at him, trying to find something likable. She tried to imagine him as a younger man. He must miss those days, she thought, high school or maybe college, back when girls would flirt with him because he was cute and played football. Or no; the girls never flirted with him, until he became the executive director of a $20 million-a-year international relief agency. He wasn't super-attractive, but he dressed nicely and his shoes (tasseled loafers—Jesus) were polished. She approved of that, anyway.

"I don't know, maybe you need glasses," she said. It was a pathetic attempt, but he brightened. She was being cheeky with him, a known big shot.

"Hey," he said. The hand on her back now gave her upper arm

a friendly squeeze. "Are you calling me old? I bet I'm not so much older than you. What are you, thirty-five, thirty-six?"

The fake smile she'd been holding slid from her face. She could feel angry tears stinging her eyes. Was he *kidding*?

"Uh-oh," he said, laughing. Had he even bothered to shave off five years, as politeness demanded? Gripping her arm more tightly, he said, "You don't look it, I swear. Listen, I was going to go somewhere better than this for lunch. Come with me. My treat. Come on, let me make it up to you."

He was so close she could feel his breath on the side of her face. That was when she looked up and saw a woman who could be her twin. Tall and broad-shouldered, like Pru, the woman was striding toward her from the other end of the hotel lobby. For a moment, Pru thought she'd caught her own reflection in one of the hotel's ornate gilt mirrors. Then she saw that the woman was enormously pregnant, and accompanied by two little girls marching side by side in bathing suits and the same dime-store daisy-toed flip-flops that Pru and her sister, Patsy, used to wear. Following close behind the woman, carrying pool toys and towels, came a nice-looking husband in a Princeton T-shirt.

Normally Pru would take one look at such a woman and dismiss her as one of those pampered, sheltered, stay-at-home types, whose only burdens were a huge diamond on her finger and a fat fashion magazine under one arm. She would have remembered her clean little apartment in the city, the comfortable arrangement she had with her attentive boyfriend, all the time she had to read books and eat at restaurants and watch movies. She would remember her friend Fiona, who complained constantly about the demands of motherhood. Or her sister, who was raising a daughter by herself on her schoolteacher's tiny salary. And she would have felt grateful for her freedom, glad she and Rudy were waiting until the time was right to get married and have kids.

But today was different. It might have been the letch she was trying to shmooze, breathing down her shirt. Or the fact that, in four more days, it would be exactly two weeks since she'd lost the job that was supposed to advance her career and let her buy a four-bedroom fixer-upper in Cleveland Park and take a nice long maternity leave in the not too distant future. Or maybe it was because Rudy had been out of town all week, at a conference for public television executives in Chicago, where he was so busy they'd only had the briefest of conversations, at night, before she went to sleep.

Or maybe it was because, as a child, Prudence had *loved* family hotel vacations. All of them together, in one room, with real silver on the room service tray, and clean sheets every night. Running through the corridors with Patsy, and riding up and down in the elevators. She'd always wanted to live in a hotel, like Eloise.

Whatever the cause, suddenly all her plans seemed pathetic and narrow. Next to the golden, fructive mother-ship before her, Pru felt like both a withered old spinster and a child. She felt hard and tired out, in her severe worsted wool suit, the sad little scarf she'd tied around her neck to brighten her face announcing her desperation. The woman before her, coming toward her like her own future—*there* was a woman who knew her place in the universe. She would go up to her hotel room tonight, after dinner, and tuck in those little girls, whose arms would linger around her neck for a moment, when she kissed their foreheads. They would smell her perfume, and she would smell their no-more-tears shampoo, and faintly, the chlorine left over from their swim. Pru could imagine it, *all* of it, entirely, all of a sudden. Her fingertips could practically feel the girls' silky hair against the pillowcase. This was a woman who had what a job would never give you. She was loved, and she would never grow old alone.

As Pru watched, transfixed and pained at the vision of herself as wife and mother, the little family moved through a ray of sunlight coming in through the hotel's atrium, so they were lit up, like angels.

Pru felt a grip of fear in her gut. Grow old alone! She'd forgotten about that! She'd been so busy at work that she'd forgotten about growing old—possibly even *dying*—alone. It wasn't so far off now. And people in their thirties got horrible diseases, all the time. What would her 401(k) do for her when she was lying in bed, immobilized by terminal cancer? She could scarcely breathe for the thought of it.

The executive director had turned around to see what had attracted Pru's attention. The sight of the blond, angelic-looking family perhaps reminded him of his own wife and children, because he quickly straightened up and gave Pru a fatherly pat on the back. "Actually, I'm just going to grab a sandwich and eat at my desk," he said. "Good meeting you." And before Pru could recover her composure long enough to give him her business card or even her last name, he was gone.

Behind her, the doors to the Gerald R. Ford Room burst open, and out came the rest of the conference attendees. They streamed from the room and around Pru, heading toward another room that had been set up for lunch. A tributary to the stream headed outside for a cigarette, and another to the bathrooms, while Pru stood rooted to the spot like an old dead tree, blinking in bewilderment, wondering how she'd forgotten to have a husband and children by this point in her life.

. . .

WELL, IT WASN'T LIKE SHE'D FORGOTTEN, EXACTLY.

In the back of her Daytimer, in fact, behind a list of her boyfriend Rudy's faults (or so he called them; she called them, more peaceably, his "pros and cons") and a list of clothes she wanted to buy, was her five-year plan. It had been unfolded and refolded so many times that the edges were soft, and nearly came apart in her hands, like some kind of historical document.

Pru was a believer in lists and plans. She'd made her first five-year plan when she was nine. It had included becoming an astronaut, a schoolteacher, and the mother of four children (two boys and two girls) before turning twenty.

She'd come up with her current, more realistic plan in college. *Married with children by 29,* she read. She remembered making the list in her dorm room, cold winter light pouring in through the window by the desk where she sat writing, a pot of tea steeping nearby. The 29 had since been crossed out, and replaced with 30. Then 32, then 34. And then she'd stopped bothering to update it altogether.

She always thought she'd have a lot of kids. She thought of herself as a maternal person, sensible and loving. She'd played with dolls long past the time when her friends had turned to other things—like Bonne Belle Lip Smackers and *Tiger Beat* magazine—and she was strict but loving with her stuffed animals, each of whom got a turn once a week sleeping next to her on the pillow. Even now, she felt the cravings on the inside of her arms, and somewhere along the base of her jaw, almost like salivary glands, when she held small babies. And she doted on her niece Annali, with her heart-shaped face, her cap of blond curls—but of course, who wouldn't, with a kid like that?

And Rudy was right there, too. He liked kids. His own childhood was a source of immeasurable, endlessly recollectable pleasure for him. He loved comic books, cartoons, and Quisp cereal (which he'd recently given up in favor of low-calorie twigs of bran). The fact that he wanted children, too, had been the most heavily weighted item on her pros-and-cons list (she'd given it five full points). And still, she hadn't been able to pull the trigger. It had now been two months since the last time they'd talked about getting married. Rudy had grown strangely silent on the subject.

She couldn't say why she kept putting him off. She told herself it was because they had a good thing going, so why ruin it? They could be together when they wanted to be, and each had an apartment to retreat to for what they called "me time." Pru had found that, dating Rudy, she needed a lot of "me time."

Being with Rudy could be exhausting. He practically had an advanced degree in pop culture, with an emphasis on his own childhood, and he needed a lot of attention, as the funny often do. Sometimes the apartment seemed so full of Rudy—of Rudy's needs, of Rudy's problems, of Rudy's therapy, his little jokes and his dirty socks.

A few months ago, she'd tried to talk to him about taking a break from seeing so much of each other. She had begun to wonder whether they had really chosen to be together or just fallen into the habit. But then Rudy went through a bad patch. He was promoted from animator to producer, which seemed at the time like a *good* thing; but then the pressure that came with assuming nominal control of the ragtag group of smart, neurotic comedy nerds he used to belong to made him anxious and depressed. It didn't seem right to leave him, just then.

And then the tables turned, and now *she* needed *him*. She'd never been fired before. Not even anything close to that. Right away, she'd thrown herself into the work of finding another job, as though that would erase what had just happened. She found herself missing Rudy, counting the hours until he would be home from work. She wasn't entirely comfortable with that. She wanted to turn the tables back again, so they faced in the proper direction.

In the darkness of the lunchtime session, she gathered up her things and slipped out before the PowerPoint presentation was over. She couldn't wait to get home and rip off her business suit. She wanted to shove it into the back of the closet and never see it again; but of course Pru would never really do that with wool crepe.

She was wasting her time at the conference. This wasn't the direction her future was taking her; she was absolutely certain of that. She had another vision of herself, this time sitting on a primary-colored carpet, playing quietly with a baby. She would wear those capri khakis, maybe, with layered T-shirts, and her cork-wedgie sandals.

Oh, this in-betweenness—how she hated it! They needed to fish or cut bait, as her mother would say. What did she need, big fat red arrows pointing the way? It couldn't have been an accident, seeing in that pregnant woman a vision of her future self. What better time, really, than now, to get married and have children? Didn't people take sabbaticals from their jobs, to write books or do research or whatever? Why not a sabbatical to start a family?

On her way out of the hotel, she happened to spot the little family again. The girls were playing at the koi pond in the lobby. This time, Pru got close enough to the woman so that she could say, "What sweet little girls you have."

"Thanks." The woman beamed. Then she rolled her eyes. They were the same gray-blue as Pru's, under the same straight brows. "Until it's time to go to bed. *That's* when they getcha."

Pru nodded. That was just what she would have said, too—the obvious pride, followed by a touch of humility. Just right, for a woman her age.

Two

"Rudy *Fisch?* God, *why?*"

McKay had a way of saying Rudy's name that made Pru picture a fat, glaring trout.

McKay didn't like Rudy because they had the same sense of humor, and, he said, because Rudy was an asshole.

Pru and McKay were having a beer at the bar under the souvlaki place next to Pru's apartment, on the Friday Rudy was due home. She was meeting him in a few hours, outside the Film Institute. She'd spent the days following her encounter with her future self making plans. (How she loved planning! Always much better than doing.) She found out that to book a wedding venue in D.C., you needed at least a year's notice. She was stunned at the cost—most places asked for $10,000 just to rent them for the day. She was toying now with the idea of a justice-of-the-peace wedding, followed by dinner at one of the nice restaurants in Georgetown for everyone: her mother, sister, and her niece; Rudy's parents (no getting out of that, unfortunately); McKay and Bill, of course; and her best friend Kate McCabe. In her Daytimer now was a newspaper ad for two-bedroom apartments in a new building in Columbia Heights, a not-too-scary but affordable neighborhood near her own neighborhood, Adams-Morgan. She'd love to stay in Adams-Morgan, but it had become so gentrified that she and Rudy would never be able to buy a place there now. There was also a new tab, marked "Stroller Research." She'd even put in a bid on a vintage double Peg Perego she'd found on eBay, currently a steal at $95.50. Sure, she didn't actually have kids, and it would take up half of her living room. The bid was also reckless, in light of the fact that she was trying to cut expenses wherever she could (she'd already canceled her membership at the upscale Y on Rhode Island Avenue, and sworn off cabs). But she couldn't resist. Maybe the stroller would double in the meantime as a plant stand or something. Doing these things made Pru feel less lonely. In fact, this was the happiest she'd been in months.

She wanted to scope out the new building, and so went out for a long late-afternoon walk. She was still surprised to see how many people were out and about in the daytime. There seemed to be no end of people whose lives had nothing to do with dingy offices and jammed photocopiers and rushing for the train home long after the sun went down. For as long as she could remember, she'd done little else besides work. She worked early, she worked late, she worked constantly. She'd carefully pursued her career path, from intern to project manager to development director, where it looked like she'd be stalling out. She'd put in countless hours. She'd spent the money she made on clothes for work, presents for her coworkers, and work-related lunches. After she was let go, she hardly knew what to do with herself. There was almost no reason to get out of bed. She could see how that could become dangerous, leading to a life of slovenly solitude.

And then Rudy left for his conference. She went the whole first day he was gone without saying a single word to anyone. She had to clear her throat to answer the phone when he called that night. Now she made herself say "Good morning" to random people on the street. She told her name to the people who ran the dry cleaners, a nice Korean couple, just to hear someone say it.

Today she was especially restless because Rudy was coming home, so she'd distracted herself by walking into Columbia Heights to see how far the nearest grocery store was from the apartment building she'd read about.

She found the new building, made some careful notes about possible view options, and then returned to Adams-Morgan. On the way home, she'd run into McKay outside his building. He was sitting on the bench in his work suit, looking morose.

She'd known McKay Ettlinger since college, in Ohio. For various reasons they'd both wound up here in D.C., neighbors. She considered it one of the luckiest accidents of her adulthood.

"It's Dolly's birthday," McKay explained, when she plopped down next to him. "She would have been twelve. This is when I'd be taking her out for her walkies."

"Oh, honey," Pru said, lamely. Dolly the pug had been dead for several months, but McKay was still having a hard time. He talked about her constantly. Her loyalty, her loving nature, her unselfish devotion—Pru had heard McKay invoke these qualities as if only one dog ever had embodied them, and not, as far as she could tell, every dog that had ever lived. It was really very sweet, since McKay in all other ways tended toward the cynical. He'd only recently put away Dolly's food dish and her plaid L.L. Bean doggie bed. But he still couldn't bring himself to wash her little nose prints off the sliding glass doors that led to the patio. The last time Pru was there, she had to fight the urge to Windex them off herself. Well, she wasn't a dog person. She put a hand on McKay's shoulder and gave it a little squeeze.

"When I'm dying," said McKay, in his soft Georgia drawl, "I want you to take all measures necessary. Do whatever you have to, to keep me alive. I don't care if all that remains of me is an eyeball on a spinal cord." He closed one eye and talked in a pinched, mechanical voice. "Hello, Prudence," he said, imitating his own future decrepit self. "Come here where I can see you."

"God, not me," said Pru, laughing. "I'm just going to take a fat handful of barbiturates, when my time comes. I can't stand pain." Or the thought of others taking care of her—a grown-up Annali or, worse, Patsy. She imagined them as creaky old women, Pru confined to a hospital bed, unable to do a thing for herself, while Patsy shuffled around ringing little cymbals and chanting healing mantras in Pali. "But I want you to have a big party. With music and dancing and an ice dolphin sculpture on the buffet table. And play Peggy Lee singing 'Is That All There Is?' as I'm being lowered into the ground. *Is that all there is to a fire?*" she intoned, in her best Peggy Lee voice. Of course, she'd had this scenario planned for years.

McKay didn't respond. He just looked at her blankly and said, "Do you think an engraved stone for Dolly would be too much?"

"Come on, girlfriend," she said, pulling him up by the elbow. "You need a drink. It's Friday, and somewhere the sun's over the yardarm, right? And I have a little time before I have to meet Rudy."

She was also thinking that a drink might help her tell McKay. She hadn't said the words out loud yet to anyone. She wanted to wait until she was absolutely sure of herself first. She hadn't even said anything to Rudy, during their brief conversations at night. And certainly, she hadn't told her sister, Patsy.

Partly, she blamed her sister for the fact that she wasn't able to make up her mind about Rudy. Patsy kept asking if Rudy was "the One." She accused Pru of being contented, of settling. Pru wasn't sure she *was* settling; but she wasn't sure she could see what was wrong with that, anyway. Rudy loved her. He told her so all the time. She never had to worry about him being faithful or attentive or responsive. But her sister had put doubts in her head.

Was Rudy the One? *Was* there even a One? If so, who was it, and where the hell was he? How would she even know, when she met him? Maybe Rudy was the One, or on his way to becoming the One. Or maybe he was One of the Ones, as she liked to tell Patsy, much to her sister's annoyance. Patsy had refused to marry Annali's father, because he wasn't the One. Pru couldn't help but feel it was a bit of a selfish decision, on her sister's part. Jimmy Roy had his problems, she couldn't argue with that. But Pru had always liked him. He seemed to sincerely love her sister, and that he adored Annali was beyond question. Was it better to wait for the One than to give your child a home with two loving parents? Pru wasn't sure. But she didn't have big emotions, like her sister.

Anyway, she was sick of wondering about the One. The question bored her. She could hear the boredom in her friends' voices, too, as she revisited the same old topic yet again. Everyone she knew, including her friend Fiona, Patsy—Jesus, even her gay friends—had moved on, long ago. She wanted new questions, like the ones the other women had: What should we name the baby? Epidural or natural birth? Dr. Maurino, Dr. Hamilton, or a midwife? Post-delivery doula, live-in nanny, stay-at-home or work? Montessori, Waldorf, or Reggio? For heaven's sake, she already knew the answers: Josephine or Benjamin, epidural, Hamilton (she'd delivered Fiona's kids), doula, stay-at-home, Montessori!

Even after her first few sips of beer, she couldn't quite get the words out. She knew McKay wasn't going to be thrilled. For one thing, she supposed, it would mean less time with him. The three of them—Rudy, Pru, and McKay—had never worked out. Girlfriend Pru and Best Friend Pru didn't seem to be the same person. It was like when Annali handed her a Barbie and a Teletubby, and demanded a story. Made-up stories weren't Pru's strong suit, much less one with two such disparate characters. (Rudy, she realized suddenly, would have known what to do. See? They *complemented* each other.) With McKay she never gave a second thought to what she did or said, but when she was with Rudy, she sometimes felt—constrained, somehow. McKay didn't like that. She knew—she could feel—that it made her a little rigid.

"Guess what," she finally ventured. "I think we're going to get married. Me and Rudy, I mean." It sounded funny, just saying it out loud.

What other people said with their whole faces, McKay conveyed with eyebrows alone. They were like two batwings that came whooshing down, in full glower, gathering to a scowling point right above his nose. McKay almost never bothered to hide his feelings, one of the things Pru loved most about him.

There was a little silence while he glared. Finally he said, "Rudy *Fisch?* God, *why?*"

"What do you mean, why? Because Rudy loves me."

"So what? Do you have to marry everyone who loves you? *I* love you, and you don't see me going around asking you to marry me." The batwings furrowed even deeper. "Is this because you got fired?"

She winced, and took a long drink of beer. She couldn't even *think* of that word without wanting to squash it down to six-point type, in her head. She hadn't done anything to deserve getting canned. In fact, in retrospect, she felt she should have seen it coming. Her boss was notoriously whimsical and sadistic. There weren't government grants for the arts, like there used to be. She slaved over her proposals—beautifully written, gorgeously punctuated odes addressing the plight of the inner-city children who lacked a proper arts education. She knew how to artfully disguise her budgets to hide the fact that a good chunk of government change was going to pay her boss's undeserved salary. Okay, so, inside, she acknowledged the utter bullshit of the endeavor: *Sorry you didn't get breakfast this morning, kid. Let's decoupage!* And yet, the grants kept coming back rejected. That she'd gotten the boot seemed just plain unfair. *Indecent,* in fact. Maybe she didn't have "A Passion for Mission!" But she'd thrown several good years at that job, and it had come to nothing.

More than that, she was simply not used to failing. She'd never doubted for a moment that she would rise to the level where she belonged. It's what you did, growing up middle class in the Midwest. She'd always climbed whatever ladder was in front of her—the swim team, the high school band flute section, her literature classes—and went up, step by step. It never occurred to her to go *down* a step, not by accident, and certainly not on purpose. People were supposed to be like bread: people *rose.*

"Not at all," she said, defensively. "Well, yes, a little bit. I mean, I'm beginning to think this whole work thing is antifemale. Antifeminist, frankly. It's so male—oh, you have to have a job, so we can define you in some narrow way. What's wrong with just being a wife and a mother? Why do I have to be some other . . . thing?" Not, she reflected ruefully, that she had any idea of what that other thing would be.

McKay looked truly appalled. "God, Pru, when did you start channeling right-wing talk-show fascists?"

"You know what I mean. There's so much pressure to do everything, have everything. I'm just saying maybe that's just another form of oppression." Now, *that* sounded good. "There's got to be something more important to do with all this equipment, you know what I mean?"

"So you're going to marry Rudy because you want to have a baby?"

"Also, you know, I love him." It came out sounding like an afterthought.

McKay was looking at her suspiciously. "You do?"

"Of course I do. I've been with him for years. What did you think?"

"I don't know, I thought you were in it for the sex."

"Girls don't do things just for sex," Pru said. "It's not that hard for us to get. Come on, honey. I gotta get this show on the road. I'm thirty-six. Oh, cut it out, you knew that."

They didn't speak, drinking their beers. In the heat of the day, it didn't take long to feel a little drunk. Then McKay loudly smacked his lips and said, "I hate to admit it, but I always thought Rudy was hot. I was kind of pissed that he went for you, not me."

Pru pressed the cold bottle to her face, pleased. Rudy *was* hot, with intelligent, green eyes and black, curly hair. And until she'd gotten to him, he hadn't known it. He'd dressed in sloppy over-sized clothes, with big plastic, geeky-on-purpose glasses. She made him buy some nice new clothes that fit, and more flattering glasses. She took him to her own hairdresser, Samuel, to have his hair cut. And she'd persuaded him to work his shtick a little bit less when out in public. He still embarrassed her sometimes, but the way he took her suggestions, his desire to please her, touched her deeply. She'd thought it a stroke of genius on her part: Rather than fight over the obvious desirable guys, she'd made one for herself.

"I did some good work on that boy," she said. "You wouldn't know him as the same person from two years ago. He's like my Eliza Doolittle."

"More like your Frankenstein," McKay replied. "So, when is this whole wedding thing happening?"

"Soon, I think. There was a kind of we-need-to-talk-tonight e-mail from him this morning."

"What kind of we-need-to-talk?"

She shrugged. "I don't know, just that. Just, we need to talk tonight."

"That could be anything, you know."

"Like what?"

"Like anything."

She'd been so happy to see that e-mail. She wasn't used to feeling out of touch with Rudy. Quite the opposite. She was usually besieged with e-mails and phone calls from Rudy, even when he was just a mile away, at his office downtown. The most she'd been able to get out of him all week was that he'd met Ken Burns in a session on documentary film programming, and that his dry cleaning needed to be picked up.

While McKay went to the men's room, she ordered another round. It was almost too bad she had to leave soon to meet Rudy. She and McKay were so comfortable together they could sit and watch grass grow. In fact, the summer after college, when McKay's roommate seemed to have unlimited access to dime bags, they probably *had* watched grass grow. God, she hadn't gotten high in ages. She didn't know anyone who smoked pot anymore. She hadn't particularly enjoyed the smell, the dirty bong, or how it made her feel—thirsty and, later, paranoid—but she liked its calming effect. And how, when stoned, you were semi-quarantined with those who got you that way.

"Hey, Rudy'll age well, too, don't you think?" she said, when McKay returned from the bathroom.

McKay rolled his eyes. "If you don't kill him first."

"You're just jealous. Always the bridesmaid . . ."

McKay snorted. "Baby, I can get married whenever I want. I can get married before *you*."

Pru smiled. McKay with his back up was preferable to McKay pining for his dog. In fact, there wasn't anything much more entertaining than McKay with his back up.

"Oh yeah?" she said. "Prove it."

"Fine," he said. "I will." He plucked his cell phone out of the breast pocket of his jacket and dialed his home number. He put it on speaker, so Pru could hear.

"Hey," said Bill's voice, after a few rings.

"Hey, it's me. You want to get married?"

There was a pause. Then Bill said, "Troy? I told you never to call me here."

"Ha-ha," said McKay. "Pru's here, by the way."

"Hi, Pru," said Bill, laughing. "Sure, let's get married. Why not?"

"But we won't have Dolly, to be our ring-bearer," McKay said. "I was going to tie a little silk pillow on to her back."

Bill ignored this. "Why don't you stop on your way home and get some souvlaki?" he said. "If you're not too drunk, of course."

"I know what will cheer you up," Pru said, as they emerged from the dark bar into sunlight, blinking like night ferrets. "Let's go to the shelter and look at some doggies. I mean, I know no dog could ever replace the Dolly Lama. But maybe it's okay just to look."

"I don't know. It doesn't feel right to me, not yet."

"It's not like you're going to have another one right away. I mean, look how long it took you two to choose paint for your bathroom." Pru had threatened to kill herself if they asked her to look at those paint chips—"Butterfrost" or "Sandy Toes"—one more time.

"Hmm," he said. She could see he was warming to the idea. "Well, maybe. I keep hearing about these rescued greyhounds. I always liked the idea of that, you know, giving an old race dog a good retirement home." They were standing at the steps in front of Pru's building. "Listen," McKay said, surprisingly serious. "If you marry Rudy, you're going to have to live with him. And his cat. Didn't you say he had a cat?"

Trust McKay to remember that Rudy had a cat. She'd totally forgotten. She'd met the cat only once, the one time she'd agreed to sleep over at Rudy's apartment. The instant she opened her eyes in the morning she became depressed, seeing the grim, oatmeal-colored Berber carpeting, a harsh ray of sun stealing around the edges of the cheap window shade. She felt someone watching her, and looked around to see Rudy's enormous, beat-up-looking cat sitting nearby, staring hard at her. She put out a friendly hand for the cat to sniff, but it hissed and spat at her as if she'd extended a dog paw. Without taking its eyes from her, the cat slowly backed out of the room. It was the strangest thing she had ever seen, oddly deliberate and menacing. The message couldn't have been clearer: *Stay away or I will claw your eyes out, girly.*

So she'd deal with the cat. She'd already dealt with so much. She'd worked hard to get Rudy to trust her, and to let down his guard a bit, when they were together. Bit by bit, he'd begun to show her more sides of himself, open up and reveal things about his childhood, how poorly parented he'd been. Pru had been well parented, and she felt it was a duty of the well-parented to help the others adjust. Just recently he'd reported that his therapist had said he was making "great strides in the trust department." Pru kept imagining Rudy marching with giant steps across the floor of a brightly lit department store, like Macy's. The trust department would be on the same floor as the mattresses and box springs.

"You'll be happy for me, right?" she said.

"Of course." McKay hugged her. "And we'll do anything you want, for the wedding."

"Thanks, honey."

"But don't put me in pastels," he said. "Pastels wash me right out."

Three

Rudy was late.

Pru was standing outside the theater, in her carefully chosen possibly-getting-engaged outfit. She'd allowed herself the fantasy that Rudy meant to surprise her by taking her to the Inn at Little Washington, where he would have reserved the banquette with the velvet privacy curtain and a view of the gardens, in order to renew his offer of marriage. She knew she had very little reason to think this might happen. Rudy was just as likely to ask her to marry him in Joe's Joe. And maybe McKay was right, and we-need-to-talk wasn't about anything more than that he'd missed her. But just in case, she'd chosen a pretty skirt and the vintage cardigan she'd found at a thrift store. She would have liked to have worn her kitten-heel shoes, but the kitten heels would put her a fraction of an inch taller than Rudy. She'd worn satiny ballet flats instead.

But when Rudy finally showed up, he wasn't dressed for anything special. He wore the French blue shirt she gave him for his last birthday, good jeans, and what he referred to as his "gay guy" glasses. No jacket, no tie. Not proposal wear, as even Rudy would know. He brushed the side of her mouth with his lips and hurried into the theater, saying that he didn't want to miss the opening credits.

Pru stood on the sidewalk for a moment, fixing her lipstick with the edge of her thumb. She had forgotten that sometimes she was the most fond of Rudy when she wasn't actually *with* Rudy.

WHEN THEY HAD FOUND SEATS THAT WERE TO RUDY'S satisfaction and had settled themselves, Pru asked, "How was the conference?"

"Let's talk later."

She was quiet a moment, then said, "Oh, money, your money doesn't money." It was one of Rudy's favorite quotes. Maybe from *The Simpsons,* she thought. She had no idea what it meant, and she always got it wrong, but it cracked him up.

This time, however, he forced a little smile and nodded his head, stiffly. "You always get that wrong," he said.

They watched an older couple choosing their seats. The pair had to loudly discuss the merits of each one, and finally settled on two a few rows away. Pru thought they looked sweet, but Rudy breathed out a loud sigh and muttered, "Thank *God.*" Rudy hated unnecessary talking during a movie.

"I fell in love with a family while you were gone," she said. "A whole family, even the . . ."

"Hon, let's just watch the opening sequence. It's the best camera work in the film." He took her hand and kissed it, a moment later putting it back in her lap.

While he watched the screen, Pru watched him. She wondered how Rudy's features would look on a child. She decided that they could have his curly, dark hair, his square jaw. Those things from him, and her basic personality structure. Nice, easy kids, not crazy, neurotic ones.

PRU HAD TO JOG TO KEEP UP WITH HIM, AS THEY threaded their way down Wisconsin toward Joe's Joe, their usual post-movie coffee shop. She was still feeling a little lost, remembering the scene where Grace Kelly turns on three lights in Jimmy Stewart's apartment as she recites her full name: *Reading from top to bottom, Lisa [click]—Carol [click]—Fremont [click].* Pru was fascinated by that third lamp, a simple pleated shade hanging from the ceiling. She'd never seen anything so beautiful in her life. While she trailed after Rudy she put together in her mind the Google search she'd use to find one just like it. Barrel shade, pendant, pleated? He scooted through the line at Joe's and sat waiting for her at a small table, near the restrooms. Rudy could be so oblivious. A table by the restrooms! She quickly scanned the other tables, then somewhat reluctantly sat down with her tea.

Rudy said, immediately, "We have to talk about something." He was sitting on the edge of his chair, jiggling his foot.

"God, Rudy," she said, "you're as nervous as a long-tailed cat in a room full of rocking chairs." He didn't even smile at her reference—another one of his favorites. Or maybe it was one of McKay's. She sometimes got them confused.

In fact, Rudy looked a little ill. She hadn't thought he'd be so worked up about asking her to marry him again, having already done it three times before. She reached out and took his hand, and gave it an affectionate, encouraging squeeze.

He took a deep breath, then said in a steadier voice, "I think it's time to take a little break, P.W."

A girl at a table behind Rudy burst out laughing. For a minute, Pru thought the girl was laughing at them. She was having trouble working out what was happening.

"What did you say?"

Rudy shrugged a little, scrunching up the skin on his jaw so that she could see the wrinkles that would one day be etched there permanently. "Not be so dependent on each other," he said. "Give each other some breathing room. Some space."

Pru frowned, and adjusted her glasses. Rudy wanted space? She didn't want Rudy to want space. She wanted him to want to marry her.

"If we do this," she said, "it's hard to see how we'd go back."

"I realize that."

She tried again. "To being a couple, I mean," she said. She lowered her voice. "To *sleeping* together. I don't know how we'd go back to that." He'd been so naïve when she'd first met him, surprised that she would go out with him, then grateful when she'd slept with him. She used to tell him to go easy on that gratitude. The rocky shoals of sexual etiquette were ones only dimly perceived by Rudy. He knew so little about it. She'd had to teach him *everything.*

"I know, Pru." He said it gently, almost . . . condescendingly.

"A break, that sounds like you want to"—she couldn't believe she was even saying it—"break up?"

"Yeah. I guess that's right. I'm really sorry, P.W."

She was still holding his hand, and it was sweaty. Or maybe it was her hand that was sweaty. Rudy reached over and put his other hand on top, sandwiching her hand between both of his. She did not like how this made her feel, like deli meat, like cheese. His hands were not much bigger than her own, but the move was accompanied by a power shift so real she could feel it. She had the wild thought to shift it back again by covering up the pile of hands with her free one. But it was all too easy to picture this game going on forever, each of them pulling out the bottom hand to place it on top, over and over. She tried to slow her breathing, and ease her hand back into her lap in a non-horrified way. She looked at the cardigan folded in her lap. *I'm really sorry.* Her boss had said that, too. He'd also said, *Your services are no longer required.* What was she, a garbageman? A hooker?

She tried to steady her voice. "You know, Rudy, when I tried to break up with you, *two months ago,* you said your therapist didn't think it was a good idea."

"Do you want to be the one to break up? That's fine. You can be the one. I don't care."

"That's not the point."

"What *is* the point?"

She couldn't come up with anything. Maybe it was the point, after all. God*damn* it, she wanted that lamp!

"I just don't understand *why.* This is all coming out of no-where."

"You're still trying to change me," Rudy said, putting his cup down so roughly that it clattered in its saucer. "I'm sick of feeling not good enough. I'm sick of feeling like, if I wear the wrong pants, we're back to square one."

She was so relieved that she almost smiled at him. She'd been afraid he was going to tell her she'd become too desperate, too—just thinking about the word made her cringe—*needy.* "Come on, you haven't done that in a long time."

"Not funny, Pru."

She looked at him. He wasn't really here, she realized. He could barely sit still while she slowly digested what he'd said. "This is crazy. What we have is bigger than all this, right?"

"I don't think so. I think this is all we're about, actually. Me working my ass off to try to please you, who is never satisfied."

Working his ass off? *Really.* How hard was it to let her choose his clothes, direct his haircuts? But at least it sounded more like the old Rudy. She knew how to talk to this Rudy—the petulant, almost whiny one. They'd had this same discussion a hundred times.

Her voice softened. "But I thought you wanted to change. I thought you *liked* changing."

He nodded. "Then I realized that I'm okay, just the way I am."

"Rudy." She leaned forward. "Who *told* you that?"

But she knew. The damn therapist.

Just then, his cell phone rang. He turned a little in his chair, but he was shouting so it wasn't hard to hear what he was saying, even above the racket of the café's espresso machine. What were those kids doing with that damn thing, banging it with wrenches? It was like being in a machine shop. "Yeah," he yelled, "I just told her. What? No, of *course* not."

Pru leaned forward. Of course not *what?* What hadn't she done?

"Who was that?" she said, after he hung up.

"Just Dr. Schwaiger," he said, as if it was a perfectly normal thing for your shrink to call you up at eleven o'clock on a Friday night. He closed the phone with a sharp snap, not looking at her. "I better go."

What a mistake that damn therapist had been. And it was all her fault! She had persuaded him to go into therapy in the first place, had even found Andrea Schwaiger for him. For the first month, he'd referred to her as "the rapist"—of course, from a TV skit. But then he'd gotten into it. *Way* into it. Dr. Schwaiger made him feel validated and confirmed. She told him everything he felt and did and wanted was okay. For Pru, Rudy's therapy had been a bitter disappointment, making him more Rudy-like, not less.

"Is this about the stupid list?" Pru said.

"It's not about the list. Listen, I have to go. Are you going to be all right?"

Pru straightened up in her chair. She smoothed her skirt with her hands. It was a very good skirt, new, with sharp pleats. It looked solid black until she moved, and then you saw white inside the pleats. It was the last thing she'd bought before losing her job, at Edie's on Connecticut. How she wished Edie's was open right now! "All right? Of course I'm going to be all right."

"See what I mean?" Rudy said. "We've been together for years, and you're acting like nothing big is happening. That's exactly what I'm talking about. You're a very *shut-down* person, you know that?"

She was silent, stung. Shut-down? She was shut-down? How long had she been waiting for him to come home? That shit. She'd had dozens of reasons to leave him, and she never had. Except that one time, two months ago, when she'd tried, and he had pleaded with her not to, and so she hadn't.

Rudy stood. As Pru began to rise he quickly leaned over to hug her, crouched above her chair, in an awkward squat. "Take care of yourself, P.W.," he whispered. Oh, that stupid nickname. He got it from some Pee-wee Herman movie, and thought it was hilarious to call her that. Pru smiled and said, too loudly, "And you take care of yourself, too!" Her own phony tone rang in her ears.

She sat back down and made herself slowly finish her tea. The girls at the next table were laughing again. After a minute, she started to relax. Rudy didn't really mean any of this. It was probably something his therapist had suggested, and he had taken it out of context. Rudy was highly impressionable. When they were calmer, they'd talk things out.

But in the cab home (screw the cost, she'd thought, flagging it down with her purse) she started fuming. What was she supposed to do now? Damn it, how were they going to make this up? How long would he wait before calling? He never went to sleep without calling to say good night first. Surely, with the sight of her before him, he'd have to think about what he'd done, and call her, begging her to forget it all. Anyway, that's what the Rudy she knew would do.

She looked out the window at the passing lights of Dupont Circle. He said it wasn't about the list but, naturally, it was. He wasn't supposed to have seen it, of course. It was meant to be private. It was just how she did things. She liked to look at all the angles, laid out in two columns, side by side. She didn't seem to have strong gut feelings telling her what to do, like other people. And wasn't who you loved one of the most important decisions of your life? But when she saw him charging out of her bedroom with her planner, his face contorted with rage, she knew she had been wrong to do it.

"*Number three,*" he read, his voice shaking. "*Unpredictable and sweaty.*"

Pru was horrified, ashamed, and sorry; but also annoyed, and not sorry. She said, in a conciliatory way, "Okay, now, that was when you first started the meds. That's gotten *way* better."

"*Immature and embarrassing.*"

"What about the pros? Did you even look at the pros? Dependable, loving, and committed?"

"Disaster, nightmarish, possibly sociopathic parents."

She didn't know what to say about that one. Even if she'd been twice as much in love with Rudy Fisch, she would have thought long and hard about joining a family like *that*. Anyway, Pru had been nice to them. She'd even told Rudy that they weren't as bad as he'd made them out to be. Wasn't she allowed some private thoughts? It wasn't like she'd taken out an ad, for crissake.

She had the cab driver drop her off at the video store next to her building. She loved her block and instantly felt better just being there. There was a Turkish carpet store, the souvlaki shop, the Korean dry cleaners, where someone carefully wrapped the buttons of her sweaters in foil before cleaning them, and, occupying the corner lot, the Kozy Korner, a divey little eggs-and-coffee shop. McKay had told her that the place was supposed to have been bought recently by Starbucks, but somehow the deal hadn't gone through. McKay seemed to know, through his network of gay friends, just about everything happening in the city. Pru had been a little disappointed about the Starbucks falling through. It might have driven the offensive Cluck-U Chicken out of business.

The Cluck-U was on the other side of the video store from Pru's building. Its exterior signage featured not a chicken, but a flashing neon bantam rooster smoking a cigar. The bird was leaning toward the pedestrians on the street and winking, as its nauseating yellow light flashed away. The lurid sign had almost been enough to make her pass on the apartment, initially. She wondered what it was about a rooster smoking a cigar that said to people, *Come on in and eat poultry!* She tried not to see it, the many times she was forced to walk underneath it every day. But the rooster had an insidious way of drawing her attention. She could practically smell its disgusting cigar-and-pellets breath. She went into the video store and straight to the "Great Directors" wall. She had a sudden yen for the extreme violence of Don Vito Corleone and his brood. She would spend the whole weekend watching them blow one another's brains out.

When she put the trilogy on the counter, Phan gave her a knowing look and said, "Uh-oh."

Today Phan's spiky, usually black hair was dyed green, and he wore a Pat Benatar T-shirt. It showed a pair of red lips and the words HELL IS FOR CHILDREN! Phan's bony chest was like a rotating billboard of artifacts from Pru's young adulthood, years and years before his own.

"What 'uh-oh'?" she said. She had a little crush on Phan. Mostly it was because of how Phan's girlfriend looked at him, from her seat on the milk crate behind the counter, where she sometimes sat while he worked. Phan's girlfriend wore striped knee socks and a pair of ponytails, like a child. Pru thought her name was something like "Chuckie." She looked at Phan with such open adoration that Pru had to wonder what was behind it.

"Man, every time you break up with someone, you come in for *The Godfather.*"

"No, really?"

Phan consulted the computer screen in front of him. "Five times in six years," he said.

Pru counted them off, in her head. Phil, Jack, Steve, Gay/Not Gay David, and Nate. Now Rudy. Pathetic, wasn't it, when the guy at the video store knew your own love life better than you? And so many of them! Maybe Patsy was right. Maybe she was indiscriminate.

"Well, I like the violence. Is that so wrong?"

"So what's up with Rudy? Did you toss him out?"

Pru pulled her wallet from her purse. "I don't know. We're working on some things."

"Too bad. I liked Rudy." Phan shook his head, as if recalling something particularly hilarious. "That guy cracks me up."

That's what everyone said about Rudy, even McKay. Until recently, anyway. As much as she hated to admit it, he'd been happier drawing all day and thinking up stupid jokes, with bad hair and glasses and the sloppy clothes. Pru tried to remember if he'd started a new antidepressant med lately. That would certainly account for his behavior tonight. It always took his brain a few weeks to settle down, whenever Schwaiger adjusted his meds. When he was on Wellbutrin he used to chew his fingernails down to the quick.

"Listen, girlfriend," said Phan, handing the change to her. "I can get you some good drugs."

"Next time," said Pru. "Anyway, doesn't that just make you more depressed, in the end?"

Phan shrugged. "I'm a Buddhist. We don't get depressed."

"What do you mean? Everyone gets depressed."

"Yeah," Phan said, "but not Buddhists."

"Why not?"

"We know how to suffer."

She took the videos from him. "Okay. How?"

"Very carefully?" he said, smiling at her, so she could see the tips of his white teeth. "Also, I like Ecstasy."

AT HOME, SHE COLLECTED EVERYTHING THAT HAD BE-
longed to Rudy, including two half-eaten boxes of his diet cereal, a SpongeBob SquarePants toothbrush, and three Brooks Brothers

shirts he kept in her closet. She put it all in a shopping bag by the door. Brooks Brothers! When she met him he was still wearing "no-iron" shirts from JCPenney. It was all her fault. She'd turned him into a pompous ass. She should have left some of him the way she'd found him, eager and unfinished. That was just the problem: He *was* unfinished, still. Hot, but unfinished. Or finished badly. McKay was right—she'd created a monster. A hot monster.

She'd thought it was so clever of her, fixing him up. But now she felt twinges of something having been not quite right. Maybe it just didn't work that way. Like how her grandmother could never eat the food she herself cooked, never enjoying a meal as much as when someone else cooked it. Maybe it was impossible to look at your own creation the way Phan's girlfriend looked at Phan from her seat behind the counter in the video store, mute with admiration.

In the bottom of her linens trunk she found a set of sheets, pale green and purple flowers, that she couldn't remember using with Rudy. She changed her bed, throwing the old sheets in the wash. It was almost midnight. He still hadn't called.

She watched *The Godfather* until Moe Greene got it in the eye, then put on clean pajamas. The pajamas refreshed her, as did cleaning up her apartment and watching Mo Green get it in the eye.

She lay in bed listening to the bass *thrum* from a passing car seven floors below. Her windows looked over the busiest part of the busiest street in Adams-Morgan, what some hopefully called the "Greenwich Village" of the District. It was a stretch, even Pru had to acknowledge. There was no Cluck-U Chicken in the Village, as her friend Kate McCabe never tired of pointing out. Kate was a true New Yorker who happened to have grown up in Ohio, two streets over from Pru. A couple of times a year Pru would take the Chinatown bus to see Kate, or Kate would visit

Pru. Between D.C. and New York it was only $14 each way, and someone always gave you a greasy homemade dumpling in a paper bag.

The phone rang. Pru saw Rudy's number come up on her caller ID display, and something she'd been holding in her belly seemed to settle. She put the handset on her chest, and let it ring again. She knew he would call. *Knew* it. Knew Rudy really wouldn't leave her.

After all, that was the *whole point* of Rudy.

She let her voicemail pick up, waited a decent interval, then dialed the voicemail access number. This would be good for them, she thought, listening to the mechanical voice telling her there was one new message. The ebb and flow, the up and down of the grown-up relationship. It was something Rudy had only very limited experience with. He'd see how going through a rough patch together, swallowing their pride and forgiving each other, could deepen their relationship. They'd see the tender goodness in each other, how they were each, in their own way, doing their best.

She wondered what she should say. Should she call him right back and forgive him tonight, or wait until tomorrow? It depended of course on his apology. He'd *absolutely* have to find another therapist, that was the first thing . . .

"Hey," said Rudy's voice, "how are you? It's Rudy. Listen, I forgot to ask you about the TV. I know you don't use it much, anyway, and it set me back a couple K. I guess I could pay you for it, if you wanted. It's used now, but, well, let me know what you'd want for it. But I'm also happy just to come and take it off your hands. I know you don't use it much anyway. Okay, hope you're well. Bye."

She punched the button to delete the message, hung up the phone, and turned out the light. Then she sat up and turned the light back on. She threw off the covers and jumped out of bed. She shuddered, although the room was hot and stuffy. How stupid she had been. What a *fool* she'd been.

She threw on her bathrobe and slippers and took the elevator down to the basement. She found the moving dolly stored there for new move-ins, and wheeled it back upstairs. The thirty-seven-inch plasma TV Rudy had given her for Christmas stood in its place on the far side of her living area. "A couple K." Had he always been like that?

She yanked the TV's electrical cord out of the wall socket, unhooked the cable, and hoisted the set onto the dolly. She pulled it into the elevator, through the front lobby, and out the front doors of her apartment building. She barely noticed that it was after midnight and she wore almost nothing under her robe.

How would anyone ever love her again? she thought, bumping the dolly down the front stairs. They'd find out, sooner or later, that she'd slept with *him*—indecent, unkind, ridiculous Rudy Fisch. They'd be walking down the street, she and her new love, and they would run into Rudy, bouncing along happily. "Who's that?" the new love would say, and she'd be forced to admit it: "An old boyfriend." Whoever was loving her until that moment would suddenly see her in a new light and think, *Is that who I'm to follow? Does she have no standards at all? What does that say about me?* No, it was impossible. Rudy Fisch had ruined her life forever. She felt as if he'd left her with some kind of horrible disease.

She had almost gotten the TV down the front steps of her building when she got stuck. She was hunched over as far as she could, but the dolly wouldn't budge. Hell, she thought, just let it go. She was about to let it smash into fifteen thousand pieces, when, suddenly, there were feet on the other side of the dolly, and the television's weight was being eased from her straining back. She looked up and saw a face attached to the feet. It was a man's face. She knew him from the neighborhood, but in her overwrought state she couldn't remember exactly where. She let go as the man took the dolly and eased it down the last step. "Funny time to be moving," he said. He was wearing a pair of stained, baggy chef's pants. They made him look like a half-dressed clown.

"Thanks," Pru said. "I can get it." She took the dolly from him and dragged it to the curb.

"Are you just going to leave it there?" he called after her.

"It belonged to my boyfriend," Pru said, over her shoulder. "My *ex*-boyfriend."

A battered old Chevy Impala sped by, slowed, then backed up. The Impala's back fender hung at an angle. The car stopped and two young, lean guys got out. They nodded in a brisk, professional way to Pru, picked up the TV, and put it in the car's trunk.

"Hey, wait a minute." The man in the chef's pants started to move, but Pru put up her hand. She said, "No, let them." She felt like Sonny Corleone.

It was as if everything had been pre-arranged. The two guys got back in the Impala and drove away, Rudy's TV peeking out of the trunk.

Suddenly, Pru was exhausted. She remembered the puzzled look on her mother's face as Pru was opening the enormous box on Christmas morning. A television wasn't considered a proper gift in the Whistler family. Rather, it was one of those necessities that couldn't help being as awful as it was, like the toilet plunger. Still, Nadine was hopeful about what such a costly thing must mean. Finally, a serious prospect, for Pru. Not just another one of those losers she seemed to attract, like flies at a barbecue.

She stood in the neon light of the flashing Cluck-U Chicken sign, watching the Impala bounce away. She could feel the glare of the bantam rooster behind her, mocking her. It was a rather shallow victory, after all. Rudy would just buy another TV. But she would never get back what she had lost. Everything she thought she was working for, gone. No job, no boyfriend. And no babies, anytime soon. Her hands went to the belt on her bathrobe. Was she even dressed? She couldn't remember.

The man in the stupid pants was still standing there, watching the Impala's rear lights fade in the distance. "Do you think he's going to be upset?" he said, turning to her.

"I certainly hope so," said Pru. Her eyes and nose were beginning to burn. *Oh no,* she thought.

"Hey," he said. He was looking at her with concern. She realized what a figure she must cut, out there in her robe and slippers, her glasses slipping down her nose, with its layer of grease. "Gee, I'm sorry," he said gently. "You must have loved him a lot."

"No." Pru shook her head. "Not really. Not hardly at all."

Then, to her horror, she burst into tears.

Four

Of course, she had cried when her father died.

She just hadn't cried at the cemetery. While her mother and Patsy wept, without restraint and copiously, on either side of her, Pru's attention had landed on a nick that ran down the left side of her father's casket. The nick wasn't there before, when they showed her the casket at the funeral home. Leonard wouldn't have cared about it at all, himself. But Pru couldn't hear a word of her father's eulogy, she was so troubled by the thought of him going to the hereafter with a nick in a casket that had cost almost a thousand dollars. As her sister and mother sobbed and clutched at her hands, Pru sighed deeply. There was nothing she could do about it now. She straightened up and put one arm around her mother and the other around her sister, then turned them slowly away from her father's grave and to the graveled path that led back to the cars.

Now, standing out on the street under the glow from the Cluck-U Chicken at midnight, wearing her old bathrobe, she started crying for her father all over again. She cried so hard that she couldn't breathe. She gulped noisily. Then she cried because Rudy had deserted her and her boss had fired her for no good reason. She moved on to cry about those babies which wouldn't be happening in the imaginable future, and because there was no one anywhere to take care of her. Finally, she cried because her niece Annali didn't have a father and because children all over the world were starving. It felt like she had to cry for all the things she hadn't let herself cry about since the last time she'd cried. This was why Pru didn't cry often, especially in front of other people. It was such a wracking, gruesome affair.

When she ran out of things to cry about, she stopped and looked around. She felt quite calm. The guy in the chef's pants was still standing there, staring at Pru as though she were a car that was giving him trouble.

"Is that it?" he said, hopefully.

"I think so," she said. She did a little check, to see if another sob was on the way. When one didn't come she said, "Yes. Seems to be."

"Well, I don't know what your ex did, but whatever it was, he must be a jerk."

She wanted to agree, to give him specifics on exactly how much of a jerk Rudy was. But somewhere in her gut she knew that Rudy hadn't been entirely without good reason for dumping her. Not entirely. Something was lacking in their relationship, something he probably deserved. She was too tired to think about it now. Later, when she would sift through all this, she'd have to look at it then, and she had the feeling she wasn't going to be too thrilled with what she saw of her own behavior.

"My name is John Owen," the man said, putting out his hand. Pru looked at his face for the first time. Small eyes and a square chin, a bit of stubble. Of course, he'd be handsome, in addition to being kind. She relaxed a little when she saw the wedding band on his finger. If she was going to meet a handsome man in this pathetic state, best that he should be unavailable.

"Prudence. Whistler," she added, because she didn't know if "Owen" was a double first name, or a last name. She shook his hand. "Thanks for stopping to help me."

"You're welcome," said John Owen. "Are you going to be okay?"

"Oh," she said. "Yeah. I never watched much television, anyway." She hadn't gotten to finish *The Godfather*. That was a loss, right there. Well, she could get the DVD and watch it on her laptop, in bed.

Bed. It seemed that she couldn't wait another minute to get there. She turned and walked up her steps, with as much dignity as she could muster, in her ratty old slippers.

JUST BEFORE DAWN SHE WOKE UP FROM A DREAM WHERE she was falling from the sky. In the dream, she had jumped out of an airplane only to discover that the pack on her back held not a parachute, but a bologna sandwich. She watched in horror as the bread and the bologna floated away, the slice of yellow American cheese falling uselessly to the ground like a thick yellow blanket. It was a dream Rudy would have loved.

Pru got up and opened the window, letting in the humid night air. It was raining lightly. She could hear the bums below having an argument. Their voices were drowned out by the rumble of a passing bus, the peel of its wheels on the pavement. She remembered that her sister Patsy had gone around the house burning some kind of herb when her boyfriend, Jimmy Roy, took off for the Antarctic, just after Annali's second birthday. Pru hadn't seen her doing this, but it wasn't hard to conjure up the image of Patsy stomping around their mother's little house waving the smoking sheaf of dried leaves, in the military boots and overcoat she preferred at the time, looking like some kind of New Age angry villager.

In general Pru found her sister's belief system to be a bit specious and random, a sort of half-baked mishmash of pseudo-Oriental beatnik mysticism, but right now watching something go up in flames didn't sound so bad. And if it drove Rudy's presence out of the apartment, all the better. She went into the kitchen, but all she could find was some old garlic salt and a bottle of Mrs. Dash. Somehow she didn't think you were supposed to burn Mrs. Dash in your apartment to rid it of ex-lovers' spirits. And anyway, it had been Rudy's. He liked to sprinkle it on his scrambled egg whites. Since becoming hot, Rudy watched his weight with the vigilance of a teenage girl. Egg whites, not yolks. Brown rice, not white. Sauces on the side, please. He'd grown more and more vain, spending long hours at the gym, looking askance at Pru when she ordered the occasional cheeseburger and fries.

"Please," she would say. "I happen to know you were raised on Hostess Ding Dongs."

"Exactly," said Rudy. "Which is why our kids will eat nothing but spelt."

"And no TV, right?"

"Oh, no. There's nothing wrong with television. Why, that's the best part of being a kid!"

They used to talk like that all the time. They'd already had fights about baby names. She wondered how much of that had been because they'd been unhappy. Had they really wanted children together, she wondered, or had it only become a way of filling up the empty space between them? She had a vision of Rudy and herself as George and Martha in *Who's Afraid of Virginia Woolf?*, drunkenly shrieking at each other about their imaginary dead son. Except, of course, Rudy never drank anything stronger than chocolate Yoohoo.

She tossed the Mrs. Dash bottle into the trash, then took all the bags of Rudy's things she'd collected and threw them down the chute in the hall. She'd wait until morning and call Patsy to find out what herb it was she was supposed to burn.

And that would be it for Rudy, she thought, getting back into bed. She'd been through this before. Five times in the last six years, as Phan had pointed out. She knew it would hurt for a few days or so, and she'd feel sorry for herself for a few days longer. Then she'd move on. These hadn't been huge losses in her life. They had left her lonely, and blue, and with the sense that maybe she was going through all this for what had been not such a great relationship, to start with. Already, she was feeling she was over Rudy. She wasn't longing for him. For someone, yes, but if she was being honest, she couldn't say that it was *Rudyness* that she wanted, that she missed. McKay was probably having a harder time tonight without Dolly than she was without Rudy.

Somehow, that wasn't as comforting a thought as it should have been.

"OH, YOU TOLD HIM RIGHT FUCKING OFF, DIDN'T YOU?" her sister Patsy yelped into the phone, later that morning. "Tell me you told him right fucking off!"

"Sure, I told him right fucking off," Pru said. "You know me. Just try and stop me from telling people right fucking off."

"God, it's like an alternative universe," Patsy said. "Rudy breaking up with *you*. I just never would have imagined it, in a million years. He was weak, Pru," she concluded. "Beware of the weak. They'll throw you overboard first, if you know what I mean."

Pru crawled into the window seat where she could look out onto Columbia Road. The neighborhood was just getting moving. One of the Manoushian brothers was opening the Manoushian Brothers carpet shop across the street. And today was the day they set up the farmer's market in the bank's parking lot. Soon the street would be crowded with people, shopping. With *couples*, shopping. She and Rudy used to be among those couples, vetting vegetables for Saturday-night dinner, holding hands loosely as they moved through the stalls.

"What's going on with you guys? How's my baby girl?"

Patsy ignored her. "They *hate* it when your chi dominates theirs. It was bound to happen. You have to find someone who has chi equal to yours. Rudy's chi was for shit."

"I'll have to start asking if I can see a guy's chi before going out with him."

Pru had waited to call until her mother's Saturday-morning Senior Scrabble, but now she could hear her voice in the background, saying anxiously, "Rudy? What about Rudy?" Patsy had her own house, just down the street from the house where they'd grown up, and where Nadine still lived. But she was almost always there, anyway, doing her laundry and, Pru suspected, mooching whatever she could.

"That pig," Patsy continued, ignoring Nadine. "I can't believe he took you to a *movie* first."

"You would have laughed. It was hilarious."

That's what she'd decided to tell everyone: It was hilarious! The whole thing was just a big, comical spoof. With her family, it was always the best tack to take. There was no sense in getting everyone riled up. Patsy and Nadine were ready to be riled up at the drop of a hat, when it came to such things. Her father used to help keep a lid on their extremism, with a dry comment or two. Best to downplay things. Otherwise, she'd be hearing about Rudy Fisch when she was sixty.

"What do you mean, hilarious?" Patsy said. "Yes, Mom, Rudy broke up with Pru."

"Oh, come on, don't get her all worried," Pru said. "Tell her it was no big deal. Tell her it was *funny*. What's she doing there, anyway?"

"She won early and decided to come home. She opened with 'quartz' on a double-word. And what do you mean, no big deal?" Patsy demanded. "I thought old Rudy was going to be my brother-in-law. I even started watching *The Simpsons* so I'd have something to talk to him about."

"Oh, Lord, no," Pru said. "I was the sous-chef on this one. I just got him ready for someone else."

"Come on. You don't have to be such a tough girl, for me."

"Okay, well, maybe I was sort of keeping him in my back pocket."

"In your back pocket," Patsy snorted. "A person isn't a comb, you know."

"No," Pru agreed. "You'd get more use out of a comb."

Luckily, Patsy laughed at that, and Pru was able to move the conversation along to their upcoming visit. Once or twice a year, Patsy came without Annali, to shop and carouse and do the museums. Pru always enjoyed these visits, although by the end of the weekend, she was ready to see her sister leave. Somehow, when she stayed in Pru's apartment, Patsy seemed to take up a space many, many times her actual size.

· · ·

THEY WERE IN THEIR CUSTOMARY PLACES, PRU ON THE couch next to McKay, Bill in his enormous, soft reading chair. She was telling them the same thing she'd told Patsy. They were drinking something Bill made called the Billtini, and passing around a package of Rainbow Chips Deluxe.

"Rudy," Pru said, widening her eyes. "Good riddance, huh?"

Bill and McKay exchanged looks. Rather, they very purposefully *didn't* exchange looks, which was actually more pointed than exchanging looks.

"Okay, *what*?" Pru said.

McKay put down the remote. "I hate to say it, honey, but you had that coming."

"What do you mean?"

"Rudy was a sinking ship and he was only going to take you down with him."

"Come on, that's not fair. I was giving Rudy a chance. Who says it's easy? Any good relationship takes work, right? Emotional work?"

Now it was Bill and McKay's turn to look uncomfortable. They were, after all, men, Pru reflected. They had their limits. Anyway, what did they understand about the struggle between men and women? Lord, they've all slept with each other and remained good pals. That tells you right there about the huge canyon between gay and straight relations, she thought.

"Did I mention I saw Gay/Not Gay David?" she said. "Turns out he's more gay than not. I ran into him in Fresh Fields with a guy, and he didn't say he was his boyfriend, but you could tell."

"Were they in the crème fraîche aisle?" said McKay.

"I was going to say 'endive,'" Bill said to McKay, and they beamed at each other.

"So, later, he calls me and asks if it had upset me, seeing them together. Wasn't that decent of him? And it didn't bother me, because he really looked happy. So I told him that, and you know what he said? 'Well, you have a lot more sex being gay.'"

"Oh, hush, you," McKay said, before Bill could open his mouth to speak. "I don't care why, but I'm glad Rudy broke up with you. We thought we were going to have to instigate an intervention. You *never* would have left him, would you?"

"God," Pru said, sloshing her Billtini on her hand as she put her glass on the table next to the couch. McKay threw a towel at her and she mopped it up. "Was he really that bad?"

"Dear, he was the bad dress of men—a bit too short and clinging to you in all the wrong places."

"He wasn't *that* bad. And you're not a single woman," she added. "You don't know how hard it is."

"You're pickier about what you wear than you are about who you sleep with," said McKay.

"*Me?* What about you? I can name names, McKay Ettlinger." Ouch, she thought. He's *right*.

Bill stood up. "I think I'll go make another pitcher."

She turned back to the TV. Sara Moulton was demonstrating how to debone a chicken. Was Pru the only one who hadn't seen Rudy for what he really was? Why hadn't anyone told her? Weak chi . . . a bad dress . . . She felt like she was standing in light, a really nasty, too-bright light, the kind in the dressing rooms at the lesser department stores, where you always find pins and a Kotex strip on the floor.

Rudy wasn't her dream man, okay. If you'd asked her at the age of six who she'd grow up to marry, she wouldn't have said a neurotic, culture-obsessed, insecure cartoon producer. But she'd thought him decent enough. Until the TV thing, of course. Obviously, she hadn't been as clued in as everyone else. David *had* turned out to be gay . . . Peter *had* cheated on her . . . Phil had so many problems, she didn't know where to start. None of these, in her mind, had been casual relationships. She'd been looking for Mr. Prudence Whistler for a long time, and she was beginning to have grave reservations about her judgment. It had served her so well in other areas—she'd blazed her way to this point in life. Why was he abandoning her now?

"Will you guys have a baby with me?" she said, as Bill came out of the kitchen. "I'll raise it and everything. I just need the sperm. And let's face it, you two have lots extra floating around here."

"We've talked about that before," Bill said, refilling her glass. "I'm all for it."

McKay raised his hand. "And I'm agin' it."

Pru sat up. "Really? Did you talk about me as the birth mother?"

"Of course," said McKay. "Of all the women we don't want to sleep with, babe, you're number one."

"But you wouldn't have to do all the caregiving yourself," Bill said. "We'd want to be involved fathers."

"You know," said McKay. "We'd want to see it before you bring it up to bed at night. *Briefly.*"

"By 'it' he means 'him or her,' " added Bill.

LATER, IN THE STRIPED COTTON PAJAMAS McKAY HAD given her to sleep in, safe and cozy under the seersucker bedspread, she wondered, *Why not?* McKay and Bill would be great fathers, attentive and gentle and fun. She'd be the mother and housewife. She'd remember to bring McKay's empty glasses of Diet Squirt back to the kitchen, and have dinner waiting for them every night. They'd show up at PTA meetings together and chaperone the prom as a threesome. They would grow old together, reading the kids' letters out loud to one another, trading quips and playing board games.

The next day, after breakfast, Pru and McKay drove to the D.C. Humane Society. It was in a strip mall in one of the worst neighborhoods she'd ever seen. The entire block looked like it had been hit by a bomb. There were only two other storefronts occupied: what looked to be a Mylar balloon shop, and something called Deondre Dress. Inside the animal shelter, a handful of dogs kept up a constant racket. Others lay about despondently in the heat. It was about a thousand degrees inside, and smelled of thick, warm pet smells. She couldn't stand the naked need of the puppies in what was called the Puppy Playground, and quickly left McKay to wander around.

She found herself in the Cat Condo. It was a sad, lackluster place. The few people who'd come to look at felines were all in the Kitten Kastle, oohing and ahhing over the tiny, mewling babies. Here, the elderly cats were left to nap, undisturbed. A few regarded her with distant, cool eyes. She was about to go back and find McKay when the sight of a cat in its cage stopped her. It was a huge tabby, absolutely massive. It had a notch in one ear, and it sat back on its haunches, sleeping, like a bum on the street. It looked exactly like Rudy's cat, the cat that had menaced her the one and only night she'd slept over at his place. She took off her hat and her sunglass clip, to get a better look at the cat. He was so large that there almost wasn't any room for him in the cage. Pru couldn't remember his name, so she said, "Rudy?" The cat's eyes opened. They were the same amber as Rudy's cat's eyes, and they wore the same utterly blank expression with which they'd always regarded her. No doubt about it; this was Rudy Fisch's cat.

But what on earth was it doing *here*? Rudy was ridiculously devoted to the beast. If he was spending the night at Pru's, he'd stop at home after work to feed the cat and play with it. He did this even though it took him an hour out of the way. She'd thought of it as a good sign, when they'd first met, and, in fact, HAS CAT was listed in the pro column of the Rudy list. It meant he could care for something. Of course, the morning after it spat at her, HAS CAT appeared on the con side, too, thereby canceling itself out.

McKay wasn't in the Puppy Playground. She found him in the Doggie Den, kneeling in front of what looked to be a dirty dust mop on four legs. Like the Cat Condo, it was much quieter here, almost eerily so. The cage behind them was opened, and McKay was letting the dust mop lick his hand.

"What are you doing?" she said.

"Nothing," he said, mock innocently.

"I think I saw Rudy's cat, in there. In fact, I'm sure it was Rudy's cat. In the Cat Condo."

"Rudy Fisch? What's his cat doing in the Cat Condo?"

"I don't know. Playing shuffleboard?"

"Do you think Rudy dumped him?"

"I wouldn't have thought so, but I can't imagine how else he'd get here. I've never seen the cat leave the couch, much less the apartment. I guess maybe he did. He's in something of a dumping phase, isn't he?"

"So, what did you do about it?" McKay said.

"About *Rudy's* cat? Nothing."

McKay looked genuinely appalled. "Prudence Whistler. You just left that poor thing there?"

"*I* didn't dump the cat. Hell, it never even lived with me. Why is this my problem?"

"I don't know, but it is."

"I'm not really a pet person."

"So? Just call Rudy and tell him it's there. Maybe he doesn't even know."

"No," she said firmly. "No way. I wouldn't call Rudy if I'd found his *mother* in a cage at the Humane Society. Although, frankly, it would be easier to understand."

McKay shrugged. "All right," he said. "But this is on your head. Look at her eyes," he said, raising the dog's face so Pru could see. "Aren't they intelligent? Huskies are supposed to be very smart dogs."

The husky's fur was matted and gray. She performed no tricks, emitted no grunts, exhaled no sweet warm puppy breath. Her teeth were yellow. She sat there and panted, wetly. Leave it to McKay to choose the dog that looked most ready to keel over. He really was a ridiculously soft touch.

"You're not getting attached, are you?"

"Oh, no. Of course not."

"I *promised* Bill . . ."

"Just relax. There's something going on between me and this here girl."

McKay stood and moved a short distance away, then snapped his fingers. Slowly, the dog stood and obediently dragged herself over to him, then sat at his feet, swaying a little.

"Look at that," McKay said, delighted. "She already obeys me."

"Stop," Pru said, dryly, automatically. "You are not going home with this dog."

"Don't be silly," said McKay. "They kill animals that are left here, you know. I can't do that to poor Oxo."

"What's an Oxo?"

"Her name!"

Pru looked at the tag on the cage. "It says here 'Debbie.'"

"Well, now it's Oxo."

"You're naming her after a can opener?"

McKay bent low to the dog, running his hand over her head and cooing, "You're coming with me, aren't you, girl? Aren't you, girl? Yes, you are! Yes, you are!"

Five

On Monday morning she sat at the little desk in her living room, chewing on her pen and staring out the window. She'd made herself change out of her pajamas, into her comfiest pair of Lucky jeans and a peasant blouse. She'd even made herself put on shoes, the ones that laced up her legs, under the jeans. She thought she looked very work-at-homey. It was cooler than it had been in weeks, but still warm enough that she kept the windows open.

She used to love this time of year, back-to-school time. She loved the smell of sharpened pencils, the clean sheets of paper in her three-ring binder. The night before the first day of school, she and Patsy would sit at the kitchen table, folding book covers out of brown paper bags and decorating them with magic markers. Everything would be new and shiny and ready for the next day. She'd have picked out her outfit for school before she went to sleep.

But now she was feeling restless and antsy. Since she'd lost her job she'd had the odd sense of carrying around a big bucket of water. The bucket was filled to the brim and almost too heavy to lift, and she couldn't figure out where to put it down. Ordinarily she would have left it next to her desk, at work. Or she'd have given it to Rudy. But now she just had to keep slogging that bucket around with her, from one place to another, everywhere she went.

On the drive home from the Humane Society, while McKay talked to the happy, loudly panting dog in the rearview mirror, she'd come up with a better plan than finding another full-time job: consulting. She liked the dignified sound of it. She'd be her own boss, and she could do almost all her work out of her apartment. Maybe she wasn't cut out for an office job after all. It was true, she missed her old desk, with its neatly arranged surface. She missed her commute, across the bridge to Woodley Park Metro station. She missed the structure the job had given her, the sense of purpose. And of course, some of her business clothes. Not the tired old interview suit she'd worn to the conference last week, but the pieces she thought of as "business sexy," clingy silk wrap dresses and Italian high heels and dozens of leather commuter bags. But she was getting used to being at home. She was comfortable here. She liked being out in her neighborhood in the daytime, able to see what everyone was doing.

And consulting would let her expand her horizons. So, fine, she had no real passion for fund-raising. Her passion. She'd never thought of herself as passionate. She chewed her pen and looked around at the drab, nothing-colored walls of her living room. The corner where the TV had been was empty and cobwebby. She wished she was back at McKay and Bill's, lying on the couch and watching cable TV cooking shows. That, she could do all day. *I have a passion for wasting time.*

She couldn't work in a room with such a dismal corner. She jumped up and grabbed a feather duster and began cleaning. Somehow the walls had gotten all scuffed up, probably when Rudy had hoisted the massive television up on its stand. Really, she should paint the living room. Preferably before Patsy came, on Friday. Her sister was very sensitive to her surroundings, and would surely have something to say about it, such as *How like you, Pru, to live with nothing-colored walls.*

Probably she should take the week and do the whole apartment before buckling down to work, she thought while walking through the rooms. With e-mail now, everything happened so quickly. She wouldn't want to start painting only to get a job offer the very next day. Maybe she'd even get a break on the rent, for the new paint.

She grabbed her jacket and purse and headed out to the paint store on Seventeenth Street. That could be part of her consulting work! She could hire herself out to the other condo owners in the building, painting, spackling, doing whatever was needed. She could be a sort of Jill-of-all-trades, getting by on her sweat and her labor. Then she remembered that laborers worked hard, and she wasn't sure she would like that very much.

Definitely, though, she'd paint the apartment, for Patsy.

SHE GOT RIGHT TO WORK. SHE WAS SO EXCITED TO SEE the pale lavender she'd chosen for the living room actually up on the walls that she didn't even bother to prime them first. When McKay came to inspect her work, later, he scolded her for that. But then he helped her choose a soft sage green for the bedroom, and insisted on hand-mixing it himself. She spent the whole week painting. The days flew by. She loved doing the cutting-in around the trim and the ceiling, in particular. It required concentration and attention and she had plenty of that. She'd gotten an audiobook called *The Voice of Winston Churchill*, and she listened to it while she worked.

Never give in. Never give in. Never, never, never, never—in nothing, great or small, large or petty—never give in except to convictions of honour and good sense. Never yield to force; never yield to the apparently overwhelming might of the enemy.

She didn't give in, to boredom, to frustration, to the dizziness in her head when she was forced to stand on the top step of the ladder nearly upside down, to reach the molding. She didn't give in to the stubborn patches of drywall that refused to absorb the paint. She didn't give in to her impulses (many, many of them) to put the paintbrush down and go have a drink with McKay. While listening to Churchill, painting the walls of her apartment felt inspired, absorbingly religious. Sounds from the street below came in through her open windows. "Hey, *chollo!*" "I'm like, darling, we're not going *there,* are we?" "Christopher Anthony, you get your butt back here this minute!"

She finished the last wall of the bedroom on Thursday afternoon. She cleaned the brushes and the paint trays and brought the ladder back to the basement. She put all the furniture back and swept the floor and looked around. The colors made her feel better. The colors, and Churchill's speeches. Not happy, but better.

It was four o'clock in the afternoon. A time she hated. A time for nothing. The sun was setting, at an angle she found painful. It wasn't time to eat. She didn't feel like taking a walk. McKay was at work, *all* her friends were at work. It was a Thursday—not a party night, not a laundry night. She sat on her couch, looking at her newly painted walls, and feeling, slowly, the return of the bucket of water she'd been carrying.

. . .

PATSY WAS WEARING ONE OF HER OLD ARMY COATS AND a pair of white hairy yak boots, when Pru picked her up at National Airport the following day. She had a new piercing, in her right nostril, and her long, dirty-blond hair was piled on top of her head. It looked like it might have included some dread-locks. They went straight to Chinatown, stopping at Pru's only long enough to drop off Patsy's knapsack. Chinatown was Patsy's favorite place to shop when she was in D.C. She liked the cheap straw hats and silk shirts and combs for her hair, anything that looked sparkly and pretty and not made in Ohio but, Pru couldn't help pointing out, in some third-world sweatshop.

On the Metro, Patsy said, "What am I supposed to be feeling here? Grief? Relief? I never know where to stand with you." She pulled back so she could look at Pru. Patsy was actually the taller one, although younger by four years. The fact that she mistakenly got pregnant out of wedlock added to Pru's impression of Patsy being even younger. But now that Patsy was a mother, she felt entitled to seize the role of the older sister. She acted bossy and knowledgeable. Pru found it quite irritating, and wondered if this was how Patsy had felt, growing up.

"Tell me the truth, now," Patsy said loudly, in her stern, moth-erly way. "Were you even in love with Rudy Fisch?"

"Of course." She didn't want to hear again what a loser Rudy was. She thought maybe if she kept her answers short, Patsy would grow bored and eventually stop.

"See? I couldn't even tell. Okay, so what did you love about him?"

"I don't know. He made me laugh."

"He made you laugh," Patsy repeated flatly. "He was squirrely, and short, and needy. But he made you laugh."

"You don't understand. I *really* love to laugh. Anyway, he wasn't so short."

"What else?"

Pru thought for a moment. What she wanted to say—that she never worried about him leaving her—seemed ridiculous now, in light of his doing exactly that. "It just made a lot of sense," she said finally. "That's all."

"You are all *this*," Patsy said, circling Pru's head with her palm. "And no *this*," indicating Pru's torso.

"Oh, I'm plenty of that," Pru said. Patsy didn't have to do a thing to keep slender, but Pru didn't find it that easy to stay at her ideal weight. It was easier without Rudy. Even though he was always dieting, they spent a good deal of their time together focused on food. What to eat, what not to eat, where to eat. Another bad sign, she thought. How hadn't she noticed this before?

"You can't *think* about love, Prudy," Patsy was saying. "You think too much. You probably made a list to help you decide if you were in love with him or not."

"What's wrong with that?" Pru was startled. Was she really so predictable?

"You wouldn't need it, if you'd learn to listen to your body. The body knows. Your body decides these things, not your head. Your toes tell you when you're in love. Your *pelvic floor* tells you."

"A little louder?" Pru said. The man in front of them had turned his head partway around.

Patsy ignored her. "You have to learn to go with your gut. Why, within two minutes of meeting a guy, I can tell you if I'm going to go to bed with him, fall in love with him, or have nothing to do with him."

The man in front of them turned around fully now, to look at Patsy. Pru saw a boyish face, a sly grin. Patsy stared right back at him.

"Hello," he said pleasantly. "Let me know when you decide what you're going to do with me, okay?"

"It hasn't been two minutes yet, has it?" said Patsy, archly.

The man looked at his watch. "I can wait."

"Just because I know doesn't mean I'm going to tell you," said Patsy.

Pru saw plenty of guys around D.C. like this one—handsome, well-dressed, confident. It was a type she particularly didn't like, the Ivy League frat boy with thick hair and good connections. No doubt he'd been handed a position in one of the big law firms by one of his daddy's friends. She didn't think he'd be Patsy's type, either. She couldn't see one single tattoo, for example.

The man turned to look at Pru, too, and she wondered whether he saw what she saw, reflected back in the Metro car's window: the same face in two vastly different orientations. Pru's stark and unframed because her hair, as usual, was pulled back in a smooth ponytail; Patsy's surrounded by the wisps and tendrils escaping a knot that was secured with chopsticks. Pru's face smooth and bland, unadorned; Patsy's punctuated by the diamond stud that drew attention to her pretty nose.

The man was now telling Patsy that she looked like Heather Graham, and before Pru knew it, they were having a full-blown conversation about the state of independent filmmaking. Pru watched their reflections in the window, thinking about what Patsy had said about her gut. She didn't really know what that meant. Her gut wasn't really something she consulted for reliable information. More often than not, her body disappointed her, with its bulges, its smells, its refusal to conform to the way she saw herself. It was the dumber, ruder, embarrassing part of her. With its desires, its fears, its needs, her body was hardly a source of trustworthy information.

When they reached Foggy Bottom station, Pru watched as a young man stood to give his seat to a young woman struggling with a baby stroller. Ever since the encounter with her evil pregnant doppelgänger, as McKay called the woman, Pru had been seeing babies everywhere she went. There were babies riding in strollers on Columbia Road, trundling on stout legs in the little park next to her building, nursing in the café where she met Fiona for coffee. It made her think of a line from the book she'd read to Annali so many times that she had it memorized by now: *Fat babies, thin babies, small babies, tall babies, winter and spring babies, summer and fall babies. Everywhere babies!* Even the celebrities had babies, as she saw from the tabloids at the checkout line at Safeway. As if they were as easily obtained as the ubiquitous Kate Spade handbag.

Patsy and the man were still chatting away. Well, they'd lose him at the next stop. After shopping, she'd take Patsy to the upstairs restaurant they liked, the one that overlooked H Street, and they'd look at the lights of Chinatown and drink mai tais. Then on Saturday they'd hit the Smithsonian museums. They'd have to get there early, since she'd heard there were lines for the de Kooning show at the National Gallery of Art. Saturday night, they'd have dinner at City and see what was playing at the Uptown; and, on Sunday, a long, chatty breakfast with McKay and Bill someplace in Dupont Circle, before Patsy's flight home. Before they'd gotten off the train, Patsy had given her number to the man in front of her and Pru was making a mental note to call ahead for brunch reservations.

.   .   .

THE NEXT DAY, PATSY CAME HOME FROM HER RUN AND announced that she was having dinner that evening with the guy from the train. *Jacob,* she was calling him now.

Pru was lying on the couch, headachy and blue. Patsy stood over her, grinning and panting from her run. Right there was the difference between being thirty-six and thirty-two, Pru thought. Patsy seemed to be in about one mai tai better shape than herself.

"You don't mind, do you?" Patsy said.

Pru didn't answer. Well, *of course* she minded. They hadn't made it to the de Kooning exhibit that morning, and now it wasn't looking good for the Uptown. And what was Patsy doing, dating in *her* town? She followed Patsy into the bedroom.

"What do you even know about this guy, Pats? I have to say, I'm surprised. He seems so not your type."

Patsy was rooting through the "dressy" side of Pru's closet. Pru hadn't opened that side of the closet in a long time. Watching Patsy flip through her clothes made her jealous and possessive. Not that one, she kept thinking. Keep flipping, missy.

"He's a doctor, at GW Emergency, he said. See? I bothered to find that out." She held up Pru's best dress, a light-brown silk with a cornflower-blue print. It was her only designer dress, a Marc Jacobs that she'd gotten on eBay. "This here?" she said. It was sweet and feminine and, Pru had to admit, perfect for Patsy. It would provide interesting contrast to the nose ring and the dreads.

"What am I supposed to do while you're out?" she said, but Patsy had already disappeared into the bathroom and closed the door behind her.

Pru poured herself a glass of wine, feeling rather petulant about this turn of events. She could hear Patsy singing in the shower,

The wheels on the bus go round and round, round and round, the gays on the bus go swish, swish, swish. Pru drank her wine and watched the rain falling outside. The days were getting shorter, she realized. Well, thank goodness. Fewer daylight hours to get through.

She felt shy when Patsy's date came to the door, and she withdrew to watch them from the other side of the living room, in the bay window seat, with the new pile of blue and lavender silk pillows that she'd bought to match the walls. Jacob didn't hide his admiration of Patsy, who beamed with pleasure.

Everything was right there, in their full, open smiles.

They were like children at the circus, so openly happy and excited. It was a very different and strange way of doing things, from Pru's point of view. She was used to a style of dating that was more like buying a used car. Any outward show of eagerness only put you at a disadvantage, when it came time for negotiations. Pru felt jealous, and annoyed at herself for feeling jealous. For heaven's sake, Patsy's last date in Akron had taken her to the Olive Garden, where he'd eaten three baskets of "never-ending breadsticks" before his pasta entree, according to Patsy.

Pru suddenly wanted to go to them, to shake Jacob's hand and kiss Patsy. She wanted to say "Have a good time!" and see them to the elevator. She wanted them to insist that she come along, too. But Jacob was helping Patsy on with Pru's good raincoat, and they were already insulated in the cocoon of their date. Pru stayed where she was and waved to them from the living room, as if from the other side of an airport security gate.

SHORTLY AFTER PATSY LEFT, THEIR MOTHER, NADINE, called.

Just hearing Nadine's voice brought to mind her soft, freckled

hands, her broad shoulders, her devotion to the kinds of outmoded products you could get only through the Vermont Country
Store catalogue: pastilles and peanut chews, Silver Fox shampoo
and Lotil hand cream, Lanz of Salzburg nightgowns and loose
face powder and Tangee lipstick, the "secret of beautiful women
for over seventy years . . . the orange lipstick that goes on clear
and transforms into the perfect shade for you!"

"Is Patsy there? Annali really wants to say good night to her
mommy."

Pru thought perhaps she shouldn't say that Patsy was out with
someone she'd picked up on the train, so she hedged.

"She just ran out for food," she said, trying to lie as little as
possible. "How long will Annali be up?"

"Not long," said her mother. "Are you girls having fun? What
are you doing?"

"Nothing much. We're being low-key tonight."

"Make sure Patsy has a good time," Nadine said. "She really
deserves a little fun."

"Yeah, it's hard making sure Patsy has a good time," said Pru,
dryly.

Her mother chuckled, and said, *"Well . . ."*

Her response to almost anything these days seemed to be a
low chuckle, followed by a long, *"Well . . ."* that never went anywhere. There was a vagueness about her, since Leonard's death.
As though she couldn't quite remember what she was doing at
any given moment. Except when she played Scrabble, which she
did every night with an online group. She won consistently,
skunking her opponents with twice as many points. Pru figured
that her mother must be in good mental shape, if she could keep
winning like that. Nadine and Leonard had been older than her
friends' parents, almost grandparently by the time Pru entered

high school. Still, her father's death, at seventy-eight, had taken them all by surprise, and Pru couldn't help feeling anxious over her mother's odd new behaviors.

"How are you, Mom?" said Pru, pointedly.

"Me? Just fine. I had a four-hundred-point game the other day. Cleaned Maudie's clock. One of my best."

"Have you called any of those people about the basement?"

"Just a minute," Nadine said. Pru heard her cover up the phone and say to Annali, "Find your hat, pumpkin. Then it's bedtime." Then, back to Pru: "What people, hon?"

"To come and clean out the basement. I left you some numbers to call, remember?"

Her mother sighed. "No. I don't know where I put it, now. I'm sure it's here somewhere . . ."

Exasperation rose in Pru's chest. She'd left the list with her mother months ago, tacked up on the bulletin board in the kitchen. It had been more than a year since Leonard had died, but the basement was still full of his things. He'd liked to collect useless antiquities: broken clocks, pocket watches, old black telephones, manual typewriters that typed in script. It was the same impulse that had inspired in him his daughters' antiquarian names, Prudence and Patience. After he'd discovered eBay, during the last year of his life, the stuff had multiplied exponentially. There were packages from Florida and Minnesota that he'd never opened. It was nothing you'd make any money from, and Nadine couldn't bear to just toss it all in the trash. Pru made a mental note to find the list, the next time she was home, and moved on to the next topic.

"Well, did you ask Mrs. Kovaks about selling the house?"

"Oh, Pru. I'm not ready to leave here yet. Not with Patsy and Annali just down the street."

That was always the reason Nadine gave. Pru wished she lived closer, so she could help Nadine with some of these things. Patsy, of course, was there every day for dinner, and could easily be helping. But it didn't seem to bother her in the least that the house was losing whatever value it might still possess while her mother read *The Official Scrabble Players Dictionary* and ignored the unmoving disaster in the basement, the crumbling roof, the clogged radiators.

"And what about your health?" Pru asked. It was an obligatory question; she knew she would never get any other answer than the one she got:

"Fine, fine."

"Are you going to confession?"

"Oh, yes," her mother said, with interest. "Are you?"

"I'm not actually a Catholic," Pru said.

"Oh, that's right," her mother said. "I keep forgetting. Why did I let your father talk me into that, I wonder? Confession's a wonderful thing."

"What do you even have to confess?" Pru asked, with a smile. "Tell me. I really want to know. Cleaning Maudie's clock?"

"Oh," said her mother. "This and that. My life isn't as exciting as you girls'."

"My life isn't exciting, Mom."

There was silence.

Then Nadine chuckled. *"Well . . ."* She heard Annali in the background, beginning to fuss.

"Well, what, Mom?" she pressed. Maybe her mother was getting ready to tell her something about herself, something Pru didn't know, that would explain how she'd ended up alone on a Saturday night, again, jobless, loveless, and hungover. She held her breath, waiting.

"Hon, I better get our Peachy off to bed."

"Okay. I wish you were here with us, Mom."

"Oh, me too, honey. Me too. Call us in the morning, all right?"

PHAN, AT THE VIDEO STORE, WAS WEARING A 1980S Journey T-shirt with the sleeves ripped off, when Pru came in later that night for a DVD to watch on her laptop. The hair was still green. He smiled at her, and Pru wondered what it would be like to sleep with him. Since the breakup, she'd begun to do that more than was normal, she felt. Anyone she looked at, she wondered what they'd be like in the sack. The driver of the 42 bus. Her neighbors. Men in the elevator. The silent woman behind the counter at the souvlaki place. Apparently, her loneliness knew no bounds, had no preferences as to gender or age or attractiveness. It was loneliness that could unhinge you quicker than anything, she was beginning to think.

Coming out of the video store, she almost ran straight into the man who had helped her ditch the TV. John Owen, she remembered. He was again wearing chef's pants, splattered with grease, and his hair was messed up.

"Hi, Prudence," he said. He looked tired, and the smile he gave her was rather lifeless.

She felt some instinct to hurry away. She was still embarrassed about the night she'd met him.

"I've been thinking about you," John Owen said, falling into step with her. "I sort of thought you'd show up at the café."

"The café?" she said.

"The Kozy Korner," he said, gesturing down the street. "It's my place."

The divey eggs-and-coffee place. She'd sometimes stopped in

there for a coffee on her way to the Metro station, back when she had a job. "Oh, that's how I know you. So you're the guy who saved us from Starbucks?"

"With my very last dime," he said. "And I'd do it again."

"Listen," she said, "I am so sorry about the other night. I'm embarrassed, really."

"I wish you wouldn't be. How have you been?"

"Oh, you know," she said. "I'm getting really good at pool."

"You play pool?"

"No," she said. "I mean yes, but I just meant . . ."

"Ah," he said, apparently not even listening to her. "So what happened that night?"

She'd like to have said something funny. But she couldn't think of anything, and clearly he wasn't the jokey type. "My boyfriend broke up with me."

He nodded. "That part, I got. It was just that you said you didn't love him very much. I was wondering why you were so upset, if you didn't."

"Well, I'd just lost my job, too. I just can't figure out where everything went wrong. It seemed like it was all going along according to plan. Then, kaplooey."

"I know kaplooey," he said. He held up three videos. "Any idea why a happily married woman would rent these?"

She was a little afraid of seeing pornographic titles, something bizarre and relationship-ending. Instead, they were *Shirley Valentine*, *The Hours*, and *A Doll's House*. The common theme being: women desperately unhappy in their horrible, dying marriages.

"Your wife's?"

"I believe so. Yes. I mean, I knew she was unhappy, or she wouldn't have left me, would she?"

"I'm sorry—I'm confused . . ."

"Oh, sorry. First, she left me. Then I found these in the drawer of her bedside table. It's funny, I have never in my life looked in her bedside table. I wouldn't dream of it, you know, and why would I? Not that it's that private, but it was hers. So the other night I'm lying in bed and I think, why not? She's gone, and it's all mine now, right? So I just went through all her stuff. These were all I found, of course. Not that I was even looking for anything. It was just for the *sake* of it, do you know what I mean?"

"I—" She hardly knew what to say.

"No, look—I'm sorry. I must sound insane. I'm just laying all this on you because I have this idea that you understand. I'm having a horrible time being with people right now. I feel like I'm okay, then I hear myself talking. You know, seeing you fall apart that night, it was just how I'd been feeling, inside. Just ripped open, raw, you know."

She cringed at the words "fall apart." She hadn't *fallen apart.* She'd just cried a little bit. Okay, she'd cried a *lot.* But for heaven's sake, since when was crying the same as *falling apart*? She felt very annoyed with him. And he was separated! She'd done that in front of someone soon to be single! Of course, she wasn't in the market for another relationship, not yet. But she might as well cross this one right off the list. Already there were two strikes against him: "too handsome," and "seen me in my bathrobe." No, three: "lonely and predatory."

They were at her building. "The mornings are the worst, aren't they?" he went on, ignoring her silence. "I'm still not used to it. You should come by in the morning, if you want. It's just us lonelyhearts, at that hour."

"Oh, I quite like being alone, now," she lied, brightly.

He was looking up at her building. "Do you have one of the balcony apartments?" he said.

"No," she said. "I'm on the top floor."

"I bet it's a great view."

It sounded like a line. She didn't say anything.

Still, he didn't move to go.

"I better go in," she said. "I hope you feel better." That didn't seem right, but the conversation was well beyond her now. She felt tired and overexposed, hurrying up her steps to get away from him.

SHE TRIED TO WATCH THE MOVIE PHAN HAD GIVEN HER. It seemed promising in the store, but paled in comparison with *The Godfather,* once she started watching. She found herself missing James Caan and Al Pacino and Diane Keaton. She turned it off and went to take a shower.

She used a new shampoo she'd just bought. It was something of a splurge, but it had a wonderful coconut smell that reminded her of the beach. While she was in the shower she left the radio on to *Prairie Home Companion,* so as to have a little company. She wrapped her hair in a towel and put on her pajamas and slippers, then sat down and ate leftover Chinese food from the night before, listening to the end of the program. While she ate, she contemplated what it would be like to sleep with Garrison Keillor. The chopsticks made a harsh scraping noise against the paper container, making her teeth itch.

Maybe she should have invited John Owen up. It would be nice to have some company. But, lord, had he made her nervous. He was like a raw, gaping wound, and she had only just started to scab over, herself. No, it was a bad idea. Best to keep her distance from such need.

She finished eating and threw away the containers and washed the chopsticks and put them in the drainboard next to the sink. She found the Churchill biography she'd borrowed from the library, and took it to the other room to read while waiting for Patsy.

A few minutes later, she put the book down. Patsy's things were spread out all over the room—her green knapsack, her few clothes, the hairy yak boots she'd arrived in, makeup and books. Patsy had not been impressed with Pru's paint job. "What is that?" she'd said, so close to the wall that her nose was almost touching it. "Just plain white?"

"It's lavender!"

"No, Pru, lavender is a *color*," Patsy had said.

Pru went to work piling Patsy's things neatly in the corner that used to hold the TV. She looked at the titles of Patsy's books— *MORE Zen Koans; Kabbalah, Re-Mystified;* and, with many of its pages dog-eared, *Your Two-Year-Old.* Pru smiled and stacked the books next to the pile of things she had made. She should see more of Annali, she thought. Soon she would be in school, then a teenager, and Pru knew so very little about her, really. On one of her visits home, Annali was just a little peanut in a striped receiving blanket. Then, the next time, she was starting to walk, stumbling around in her lurching gait, her hat-lovey clutched in one hand. Then she was actually speaking, saying "Hello, Aunt Pwoody" into the phone, and it seemed Pru had missed out on everything she meant to do.

She picked up *Your Two-Year-Old* and read for a while, running her fingers through her damp hair to dry it. Two-year-olds sounded rather scary. The author used words like "impulsive" and "accidents" and "moody." When she could barely keep her eyes open any longer, she put the book down. She sat up and yawned and stretched, and looked at the clock over the little stove in the kitchen. It was almost one, and Patsy still wasn't home. The apartment was perfectly still, and clean, and neat. There was nothing else to do, then, but go to bed.

In her sleep she kept rearranging Patsy's things in her apartment. The knapsack here, the boots there. Over and over, like a Rubik's Cube, she moved her things around in her mind. Finally she woke up just in time to see the sun beginning to come up, and she watched out her bedroom window as the black sky became perceptibly lighter, until it was gray, then almost smoky white. Finally, when she was thinking she would have to call the police, she heard the front door open. She got out of bed and went into the other room.

"Did you eat?" Patsy said, slamming the door behind her. "I'm starving. What time is it?"

"Just after six," said Pru. "Let me see the dress."

With an aggrieved, insulted look on her face, Patsy opened the raincoat. Pru made her turn around so she could inspect the back, too.

"So," she said, trying to sound disinterested. "How was it?"

Patsy had disappeared inside the refrigerator, where she was rummaging around. "God, let's eat first. Do you have any eggs? Oh, you do." She pulled out a carton of eggs and the milk. "Where's your whisk?" Patsy began opening all the drawers, pulling everything out. "I've never met anyone like him. Why can't I find a friggin' whisk?"

"Here," said Pru, closing the drawer Patsy was digging through and opening the one below it. "Let me do it."

"Okay, but you let me clean up. Can I take a shower? I'm freezing. Don't cook the eggs too much, okay? Oh, and make the coffee really strong, put in one more scoop, please. And don't let me forget to call home." Then she disappeared into the bedroom.

Pru toasted bread and cooked the eggs, the little coffeemaker gurgling away contentedly. She was trying to shake off her annoyance at Patsy. They'd hardly spent any time together. Wasn't the point of this little visit to cheer Pru up and keep her company? Or to make sure she wasn't contemplating some horrific, desperate act? Everyone took her sanity for granted, she thought, shaking salt and pepper over the eggs. She *could* be going off the deep end, here. Anything could have happened last night, while Patsy was out on her little tryst. She could have done something stupid. Hunted Rudy down and beaten him with a club. Jumped off the Woodley Park Bridge. Anything at all. She turned off the burner, plated the eggs, and dumped the skillet into the sink, filling it with hot, soapy water. She glanced up at the kitchen clock. It was still early. They could still make the zoo before Patsy's flight, if they wanted to.

Patsy came back from the shower, talking as if she had never stopped: ". . . what time my flight is?" She wore Pru's white bathrobe, a towel around her neck. She was using one end of the towel to clean out her ear. Pru admired her sister's physical ease. She seemed so perfectly at home no matter where she was.

"Your plane leaves at two," Pru said. "We have plenty of time."

Patsy sat down at the little table. She was clean and shining with happiness. Pru brought the eggs over and put them in front of her, then poured two cups of the strong coffee. Patsy ate ravenously. She never stopped chewing, even to answer Pru's questions.

"So?"

"There's not much to tell," Patsy answered through a mouthful of eggs. "This is it. It's him. Do you have any ketchup?"

"What's 'him'?"

"Him is it. You know, *it*."

"It?"

"Yup. You know . . . the One."

"He's the One? Like, the One, the One?"

"You got it." She touched Pru's hand. "Ketchup."

Pru went to the refrigerator for the bowl of restaurant ketchup packets she kept on the door. She put the bowl in front of Patsy. Patsy tore a package open with her teeth. Pru continued to stand over her. "And, what, you just know this?"

"Yup."

"How?"

Patsy squirted ketchup on the eggs, making a squiggly pattern. She shrugged. "I don't know. What they say is true," she said. "You just know."

Pru looked down at Patsy's tousled blond head. She was tempted to reach out and yank on her hair. Or push her face into the plate of eggs. "And does he feel the same?"

"I don't know, *Mom*. But if I had to hazard a guess, I'd say yes."

Pru didn't know what to say. Patsy really wasn't the type to go around making declarations of love. She liked to think of herself as the proverbial bird that must be free. As soon as a guy began to fall for her, she began bashing herself against the imaginary bars of her cage. Pru felt even more annoyed, though she forced herself to sit down and listen to the details of Patsy's night.

As Patsy told it, they'd packed a whole month's worth of dates into less than twelve hours. They'd eaten at Mira, had a salsa lesson at Brazilia, and driven around looking at the monuments by moonlight. They hit a midnight show at a jazz club, and at three in the morning they were having pie and coffee at a diner in Georgetown. They'd sat on Pru's front steps to watch the sun come up and finish finding out every last little thing about each other.

Jacob was adventuresome and smart and ambitious. He had a strong, intelligent mother and many women friends—an extremely good thing, in Patsy's book. He wasn't a typical Yalie. He had *depth*. He'd met Lou Reed at a club in New York, when he was a med student by day and a punk scene hipster by night. He knew of a remote island in the Caribbean you could get to only by chartering a private boat. He could actually talk intelligently about Kabbalah. He was confident and exciting, and being around him made Patsy's head spin.

"He's all Aries," Patsy said. "Pure energy. He likes the intensity of emergency medicine. Oh, and guess what—I'm coming back next weekend. With Annali. He wants to meet her."

"Next weekend," said Pru, startled. "Really?"

"And guess where we're going—the beach house! Remember, Grandma's beach house, in Rehoboth? You know it's only three hours from here? Why don't you ever go there? I swear, if I lived here I'd be there all the time." She shook Pru's knee. "So, thanks for the invite, but we won't need to stay with you."

"Since when do you need an invitation?" Pru said.

"That was irony, honey," Patsy said. She wiped her plate with a piece of toast, finished her coffee, and burped.

"Very nice," said Pru.

Patsy laughed. "Prudy Prudy," she said. She stretched her arms above her head. "I better get some sleep. I'm exhausted." She stumbled off to the bedroom before Pru could even mention the zoo.

She knew she should feel happy for Patsy, but she didn't like it, this guy popping up all of a sudden, making claims on her sister and, now, on Annali. Whom he'd never even met! What was the idea, one date, and now a road trip to their family vacation home? And this from *Patsy,* who never liked anybody, *ever*?

She went out and got the Sunday *New York Times* and leafed through it while Patsy slept. She didn't really like the *Times,* but she wanted to look at the pictures of the people who were getting married. What was their secret? What did they all know that she didn't? She thought of that party game where you went through the whole evening trying to figure out who your "partner" was. She couldn't really remember how it worked, but everyone was paired up at the beginning of the party, and you were supposed to ask questions about all the guests until you found your mate. One time, at a party, Rudy and she had started to play, but Rudy got a tension migraine and they left early.

She examined the photos of brides and grooms closely, to see if there were any clues to be found. How had they known each other? Was it something in the eyes? The forehead? Did everyone already know what it was they were looking for, a shape of earlobe, a smell? What was it? In the pictures, the brides-to-be had had their teeth whitened and their hair done, while the guys looked as if they pretty much wore whatever they'd had on that day. Most of them matched, more or less, in terms of personal attractiveness. If there was an imbalance—her friend Kate referred to it as "couple inequity"—it was the woman who was more attractive than the man, never the other way around.

Otherwise, they all looked different. She had no idea what had attracted them to each other, or how they'd known their partner was someone they could live with for the rest of their lives, and not someone it would be depressing to wake up with a year later. She suspected that nobody ever knew, not really. Still, Patsy had seemed so certain. So certain that it almost bored her to talk about it. Pru wanted to know what that felt like, that surety. She had never "just known." Never. Not once. It always felt the same—the fizz of attraction, a few fun weeks, then a long, miserable slowing, like a train pulling inexorably into the station at the end of the line, way past the time it should have arrived.

She read the book reviews and the fashion section. She picked up her biography of Churchill, saw that she had only fifty pages left, and put it down again. She would take her sister to the airport, see her to the gate, and watch her plane fly off. Then she would come back to her neat, clean, empty apartment. And then what? The rest of Sunday stretched before her like an endless, dry desert.

WHEN SHE GOT HOME FROM THE AIRPORT, MCKAY WAS sitting on her front steps. Just seeing him sitting there made her happy, and she hurried to meet him. He had a formal and almost stiff way about him sometimes, back erect, hands on knees. Oxo was lying at McKay's feet, panting. Oxo always panted, in her heavy fur coat. Just lying still, she panted.

"Did you get my message?" McKay said, as Pru bounded up the steps.

"No. What's going on?"

"Tomorrow is the last day in the shelter for Rudy's cat. I asked the kid at the counter to let me know, and he just called."

"McKay, I'm in no shape to take care of a cat. I can barely take care of myself."

"That's ridiculous," said McKay. "I don't know anyone who's better at taking care of herself than you. I already told him we were coming. I'll pick you up in the morning, at nine. Unless you have other plans, of course."

"What other plans would I have?"

"Well, exactly."

"McKay," she said, "I don't want a cat."

"But this cat needs a home. And you need something to love."

She opened the door to her apartment. It felt even emptier without Patsy and her things. She put her keys in the silver bowl she kept near the door. It was so quiet she could hear the electric buzz coming from the clock in the stove. Whenever you opened McKay's front door, a dog came running to you. Cats didn't really do that, did they? Cats came over to you in their own time and rubbed up against your leg, purring. Well, maybe that was better, actually. She didn't really feel comfortable with how quickly a dog fell in love with you.

She started to get ready for bed, and then realized it wasn't even time for dinner yet. Maybe McKay was right. Maybe she and the cat were meant to find each other. She had to admit, she'd felt for the poor thing, in that miserable cage. Dumped by Rudy, when he'd gotten sick of it. Maybe the cat, too, had lost *its* job and had gotten too needy.

She made a sudden, uncharacteristic decision: She'd save the cat. She'd give it a good, loving home. How hard could it be? Plus, the scheme held the appeal of trumping Rudy. Rescuing his cat would show the world who was the real decent human being in all of this.

Six

When the kid in the cutoff shorts brought out the carrier cage holding Rudy's cat, Pru faltered.

The kid was struggling with the cage. Its apparent weight, coupled with the fact that the cat inside kept scrambling around, forced him to use two hands to haul it up to the counter. As soon as he was settled, the cat bared its teeth and let out an ear-piercing yowl. The sound made Pru want to turn and run out of the building. McKay grabbed her arm and held her there.

As Pru and McKay peered inside the cage, the cat thrust a vicious-looking yellow paw between the bars of the front of the cage. They drew back, clutching each other.

McKay was nearly beside himself, trying not to laugh. "Wow," he said, at last. "He *is* a beast, isn't he?"

The cat gave a sudden leap, hitting the top of his container.

"It's okay, boy," said the kid soothingly. "You're going home, now."

"Wait a minute," Pru said. But she'd already filled out the

paperwork for the cat and paid for it—paid for it! Ninety-six dollars! The cat gave a low growl and hissed at her fiercely, before backing himself into an angry ball of fur in the farthest corner of his cage.

The kid said, "He'll be okay once you get him home. They always do this in the carrier. They don't like the movement. He's just scared, is all. Aren't you, boy?"

"Are you sure?" said Pru, uncertainly. "He looks dangerous."

"No," said the kid, very seriously. "He's not dangerous. He's not feral or anything."

She looked at McKay. He had an index finger pressed to his lips, in an apparent attempt to stay straight-faced. "He's not feral," he repeated softly, his eyes shining with barely restrained glee.

"Okay," said Pru. "But if he doesn't calm down, you know, I might have to bring him back here."

"No worries," said the kid. He smiled at McKay.

On the way out they passed a father and a little girl with a small white kitten in her arms. As Pru walked by with the hissing, lurching cage, the girl's daddy drew her back behind him, protectively.

Pru put the cage in the backseat of McKay's car, then got into the front passenger seat. McKay was trying so hard not to laugh that his eyes watered with the effort. McKay wiped his eyes and then started the car. "You're doing such a good thing!" he said. In the backseat, the cat, which had been silent, began to howl in despair. Pru turned toward McKay and stared at him, not saying a word. "I'm sure it'll be fine!" he said, through tears.

McKay found a parking space outside her building and they brought the cat upstairs. Inside the apartment, they put the cage gently on the floor. As soon as McKay opened the door, the cat banged its way out of the cage and ran straight under the couch.

There it stayed, staring out at them with fierce yellow eyes. Pru squeaked the squeaky toys and dangled the dangly toys. McKay tried to make helpful suggestions but Pru finally told him to leave.

The cat hid under the couch all day. It ignored the bowl of food Pru put out, and the little trail of "tempting kitty morsels" she'd made to help it find the litter box in the bathroom. Finally, she gave up, and sat at her desk for a while, trying to come up with a "look" McKay said she had to have for the "identity package" that Bill told her she had to have, to be a real consultant. After a few minutes, she got up and grabbed her swimming suit and gym bag. She was out the front door and pressing the button for the elevator before she remembered that she'd canceled her membership to the Y.

She could go back to change into her running things. But she didn't want to run. She wanted to be immersed in a pool of water. She wanted to feel it under her, all around her, holding her up.

She thought about her pregnant doppelgänger, and the pool at the Sheraton. Would anybody care if she used it, just for a quick swim? It wasn't like she'd be any trouble. She even had her own towel, in her gym bag. She could just pretend to be another hotel guest. When the elevator door opened she jumped in, excited by the prospect of having something new to do. It made her feel a little dangerous, a little bad, a little like the Artful Dodger, living by her wits alone.

WHEN SHE RETURNED FROM HER SWIM (NO ONE HAD SAID a word to her, and she'd had the Sheraton's glorious outdoor pool all to herself!), there was still no sign of the cat. She thought he might have eaten some of the food in his bowl, but it was hard to tell.

There was no sound until four in the morning. At first she was scared, but then she remembered the cat. She staggered up out of bed and chased it into the other room, slamming the bedroom door between them. She fell back asleep, but in half an hour she awoke again. The cat was vigorously pawing at her bedroom door, making it rattle in its frame. Pru got up again and, in a sort of predawn haze, decided that a better place for the cat would be the bathroom. She managed to catch it after cornering it in the kitchen. She got a good swipe on the forearm for her efforts.

Just as she was beginning to drift off, the cat took up yowling again. It was an unearthly sound that reverberated against the porcelain tiling. Pru pulled the pillow over her head. The cat yowled for a bit more, then began flinging himself against the bathroom door. The door rattled in its frame, each time he threw his massive weight against it. It unnerved her so much that finally Pru got up and opened the bathroom door. The cat flew past her, straight to a spot under her bed where it was impossible to reach him. It wasn't even five in the morning yet, too dark for a run, so she lay in bed awhile, cursing.

At first she cursed McKay for talking her into rescuing the cat. Then she cursed Rudy, first for having chosen such a ridiculous animal in the first place, then for having stuck her with responsibility for the damn thing. The cat spat and growled from his hiding place under the bed. Finally, just before six, she dressed and left her apartment.

It was so early that no one was out yet. Columbia Road was strangely quiet and empty. The 7-Eleven wasn't open, but it looked like maybe there were lights on at the Kozy Korner, at the other end of the street.

She pushed open the door to the café. Inside, it was warm and welcoming. John Owen stood at the counter, reading. When he saw her, he looked up and said, "Hey, Prudence."

For some reason, "hey" instead of "hi" caught her off guard. It made her feel as though he'd been expecting her. She took a seat at the counter and looked around. They were the only people in the café.

"How are you?" he said, folding up the newspaper. "Are you a coffee drinker?"

"Coffee, yes. I'm, you know, fine."

"'You know, fine,'" he repeated, placing a cup and saucer in front of her. He filled her cup with coffee, strong from the look of it. "What's 'you know, fine'?"

She shook her head. "I don't want to get into it," she said.

"Oh, come on," he said, sitting back down. "What's going on?"

She looked at him. He was waiting for her to say something. "Okay, well, remember how, the first time you saw me, I'd just been dumped? Maybe there was a good reason for that. I took in the cat that my ex—Rudy—dumped at the same time, and it's certifiably insane. Things have pretty much gone from bad to really, really, *really* bad."

"It's just a cat," he said. "How insane can it be?"

She showed him the scratch across her forearm. "I'm telling you, it's the Charles Manson of cats," she said. "It should have a little swastika carved in its forehead. I can't believe they actually sent him home with me."

He was laughing. "Where did you get him?"

"The Humane Society."

"So you throw out a two-thousand-dollar TV and keep the cat? What a deal." She hadn't seen him laugh before. Immediately she wondered if his wife had taken him back.

"You seem good," she said.

"I'm feeling good. Better. Definitely better. And, it's nice to have someone in here. You should eat something," he added.

He brought her a cinnamon bun, but she was too tired to do more than poke at it. She drank her coffee and fell into a melancholy stupor, watching John finish his crossword puzzle. Every now and then the door would creak open and someone would come in. John would disappear for a few minutes, then return. Little tiny epiphanies, like mini electrical shocks in the brain, kept pestering her. She missed Rudy. Unfinished, uncouth, vulgar old Rudy. She missed him. She missed waking up with him, she missed his crisp, starched shirts in her closet. She missed walking to the Metro with him, holding hands. She missed having someone who would call at the end of the day, and say, So, how'd it go? Someone who didn't make weekend plans without her. She felt unloved, unlovable. She deserved to be fired, and dumped, and to have a disgusting cat. Picturing John Owen, who stood frowning at the crossword puzzle, in the sack was not a difficult thing to do. Even easier, in fact, than the silent woman behind the counter of the souvlaki place. The cinnamon bun he'd given her was stale.

Things like that.

THE CAT WAS NOWHERE TO BE SEEN WHEN SHE GOT back. She turned on her computer and got to work designing her identity. First, business card.

She got a little sidetracked searching the Internet for a font. She wanted something that resembled handwriting, something casual but not sloppy, and after an hour or so she found what she was looking for. But when she tried to get her computer to use it, something went wrong. The computer was suddenly an older version of itself, taking forever to load. Watching the desktop icons struggling to come up on her screen was like being at the Safeway checkout line behind some ninety-year-old sorting through her coupons.

She ran out to the local Radio Shack and the guy there told her to install more RAM. She managed to open up the computer, find the slots where the RAM was supposed to go, and put everything back together. But it turned out to be the wrong kind of RAM—it took her most of the evening online diagnosing this, so in the morning she went out for the right kind of RAM and started all over again.

Somehow she managed to stretch out the business card project over another three days. She'd work on it until midnight, moving the image around, adjusting the fonts, making up names for her business. When she could no longer blink without seeing the ghost of her computer screen burned into her retina, she'd stuff her ears with the foam earplugs she'd bought and go to sleep. The earplugs didn't keep her from waking up to the sound of the cat every night. But they helped. If she was lucky, she could get two or even three hours of sleep before the cat started his scrabbling. Then she'd get up out of bed, stagger around chasing the cat until she cornered him, and throw him in another room. Then she'd lie in bed, listening to the cat's rage at his banishment, until six, when John opened the Korner.

She got to recognizing the other early-morning regulars. Pru felt that anybody looking at them could tell that the one thing they had in common was not having a significant cuddler at home in bed. Their loneliness, their isolation, was practically a badge on their chests. There was the woman in the bad nylon dresses, the old man who scurried in to refill the same old tattered paper cup. A guy who owned an endless supply of pilled sweaters. They would eat their pastries and read their newspapers in silence, chatting in turn with John, who was stationed behind the counter. Every morning he greeted her with, "Hey, Prudence," and she would sit at her place at the counter. He'd bring her coffee and they'd discuss the quality of that particular morning's loneliness. They ranked it on a scale of one to ten. "About a six," she'd say. Or: "Nine, today," he said one morning. "I had to go to my first dinner party as a bachelor. The hostess's sixty-five-year-old mother was my 'date.'" "How was that?" she'd asked. "We kissed, but I didn't feel anything." Pru had laughed, but she had the sense that his was lessening, while hers was getting worse.

Over time, she'd gotten more comfortable confiding in him. It seemed that, somewhere along the line, she'd stopped talking to straight men like she did her gay and women friends. It surprised her that she and John could talk openly like this together, without worrying how their personal allure might be compromised by these unsightly feelings. Oddly enough, the opposite seemed to be happening. Sometimes she was so excited to see him in the morning that she didn't even get angry at the cat for its noise. She recognized that something familiar and yet new was happening to her. Lust and admiration and pure affection were all converging in one horrible, irresistible package. And oh, he was such a bad, bad bet. Formerly happily married, forced into a separation he didn't want. So adrift, so rudderless. That boat could end up on just about any old shore.

AT THE END OF HER FIRST MONTH OF UNEMPLOYMENT she was no closer to finding a job. Between the morning paper and the puzzle, the cat, her friends, and the problems she was having with her computer, she hadn't even produced a decent résumé and cover letter. *How did people work at home before the Internet?* she wondered, after logging on one morning to find thirty-two new e-mails. Presumably, they must have actually *worked*. Pru had her hands full just maintaining her relationships. Kate McCabe was keeping her busy analyzing the actions of the unattainable man she had her eye on, and the unavailable men eyeing her. Kate told her everything they said, and Pru and she then parsed every word and nuance to see if any intent or purpose could be reliably surmised. Pru was also in a rapid-fire e-mail group with McKay and three other friends from college. They all had desk jobs, and kept a constant flow of messages circulating, most of them full of nonsense, LOLs, private jokes a million years old. Then there was Patsy, who needed to talk about the progression of her long-distance relationship with Jacob, which did indeed seem to be progressing, mainly by phone. They talked so long and late into the night that they kept falling asleep on the phone together. Jacob was still The One, Patsy maintained. Her soul mate, the yang to her yin, the fizz in her gin, the Brad to her Angelina, the moon to her ocean. She announced they were contemplating matching tattoos, "our names, in each other's handwriting!"

"Wait," said Pru, "your name in his handwriting?"

"No—his name on me in his handwriting, and mine on him with his."

"Your own name on yourself? I don't get it."

"No—my name in my handwriting— Oh, shut up."

And, of course, there was Pru's secret hobby, which she came across by accident one day when she mistakenly typed "Couch leather bag" in the search box on eBay. She found several "Couch" bags for sale, and although she wasn't sure of the ethics of the situation, placed a bid, and won it, for ten dollars. Surely it wasn't her fault if some eBay seller had failed to carefully proof-read her listing?

After her e-mail, she opened her to-do list and stared at it. The to-do list had by now taken on a life of its own. Usually, just looking at it was enough to discourage her for the rest of the day. She'd organized her tasks into categories and subcategories, hav-ing spent many hours scouring the Internet for appropriate kinds of list-organizing software and testing out each one. Each task was color-coded and prioritized, and with each passing day that she didn't actually do any of the things on the to-do list, the longer it became, and the more her anxiety increased, the heavier that bucket in her arms became, and the more often she found herself wondering about the possibility of supporting herself by reselling the misspelled designer wear she found on eBay.

She still hadn't taken Rudy's cat back to the Humane Society. She wasn't sure what was stopping her. Certainly, it wasn't because the cat had become any easier to live with. If anything, the situa-tion was so entirely out of hand that she hardly knew what to do. For one thing, he had begun eating everything in sight. He would emerge from his hiding place while Pru was out of the house and eat all of the canned cat food she'd left for him that morning, and anything of hers she might have left out, too. An open sleeve of saltines. A packet of cream cheese. Entire loaves of bread. One night, when she got home from the Hilton on P Street, where she was now stealing her swims, she found a bag of bagels ripped open and half devoured on the kitchen floor. There were crumbs all over the floor, and somehow in the process a cup of coffee dregs had been spilled over the stack of bills she'd neatly piled on the counter, waiting to be paid.

Even worse, her apartment was beginning to smell like the lit-ter box. Actually, it smelled of a cat *not* using its litter box. She could smell it as soon as she stepped off the elevator. She kept her hat pulled low over her eyes as she keyed into her apartment, and if anyone else happened to get off the elevator at the same time, she would look around in disgust with them, as if she, too, could not *believe* someone would stink up the hall that way. McKay, coming in with her one night, announced, "If you can stand the cat piss, folks, you can stand the show."

Still, she couldn't bring herself to dump the cat again. Part of it had to do with the logistical difficulties. She just didn't feel up to the task of getting the cat back into its cage, which would require picking him up and holding him. She'd gotten used to picking him up long enough to fling him into the bathroom or the closet, but couldn't imagine actually managing to stuff it back into the tiny carrier. If McKay refused to drive her, which was likely, she'd have to take a bus, possibly with a transfer, back out to Northeast D.C. And then she'd have to face the kid in the cut-off shorts and explain that living with the cat was impossible.

It was all too much for her current state of unhappiness, running pretty much at a constant level seven, by her best estimate. She felt like she had a continual head cold, without the runny nose. The problems of her to-do list, her income, where she was going in life, seemed like someone else's problems. She knew she should be attending to these things, but as long as her severance held out, drinking coffee and commiserating with John, reading about the Battle of Britain, and playing pool with McKay seemed infinitely preferable. Besides, it was impossible to work from home, when your home smelled like the bathrooms at Camden Yards.

One night when the cat was shut in the hall closet, the location furthest from her bedroom, she woke up to the familiar *thud, thud, thud* as the cat heaved itself against the closet door. Then suddenly there came a desperate, strangled yowl and a horrible crash.

She rushed to the hall closet and pulled open the door. The cat, clearly unharmed, came flying out and dashed to its hiding place under her bed. Her heart still pounding in her chest, she peered inside the closet. The hanging rod and the shelf above it were now on the ground, on top of the coats and shoe boxes they'd once held.

Her leather coat was on the ground. She picked it up, fingers trembling. It was perhaps her most treasured item of clothing, which made it her most treasured item, period. She'd gotten it one weekend in Greenwich Village, after seeing *The Matrix* with Rudy. It was perfectly cut, its leather buttery soft. The entire left side of the coat, from breast to knee, had been shredded, in the cat's fall. The wine-colored lining peeped through, in places where the cat's claws had gone in the deepest, as if the coat were bleeding.

"THE CAT HAS TO GO," SHE SAID TO JOHN, A FEW HOURS later, "or I do."

He was pouring her coffee. She put her head on the counter. "My most prized possession in the whole world," she moaned. "Destroyed."

"We'll find you another coat," he said.

"You don't understand. That wasn't just *some* coat. That was my *Matrix* coat. I could never afford something like that now. Fucking cat!"

"The poor thing," John said. "He's just traumatized because Rudy abandoned him. I mean, imagine it, one minute you're, you know, on the pillow, the next, you're in a cage at the pound. Sure, he's going to be angry."

She looked down at her shoes. She thought perhaps she'd forgotten to put her contacts in, everything was so fuzzy, but she was pretty sure she was wearing one loafer and one ballet flat. "My shoes don't match," she said.

John peered over the edge of the bar. "So go home and change them."

She picked her head up off the counter. It was heavy with fatigue. When was the last time she'd slept for more than four hours? "Okay," she said, through the cotton of her head. "Where do I live?"

John managed to convey a look that reached out and ruffled her hair, without actually reaching out to ruffle her hair, which would have only annoyed her. She liked the kind of friends they were. But another part of her feared that if something didn't happen soon they'd end up at the point of no return, neutral chums between whom there wasn't anything more than a faint echo of a romantic spark. Or, worse: Something would happen soon. The thought gave her a grip of fear in her stomach. What, then?

Pru stayed at the café later than usual, reading the *Post*. Finally, at ten, she decided she should brave the situation at home. The thought occurred that she might just grab her laptop and come back to the café to work. She was weighing the pros and cons of such a bold move when the door opened and another girl came in.

The girl headed straight for the counter, calling out flirtatiously, "Owen! I have a bone to pick with you!" John looked up and smiled at the girl. He put his arms over his head, as if to defend himself, and the girl raised her fists. She took the seat Pru had just vacated and began scolding him, while he continued to pretend to cower.

"Mea culpa!" Pru heard him say.

Pru made herself keep walking out the door and away from the café. What was *that* all about? She didn't think the girl had been John's estranged wife, the elusive Lila. People in the middle of a divorce weren't exactly playful with each other, but there was definitely something between these two. She wished she could return and see what was happening now. The café had been nearly empty. Anything could be going on in there now, anything at all.

The cat was in the middle of the floor when she got home. He looked up at her, a greedy, hungry glint in his eye. He was hunched over her vintage cream-colored cardigan, eating one of the rosebud buttons.

Pru stomped her foot and shouted and the cat sprang up and ran away. She picked up the sweater, which she hadn't worn since the night Rudy broke up with her. The cat had chewed two large holes in the front and the right cuff had been shredded. The delicate rosebuds had all been ripped from the placket.

The cat was destroying her favorite clothes. As if it knew exactly what it was doing, it was taking out its vengeance on her rarest, most treasured things.

AS PREDICTED, MCKAY SAID HE WOULDN'T HELP HER take the cat back to the Humane Society.

"Then I'll take a bus," she said.

"No, no," he said. "Wait. I have a better idea."

"McKay."

"Come on, I'll buy you lunch. Where do you want to meet?"

She thought of the girl and John Owen, alone in the café. "I don't know," she said, trying to hide her eagerness. "The Korner?"

An hour after she'd left, she was back at the café again. The girl was still at Pru's usual spot at the counter, pretending to read a book but watching John slice a cheesecake. McKay sat across from Pru, writing out a name and phone number on a paper napkin in his crisp design-school handwriting. He pushed the napkin across the table to her, obviously pleased with himself.

"Who is this person?" she said, after reading the napkin. She had been trying to make out the title of the paperback the girl held in her lap. The girl looked extremely fit, with defined muscles in her calves and shoulders. John gestured to the cheesecake with the knife, and the smile the girl flashed him was blindingly white.

"Bradley Bond. Our pet therapist?" McKay sounded exasperated. Clearly, she was supposed to have remembered Bradley Bond. "He helped us with Dolly's end-of-life decisions? He's fabulous. The Brewster-McCallahans' cat was acting the same way, spraying everything, and Bradley put him on some kind of kitty Prozac. It's supposed to work wonders."

She pushed the napkin back across the table at him. "I'm not getting therapy for a cat," she said. "Christ, look what it did to Rudy!"

"Not therapy," said McKay. "Just drugs. You have to have one appointment with the pet therapist to get the drugs. But then you don't have to go back if you don't want. It's not *analysis.*"

Pru's attention was brought back to the girl, who was having a huge reaction to John's cheesecake. She rolled her eyes and moaned and exclaimed and wagged the fork at John accusingly. This was her trademark thing, Pru decided, this cutely accusatory, good-natured contentiousness. It was the kind of attitude you might expect from a sorority girl in college. It meant she was a girl who was willing to wrestle. Those kind of guys, the frat guys, probably loved this routine. But Pru didn't think John Owen would be so taken with it, and for a moment she was satisfied to see him turn away abruptly from the overexclaiming and point-ing, to answer the phone. The girl was left looking rather foolish, uncertain how to shift into some other behavior. She looked around a little self-consciously, wiping her mouth. Pru felt sorry for her then. She had half a mind to rescue the girl by going up to her and asking what she was reading. But just then the girl picked up her book and Pru saw the title: *Even Cowgirls Get the Blues.* That made her not want to rescue the girl anymore. Why not just carry a sign: "I'm a sexy girl! Reading a sexy book!"

"Pru," McKay said warningly, "you owe him at least that."

"The cat? I owe the cat? How did I end up owing the cat?"

"Just by loving him."

"I don't love him! I hate him! He ate my sweater! I'm going to the bathroom."

Just as Pru stood up, the girl too rose to leave. She had one of those yoga bodies Pru envied, pliant and long-torsoed, with a little pooch of a butt. John, who was passing behind the yoga queen, put a hand on her hip, close to the butt pooch. She smiled and said, *"Adiós, amigo."*

"So, let me know, okay?" John said.

Let him know what? Pru wondered, pushing open the door to the ladies' room. She could only think of romantic situations: *If you're free for dinner . . . If we're still on for some sex later . . .* Nothing innocuous suggested itself, with a sentence like that.

To her surprise, when she came back from the restroom, John and McKay were sitting at the table together, chatting away like a couple of old pals.

"You know each other?" Pru said. She looked from one to the other, alarmed. McKay was eating a piece of cheesecake, inno-cence itself.

"I work out at the gym with Bill," John said. "Is he going tonight?"

"I think so."

"Did he tell you he benched two-ten? I was spotting him."

"Lord, yes. He gloated all night about it."

"Wow," said Pru, just to keep herself included. She was still trying to puzzle it out, what it meant that McKay and John Owen knew each other. She hadn't told anyone about her friend-ship with John. Not that there was anything *to* tell. But McKay was tricky. He was always doing stuff like this, staying one step ahead of her, somehow.

John saw the napkin on the table and said, "Bradley Bond, I know him. Oh, for Rudy's cat. That's a great idea."

Pru cut a sliver of cheesecake with the fork and said, "I'm not sure what I'm doing. You know, maybe it's kinder to just have him put out of his misery. He's obviously a deeply disturbed cat. Maybe he takes one look at me and sees, you know, Cloris Leachman in *Young Frankenstein*."

"Who doesn't?" said McKay.

She let the cheesecake melt in her mouth, looking at John to see how he'd respond to what McKay had said, which was exactly what Pru had expected McKay to say. In fact, she had handed that one to him. She didn't know quite how they did it. They kept themselves amused, and yet there were boundaries, things they would never say to each other. But sometimes their teasing put other people off, the people who didn't understand how ridicu-lously devoted they were to each other. But John just reached behind and pulled a chair up to the table for himself.

"You know, you could always just call Rudy and tell him you have his cat," John said.

He'd put his feet up on the rungs of Pru's chair, rather possessively, she thought. McKay was looking at her, she could feel his interest and delight, his brain working out this new equation: Pru plus John equals . . . She finished the cheesecake, feeling slow and languorous, in the stretch of this moment, when nothing was happening except the contemplation of John's comment, the anticipation of what would be said next, the living vibe between the three of them. Who could go back to work when there was this, John's feet under her chair, McKay to process it all with later, when they were alone? *I could spend all day doing nothing but this,* she thought.

"Well," she said aloud, "that certainly puts it in perspective."

"YOU KNOW HE'S GETTING A DIVORCE," SAID MCKAY, when John Owen had left the table to return to his usual spot behind the counter. The batwings over McKay's eyes moved up and down, suggestively.

"Forget it," said Pru. "He's totally unavailable. It'll be years before he gets over Lila."

"Please," McKay said. "No, it won't. You need to give him a little motivation, that's all. Why don't you ask him out?"

"Oh, okay," she said, "I'll just ask him to the Sadie Hawkins, after social studies. What's his wife like?"

"Nothing special," said McKay. "I've only seen her a few times. She's pretty."

"Pretty pretty? Or just pretty?"

"She's pretty, Pru."

"You should hear him talk about her. He makes her sound, I don't know, like Sophia Loren or something. All alluring and mysterious and un-havable and perfect." She chewed her bottom lip thoughtfully. "That's it. I'm too havable. There's no real challenge here."

"You don't have to sleep with him, you know. Just go to a movie together. See what it's like to date a nice guy."

She shook her head. "I'm not ready to date. All that hope and expectation, I'm not ready for it yet."

"Right," McKay said.

"I'm serious."

"Honey," he said, "tell that to your uterus."

When they were leaving, he picked up the napkin with the pet therapist's phone number on it and tucked it into the back pocket of Pru's jeans. "Don't forget this," he said. "Show me the good person I know you really are, inside."

Seven

Dr. Bond's waiting room was like a spa, with its soothing, dark green walls and a little trickling fountain. Pru went to the receptionist's desk, where she was given a thick clipboard of papers to fill out. She sat on a modern white plastic chair next to two other "parents," a lawyerly-looking woman about her age and an older gentleman, both with dogs straining at their leashes. In the cage at her feet, the cat spat and hissed at the dogs. It took her forty-five minutes to fill out the forms she was given, even though she had to skip over most of the "demographic" information. When she came to the daily diary, where she was supposed to list the cat's minute-to-minute activities, she was a bit light-headed as she wrote: 2:00–5:00 AM—HOWLING, FLINGING SELF AT DOOR, WAKING UP PRU, ETC. 2:00 PM—EAT SWEATER, PEE ON BOOKS, NAP.

"You didn't put the cat's name on here," the receptionist said, taking the clipboard back from her. "What's the cat's name?" The receptionist wore a loud turquoise-and-black outfit, with turquoise jewelry. She had pictures of a curly-haired puppy, with red eye in every photo, covering the walls of her area.

Pru glanced back over her shoulder at the cat, who was still emitting low, threatening growls from his cage. She never called him anything. What came to mind, looking at him, was *big*. *Big Whoop,* she thought. For the entire year that Patsy was in seventh grade, every other word was "Big Whoop," accompanied by a shrug, a hair flip, or a sneer. "It's Big Whoop," she said to the receptionist, who made a note on a folder she'd slipped all the sheets into.

Of course, Pru had had pets as a kid—a series of dogs that ran away or got hit by cars. Only one cat, though, a stray her mother had found on Bearswamp Road. They called the cat Annie Bearswamp. Every night when Pru was eleven years old Annie Bearswamp slept curled up in the crook of her neck. One day Annie Bearswamp simply disappeared. Months later, Leonard took Pru and Patsy down to the basement, where he showed them what he'd found: a pile of dainty white bones, behind the dryer. Not a lesson in personal responsibility, or anything like that, dead-cat bones; but a fascinating and educational discovery, in his opinion. Patsy had cried, and written a prayer to recite over the shoe box they buried the bones in. It wasn't even Patsy's cat. "It wasn't even your cat," Pru had said. She wondered about the smell. Shouldn't they have smelled it decaying? Nadine had given them ice cream that night before bed.

That was when she'd understood. She was lying in her bed, looking up at the swirls in the ceiling plaster, and decided she would never give one of her children something that would decay and die. What was the point? Pets were too expendable to love. Let them roam around outside, but don't tell them your secrets. Don't get used to them on your pillow. Better you should love only things that will last forever, like the color blue and swimming and *Little House in the Big Woods* and Steve Martin records.

The receptionist called out, "Big Whoop Whistler?" Pru stood up. She picked up the carrier, and inside the cat began to howl, sadly. She followed the receptionist into a large office covered in bright, floral wallpaper.

Dr. Bond came into the examining room. He was tall and unsmiling. He looked like someone who actually could have finished medical school. Somehow she'd imagined that pet therapists were sort of like tarot card readers. Dr. Bond looked like he'd be right at home in a surgeon's lounge, with his long legs, his impeccably pressed dress shirt with glinting cuff links. She could see the outline of his chest muscles underneath. She had wanted to say something along the lines of "I'm having a hard time getting him to open up to me, Doc," but decided to keep her mouth shut.

The cat emitted a low, threatening growl. "Let him out," Bond said. Without taking his eyes off the forms she'd filled out, he opened a low cupboard beneath the examining table. Once she got the little door to the cage open, the cat dashed straight for the cupboard.

Dr. Bond closed the cupboard door halfway and went back to reading the forms. When he finished a page, he turned it in an abrupt, final manner, pinning the completed page to the table with a strong, square-ended finger. Pru sat and waited. She wondered if she should bring up the kitty Prozac or let him suggest it.

Dr. Bond frowned and looked up at Pru. He was reading the daily diary, where her tone had become a bit tongue-in-cheek. "Well," he said, in his deep rumble, "I think I see what part of the problem is."

"Ah," Pru said. She had decided to follow his lead and say as little as possible.

He closed up the folder and crossed his arms. "So, why are you here?"

Look in the friggin' chart I just spent an hour filling out, she thought. "Well, he's a really bad cat."

"Cats are neither good nor bad. They sometimes have impulses they can't control," Dr. Bond said, pinching an invisible thread off his spotless white trousers. "Go on."

"I was going to bring him back to the Humane Society, where I got him, but I wanted to try this first. My friend says you can give him some kind of kitty Prozac?"

"Why did you get this cat?"

"Sorry?"

"Why did you get this cat?" He looked up at her with clear, sharp eyes.

She faltered. Nothing she thought of sounded quite right. "Oh . . . the usual reasons, I guess," she said.

"And what is he doing that's objectionable, specifically?"

"Peeing. On everything."

"Is he peeing or spraying?"

Peeing or spraying. Did he think she was on her knees, watching the cat soiling the bookcases? "I don't know," she stammered. "Is there a difference?"

"Yes," Dr. Bond said briskly. He pulled a clean piece of paper from a drawer in the examining table and turned it over on the table. He took a gold pen from his chest pocket, screwed off the cap, and handed it to Pru. "Let's take a look at your setup. Will you draw a map of your apartment?"

She drew the outlines of her apartment, indicating the bedroom, living room, kitchen, bathroom, and the hallway. "It's bigger than it looks," she said, self-consciously.

"That's fine," Dr. Bond interrupted. "Now, let's indicate where kitty is allowed to go during the day."

"Here. Just the kitchen. Since the whole closet incident, you know." Her friend Fiona had given her a baby gate to stretch across the doorway of the kitchen, and the cat hadn't yet managed to haul his massiveness over it.

Dr. Bond frowned. "Is that it? Okay, where is he at night?" She circled the tiny hall closet. She didn't like looking at the map. It made sense when she was at home, but here, the limits of the cat's domain made her uncomfortable.

"That's not much room," said Dr. Bond. "Does he go outside at all?"

"No."

She was feeling accused and defensive. But why should she? Wasn't she here, spending two hundred bucks to try to save the damn cat's life? She hadn't thrown him out on the street, or taken him back to the shelter . . . didn't she deserve some points here? Animal people, Pru thought sulkily. They never have nice furniture, and you can never please them. Not really.

The cat finally stuck his head out from the cabinet to see what was going on. Dr. Bond ignored him and said, wearily, "I see you're using pine litter. How did you choose pine?"

"I like the smell, I guess."

"*You* like the smell," he repeated, significantly, making a note. "And his food? You feed him . . . canned? Why?"

I like the smell, she thought. "Isn't that what you feed cats?"

"Sometimes." Then it seemed he'd noticed that the cat had come out and was sniffing the air. Dr. Bond reached a long finger down to hover just above the cat's nose, and said, in a completely different tone, "How you doing down there, big guy?" Suddenly he was softer, kinder. He scratched the cat gently between the ears. "Good boy, handsome boy," he said. The gesture made Pru a little sad, and a little envious. She wondered when was the last time either one of them had been touched like that. She had the impulse to push her head under Dr. Bond's hand, too.

He straightened up again. "Here's what I'm going to recommend. For starters, you need to let him out of this confined area." He held up a hand before she could speak. "I know, he'll spray everywhere. And yes, he will, for a while. He's spraying because he's anxious and unhappy. But cats interpret those feelings as threats, and when male cats are threatened, they spray."

"Oh," she said, nodding vigorously. "Ah." She tried to look interested.

"Locking him up is compounding the problem. He's going to keep marking until he feels safe. We need to work on what's threatening him, so he won't have to spray anymore. And in the meantime, we have to reduce some of the stresses on him. Understand?"

Pru nodded, as if she could possibly comprehend what might constitute cat stress. Sleep, eat, sleep. Sure.

She listened while Dr. Bond explained how to clean the entire apartment with a special enzymatic cleaner, and then cover the bookcases and the cat's other favorite spraying spots with plastic tarps. She would have to keep the tarps clean, too, throwing them out if they became wet and replacing them with new ones. He stopped then and said,

"How is this so far?"

Like too much work for a cat I hate, she thought. But there was something commanding and reassuring in his tone, so she nodded for him to go on.

"Let him have his run of the place during the day—even your bedroom. It's a special place to him now, off-limits, which is why he wants back in there so desperately. I understand your need to sleep, so you will have to confine him at night. But during the day, Whoop is allowed to go wherever he wants. Put all your food and your"—he consulted her folder again—"vintage cashmere sweaters out of reach.

"Next, let him eat whenever he wants. I think maybe he's attacking your food because he's hungry, or he perceives he's hungry. You need to leave a bowl of dry food and one of fresh water out for him at all times."

"So, basically, let him do whatever he wants."

"That's right."

"But look at him," Pru couldn't help saying. "He's so fat he's going to explode. Isn't it really unhealthy for him to eat all day?"

"You were going to bring him back to the shelter, where he certainly would have been euthanized. Does it really matter how he dies?"

At this point, the cat himself ventured out from his hiding place. His tail was pointing straight up in the air, giving him a very smug look.

"Oh, hush, you," Pru said.

She could have sworn Dr. Bond had grinned slightly at that. But he quickly turned somber again, and said, "Last, and this will probably be the hardest thing for you, I want you to play with Whoop whenever you can. Drag a string for him, rub him between the ears, let him bat around a foil ball. Don't just leave things out for him, or he'll get tired of them. Get down there and play with him. I think you'll find that if you pay attention to him during the day, he won't be so needy at night. And it'll be good exercise for him. Since you're so concerned with his obesity."

Although she didn't particularly like his recommendations, she found herself pleased that he was telling her exactly what to do. It sounded so clean and orderly, his plan. Finally, someone who had the answers. She watched the silver pen in his hand flash as he made his notes. She wanted to throw out her other problems, just to see what he'd say. Just to watch that beautiful pen spell out the detailed, easy-to-follow plan he would create for her. "What about me?" she wanted to shout. "I'm stressed, too! I'm a good girl, a handsome girl!"

The cat chose that moment to do something he'd never done before: He came over to Pru and rubbed up against her legs. *Suck-up!* she thought.

"See?" said Bond, more pleasantly. "He's really not so bad. Are you, big boy?"

She cleared her throat. "What about the Prozac?"

"I don't think it would do him any good. Let's make these adjustments first and see what happens."

Dr. Bond showed her how to lure Whoop backward into his cage and close the door without alarming him. Dr. Bond gave her a couple cans of diet cat food and some cat toys and said she should call him in two weeks to report on their progress.

The cat had settled right down in his cage and was beginning to wash himself. As she was leaving the office, two women stood talking together in the outer lobby. One of them had a small beagle sort of dog on a leash that kept leaping up to nip the other woman in the crotch. Neither woman did anything about it. The woman being nipped didn't even put a hand down to shield herself. There was a wet smear on her skirt from the dog's nose, but they both continued to talk and pay it no mind.

Pru just couldn't understand that. Was that where she was headed? Would she, too, slide so far down that spiral that soon she'd be walking around with kitty pictures in her wallet and a rear end covered in pet hair? From there, it was the tiniest leap into total and complete acceptance that the good life, as she'd known it, was over. She could kiss her self-esteem good-bye, along with any remaining impervious pieces of her heart.

COVERED IN THE PLASTIC TARPS, HER APARTMENT ENDED up looking like an auto detailing shop, and not the funky artist's loft she'd hoped that it would.

"Here we go," she said to the cat, unlocking the door of the cage. The cat hesitated, then came bounding out. He was making his usual beeline for under the couch, when he spotted his supper dish. It was an oversized Tupperware that was designed to hold, by the look of it, six or seven lasagnas, and now contained eight and a half pounds of Science Diet Hairball Control Light. He approached the bowl gingerly, not daring to believe his incredible bounty. He sniffed, then began wolfing down the food, glancing up at Pru to see when she was going to get up and snatch it from him. Pru sat down at the table with the newspaper and began reading. She stayed where she was while the cat lapped at his water, sniffed at the tarps, and ran through the apartment a few times. He hid from her when she folded up the paper and stood up, but, as she was preparing her dinner, he crept out and began bounding around again. He even came into the kitchen area to sniff at the can of tuna she'd opened for her dinner.

"What do you want?" she said to him. "Tuna?"

The cat licked his lips and bobbed his head once, as if to say yes.

"Why the hell not," she said, tossing him a chunk. "I was going to have you euthanized, after all."

Finally the cat settled himself on the couch, instead of under it, and began to wash himself. She tried to interest him in some of the cat toys, but he was still too scared of her to play.

Before going to bed, she was supposed to put the cat in the bathroom. She approached him as Dr. Bond had instructed, from behind, while talking in a low, soothing tone. "I'm sorry to have to do this, um, Big Whoop," she said. To her surprise, the cat allowed himself to be picked up and brought into the bathroom. There wasn't much room in there for him, with the three boxes of cat litter—sand, clay, and pine—that she was to offer to him until he made his preference known. He threw himself into a corner of the bathroom and regarded her resentfully as she closed the door.

She was about to turn out the light when McKay called to see how it went.

"What did you think of Bradley?"

"*Not* what I expected."

"You should see his Donna Summer."

"He's a drag queen?"

"I'm sure it's called something a little more P.C., like gender illusionist."

She tried to imagine Dr. Bond in a sparkly wig and lip gloss. Oddly, it was not impossible. "I'm glad you didn't tell me this before my appointment."

"So? Did he give you the Prozac?"

"No. I'm supposed to do the opposite of everything I was doing. I'm supposed to give him everything he wants, whenever he wants it, until his anxiety eases."

McKay made approving sounds. "He's very Zen in his approach," McKay said.

The cat still woke her up at four o'clock in the morning, but he'd stopped hurling himself against doors. When she came home from breakfast at the Korner—no sign of Sexy Yoga Babe, thank heavens—he was sitting on her bed. She changed the water in his bowl, then sat at her desk to work. A few days later, when Pru brought home the new laser printer, he played at batting around the Styrofoam inserts from the box. He sat and watched as she set up all the cords. Presently, he came closer to bat at the pages, with curious fascination, as the first batch of her business cards came rolling out of the printer.

Prudence Whistler
GRANTS, FUND-RAISING, GRAPHIC DESIGN,
LIFE COACHING, ORGANIZATION

She didn't really know what she meant by "life coaching" and "organization," but they sounded like things she'd like to try. She'd had to hold herself back from including "on-air talent." Rudy (oh Rudy, that *shit*) used to tell her all the time that she should be on public radio. Oh, he'd told her so many things she'd been all too happy to believe.

She separated the cards from the sheets, and felt a wave of disappointment. They looked cheap, and unprofessional. There were little tufts of perforated paper hanging off the edges. They looked desperate. She wouldn't hire a person with such a card to come toss out her urine-covered plastic tarps, much less do anything professional. She canceled the rest of the print job and threw the cards in the trash. A week's worth of work, right there.

At dinnertime, she went into the kitchen for her usual can of tuna. She was feeling defeated and low. The cat followed her in this time, and was sitting up on his haunches, waiting for his scrap, before she'd even opened the can. They had a little routine, she realized, and threw him some. She took her tuna and a sleeve of crackers to the couch, and tried to watch *GoodFellas* on her laptop. Eventually, though, the violence was too much. Not even the lure of Lorraine Bracco's dresses could offset it. She winced at every gunshot, until finally closing up her laptop for good. The cat sat nearby, washing. The only sound was the gentle scraping of his rough tongue against paw pads. Now she was regretting having dumped Rudy's TV set. She would give anything to fill the emptiness around her with the cheerful blather of this season's young and beautiful, the electronic mirth of a laugh track, the gentle assurances of tampon commercial voice-overs or the entrancing spectacle of B-list celebrities gasping their last on some reality show. Anything but this, the white silence of her loneliness.

On her way to the bathroom to brush her teeth, she noticed that the box filled with clay litter had been used. She threw out the other two boxes, thinking how ridiculously obvious that should have been to her. That night, she put him as usual in the bathroom but didn't shut the door. Sometime after midnight she woke up to find the cat on her bed. She could feel him sitting there watching her. When she didn't kick him off, he got up and came to sniff the blankets. Then he sniffed her hand. She could feel his whiskers tickling her wrist. After a while, he settled himself and, tentatively, pushed his head under her hand.

She worked her fingers in a little circle on his head, between the ears. A low rumbling filled his body. He was purring. It was the first time she'd heard that since he'd arrived. She found a spot in front of his ear that made him dip his head with pleasure. He rolled heavily onto his side, paws flexing in the air. He looked so fat and happy that she smiled.

Tomorrow, she would go to the stationer's on Eighteenth, where Fiona got her wedding invitations, and have them make up new business cards for her. It would cost a little, but she was sure it'd be worth paying to have them engraved. And matching letter-head, she thought, warming to the idea. On some lovely, textured vellum paper.

She closed her eyes, and after a long while of scratching Big Whoop's head, while he flexed and purred, she fell asleep.

Eight

Annali was showing Pru her new baby. Pru recognized it as Dipsy, the green Teletubby with the halo. They were sitting on the deck of Pru's grandmother's beach house in Delaware, eating strawberry Jell-O Jigglers and watching Patsy and Jacob as they made their way down the beach.

Pru hadn't been in the beach house in years. When she and Patsy were kids, they would visit the house every summer, even after her grandmother had died. But Nadine and Leonard seemed to slow down drastically when Pru was in college. They found the ten-hour trip difficult, between the packing and the driving and opening and closing up the house. Pru was surprised to realize the house had been, for the past ten years, largely unoccupied. She'd actually forgotten about it until Patsy brought it up. Annali called the Dipsy "PBSKids" and stuck it under her nightgown to nurse. Pru thought that her niece looked like a child from a Robert McCloskey book, a girl named Sal, maybe, or Jane. She looked as though she should be digging for clams on a beach in

Maine, or squatting to pet a duckling. Annali had a tight cap of coarse, curly blond hair, and pink cheeks. Her face was round and shining, and she always looked a little bit sleepy. It had been such a relief when she'd run up to Pru in the airport. Pru hadn't fully realized it at the time, but she'd been afraid Annali had forgotten who she was.

Annali was holding the little knit hat she carried with her everywhere she went. It was the hat Pru's mother had made for Pru when she was a baby. The yarn used to be white with colored flecks in it, but Annali had loved it until it turned a sort of speckled gray. Annali fingered the hat when she sucked her thumb, and rubbed her knuckles against it as she fell asleep.

Labor Day weekend was the best one in Rehoboth Beach— still warm and beautiful, the last gasp of the season. From the window of the Peter Pan bus she'd taken up from D.C., Pru saw the same boardwalk she'd remembered as a kid, the huge red sign for Dolle's Salt Water Taffy. All the same places were there, with their ancient, faded signs: Starkey's Cones and Sundaes, Gus & Gus Place Hamburgers French Fries and Fried Chicken, and the Playland/Virtual Fun Redemption Arcade.

"PBSKids wants more Jell-O," Annali said, pushing Dipsy's head into the bowl.

"PBSKids needs something to eat besides Jell-O," said Pru. She was already planning the wholesome meals she'd prepare during Annali's stay. She was taking her back to D.C. with her in the morning, so Patsy and Jacob could have some "grown-up" time together. Annali's diet seemed to consist solely of Jell-O and "lollipops," big spoonfuls of peanut butter. She didn't think she once saw the girl eat a vegetable or anything made with a whole grain. And Pru herself could do with something other than tuna and crackers.

The house was situated on a relatively isolated strip of beach just north of town. She could still make out Patsy and Jacob, two black scrawls holding hands, coming toward her down the beach. The shawl Patsy had tied around her waist whipped her legs in the mild wind, and her hair blew long and loose.

Since Pru had arrived last night, Patsy and Jacob hadn't stopped talking for a moment. Their ongoing dialogue ranged far and wide—Tibet, the perfection of the arch of Patsy's foot, Sid Vicious, the origin of the word *salacious* (whether Greek or Latin), getting Annali to swim. Although the subjects changed frequently, Pru noticed, there was a single connecting line: Things Patsy and Jacob See in Exactly the Same Way.

There was a second favorite topic: Things Patsy and Jacob Don't See in Exactly the Same Way, and Why One or the Other Is Completely Wrong.

They were enthralled with each other. When Pru didn't feel invisible, she felt like a groupie. She felt she was being called upon to appreciate their specialness. She didn't want to dislike Jacob, but she couldn't help it. Pru found it hard to trust someone so clearly fortunate in all ways. But, then again, maybe she was just jealous.

The fact was she'd never seen Patsy so happy. She'd hardly dated at all since having Annali. The daily life of a single mom with a young child wasn't so attractive to most guys, especially the ones still hanging around Nome, Ohio. They were stuck in a kind of time warp, drinking beer at the same bars, their car stereos still programmed to WMMS, Home of the Buzzard! Playing the Rock You Grew Up With.

Annali shoved the Teletubby into her lap and said, "Auntie Pru, I have to burp."

"So, burp," Pru said.

Annali opened her mouth and a thick, red stream fell across the white patio table.

For a minute Pru thought she was playing a trick on her. As she watched the blood drip through the cracks in the table, her stomach clenched.

"Aunt Pru?" Annali said, in a frightened, quavering voice. Pru raised her eyes from the table. Annali's eyes were round and glassy. Pru stood up and the chair behind her clattered to the floor.

She ran to the balcony and screamed Patsy's name as loud as she could. They were much closer than she'd expected. Patsy looked up, dropped Jacob's hand, and broke into a full run. She came thundering up the wooden stairs, Jacob right behind her.

"What happened? Jesus God," she said, when she saw the table. For a moment, they were all mesmerized.

Then Patsy recovered, throwing her hands in the air and crying, "Oopsie!" She sang it out in this trilling, *Romper Room* voice, like *Oopsie, you spilled your juice!* And not *Oopsie, you just threw up your own liver!*

Jacob stepped forward, stuck a finger in the pool of blood, and brought it up to his tongue. The expression in his eyes was calm and medically professional. Pru felt her throat close, in protest.

"It's Jell-O," he said. He held up the finger. "Red Jell-O," he said, tasting it again. "Maybe strawberry?"

Patsy started to laugh. "Oh, you monkey!" she cried, catching Annali up in her arms.

"You gave us such a freakin' scare! *Jesus!*"

Pru sank into a chair. She had been so afraid that she'd been unable to move. She hadn't known what to do after yelling for Patsy. It left her shaken, and confused.

"It's the wrong viscosity for blood," Jacob said, pleasantly, after Patsy had taken Annali inside to get cleaned up. He poked at the pool again, to illustrate. "Blood from the gut is dark and grainy, like coffee grounds. You can see this is totally smooth."

"Jacob," she managed to say, "thank you."

"See? A guy like me can really come in handy. I also make a good cocktail, if you're ready for one."

"Lord, yes," said Pru. "Nothing strawberry, please."

"HERE WE GO, ANNALI!" CRIED JACOB. THEY WERE standing at the edge of the water, but she was refusing to get so much as a toe wet. He was doing sort of a loopy Dick Van Dyke routine, gesturing with his arms toward the ocean, saying, "*Into* the water, now! *Into* the water! Here we *go!*" While he splashed, knees high, into the surf, Annali turned and walked in the opposite direction. Pru and Patsy burst out laughing.

Late afternoon at the beach hadn't changed in all these years, either. There were never many people on the strip of beach in front of the house, closed off from either side by two rock formations, and even fewer at this time of day. The beach ran to the left and to the right of the house, undisturbed, undeveloped, as it always had been. The houses were the same, too, two- or three-bedroom clapboard sea shanty–type houses. The hotels hadn't invaded this far down the beach yet. Pru wondered how long that could last. She tried to come up with anything else in life as unchanging as that beach. Her mother's house, perhaps—the tiny, dark one-story home where she and Patsy had always shared a bedroom. The only changes made over the course of thirty years had been a new refrigerator, the addition of high-speed cable, which her mother had had installed once she discovered online Scrabble, and the absence of her father, his basement workroom crowded with unopened boxes.

And now it was Annali at the water's edge with Jacob, while Pru and Patsy sat on the striped lounge chairs under a big cobalt blue umbrella, like a couple of queens. They flipped through their magazines and watched Jacob try to coax Annali into the water. Whenever a wave rolled in, Annali ran away from it, shrieking with laughter. Jacob had a nice way with her, Pru had to admit. She let out a contented sigh, and Patsy turned to smile at her.

"Glad you finally joined us," Patsy said. "Another minute of your crazy city energy, and I was going to have to hit you with a stuffed marlin."

Pru put her hand up against the glare. Jacob, lean and sinewy in his swimming trunks, water dripping from his head, was lifting Annali up and carrying her toward the water. She shrieked and clung to him. Slowly, talking to her all the while, he walked out into the water. When a wave came, he held her up above it. She loved it, laughing and screaming, scared and thrilled at the same time.

She needs a daddy, Pru thought, and instantly felt horribly guilty. The Whistler women had agreed, silently, never to mention this among them. Even though they'd never spoken about it, she knew her mother and sister had worked hard to make up for the lack of a father figure, especially after Leonard had died.

Now, seeing them together, she remembered what it was about a daddy that Annali was missing. A daddy who could lift you up in his arms, a daddy with all that warm, salty skin to hold on to, a daddy never too tired or too busy or too worried or too angry to carry you as long as you wanted, wave after wave after wave after wave. A mommy wouldn't let you be afraid in the middle of the night. But daddies could actually *do* something about it. Even a daddy like Leonard, who, Pru was sure, had never raised his fists against anyone in his life. Daddies, everyone knew, could hold you safely up above the whole world, with their strong arms.

AT DINNER THAT NIGHT, IN ONE OF THE SEAFOOD RES-taurants in town, Jacob cracked open his lobster and said, "The first time I saw a cadaver, I couldn't wait to touch it."

He had little ways like that of surprising you, Pru was learning. He could be so earnest. Despite his obvious advantages, he so clearly wanted to be liked, he might have even been a little in doubt of whether or not anyone *should* like him. She turned to him. "So why aren't you doing autopsies, or something like that?"

"That's a little more distance than I really want from my patients." He dragged a piece of lobster flesh through the butter and popped it in his mouth. "I wouldn't want to see the same person day in and day out, but only the deceased?" He shook his head. "Plus, you get to see everything in Emergency. *Everything.* Then they go home, and you play video games with the ambu-lance drivers until the next lot comes in."

"Like what do you get to see?"

He ran a finger under the neck of his lobster bib, loosening it. "Last week? I saw a post-op transsexual whose surgery hadn't gone so well."

"Hadn't gone well how?"

He withdrew a pen, then drew a rough sketch on a napkin, making circles and arrows, showing Pru exactly what should have been where, and what really was there. She grimaced.

"It's all a matter of taste, if you ask me," he said, putting down the pen. "Who says what we should and shouldn't look like?"

"Well, there are sort of minimum acceptable standards, aren't there?" Pru said.

"You'd be surprised. People have all kinds of arrangements. All kinds."

She might have been imagining things, but the air between Patsy and Jacob suddenly seemed charged. Patsy was just sitting there, drinking her beer, with Annali in her lap, quietly coloring on the restaurant's paper place mat. Nobody said anything, while Jacob continued to crack open his lobster. But it seemed to Pru that something had been transmitted between them. He'd been talking about arrangements—probably it had something to do with Patsy's newly unveiled plans to move to Rehoboth, Pru decided. Maybe he wasn't so thrilled about it? Or maybe she was annoyed that Jacob hadn't asked her to move in with him, in D.C.? Whatever it was, Patsy wasn't happy. Pru could see that, plain as toast.

Later, when Jacob was outside making a phone call and Annali was all but asleep on her lap, Patsy said, "I'm glad you finally eased up on him. It means a lot to me."

Pru stared at her. "What'd I do to deserve that?"

Patsy shrugged. "I know you didn't like him. He knew it, too."

Pru couldn't deny that, but she didn't like to think it had been so obvious. Jacob brought out some unsavory side of Patsy, a side that was just a bit smug, a bit satisfied. It was as if their love confirmed Patsy's long-held suspicion that she was a touch more special than ordinary people. That she was destined for a kind of love exactly like this—sudden and true and deeply spiritual. She met a doctor on a train when he'd overheard something clever she'd said about sex—a story bound to appeal to Patsy. And this wasn't looking like a short-term thing. Pru had the feeling she'd be living with the Specials from Planet Special for a long time.

Patsy was watching her closely, waiting for her reaction. She really was afraid of something, Pru realized. Her annoyance faded. Possibly she'd been on the mark, with the idea that Jacob and Patsy had different opinions about whether they should move in together.

"I just had some reservations, is all. Come on, I'm protective of you guys. So sue me," Pru said.

"What about now?"

"Look, I see the attraction. He's great. And great with Annali. But"—she had to choose her words carefully, she knew—"you know what you're doing, right?"

"Here we go."

"What?"

"Here's where you make me feel like shit."

"I don't want you to feel like shit. I'm just saying, make sure you can trust the guy. Sure, today he's great with Annali, but that doesn't mean he's in it for the long haul, you know." She hated how she sounded, sometimes, with Patsy—all cautionary and "long haul" and all that. What was it about her sister that made her suddenly become a TV-sitcom dad?

"Thanks for your concern," Patsy said, bitterly, "about *Annali*."

"Come on, I'm worried about you, too. I don't want to see you get hurt."

"I haven't done one thing in two years without thinking first of Annali," Patsy said. "I wake up in the morning: Annali. I drive myself to work: Annali. Maybe I'll take a vacation: oh, right, Annali. Do you have any idea what that's like? Any idea, Pru?"

Pru didn't reply. When they both lived at home, she and Patsy had certainly had their fights. Screaming names, pulling hair, throwing clogs—the works. Maybe it was living alone for so long that made her unable to engage in it, but now she felt cowed by the prospect of a toe-to-toe with Patsy. She didn't know why. "I haven't had it so easy, either," she could have said, to which Patsy would have answered, "What does that mean?" And Pru would say, "It's not so easy being alone. Do you think I like being alone?" But then Patsy would probably snap, "Oh, I think I know alone, Pru. I think I know alone better than most." She pressed her lips together and stared at the aquarium under the bottles of liquor at the bar.

Pru *had* meant to do more, after Annali was born. She sent clothes and little gifts for both of them, just so they'd know she was thinking of them. But it had never felt like enough. She was never called upon to babysit, never asked to help with Annali's expenses. She'd gotten off far too easily, and her own conscience hadn't picked up the slack. She was glad Annali was coming home with her the following day. It would give her a chance to make up for all that, and to get some veggies in the girl, to boot.

Patsy drank her beer moodily. She kept glancing to the door where Jacob had disappeared to take his call. Pru tried to turn the conversation to the afternoon at the beach, how it reminded her of their childhood and their father. She wanted Patsy to remember the bathing suits they wore with the cinching strings up the sides, but Patsy ignored her. A wall had risen between them. Jacob came back from his phone call—a scheduling problem at the hospital, he said, and he needed to be back to the city sooner than he'd thought. Pru would still take Annali to D.C. in the morning, but just for the one night, not two. They were silent the whole way home.

In the morning, as she was getting ready to leave, Pru went into the bedroom where Patsy was packing up Annali's suitcase and put her hands on her sister's shoulders. "I love you, you know," she said, and Patsy said, "Oh, shut up." But she let herself be hugged, and everything seemed back to normal again. Still, Pru made a silent vow to stay out of this business with Jacob. Where he was concerned, she'd keep all unsolicited opinions to herself and concentrate her efforts on Annali. She had much to make up for there, and she thought she would be a good influence. Steady, and calm. Patsy was only all too eager for the help. Jacob was a touchy subject. She and her sister were closer now than they had been in years, and she didn't want to do anything to jeopardize their fragile new alliance.

Nine

When they arrived at Pru's apartment the next day, Annali dashed right after Big Whoop. He backed away but, to Pru's surprise, let her pick him up and cuddle him. He was so big that Annali could barely get him off the floor.

There was a note on the kitchen table from McKay: "Love your boy. Call me when you're back."

"He likes this one the best," she said to Annali, giving her the toy that looked like a spider on a long, thin wire. Annali waved it in front of Whoop, who jumped and snatched it out of the air. Annali let out a shriek, and dropped the toy.

While Pru unpacked, Annali wandered around the apartment. She said, in her slow monotone, "Aunt Prudence, where is your TV?"

"No TV," Pru said cheerfully. "What should we do instead?"

Annali shrugged and said, "I don't know."

She tried to remember what she'd seen her friend Fiona's kids doing. "Well, how about Go Fish? Would you like that?"

Annali nodded. They sat on the floor and Pru dealt out the cards. Annali fingered her knit hat and sucked her thumb until Pru told her to pick up her cards. It quickly became apparent that she had never in her life played Go Fish. "I'll start," said Pru. "Do you have any sixes?"

She solemnly nodded.

"So, you give them to me."

She looked at her cards carefully, then handed Pru a card. It was the jack of hearts.

Pru looked at Annali's cards. "You don't have any sixes. You say, Go fish."

"Yes, I do."

"No, you don't. Okay, I'm fishing. Now it's your turn."

"Do you have any sixes?"

"Annali, you don't have any sixes, so you can't ask me for sixes. You have to have something to ask me for it."

"Go fish," Annali said.

Pru began to gather the cards. "I know," she said, "let's play matching."

She showed Annali how to turn all the cards face down and match them. After a while, Annali went back to her thumb and her hat, and watched Pru match up all the cards.

Annali looked up and suddenly said, "Tell me a story."

Pru frowned. She could never tell a story on the spot like that. Her mother was the one with the knack for inventing little adventure tales. Whenever Pru would try, she ended up using something they'd just seen in one of Annali's videos. In her stories, Annali was always climbing up a tree to retrieve her honey pot or making friends with a big red dog. Besides which, she found herself irritated that Annali wouldn't let her finish the matching game.

"Let's play something else," Pru said.

"Okay, let's make believe."

"That sounds good." But her heart sank. She didn't really want to do any of these things. What did she think Annali was going to say, Let's read the last three weeks of *The New Yorker* and go to bed early?

"You be Mary Poppins and I'll be Jane Banks."

"Okay," said Pru.

They sat there staring at each other. Annali's mouth made little sucking sounds around her thumb.

Pru couldn't remember much of *Mary Poppins*. She'd seen it only once in her life, when she was six. "Spit-spot?" she ventured.

The thumb came out. "Make me take my medicine."

"Here's your medicine."

"No!" Annali cried. "You have to say, Children who get their feet wet must learn to take their medicine. Then I say, Cherry cordial, and you say, Rum punch."

They did that, then did it fifteen thousand times more.

Finally it was time for Annali's dinner and blessedly early bedtime. Although Pru had meant to stuff fresh veggies into the girl, Annali absolutely refused to eat the steamed spinach and carrots Pru put before her. Pru was forced to prepare mac and cheese she'd gotten from the health food store, but Annali rejected it, too, saying it was the wrong kind of mac and cheese. At bath time, the shampoo Pru used to get the sand out of Annali's hair burned her eyes and made her cry, and then they got into an argument over whether Annali was supposed to get five books before bed, or four. Lord, but Patsy had spoiled that child! Annali definitely wasn't the same kid she was six months ago, when she was still delighted by anything Pru did. "Lie down with me!"

Annali cried, when Pru turned off the lights. "Open the door! More, more!"

"It's a good thing you're so dang super-cute," Pru said. "Otherwise I'd eat your head."

Annali giggled and made room in the bed. Pru sighed, then crawled in next to her. She'd been warned that Annali absolutely would not fall asleep without a grown-up. She'd had secret thoughts about breaking Annali of that habit, too, but she was tired. She'd already tested her willpower against Annali's, and was found wanting.

Annali sang softly and played with her hat for a while, pushing her feet into it and stretching it out, until Pru said to stop and go to sleep. When Annali's mouth had fallen open and her breathing was deep and slow, Pru slipped out, and began to search the kitchen for a drink. She felt the need to exercise, however tenuously, her prerogatives as a grown-up. Which meant, in this case, getting a little drunk while looking at the new Pottery Barn catalogue.

Just as she was about to sit down with her usual dinner of tuna and crackers, she heard shrieks coming from the bedroom. Pru jumped up and hurried to the bedroom, her heart pounding in her chest. Annali was sitting up in bed, crying. There were monsters under the bed, she said. She *saw* one.

"It was just the cat, honey."

"There was a monster!"

"You know there's no such thing as monsters," Pru said. Annali cried harder.

"Spray them!" she yelled, bouncing up and down on the bed. "Get your monster spray and spray the monsters!"

"What?"

"You have to spray them," she sobbed, falling to her knees.

Something from *Mary Poppins* came back then: *Not another word, or I shall have to summon the policeman.* Brisk, kindly, firm. "Annali Whistler, you calm down. You *know* there's no such thing as monsters." With that, Pru began to leave the room.

"Stay with me!" Annali yelled, lunging at her and clutching at her sweater.

"Oh, all right." Pru lay down on the bed and Annali wrapped both arms around her neck. After a while her sobs subsided and her breathing slowed. Every now and then she would hiccup. Pru fell asleep, too, and when she woke up later, the little arms were still holding on tightly to her neck. The phone next to the bed rang and Pru snatched it before it could wake up Annali.

"Hello?" she whispered.

"How'd it go?" Not Patsy, but their mother. "Is she asleep already? I was going to call earlier, but then I thought it might upset her to hear my voice."

Pru untangled herself from Annali's grip and brought the phone out to the living room.

"She freaked out about monsters."

Her mother laughed and said, "That's a big thing right now. Did you spray?"

"What *is* that?"

"She can't go to sleep until you spray for monsters."

"Patsy didn't mention anything about monster spray."

"I just use my deodorant."

"Why are we indulging this? I mean, is it healthy? What if she gets dependent on it?"

"Nobody's ever gone to college needing monster spray," said Nadine.

"If she even gets *into* college."

"Prudence. She's *two*. When you were two, I used to have to sweep out from under your bed every night with a broom."

"Really?"

"You had terrible fears. Always did. We used to keep a pallet on our floor so you could sleep next to us. Until Patsy was old enough to share a room with you, anyway."

What a funny thing not to know about yourself, Pru thought, tucking her feet under her. A pallet, next to her parents' bed. It made her sound like a servant child.

"Annali told me she gets ice cream when she has nightmares. Is that true?"

Nadine sighed. "Well . . . sometimes, yes."

"Come on, that can't be a good thing. A sundae, every time she says she has a nightmare? What is Patsy thinking?"

"She says it's to give Annali something happy to think about when she remembers the nightmare. So, tell me about Jacob."

Whoop jumped up on her lap, bringing with him a cloud of clay litter. Pru began to scratch him in his favorite place, on his belly.

"Well, he certainly seems to love Patsy. And Annali."

"Patsy says he's great with her."

"I guess." This was followed by a little silence. Where, Pru guessed, she was supposed to rave about Jacob.

"Don't you like Jacob?" her mother said, now worried.

"I do," Pru said, slowly. "It just seems that it's moving awfully fast. You know, she's so taken by him. She's even more impulsive than usual. I mean, the whole thing with Jimmy Roy—"

"We don't know what happened with Jimmy Roy," her mother interrupted. "He had qualities. You remember how he was, when Annali was born. You saw him."

"Deer in headlights" was the phrase that came to mind, when she recalled Jimmy Roy at the birth of his daughter. He'd seemed much younger than twenty-five, almost teenagerlike. Patsy's midwife had let him pull the baby out and cut the umbilical cord. He would hold the baby and stare at her for hours, without saying a word. In Pru's opinion, he might have been irresponsible, but you couldn't say he wasn't affected by the birth of his baby girl.

"Patsy knows what she's doing," Nadine said. "She follows her heart."

"Her heart doesn't always have the best sense of direction."

Her mother laughed. "Did you get a new TV?"

"Not yet."

"Well, you might want to take Annali to the swings, after breakfast. Mornings can be hard."

She wondered if she should have told her mother that Patsy and Jacob were actually talking about Patsy and Annali moving to the beach house. But she knew it would break her mother's heart to hear that news. And maybe it was just talk, anyway. You didn't want to act too quickly on what Patsy said. Patsy said a lot of things.

FOR THE NEXT THREE WEEKENDS, ANNALI STAYED AT Pru's while Patsy and Jacob worked on the beach house. They bought all new furniture, replaced the thin, leaky windows with weatherized, double-paned ones, and recarpeted in the bedrooms. Patsy never said so, but Jacob had to be paying for everything. Patsy's small teaching stipend barely allowed her to cover her own rent on a little two-bedroom house down the street from their mother's and to keep up repairs on her battered old hatchback. Although Pru was worried about the arrangement, she kept her mouth shut. She figured her part in all of this was to keep Annali happy.

Which wasn't an easy job. For one thing, Pru found the occupation of child watching unbearably dull. She hated, for instance, Annali's main delight, the swing set at the scruffy little neighborhood playground near her building. This morning, the third Sunday in a row Annali was a visitor to Pru's apartment, there was a definite chill in the air, announcing the beginning, at last, of D.C.'s brief autumn. Patsy had promised that this would be the last time she'd ask Pru to watch Annali, until almost Thanksgiving. Pru shivered in her sweater. The chains of the swing made a forlorn, creaking sound, threaded through with the sad notes of the little song Annali liked to sing to herself. *My heart,* she sang, *love to my heart* . . . The street was empty, except for the occasional homeless person shuffling down the street.

Kill me, Pru thought, giving the swing a sharp push. *Somebody, please, kill me now.* God, her mother hadn't been kidding—mornings were *deadly.* Annali got up dreadfully early, just as Whoop was allowing Pru to let her sleep later. So by seven A.M., she'd exhausted what turned out to be a pretty limited bag of tricks to begin with. She still couldn't get over how hard it was to take care of a two-year-old. Annali demanded constant attention. She couldn't stand it if Pru tried to go to the bathroom by herself, or tried to sit down with a cup of tea and a magazine. Pru prayed this was just a phase of Annali's, a result of her being without her mommy, whose attention was, for the time being, elsewhere.

Because this could not be what mothering is all about. Simply *could not* be. The female gender would have done itself in long, long ago if this was all there was to child-rearing, this endless need for amusement, attention, and sippy cups. Pru as she knew herself ceased to exist when Annali was there. If she was on the toilet, there was Annali. In bed at night, there was Annali, tossing and turning so that, once again, Pru couldn't sleep. She couldn't shower, either, with Annali around, and a whole day could go by that she didn't run a comb through her hair. No wonder Patsy had looked like a wrung-out sponge for an entire year after Annali was born. It had shocked Pru, at the time. She had known—she had *thought*—that this would never happen to *her.*

She scanned the playground, desperate for any kind of adult contact. If one of the homeless people had slowed down to pick a cigarette butt off the street, she would have pounced on him. Finally, after much negotiating, she managed to persuade Annali off the swings and out for breakfast.

They slid into a booth at the Korner and ordered pancakes. Annali looked around, as if to say, You expect me to eat in a place like *this*? John smiled and waved from behind the counter, where he was organizing the Sunday-morning rush, such as it was. Ludmilla, the new, curvy, silent waitress, brought her a cup of coffee, and Pru felt her shoulders relax back down from her ears. Here were people! Grown-ups! Lovers right out of bed, gay couples meeting for breakfast, a couple of lost-looking tourists. Annali drank from her sippy cup while Pru savored her coffee, both of them watching the scene with hungry interest. She had the urge to run around and ask everyone what they'd done last night. A harmless but odd-looking elderly woman whom Pru recognized as one of the diner's regulars came over to the table. She wanted to talk to Annali. Her mouth was crooked, with a jutting-out jaw, and she wore a damp, dank wool scarf wrapped around her neck. She stood too close to Annali's side of the table, overwhelming her with her strange old-lady smell, her loneliness, her need to make Annali smile. *Me, after ten more years of being alone,* Pru thought. Annali turned away and began to cry. Pru could have done the same thing. She put an arm around Annali and pulled her closer.

Annali wrenched herself away. "I want my mommy!" she cried.

"Mommy will be home soon," Pru said. "Before lunch!" she added brightly. Annali began to howl.

"Hey," she said, snapping her fingers, a diversionary tactic that had worked once before. "Hey. I'm going to eat your head!"

The sound of Annali's wailing filled the café. It seemed to enter Pru physically and burn its way along all the neural pathways in her body. She wondered if she could just walk away, pretend to have nothing to do with this horrible child.

The next thing she knew, John was there with the pancakes. "I wanted *waffles*," Annali cried, kicking the table leg and making the cups and saucers rattle.

"I'm sorry," Pru said to John. "I think we better skip breakfast and go on home." At this, Annali began to kick her feet rhythmically, in time with her crying.

"How about a pancake on my head?" John said, trying a diversionary tactic of his own. He put one of Annali's pancakes on his head. "Now, where did that pancake go?" he said, pretending to look around.

Pru laughed, thinking he looked like a Swiss tourist, and so that he wouldn't feel bad. But Annali's face crumpled and her legs went rigid. "My pancake!" she wailed.

"I don't know what to do," Pru said. Annali was listing to one side now. Pru could see she was heading for the floor, where she could have her tantrum in comfort. People were looking at them.

But Pru didn't want to go home, to her lonely, messy, boring apartment. *Please,* she pleaded silently. *Knock it off.*

They watched Annali, still howling, sinking under the table. Pru was beginning to wonder if she had some serious behavioral problems—and worse, how she would get her out from under the table without someone calling child protective services—when John said, "I know. Will you guys go upstairs and feed my fish? I have a Nemo fish."

Annali stopped crying instantly. She sat up straight and the thumb returned to the mouth. Her eyes were red. She sucked and hiccuped.

"You like Nemo?" John said, clearly pleased with himself. "That's great. Nemo is probably *starving* by now. Here, we'll take your breakfasts. You guys can eat up there."

He balanced the tray with one hand and led them through the diner.

"What does a two-year-old know about Roman emperors?" Pru whispered.

"That's Nero," John said. "This is Disney. It's a universal language. Like Esperanto for kids." As they made their way through the kitchen, two men looked up from their work. "This is Juan and Raul. Pru and Annali." The Hispanic chefs John employed returned Pru's smile. She noticed them exchanging looks, as the three of them went up the stairs that led to John's apartment.

"How do you know this?" Pru asked. "The last Disney thing I remember is *Fantasia.*"

"My sisters have kids. We saw the video fifty-six thousand times, by my count, last Christmas." He opened a door at the top of the stairs, and in two steps she was inside John Owen's apartment.

The apartment was large, sunny, and almost completely empty. In the dining room, which alone was as big as Pru's kitchen/

office/living room, there was a long wooden table and two chairs. The living room, where Annali found the fishtank, was even bigger. It held only a small, old futon, a stereo, and speakers.

"Mi casa," said John. Pru winced, thinking of the Yoga Babe's parting words, *"Adiós, amigo."* Was this some new verbal twitch he'd gotten from her? "Make yourselves at home. As much as you can, here," he said, looking around as if he'd only now noticed the spare furnishings.

"Are you sure this is okay?"

"No problem," he said, unloading the tray of food he'd brought up for them. "Stay as long as you need to." He showed Annali how to carefully tap food into the top of the fishtank. All the fish came darting over, to her delight.

"Thanks," said Pru, wishing he would stay. To keep him there another minute she said, "I feel like I'm doing everything wrong with her."

"I don't know if you can do anything wrong with kids."

"Lock them in your apartment and fly to Guadalajara?"

"Well, that would be wrong." They smiled at each other. Don't say "I better go," she pleaded, silently.

But then he said, "I guess I better go."

When John left them, Annali was perfectly calm and happy, inspecting the fishtank, all thoughts of her mother vanished into thin air. Pru was going to insist she stay home with Grandma next weekend. She knew her mother's arthritis made it difficult for her to care for Annali, but Pru needed a break. There was a dirty plate on the table, and she found herself wanting to examine it, curious to know what John had eaten for breakfast.

While Annali sat at the table, eating her pancakes, Pru walked around the apartment, snooping. She didn't see any trace of a female, no clothes or shoes or handbags lying about, nothing that would suggest that a woman had ever lived here. How could someone disappear so completely? Hadn't she left anything behind? Hadn't he kept something of hers to remember her by? She didn't know which would be worse, that he had or that he hadn't.

John's apartment had three bedrooms. Two were empty, except for some moving boxes and a few odd pieces of furniture. The smallest had been half-painted a happy shade of yellow. It looked like whoever had done it had stopped in the middle of the job. In the biggest room was the only bed in the place, a simple mattress on the floor. She saw the bedside table he'd talked about, the one where he'd found Lila's videos.

The covers were thrown off the mattress, revealing the place where he'd been sleeping. She knelt down next to it; then she lay down. She took an exploratory sniff of his pillow. It had only a pleasing, fresh laundry smell. John's bed, she realized, was situated to face the same direction as her own bed at home. She was musing that they were practically lying next to each other, on opposite ends of the same block and separated by only a series of brick walls, when she heard the front door open. She jumped up and hurried back down the hall.

"I thought I'd see how you're doing," John said. "It's pretty slow down there." He started collecting the breakfast plates, then put them down. "This place is kind of pathetic, isn't it? I hadn't realized it until now."

"I don't know," Pru said, looking around. "It's a beautiful apartment. But I get the feeling you haven't spent much time here."

He was quiet a moment. "No," he said. "The diner takes up all my time. *All* my time. It was my wife's big complaint." Suddenly he seemed angry. "I need to get out," he said. "Someplace that's not this building. Outside of the city. You want to go for a hike somewhere? Like, Shenandoah?"

THAT AFTERNOON, AFTER HANDING ANNALI OVER TO Patsy, Pru and John drove all the way out to Shenandoah National Park, two and a half hours outside the city. John's van was old and very dirty. The front end of it was perfectly flat. The cars in front were so close that Pru kept grabbing the dashboard. The radio was completely devoid of any kind of bass range, the interior upholstery was ripped up, and John looked utterly relaxed and happy, for the first time she could remember, as they bumped off the beltway and out of the city.

It was a gorgeous day, crisp and bright, and Pru was glad to ride quietly and look out the window at the changing scenery. She was still sad, from saying good-bye to Patsy and Annali. Patsy had come after lunch and they'd left for the airport, all in a hurry, because they were late, as usual. Pru always hated saying good-bye, but these Sundays were the worst. She gave Annali long hugs and kissed her face over and over.

When they drove up to the park ranger's station, it was past three o'clock in the afternoon. The scenery was spectacular. Sunlight played in the trees, showing to advantage the leaves in the throes of autumn, preening about in golds and pear and sunburn. It was as if, knowing that death was near, the leaves had finally gotten their act together, and burst forth into their full, glorious color.

John sprang into happy action, racing up a trail, circling back to her when she lagged behind, pointing out various things in the forest that had caught his eye. She'd never seen him so lively. Any trace of his former sadness was gone. Here he was in his element. He was like a frisky puppy, jumping everywhere.

She'd changed into the Lucky jeans and Doc Martens lace-up boots before John had picked her up, the only thing close to "rugged" she could find. But the Doc Martens weren't really meant for hiking, and by the time they stopped to eat, an hour later, her feet were hot and sore. She took off the boots and they ate the food John had brought: boiled eggs, a loaf of French bread, grapes, crackers and cheese, and carrot sticks.

The carrot sticks were what got her. Not baby carrots, but regular carrots peeled and cut into strips. He'd put them in waxed paper bags, just like her mother had used for their school lunches. He said he'd found the bags in the Latino supermarket in Mount Pleasant, where he liked to shop. Pru had been in there once, when she and Rudy were out walking and he'd wanted a bottle of water. Rudy had pinched his nose and said "pee-yoo" as soon as they'd walked out. It was true that the Latino market had a funny smell, but Pru had pretended she hadn't noticed. Surely it meant something, that John had gone to some trouble with the carrot sticks? Had he been thinking of what might please her?

"Lila called me this morning," he said, while they were eating. It took Pru a moment to realize he was talking about his wife. She'd forgotten that such a person existed.

"She's got a new boyfriend," he said. "After six weeks, she's dating again. And I'm still sleeping on one side of the bed." It was true, Pru knew. She'd seen his bed. Half of it was still made.

"That's harsh," Pru said. "I'm really sorry."

They put the lunch things back in John's knapsack and continued up the path they'd been hiking. John's sad looks were back, and he didn't say anything, so neither did Pru. She was vaguely aware of the time, as she always was, and there was a little anxiety in the back of her mind. The sun had gotten very low in the sky. But surely John knew that. Just when she was about to say something, he seemed to come to his senses. He looked up at the setting sun and said, "We'd better find our way back, huh?" They turned around and started back down the mountain. In a matter of minutes, though, it had gotten visibly darker. They began to hurry through the woods. Suddenly John stopped, at the intersection of two trails.

"Do you remember if this is right?" he said to Pru.

"I'm afraid I don't," she said, trying to swallow her nervousness. He frowned, and they kept going. "I think it's right," he said.

There were only traces of the sun's rays left. In another moment, she realized, they would be plunged into darkness. They were running so fast now that she stumbled. He reached back and grabbed her hand, pulling her along the brambled trail.

That was the next telling moment, after the carrots in the wax paper bag. The hand. As soon as it was holding hers, she had a feeling about it that didn't fully make sense. It was a nice enough hand, dry, with sensitive fingertips. Through it she could feel his worry, and his wish to reassure her, and his heartbeat. She was glad to have it guiding her along, in the darkness that at last had begun to close in on them. But it gave her an eerie feeling, too, of something familiar, something she had forgotten but now remembered. Like when you looked under your bed and there was your watch, which you hadn't even noticed was missing.

"Look!" shouted John. Somehow, they had found their way back to the ranger's station. Pru was discombobulated from the setting sun and the hand-holding. He dropped her hand when the van came into sight. They got in and both started laughing. "That would have been really smooth, huh?" John said. "I take you out and get you lost in the woods."

He put the key in the ignition and turned it. Nothing. He tried it again. Still nothing. They looked at each other. On the next try the engine rolled over once, gagged, and fell silent. Even more silent, it seemed to Pru, then before. Then the dashboard lights flickered, and faded. When John opened the door, the overhead light didn't come on. He went to pop the hood while she rooted in her bag for her cell phone. She could see him out there, the white of his T-shirt standing out slightly against the other gray forms.

"I can't see anything, and even if I could, I wouldn't know what to look for," he said, getting in the van. "You getting anything?" She had taken out her cell phone and had turned it on. It glowed blue, but she couldn't get a signal.

"No," she said. "Nothing."

John sat back in his seat. "Shit," he said.

"What do we do?"

They were at the park ranger's station, in the absolute dead of nowhere, with no phones, no food, and no *bathroom*. Just stay calm, she told herself.

Then John said, "Wait here."

He got out of the van and Pru watched him try the doors of the ranger's station. He walked all the way around the outside of the building, searching for a call box, a stash of emergency flares, she didn't know what. He went back to try the doors again, and all the windows. Then he came to the van, his hands shoved in his jacket pocket, a scowl on his face.

He got in and said, "I think we better hunker down and wait for the park ranger to come back."

She tried to keep her voice steady. "When do you think that will be?"

"I don't know. I guess it could be tomorrow morning."

"Someone has to know we're here, right?"

"Okay, listen, don't panic."

"I'm not panicking. I'm just thinking, I'm just *saying,* that someone had to have seen the van, and realize we were still out. They wouldn't just leave while we were still out, would they?"

"I'm afraid they have."

"And listen, you don't have to say 'panicking,' like I'm some hysterical female or something. Honestly. You hardly even know me, so how do you even know what's panicking and what's, you know, regular concern? I'm just trying to get a handle on what's happening here. I could have a whole range of emotions that you're not even fucking aware of. So don't say panicking. Now try the goddamn car again."

He did. Nothing. Just a jingle of keys, then silence.

"All right," she said. "So now we know. We're stuck." She was having trouble breathing.

"It's not so bad," he said, scampering to the back of the van. "Look, we have water and food and, you know, even blankets. Moving pads, really, but they'll do. Look how thick they are! And hopefully it won't get too cold tonight. We'll be okay."

Pru wanted to be cool and cooperative but her stomach was churning. She couldn't remember the last night she'd spent outside. She didn't think she was the most *regimented* person on the face of the planet, but honestly. Shouldn't they be shouting for help, sending out smoke signals, *something*? She couldn't spend all night out here, in the wilderness. What were they supposed to do, for all these hours, with no movie theater, no restaurant, nothing? What would she smell like in the morning? She didn't have so much as a toothbrush!

Pru sat in the front seat, shivering. Her family hadn't been one of those camping families. They might take a small cottage on a lake for a week or two during summer, but never in her life had she slept out in nature. The Whistlers liked to be home, in their beds, reading well past midnight. Oh, how she wanted to be home! She needed people and running water. Dead bolts and a security system and, when she could afford it, a night doorman. John seemed perfectly content with the unexpected adventure, this rent in the fabric of the everyday. He was actually *enjoying* this. He was hopping around, making a pile of blankets, cheerfully going through the bag of food he'd brought for their lunch, rationing the leftovers.

When he saw her sitting there, unmoving, he said, "You're not okay, are you?"

"I'm fine," she managed to reply. "Good." She practically whispered it. She was furious with him. How irresponsible! How stupid! And she'd wanted so much to like him. But a man who let himself get lost, who drove a half-dead van up the side of a mountain—was this a man you'd trust to pick up your own children from soccer practice?

"We'll be okay," he said. "I promise. There's no one around for miles."

"Oh, great," she groaned. She was remembering the bits of the shower scene from *Psycho* she had glimpsed through her fingers, when Rudy had discovered she'd never seen it and decided it was an essential part of her cultural education. She also remembered how, a few nights later, Rudy actually ripped open the shower curtain while she was in there, scaring the absolute bejesus out of her. Although he apologized immediately and swore up and down he had no idea it would terrify her so, it was days before she'd even let him spend the night. And she never again took a shower when he was around.

Because, when it came down to it, Pru was an absolute *chicken*. That was why she lived in the city, in an apartment building, surrounded by people. People, people, people, please, and more people. Nothing can happen to you with that many people around. At least, if something does, there are *witnesses*.

"Okay," he said. "I've got to go."

She grabbed his arm. "What?"

"To use the facilities. The bushes."

"Oh," she said, releasing her grip. "Okay."

While he was gone she searched the glove box for anything she might be able to use as a weapon. The only thing she found was a very short screwdriver. He was away for a long time. She sat there with the little screwdriver in her hand, feeling alternately scared and foolish. He was gone so long that she finally rolled down the window and yelled his name.

"John?" she called, louder. She strained her ears. No movement, no response, nothing. She sat up, tense and alert. Her fingers tightened around the ridged handle of the little screwdriver.

"John?"

Suddenly, there was someone standing next to her, outside her window. "What?"

She almost leapt out of her skin. "Jesus!"

"Sorry."

"Don't do that again!" Her heart felt as though it would explode out of her chest.

"Okay. *Sorry.* I was just looking around the ranger's station again. This van is going to get cold, you know. I thought I might find a way inside."

He opened the rear doors of the van, and she could hear him rummaging around back there. "You get under these blankets," he said. "You'll be warm enough, I think. It shouldn't get much below thirty, if we're lucky. And these are pretty thick. You'll be okay."

"What are you going to do?"

He was climbing into the front seat. "I'll be up here," he said. "Okay? I'll lock the doors."

Pru made her way to the back of the van, and slipped between the moving blankets he'd piled up for her. They were quilted, very thick and heavy. But John was right, she was entirely warm and cozy under them.

"How are you doing?" he called from the front seat, when she was settled.

"I feel like an armoire."

"They're a little moldy, aren't they? Sorry."

"Why do you even have these?"

"What? Oh. From when Lila moved out. She took some furniture with her."

"Did you help her move out?"

"Yeah. It seemed the decent thing to do."

A new thought struck her.

"Is it okay if we fall asleep? We won't die or anything, will we?"

"No." That was all he said, that one word. No other explanation. But it reassured her. She was going back to liking him again. Already, she missed his nearness.

"Are you okay up there?" she asked, after a minute.

"Just fine." A pause, then: "Wow, the stars are amazing. Oh, *wow.* You should see Delphinus. Look, see that diamond? With nothing else much around it?"

"No."

He turned around. "Are you even trying to look?"

"I already know I can't see. I can never see constellations. I can't even find the Big Dipper. Any group of six stars make a dipper, as far as I can tell."

"No, look here. Here's the Big Dipper. Right out the front window. Can you see? Come down until you find these two bright stars. They're always in line with Polaris. That's the bowl, see? Polaris is the end of the handle of the Little Dipper. You find those three stars, you can always find which way is north. And, of course, your dipper."

She heard him moving around, trying to get comfortable. She thought of the van's front seats, their hard, lumpy upholstery. She felt a little guilty, with the lovely, warm bed he'd made for her. "Are you sure you're okay up there?" she said.

"Oh yeah, I'm fine. I can sleep anywhere."

She was thinking about insisting that he come back and take the bed for a while, but she must have nodded off, because she suddenly jerked awake. She heard John moving around and said, "John?"

"What's wrong?"

"Do you want to come back here?"

"Oh no, I'm all right," he said.

She sat up so she could see him. He was curled up in the driver's seat, shivering, with the blanket pulled closely around him.

"Come back here," she said. "You're freezing!"

He stumbled to the back and they sat up under the blankets, with their legs touching.

"What time do you think it is?" she said. It was disconcerting not to know. She almost always knew what time it was, within six minutes. It drove Patsy crazy. "How do you *do* that?" she'd demand.

"I don't know. Maybe midnight."

Pru pulled the blanket up as far as she could. "My nose is freezing."

"Try not to think about it."

"How?"

"I don't know. We could talk."

"Okay. What should we talk about?"

"Do you want to hear the story of Delphinus? Now that I'm thinking about it?"

"Sure."

"Okay. Poseidon . . . you know Poseidon, right?"

"Ship that drowned Shelley Winters. And god of fish. Or something like that."

"Close enough. Poseidon had fallen in love with one of the sea nymphs, named Amphitrite. But Amphitrite, to protect her virginity, fled to the mountains. Delphinus found her and wooed her for Poseidon. He persuaded her to return from the mountains and to marry Poseidon. So, to reward Delphinus, Poseidon put an image of a dolphin in the sky, among the stars."

"You know, that's a lot like what happened with me and Rudy."

He laughed. "How did you meet Rudy, anyway?"

She smiled, in the dark. It was actually a good story. She met Rudy when she and McKay were playing pool, at the bar under the souvlaki place next to her building. She loved watching McKay shoot pool. He took less than a second to line up the shot, then happily whacked the cue ball with the stick as hard as he possibly could. He hit very few of his shots that way, but he didn't care.

Rudy was supposed to meet a work friend, and while he

waited, he watched Pru and McKay. He told her, later, that he'd liked the "set of her jib." He and McKay traded quips for a while, until McKay understood it was really Pru he was interested in. Rudy asked if he could call her, and although he was a bit of a mess, with his sloppy clothes and his big old glasses, he seemed funny and sincere. She'd just broken up with someone *not* a mess—and not funny or sincere, either—so she'd said yes.

The next morning, at one minute after seven, her phone rang. He didn't even announce his name. It was as if he'd been waking her up every morning for years. "Don't you hate it when you forget to turn off your clock radio on Sunday, and so you wake up to NPR's *Bluegrass Hour*?" he'd said. She sat up and listened to him talk for half an hour. The very neat but insincere guy she'd just broken up with—Nate—hadn't been much of a talker, either, so it was a very pleasant change. Rudy made her feel pretty loved, that was for sure. Now that she thought about it, though, it seemed a little odd. He seemed so sure of her, so quickly. That sudden attachment, and all the proposals? What was all that about, anyway? She'd liked it, though. She couldn't deny that.

She made John tell her about Lila. They'd met at her twenty-second-birthday party. They were both doing graduate work at Columbia, and he'd been invited to the party by a mutual friend. Just before John and his friend arrived, Lila ate a piece of the cake, which someone had spiked with twenty-two hits of acid. She did her share of drugs in those days, but she hadn't known about the acid in the cake. John left the party before the acid had kicked in, but the next morning, he saw her. He was on the commuter train to the city and happened to look out the window at the next stop, where Lila stood waiting on the platform. He knew she had a job, at Sotheby's. She was wearing dark glasses and standing stock still, and even though there was snow on the ground, she wasn't wearing shoes. John had gotten off his train and brought her home, and a year later they were married.

Pru added a swing coat and a French twist and had a complete picture of John's wife at twenty-two: Audrey Hepburn as Holly Golightly, deftly applying lipstick without a mirror as she was being driven away from the city jail.

"It wasn't awful," John said. "It wasn't like we woke up yelling at each other or had affairs or anything like that. It was just sort of . . . a struggle. A little struggle, every day. Pick, pick, pick. You know.

"And then she had a miscarriage. It was early, first trimester," he added, quickly. "I had already bought the diner and we were caught up in disagreeing about that. The place embarrassed her. She hated the name, the old sign, and the beat-up furniture—all the stuff I love. She wanted me to make it nicer, serve more sophisticated food, have couches. But that all stopped as soon as she was pregnant. The baby gave her some other focus, I think. And we were happy, talking about names, painting the baby's room. That kind of thing."

He drank from the water bottle. Pru thought of the bedroom she'd seen in John's apartment, the one half-painted yellow. The nursery, she thought, sadly.

"I guess having a baby wouldn't have saved us," he said at last. "We would have gone back to being unhappy, eventually. But, you know, losing it just didn't help. And that's it, really. She moved out a little while later. Right before I met you."

"But you could see it, right?" Pru said, after they were quiet for a while. "A way that something like that actually could have turned out differently? I don't mean to sound callous, but I remember thinking that when Rudy and I were having such a bad time—this could be good. Somehow, this could make things better. Like you could show each other your qualities, you know?" She smiled a little. Her mother's word, "qualities." The night air must be getting to her. She never would have said that in the city.

He nodded. "I guess that's right. I guess that's why I feel like I have to let go. We just didn't get there. I decided I'm going to give her whatever she wants. Let this thing end, in the best way we can."

She could hear all kinds of sounds around them, the wind in the leaves of the trees, crickets and something that sounded like frogs. She heard a branch break and jumped, grabbing John's arm. Someone named Jethro creeping through the bushes, a home-made knife between his teeth. No; probably just a squirrel.

When she touched his arm, he'd quickly reached to put his own hand over hers. It was as if he'd been waiting for it. She'd had the same response when they'd held hands earlier. It was hard to even think that in that moment the nature of their relationship had changed, it felt so utterly familiar. He took her hand in both of his and rubbed her cold fingers, as if to warm them.

He said, "I can't believe it, still. I'll be divorced." He said "divorce" as though he was trying it out for the first time. It was awkward, listening to him talk about his heartbreak while stroking her hand. In another context, she would have dismissed him as something of a player. Here, in the dark van, under the blankets, it seemed perfectly natural.

"I'm embarrassed to say this, but divorce embarrasses me. It's like telling everyone you've failed, each time you announce your marital status. I never thought of myself as someone who was proud, you know, of any kind of status. But I guess being married did mean something to me, being a *husband*. I guess with my parents both dead, and my sisters with their own families . . . Well, it felt like something of my own. We were married before anyone else in our circle. Married, in graduate school, everything seemed to be going according to plan. And then . . ."

"Kaplooey?" she supplied.

"Kaplooey."

"Are you sure it's going to end up that way?"

"I think it's what she wants."

"John," she said. "What do you want? Where are you, in all this?"

He was quiet for a while. Pru moved closer under the blankets. They were pressed together, side by side. She thought maybe she was getting sleepy. She was starting to drift in and out of consciousness. Then he said, "I don't want her to stay with me if she's unhappy."

"Do *you* get to be happy?" Pru asked, drowsily.

He was quiet for so long that Pru thought he'd fallen asleep. Then came his voice: "Yeah, there's that. It's just—I'm just not used to thinking in those terms."

She started to drift off again. It was very quiet, and it had started to rain, very gently. She could smell John's shirt next to her nose. Suddenly, they were both jolted awake. Something heavy hit the roof of the van, right above their heads. Something alive, and freaked-out. Whatever it was began scrambling around. It sounded like someone was trying to cut through the roof with a set of butcher knives.

"What is it?" Pru cried.

"Just an animal," John said. "Don't be scared."

Whatever it was scrambled around some more. The sound was nails-on-blackboard awful. Pru had been so relaxed, in her sleep, but the sound made her whole body stiffen. She put her hands over her ears.

"I'll go see what it is," John said, standing.

"No!" said Pru. "What if it's a bear?"

John listened for a little while to the thing. "It's not a bear," he said, at last. "A bear would be much heavier."

"They make them small, too, you know."

He opened the back door of the van before she could say anything and stepped out quickly. She heard him shout and clap his hands. Then his head reappeared, still attached securely, she noted, to his body.

"Raccoon," he said, getting back into the van. "Cute little guy. He's gone."

She now had so much adrenaline rushing in her veins that further sleep was impossible. There were hours more to pass. The floor of the van was hard and bumpy under her, making comfort impossible. They kept up an idly meandering stream of patter, singing jingles from TV commercials they knew from when they were kids, remembering their favorite rock bands. John could remember all the songs on his favorite albums in their proper order, year of release, and cover art. She told him that her first concert was Tom Petty and the Heartbreakers; he said that his was Queen *and* Thin Lizzy, on a double bill, and his father had taken him when he was fourteen. Pru told him how her father would change the words to songs, so instead of "When she's weary, try a little tenderness," he would sing, "Buy another shabby dress." She told him about the other guys, the ones before Rudy. He laughed when she imitated Phil, who liked to narrate what was going on while they were in bed: "You're here! I'm there! The Giants win the pennant! *The Giants win the pennant!*"

"You know when was the last time I slept outside?" she said, sleepily. A wind had picked up outside. They could hear it rushing through the treetops. John was lazily tracing the outlines of her fingertips with his own, his head on her shoulder. It must be very late, now. Pru was relaxed and sleepy, saying anything that came into her mind. "Waiting in line at the Medina Ticketron for Springsteen tickets with Kate McCabe, when we were in high school. This was, like, *The River,* but we'd been in love with him since *Born to Run.* In junior high. Oh my God, you have never seen two girls so crazy in your life as me and Kate were for Bruce Springsteen. Her brother had all the albums, so we used to go sneak into his room while he was at basketball practice and listen to them." She waited for him to say something. His answer was so long in coming that she almost fell asleep herself. She jerked awake. "Hey. Are you listening?"

"Hmph? Yeah. I am now." John moved his head from her shoulder to her lap and curled up into her. She put her hands in his hair. She didn't want them to fall asleep yet. If they fell asleep, then it would be morning, and this would all be over.

"All the other girls were all about Andy Gibb, you know, Shaun Cassidy. Boy singers with blond, feathered hair. And then there's Springsteen, remember the cover of *Darkness?* He's in that T-shirt, looking stoned?" John grunted something that seemed like assent. "I had never seen anything more beautiful in my life than that album cover. 'Candy's Room' was my favorite song. I was probably the only fourteen-year-old girl in all of Ohio who got off to a song about a hooker." John snickered a little, but he was mostly asleep. Softly, she said, "I always wanted someone who'd feel that way about me. Someone who'd still love me even if I was a hooker. He wants to protect her so much, you know? That's my Springsteen, the one in the dingy T-shirt, in love with a prostitute. Did she live at Coney Island? No, that's ridiculous . . . she couldn't have . . ." Her eyes were closed and she was becoming confused. John had become very still, in her lap. Sleepily, she said, "Kate was more into *Asbury Park*. I don't know, for me that one's a bit overwhelming . . . all those *words* . . ." Then she was sitting on Josh McCabe's green shag carpet, staring at the cover of *Darkness on the Edge of Town,* the scrawny, young Springsteen in a white T-shirt, his hair badly cut in a sort of pointy V on top of his head, as bleary-eyed as if he'd just gotten out of bed . . .

Pru awakened on the floor of the van sometime in the very early morning, before the sun was up. Even her head was under the blankets, against the cold. Her arms were wrapped around John. The way the front of her body was plastered against the back of his, she might have been a drowning victim he was pulling to shore. She started to ease herself away, but he rolled over and pulled her back toward him, tucking his arm under her head. She smiled, and closed her eyes. In a moment, she had fallen back asleep inside the warmth of his body, with his breath on her neck.

When she woke up again, the sun was just beginning to rise. Her hips and back were aching but she didn't want to move. For a long time, she watched John sleeping. She wanted to reach out and touch the sweet line curving around each of his fine nostrils. She wanted to sweep his hair off his forehead and kiss him there.

He opened his eyes, blinked a few times, then smiled. "Hey," he said, gently, without moving away. She smiled back.

"Thin Lizzy," she said.

"Bruce *Springsteen,*" he said, yawning.

"It was before *Born in the U.S.A.* and that supermodel," Pru said. "You have to understand that."

"Wait a minute," he said, his body tensing. "I think I heard something."

In the next moment, the back door of the van flew open. It made a horrible wrenching noise. Blinding sunlight flooded the van. It was all so sudden and frightening that Pru felt like she'd been shot in the eye.

"That shit for brains," someone said. "What the hell?"

John threw off the blankets and sat up. "Good morning," he said, pleasantly.

The morning park ranger blinked at them, completely surprised by their presence. He held a Starbucks cup of coffee, Pru noticed, and something about that struck her as so funny that she started to laugh.

"You're not supposed to be here," the ranger said.

"Guess what," said John. "No shit."

*T*en

"Oh, no no no no no," Fiona said. "*No.* Rebound girlfriend: No." The bartender passed by them and Fiona crooked a finger at him. "Hit me," she said. It was the first night she'd had away from the kids in months, and she was going for broke.

She had had three shots of whiskey and a margarita (on the rocks) in twenty minutes, to Pru's one glass of wine. They were at the bar at City. Pru was in culture shock after her night in the woods. She'd slept all day in her flannel nightgown in a bed piled with as many covers as she could find. She couldn't get enough warmth. Even in sleep, she kept remembering John waking up in the van that morning: *"Hey."* She would have liked to wander by the café to see what he was doing, but she had promised weeks ago to take Fiona out for her fortieth birthday, and there was no getting out of it. Had something changed? She felt almost certain it had. She and John hadn't so much as touched on the way home, but when she'd gotten out of the van on Columbia Road he'd said, "We'll talk later." Did he mean to call? She wasn't entirely sure he had her number.

"Anyway, it's not like that," Pru told Fiona. She wasn't ready to get publicly excited about him, not yet. Not until she had more solid evidence that this was going somewhere. "I'm just the sympathetic listener. You know, a friend."

"Nooooo!" Fiona cried, throwing back her long ballerina neck. "The comfort girlfriend! That's even worse! Rebound, at least it's sexual. But comforter, once you're that, you're like his *mother.*" She downed the last of the margarita, and shuddered. "And believe you me, missy, that's the last thing you want to be. Somebody's fucking *mother.*"

"Anyway," Pru said, "I'm not convinced I could have a real future with a man who smelled my morning breath, without having had sex with me first."

"Please," said Fiona dismissively. "It's just a matter of time."

Pru shook her head. "I don't think so, Fi. He's seen me at my absolute worst. The man has his pride, you know."

"You go to him right now," Fiona slurred. "Right now, before it's too late, and *jump his bones!*" She punctuated these last words with a swizzle stick she'd been mangling.

Fiona clearly had a skewed idea of her life. She acted as though all Pru did was go out and meet men, everywhere she went. Married people, thought Pru, never pictured single people as they really were, eating dinner from a tin with the cat on the table. For the millionth time that day, she pictured John waking up next to her: *"Hey."*

Fiona turned to the guy sitting next to her. "Can I bum a cigarette?" she said, smiling broadly. He gave her one and slid over a pack of matches. She lit it, closed her eyes, and inhaled deeply.

"Oh, yeah," she said, exhaling a stream of smoke. "You know what I'd *really* love? A joint."

"Heroin?" Pru called out, looking around the bar. "Metham-phetamines, anyone? Nursing mom here!"

Fiona grinned and pointed the cigarette at her. "Listen, just don't let on that you're in love with him right away, that's all I'm saying. I know you don't want to hear this. I didn't want to hear it either. But you can't expect him to marry you if you don't let him chase you a little bit."

"I'm not looking to get him to marry me, Liz Taylor. So, hush up."

After another round, when Fiona stood up and started doing her Axl Rose dance, Pru announced that it was time to go home.

She saw Fiona to her door and then started up Eighteenth Street. Pru wasn't stupid. She didn't confuse love with sitting out a cold night in a dead van. Not real, lasting love, anyway. Maybe rebound love, like Fiona said. And that might be okay, she thought, as she walked. Getting-each-other-through-a-bad-time love. The kind of love that could turn from platonic to "more" to platonic again, as easily as a leaf turns in the breeze. She wouldn't even *want* him to real-love love her right now. She wouldn't trust it. She'd taken freshman psychology in college, after all, and was familiar with the way baby ducks imprint on the first adult they see after birth. Even if it's not another duck, but, say, a cow.

So, I'm *way* ahead of you here, Miss Fiona, she thought, turn-ing onto Columbia Road. Unless, of course, John really did real-love love her right now. It didn't seem entirely implausible. Perhaps a little *soon*, on the heels of his divorce. Fiona was right, one did like to put another relationship between oneself and the ex. A little palate cleanser between courses, as McKay called the little twenty-two-year-old who came his way right before Bill. An *amuse-bouche*. But what if it was happening now? What if it had happened already? Look at Patsy and Jacob and their twenty-second courtship! Maybe John felt the same way as she did, after all. Would that be so terribly bad?

She found herself standing in front of the Kozy Korner. There were lights on inside. She pushed open the door and went in. John was standing behind the counter, washing up. She noticed, with a little thrill, that otherwise the place was empty.

"Hey!" he called, happily, when he saw her. "I was just thinking about you."

"Were you going to ask me to come up and listen to your Queen albums?" said Pru, swinging her purse as she strolled toward him, smiling.

Just then, a girl came out of the bathroom. It was the exclaiming-over-the-cheesecake girl, the one who'd taken Pru's seat at the counter. Sexy Yoga Babe.

"Oh," Pru said, with more obvious surprise than she could wish. She abruptly stopped swinging her purse and it hit her in the knee. "Hi."

"Hi," the girl said, pleasantly.

The girl was in date dress—silky top and skinny jeans, sparkly, strappy shoes. Of course, with a girl like that, thought Pru, such an outfit could be a taking-out-the-garbage dress. She turned to look at John. He was in date dress, too, a black sweater and gray trousers. She hadn't noticed this before.

There was an awkward, polite pause before John remembered to introduce them. The girl's name was Gaia. Gaia stood with poise, her arms resting comfortably at her sides. Pru's own arms, for all she knew, were flapping like a chicken's.

"Maybe another time?" she said to John.

He smiled easily and said, "Sure."

She backed out of the diner and hurried home, a little stunned and now feeling the wine she'd drunk. She remembered what he'd said about Lila: *I still sleep on one side of the bed, and she's dating already.* Didn't that imply that he was *not* dating? Hadn't he said that just yesterday? What, had he gotten on the horn and lined this up for tonight, while she was in bed all day, thinking about him? He had wrapped his arms around her, hadn't he? Was that just for animal warmth, for survival? How could he be dating someone else. How?

She sat down on her front steps. Oh, God. She was doing it. Exactly what she'd hoped to avoid. She realized she was sitting in the spot where she'd first met him, the night she dumped Rudy's TV. Where Patsy and Jacob sat out talking until the sun came up. Where probably countless others had done the same thing, their little beating hearts in their outstretched hands.

He didn't real-love love her. Like she did him.

Shit.

"WELL, WHAT DID YOU EXPECT?" MCKAY SAID. "A NICE, good-looking guy in D.C., going through a divorce? That's like throwing a scrap of bacon to a pack of wild, hungry dogs."

They were sitting on McKay's front steps, while Oxo sniffed around, looking for a place to pee. It was actually getting too cold to sit outside at night. Pru wondered again that she and John hadn't died, sleeping in the van. Was that only three nights ago?

She put her head in her hands. "I hate this stuff," Pru moaned. "*Boy* stuff. I've been doing the same thing for twenty years now. When does it ever end?"

In fact, what was happening with John was a lot like the only high school crush she'd ever had. The boy had been older and there wasn't much to distinguish him from all the other boys except that his locker was right next to hers, and he had this face that she couldn't look at full-on, for whatever reason. Her crush on him was huge and preoccupying and dwindled her down to the size of a peanut, in her mind. She practically hid inside her locker whenever she saw him. There wasn't even a question of the boy liking her back. She didn't for a moment entertain the possibility that, if her hair caught on fire, he would even notice, as he stood there spinning out the combination on his lock.

But she had some reason to think that John would notice. That he had, in fact, already noticed. There was some possibility there . . . wasn't there? No. She had been foolish to think so. The carrots in the waxed paper bag—the familiar, inevitable feeling of her hand in his—none of it meant anything. When she saw him a few mornings later at the Korner, she felt one part of herself removed, watching and listening with the eyes and ears of a Soviet-era spy. He was nothing but his usual, amiable self, although once or twice she thought he was looking at her strangely.

The other thing that was like her only high school crush was the amount of John Owens–related trivia she'd amassed. He had flecks of green in his hazel eyes. He tied his apron in the back, and when he cooked, he put a towel over one shoulder. He gave free coffee to the people who couldn't afford it. He was nice to the delivery guys and beggars, everyone who set foot in his café. He had two sisters and they were always calling him on his cell phone. His heroes were Charlie Parker and Lyndon B. Johnson. He grew up wild, near the woods, and scampered over rocks like a billy goat. When he fell asleep, his body jerked exactly one time. She was like a John Owens philatelist.

Did Gaia know any of this stuff? Pru wondered. Probably not. Probably, that was the whole attraction.

A WEEK AFTER THE NIGHT IN THE VAN, SHE WAS SPEEDING up the BWI Parkway behind the wheel of Jacob's convertible. Patsy called the color look-at-me blue. It was, indeed, very, very blue.

The convertible had a stick shift and ergonomic leather seats and a subwoofer that pounded away right underneath the seat, as she drove. The sun was out as they sped north, toward the Delaware shore. Her whole body vibrated deliciously. So this is what it feels like to be Jacob, she thought.

Jacob himself was sacked out in the backseat, fast asleep. He had tossed her the keys and jumped back there as soon as she'd come down with her overnight bag. He hadn't even bothered to find out if she knew how to drive stick, much less whether she had a driver's license, or any outstanding warrants for her arrest. He lay on his back with his arms crossed over his chest, wearing scrubs and sunglasses. Pru felt as though she had kidnapped a member of Prince's band.

It was a beautiful autumn day, cool enough so that she had turned on the car's heater to warm her toes. Patsy and Annali were already at the beach house, having driven in from the airport in Baltimore in a rented car a few days earlier. This was to be their last trip before the move. Nadine knew about it now, and professed, even in private conversations with Pru, to be *thrilled*.

Climbing the bridge over the Chesapeake, she gave the accelerator a little tap with her foot and the car leapt forward, out of the shadow of a semi in the next lane. She'd never driven a car like this before. Her only experience was with old beaters that you had to coax up the slightest rise, keeping your fingers crossed that the engine didn't suddenly die.

Jacob's head appeared in her rearview mirror, just as they were cresting the bridge. He looked around, stretching and yawning, then clambered into the front seat.

"Is that coffee?" he said, pointing to a styrofoam cup in the cup holder. He pried off the lid and drank the coffee in a long, undulating gulp, as if it were Gatorade. He replaced the empty cup in the holder and began riffling through a box of CDs on the floor. He flipped down the visor. He checked his cell phone for messages. Pru held her breath and tried not to go over any bumps in the road when he pulled out a little bottle of Visine and put drops in his eyes. He had the attention span of a cricket. "That's where this went!" he said, digging a disc out of the glove compartment. He put it into the car's CD player, and they were assaulted by the Pretenders' "Message of Love."

"Like Brigitte Bardot!" they yelled at the same time. Pru's heart was racing.

Jacob turned down the volume on the radio. "We should stop and get Annali a dog," he said.

"Does Patsy want a dog?"

"Not for Patsy. For Annali. For her birthday. She's going to be three."

"Yeah, well, a three-year-old isn't going to take a dog out for walks."

"If you see a pet store, pull over, and we'll get her a dog."

So far she hadn't seen anything for miles except for farm stands and motels. "Okay, Jacob," she said. "But maybe you should check it out with Patsy first."

Jacob didn't say anything. He drummed his knees, and sang along with Chrissie Hynde.

They arrived just before noon. Jacob took the rickety beach house stairs two at a time. Pru opened the trunk and took out their bags. When she looked up at the house, Jacob had both of them in his arms, Patsy and Annali.

JACOB PUT HIS ENERGY TO GOOD USE SHOPPING, CHOP-ping, and cooking. He had an insane amount of energy. Omelets with mushrooms when they arrived, chocolate fondue and straw-berries. He banged nails into walls and drove wedges under the new refrigerator to straighten it and caulked the bathroom shower. He ran along the beach chasing Annali and played games with her in the arcade on the boardwalk. By the time dinner rolled around, Pru was exhausted.

He made beef Wellington for dinner, and then—at last, thought Pru—sat down to watch a basketball game on the tele-vision. She and Patsy began cleaning up the kitchen. Patsy was going over her plans for the move. She would have to quit the teaching job that she'd just begun, and find something new. Annali came over with a dead beetle she'd found, and they both admired it. "Show Jacob," Patsy said, and Annali scooted right off, carefully cupping her hands around the bug carcass.

Pru was dying to suggest to Patsy that the job situation gave her another good reason to wait on moving, at least until the spring, but remembered she'd promised herself to butt out. She was about to offer to help with the moving van, when there was a loud cry from the living room.

"Honey, *no!*" Pru heard Jacob yell, then: "Dammit, *Annali!*" She looked up in time to see Jacob stand up, and Annali fall gently to the floor on her bottom. Annali looked up at Jacob, her eyes wide in surprise. Jacob looked down at her, then at the hand he'd pushed her with, as if it belonged to somebody else.

"Oh, honey," he said. "Annali," he said, reaching for her.

Annali sprang up and ran from the room. Patsy put down the dish towel she was holding, and followed her into the bedroom, closing the door gently behind them.

"Shit," Jacob said, "I can't believe it. I *pushed* her."

He sat back down on the couch, muting the volume on the TV. "Christ. I feel like a monster." He put his head in his hands. "I can't believe it," he said again. He looked truly miserable.

"She'll be okay," Pru said. "Kids are tough."

But he didn't answer. Pru thought he seemed a little more distraught than the circumstances called for. He hadn't exactly pushed Annali, from what she'd seen. It looked more as if he had sort of tried to pull her to the side, but she'd become unbalanced and fallen to the floor.

Jacob kept watching the door to the bedroom, but he made no move to go to them. At last he turned off the TV and went outside. Pru finished the dishes, occasionally looking out of the glass doors to where Jacob stood at the railing, staring off at the ocean. Presently, Patsy came out of the bedroom.

"Where'd he go?"

Pru pointed to the deck. "He's pretty upset," she said.

Patsy went out to him. Pru watched them through the doors. Patsy tried to get him to look at her, but he wouldn't. Finally she pulled him by the hand down the stairs to the beach.

The phone rang and Pru went to answer it. It could only be Nadine, at home by herself.

"I miss my girls!" she said. "I'm so jealous of you all there together. How's it going?"

Pru could hear the clack of her knitting needles in the background. When her mother was agitated, she knit like nobody's business. When Leonard was sick, she made matching hats, ponchos, and mittens for Pru, Patsy, *and* Annali. The lovely, intricate patterns would have taken a normal person several months to finish. Her mother did them in a couple of weeks, sitting by his bed at home, then in the hospital, then home again, for his final days.

She told her mother about the incident with Jacob and Annali.

"Poor Jacob," her mother said. "Do you remember pushing her off the swing, last year?"

"God, yes. I think you spent more time consoling me than her."

"It's something every parent has to get used to, you know. There's nothing that shows you how *not* perfect you are like being a parent. Jacob's used to having all the answers, I think. I don't think you could be a doctor, otherwise."

"I've been thinking," said Pru. "Is she allowed to move with Annali? What about Jimmy Roy?"

"We haven't heard from Jimmy Roy in a while," her mother said, sighing.

"Really?" Pru was surprised. She knew Jimmy Roy had been gone for several months, but he'd always kept in touch, little postcards and letters to Annali. He'd sent her pictures of penguins, which were tacked up on the wall behind her bed.

"I guess Jimmy Roy could stop her from moving," her mother continued, "but I don't think he will."

"No," Pru agreed. "But do you think this is a good idea? Moving here just to be near Jacob?"

The needles paused, and then resumed.

"There's nothing for Patsy around here," her mother said at last. "She's been biding her time, you know. She's not like you, Pru. She needs to be excited by life."

"Whereas I need to have the crap bored out of me by life?"

"You just have a different tolerance. Patsy will follow her heart, wherever it takes her. I don't think it's my place to tell her where that is."

"Unfortunately, Annali has to follow Patsy's heart, too."

"It's a good heart, Pru. I don't think we have to worry. I barely knew your father when I married him."

Although she'd heard that before, it was impossible to visualize. She thought of her mother, sitting up in bed in her flannel Lanz of Salzburg nightgown, and found it hard to believe she'd ever been impulsive. It must have been just that one time, that one wild instinct that drove her to marry Leonard after knowing him only three weeks. Then she settled down to her life of making dinners and vacuuming the carpets and going to the basement of the First Christian Missionary Alliance to play Senior Scrabble.

Pru had the strange feeling that her mother was playing online Scrabble now—as well as knitting—while they talked. Sometimes her voice would fade out, or it would take her a moment too long to answer. Was she quietly typing in a word, so Pru wouldn't hear?

"You'll be sad if they move here, won't you?" Pru said.

The needles stopped again, and there was a long pause. "Oh my goodness, yes," Nadine said, at last. "I most certainly will. I certainly, certainly will."

AFTER SHE HUNG UP WITH HER MOTHER, PRU CALLED her home phone. That was another good thing about being self-employed: You could actually pretend that your obsessive checking in with all means of communications was work related. She'd managed to restrict herself to checking her messages only twice a day, which, considering, was rather valiant.

That was how she thought of herself now, self-employed. She just wasn't earning anything, that was all. But she was on the verge of locking up a couple of jobs Kate had steered her way. She now truly needed the money, and would be glad to have something to do with her days. She needed to get away from the Korner, where she was spending too much time. Some days, it was the only human contact she had.

No messages. She wondered how far into the realm of getting weird on John she'd already wandered. Was there any return? Could they go back to their easy friendship? Or was she doomed to this no-man's land forever?

No-man's land. She liked that. She'd have to tell McKay, when she saw him again.

THE NEXT MORNING, SHE AWOKE TO THE SOUNDS OF Annali shrieking and laughing in the kitchen. She came out of the bedroom to see Annali trundling through the house, followed closely by a small, pudgy yellow puppy.

The puppy kept jumping up on Annali and licking her face, to her great delight. "Look what Jacob brought me!" she yelled, when she saw Pru.

Jacob seemed somewhat abashed at himself, but pleased nonetheless. Pru could see that Patsy was pleased, too. All Pru could think of was, How are you going to get it home? And who was going to walk him during the day—Nadine, with her bad hip? Well, it wasn't her concern. She poured coffee for herself and sat down, bending to pet the puppy when it came wriggling over for a sniff.

Jacob wanted to rent bikes for everyone. For him, Patsy, and Annali, he rented a tandem with a child's seat on the back, and a red bike for Pru, upright and retro in design but with thirty speeds. Annali insisted on bringing the puppy along, but it kept getting its leash tangled in the pedals of the tandem, so they ended up pushing the bikes along as the puppy wriggled and bit them on the ankles. Their little group seemed to be the main attraction in town. People keep stopping to coo and pet the puppy, whom Annali had named Jenny. Jacob seemed to love the attention almost as much as the puppy did. "She wanted a dog," he said to everyone. "Am I going to tell her no?"

Patsy squeezed her arm and said, "This is perfect. Everyone I love best in one place. *Perfect.*" Her wildly happy aspect had returned. There was no sign of her previous anxiety. Patsy was having a good day. It was as if the dog had signaled something to her, something irrevocable.

By the end of the day, Jenny had nipped Annali on the nose at least twice, attacked the new furniture, and dragged a rotting shellfish carcass halfway up the beach stairs. Annali wanted to take the dog to bed with her, but Patsy explained that it must sleep in its crate until it was trained. When Jacob kissed her good night, Annali said, "I love my dog. Good night, Daddy."

Hearing this, Pru looked up from the sink. Patsy was watching Jacob closely, a combination of amusement and worry on her face. Jacob said, mildly, "Good night, kiddo." But as soon as Annali and Patsy disappeared into the bedroom, he rose and went outside to stand at the railing.

Pru lay down on the couch and began reading a biography of Toussaint L'Ouverture that John had given her. He said L'Ouverture was even more fascinating than Churchill, and up against even greater odds, and what was she doing reading about dead white European males, anyway? After Patsy finished putting Annali down, she went to find Jacob outside. Presently, Pru could hear their voices coming in through the window. She heard Patsy say something laughingly, but then Jacob said, in a somber voice, "I think it's a bad idea." Pru put down her book.

"Why?" Patsy's voice sounded teasing, but there was a note of anxiety, too. "Did it scare you?"

"It's just confusing, that's all. I'm not her daddy."

Pru stopped chewing the gum in her mouth, waiting for Patsy's response.

"I know that," Patsy said, after a pause. "But she loves you, Jacob. Isn't that what you wanted? Because, you know, you could have fooled me."

"Let's go for a walk," Jacob said then, and she heard their steps rattle down the stairs and their voices drift away.

Soon Patsy returned, alone. Pru put down her book. "What happened?"

"What do you mean?"

"Where's Jacob?"

She shrugged. "Walking on the beach." She began to move to the bedroom where she and Jacob were sleeping.

"Is everything all right?" Pru said.

"Sure. Why?"

"I don't know. Jacob seemed a little freaked earlier, when Annali called him Daddy. That's all."

Patsy stopped, and turned around. "Pru, don't you start," she said, in an unsteady voice.

"I'm not . . ."

"Yes you are! And *you're* going to freak him out, with all your prying and your demands and your usual bullshit!" Pru was so surprised she couldn't speak. Patsy was shaking. "Just quit it, okay?" She hissed, and then banged into the bedroom.

Pru stayed where she was, struggling to understand what had just happened. Then she went to Patsy's room and tapped on the door. When there was no answer, she let herself in.

She found Patsy sitting on the bed, plucking at a pillow on her lap. Pru sat next to her and took her hand. "I don't understand," she said. "Make me understand."

Patsy leaned back against the headboard and looked at Pru with big, inscrutable eyes. "Just be happy for me," she said. "Just get behind this. Why is everyone chasing him away?"

"No one is chasing him away," Pru said. "But, you know, we're not perfect. I know he thinks *you* are. But the rest of us—he'll have to learn to put up with our ways, that's all."

She was trying to be cheerful, but she could feel how insufficient it was. If she only knew more—but Patsy hadn't told her what was going on, and she didn't know how to ask without setting her off. Patsy had always been moody, but her present state made those days seem tame, by comparison.

"Just be happy," Patsy said again. "Look how good everything is. Just *look*."

"I *am* happy," Pru said. "Aren't you happy? Isn't Jacob?"

"Of course," Patsy said. "You see how we are together." She began to say something, then bit back the words. She looked as if she might start crying.

"Well," Pru said, at a total loss now, but determined to stay in the game. "I *am* happy. Happy, happy, happy."

Patsy pushed away the pillow she was plucking. "Okay, now you're freaking *me* out," she said. But she wasn't laughing, and her eyes were sad.

. . .

PRU AND JACOB DROVE BACK TO D.C. THE NEXT DAY. It was overcast and cold. Jacob was different, silent and rigid. He didn't play any music. He hardly spoke during the three hours it took to get back to the city, except to announce at a rest stop that he was going in for a coffee. Pru watched the light, steady rain out of her window. Every now and then, Jacob would shake his head, set his lips tightly, and grip the steering wheel, as if wrestling with something. She asked him once if he wanted to stop and eat, but he was so deeply immersed with the argument he was having with himself that he didn't answer. Pru went back to watching the rain, lulled by the sound of the wipers.

When they finally pulled up outside her apartment, Jacob let the engine idle and grabbed her bag from the backseat. Pru wished she could think of something to say. Seeing him this way made her nervous. Jacob was many things, but morose and moody didn't seem to be one of them. Everything had changed, somewhere. She didn't know what, and she didn't know how. The wipers slapped at the rain while Jacob held out her bag to her, practically wishing out loud that she would go.

"I guess I'll see you at Thanksgiving?" she said.

He looked out the window at the rain, running a hand through his hair. There was a short silence. "I might have to be in the hospital," he said. "I'll have to see."

"Oh," she said. "Well, we'll miss you." She tried to smile at him, but he wouldn't look at her.

"Yeah," he said, turning away. Two people holding newspapers over their heads dashed past the car, laughing. "You'll explain it to Annali, won't you?"

"That you're working? I think she's old enough to understand that."

"She's a great kid," he said suddenly. "I love that kid. I *really* love her."

He said it with such regret and finality that it made her shudder. Suddenly, she knew that they were not just talking about Thanksgiving. Why? Just because Annali called him Daddy? Was he *kidding*? She found it hard to believe that, given his obvious attachment to her, he'd be so alarmed at the return of his affection. What was going on?

She didn't know what to say. She listened to the cold rain falling on the canvas roof of the car. "She's really attached to you, Jacob," she said at last, a statement, a plea.

He nodded. "I know. Good-bye, Pru," he said.

She didn't move. "You're leaving them, aren't you?"

"Listen," he said. "Please—don't make this harder for me than it already is."

"Harder for you! What about Patsy? And Annali? Have you even thought about what this will do to them?" She didn't think she'd ever been so angry in her life. She wanted to grab his face, make him look at her. She wanted to dig her fingers into that handsome jaw, to hurt him, badly.

He fell silent, and turned away again. She didn't think she could continue to speak to him without screaming. Without another word she opened the car door and stepped out. The rain, heavy and chill, was beginning to come down fast, and she ran up the stairs of her apartment building. Before she'd even found her keys in her pocket, Jacob had pulled away from the curb and was gone.

Eleven

Pru decided not to tell Patsy right away about her conversation with Jacob. She really meant to keep to her resolution not to get involved. But when Patsy called her later in the week to help arrange a moving van, she changed her mind. She laid it all out for Patsy, as best she could remember.

In the car, with Jacob right in front of her, she'd been absolutely sure they'd never see him again. But now, talking to Patsy, who clearly thought no such thing, it was disconcerting to hear how shaky her conclusion sounded. Patsy was entirely unimpressed, when she was finished. Tears, shouting, accusations of lying . . . *that* Pru had expected. This blasé shrugging of the shoulders, she hadn't.

"I've heard him say that before," Patsy said, brushing it off. "Then, in the next second, he can't live without us. It just scares him sometimes, that's all. Don't worry. We're fine."

"You are? Really?"

"Really," Patsy said. "This living so far apart is just hard, that's all. It'll be so much better when we're in Rehoboth."

"He knows you're moving all the way across the country just to be near him, right?"

"It's not just to be near him," Patsy said. Pru could tell she was offended. "I can't live at home forever, you know. Don't worry, we're not going to cramp your style. I know you 'own' the mid-Atlantic."

"I didn't say I owned the mid-Atlantic," Pru said. It was so typical that this was where they'd arrived.

So, fine, Pru thought, hanging up the phone. She'd done her part. Maybe she *had* totally misunderstood what Jacob had said. Or maybe Patsy was right, this was just par for the course with them. They were passionate about each other, probably they were passionate in their fights, too. They'd never really been attracted to the same things, Pru and Patsy. She realized that when Rudy had told her it was over, it really *was* over. She wouldn't have been able to go back to him, after that. She couldn't understand how you could hang on to someone who didn't want you anymore. So her sister wanted a lover who changed on her from minute to minute—well, she seemed to have found him.

Anyway, it was Annali she should be concentrating on, Pru reminded herself. Patsy was determined to sink her own ship. Fine. She didn't need Pru. But one day, maybe when she was a teenager, *Annali* would. She'd reach her limit with her flaky mother, and show up on Pru's doorstep, gangly and gorgeous, carrying only what she'd stuffed into a backpack on her way out. Pru couldn't do anything about Jacob. But she could make sure that Annali knew her circle of love extended beyond her mother and whoever happened to be on her mother's arm at the moment. She'd see to it that Annali would never regard her aunt as a stranger, some distant relative who may or may not take her in in her time of need. She'd make sure Annali knew she could always show up on that doorstep, and she'd be as good as home.

THE NEXT DAY, WHEN SHE WALKED INTO THE KORNER for breakfast, John waved her over to one of the little tables near the large plate-glass window, where he sat with a couple she'd never seen before.

"This is Ralph and Rona Mortensen," he said, adding, with unmistakable emphasis, "and *this* is Pru."

Ralph and Rona shook her hand warmly. They were in their fifties, perhaps, and wore matching windbreakers. John explained that Ralph had been his dissertation adviser in graduate school.

"You have a Ph.D.?" she said, surprised.

"So they tell me," John said.

"In what?"

"Philosophy."

"Wow," she said. "Where was that going?"

"Well, exactly," he said.

"He's a genius," Ralph said. "I've never read a more cogent dissertation on the phenomenological aspects of Kant in all my years of teaching."

"It's just crap, really," John said, in a low voice.

"I Kant believe that," she replied.

When she went up to the counter for a coffee and scone, there was a pregnant silence behind her at the table. At least, it sounded to her like a pregnant silence. She felt that she could practically hear the exchange of meaningful glances, and felt a little light-headed, imagining they were about her.

Ralph and Rona Mortensen were what her mother would call *academics*. They lived in New York City and had come down for a conference at the Smithsonian that had to do with Rona's work on Fanny Brice and vaudeville. Pru was fascinated. Who did work on vaudeville? What *was* work on vaudeville? And did it pay anything? She was dying to ask.

In the company of his friends, John was downright giddy. This must be how others felt with her and McKay, she decided. The three of them finished each other's sentences and made quick references to things she didn't understand. Ralph and Rona called him "Johnny."

"Have you been to the Holocaust Museum, Pru?" Rona asked, turning to her.

"You know, I'm ashamed to say I haven't," she admitted. "I am just never in the mood for it. All those *shoes*."

Rona said, "I hear it's very depressing, but Ralph wants to go."

"Sure it's depressing," said Ralph. "You want happy, go to Christmas at Macy's."

"Oh, let's do something else, Ralph," Rona says. "Pru's right. I don't want to see that today."

"Do you want to visit the NPR studios?" Pru said. It was her ace in the hole, with visitors of a certain stripe. And Ralph and Rona were definitely of that stripe. Fiona's husband, Noah, directed one of the news shows, and he was always happy to get Pru and her guests in to see one of the programs being taped.

"I love NPR!" Rona said, and beamed at her. "But you have to come with us."

"Sure," said Pru. "I just have to call my friend and see if he can get us in."

At four o'clock on the nose, John and Ralph and Rona buzzed

from downstairs. Pru buzzed back, to let them in. It was turning out to be a banner day. In addition to getting to see John again, she'd finally gotten a call about some work. It sounded like a grant she could write in her sleep, and the pay was rather unbelievable. She'd been amazed at how she'd managed to sound like an actual *consultant* on the phone. She'd even said, "Hold on, let me check my book," when the director had asked if they could meet for lunch one day that week.

While she waited for John and the Mortensens, she smoothed back her hair in the hallway mirror. She'd changed out of her usual work jeans and into a sweater, skirt, and boots. Thank God her apartment no longer smelled of cat urine! She felt a twinge of nerves, as John poked his head into her apartment.

Whoop came to twine himself around her legs in an affectionate way. "So that's the beast, huh?" John said, crouching to rub him between the ears. Rona and Ralph wandered over to the bay window, as everyone did, to look at her view of the city, but John walked straight to her desk. He noted the abundance of blue objects she had placed around her desk, because she found the color calming. He picked up the cup of carefully sharpened 2H pencils Pru favored, said, "Hmm . . ." rather pointedly, and replaced it on her desk. He looked at the pictures of Annali, Patsy, her parents, and Pru identified them for John.

"Is this your phone?" he said, picking up her phone.

"Yes."

"And this is your computer?"

"Yes."

"Hmm." He leaned over to squint at her screen, and she wondered if she'd left up any offensive e-mail from her group of college friends, who tended to be extremely caustic, to say the least, in their online conversations. John sat down in her chair. "Do you sit here?"

"When I'm not standing."

"So here I am, Pru Whistler, making my way in the world," he said.

Just as she was leaning over to move the pencil cup back to where it belonged, John stood up. He almost stood up right into her. It would have been the perfect moment to kiss her. Ralph and Rona were busy at the window, trying to find the Capitol building. It wouldn't have taken but the slightest, most undetectable movement. It wouldn't have taken but a *second*.

He stepped back and looked at her like, *Uh-oh*. To hide her annoyance, she screwed up her face at him. He screwed his up back at her.

"You guys ready?" Pru said. Ralph and Rona had plastered themselves so discreetly to the window that they were practically on the other side of the glass.

PRU HAD BEEN RIGHT ABOUT BRINGING THEM TO NPR. Rona kept exclaiming over the photos of the on-air talent that lined the walls of the lobby: "*That's* what she looks like?" and "I thought he'd be bigger!" Noah had gotten them in to see one of the live news programs, which was fun to watch because they were orchestrated from a central pit, around which the recording booths stood. In the pit there was a director, who motioned cues to the readers and the engineers while keeping a constant eye on an enormous digital clock in front of him. There were mad scrambles when a piece failed to play, or the show had gotten off the clock somehow, and the director had to figure out what to cut or lengthen in order to make up the difference in time. This was something she'd be good at, Pru considered. She had an unwavering internal clock. However, she didn't think she could handle the stress. Fiona said that Noah was constantly hanging up on her, because of the time. She'd never survive in such an impolite environment.

Ralph and Rona watched it all with fascination and eagerness, even when the action slowed down during lengthy, prerecorded field reports, when the on-air talent took off their headphones and drank coffee together in the hallway, complaining about the funding environment. Ralph and Rona went out of the observer's booth after the show to meet them and shake their hands.

"I'd like to be called 'the talent,'" Pru said to John.

"I'll start calling you that," he said. "More coffee, please, for 'the talent.'"

They took a cab back to the café and John cooked eggs for everyone. Although she'd prepared herself for it, no one mentioned Gaia. Or Lila. Pru had to wonder if that had something to do with her being there.

When she left them at the front door of the café, Rona put an arm around Pru and squeezed her, whispering, "Now, *you,* we get."

You, we get. You, we get, Pru thought, going up her front steps. Was she crazy, or had Rona just told her about a dozen things she'd been dying to know? She couldn't wait to call Kate, to discuss.

She was just putting the key in the front door when a cheery voice behind her said, "Hi!"

She turned around and almost screamed. There, bouncing on his toes, hands shoved into the pockets of the trench coat that she'd helped him buy, was Rudy.

Rudy *Fisch.*

. . .

HE LOOKED THINNER AND PALER THAN SHE HAD REMEM-
bered. "You don't have a cold or anything, do you?" he said, putting his hands up in front of him. "I'm a walking Petri dish."

"Rudy," she gasped.

"Yes, it's me. Can I come up? It's not good for me to be outside for too long. Come on," he added, seeing her hesitation. "I
know I owe you an apology."

She couldn't think of an excuse, so she simply let him in. They
got into the elevator and Rudy hit the button for her floor.

"What is going on with you, Rudy?" she said. Of all the
times she'd been anxious about running into Rudy, this wasn't
one of them. In fact, she hadn't thought of him in ages, she
realized.

"I haven't been working," Rudy said. "They've put me on
short-term disability. I've been poked by every specialist in D.C.
and New York. No one knows what's going on. Multiple environmental allergies, food sensitivities, sick-building syndrome—
you name it, I may or may not have it. Oh, nothing transmittable,
so you're safe."

"Thank God," she said, feeling all the air leave her body. She
was scrupulous about protecting herself from STDs, but that
hadn't stopped her from imagining a moment very much like this
one a thousand times.

He stepped into her apartment familiarly, tossing his coat onto
one of the chairs. "They checked me for AIDS, herpes, the
works. Oh, yes, it's been a fun couple of weeks. Personally, I
think it's my office—the place is a fucking allergen factory. I'm
talking to the best mold guy in the city about an action. Did you
know there's scientific evidence linking fluorescent lights with

Epstein-Barr? The fucking lights they use in every office in the city, and it's killing everybody."

"I don't understand. Why can't you work?"

"Because I basically have the vitality of an eighty-year-old emphysemic?" He moved to sit down on the couch, rubbing his hands together. "See? Just going up your front steps, and I'm about to pass out. Do you have any purified water?"

"I have a filter on the tap. It's Brita," she added.

"No, it has to be purified. Filtered isn't good enough. Anything in a bottle?"

"I'll see."

She found some bottled mineral water in the back of the refrigerator, and brought it to him. He pulled a little plastic cup wrapped in cellophane from his pocket, and poured some of the water in it. "No offense," he said. "It's just a precaution."

"I still don't understand," she said. "Do you have a diagnosis?"

Rudy waved a hand. "I've heard everything. Nobody knows, really. Fibromyalgia, chronic fatigue syndrome, seronegative rheumatoid arthritis. None of this stuff is diagnosable, you know. Oh, we're also talking about sprue. Did I leave some shirts here, by the way? Jesus," he said, jumping a little, "you have a cat?"

He was looking at Big Whoop, who had wandered in from the bedroom to stare at them with open hostility.

"That's *your* cat, Rudy."

"Sylvester?" he said. "No, no, don't let him near me. He gets within a foot of me, I'm a dead man. Can you put him in the back? Hi, Sylvie. Hi, baby. I can't believe you found him. I can't believe you *have* him."

She tried to pick up Whoop, but he ran under the couch. She decided to wait for him to come out. She'd be damned if she'd go on her hands and knees in front of Rudy Fisch.

"Funny story," she said, taking a chair across from him. "I found him at the Humane Society."

He sighed and nodded his head. "I know, I shouldn't have done that. Pru, it's such a relief that you have him. Really. I mean that. Thank you." He looked stricken, suddenly, and to her annoyance, Pru was moved.

She had imagined seeing him again many times, but never like this. The Rudy she'd imagined held some kind of trump card over her. He'd beaten her by being the first to leave, ending the game by taking all the pieces and going home. When she saw him again, she imagined, he'd be victorious and strong and have some good, hot babe on his arm. He'd somehow be the Rudy he always should have been.

Whoop came out from under the couch and readied himself to jump on Rudy. "No," Rudy said, alarmed. "No, Sylvester, no." He pulled up his knees as Whoop pounced.

Whoop hit Rudy's knees and fell back. Pru leaned over, scooped him up, and settled him on her lap, where he glared at Rudy.

"Look at that," Rudy said. "You guys are friends now?"

"We're doing okay," she said, smoothing the ruffled fur on Whoop's back. "Do you want him back?"

"God, no. You might as well feed me poison." Suddenly he looked at her. "You probably want to, huh? Feed me poison?" He scrunched up his face, suddenly, and raised his fist to his mouth, as if he was going to sneeze, or cough, or both. After it passed, he said, "I must say, I wasn't expecting you to be so nice to me. Aren't you going to yell at me, or something?"

"No."

"Have you been upset?"

She shrugged. Whoop raised his head as she concentrated on moving her fingers under his chin.

"No," Rudy said, leaning back again. "I didn't think so."

She stroked Whoop for a while. Then she said, "Okay. Yes. I was upset. You know, I can understand your leaving me. You were right, everything you said was true. Fine, you want to find someone else. Fair enough. But you know what really hurt? You never even called me to see how I was doing. I could have been dead."

"You're absolutely right."

"You left me feeling—unlovable."

He closed his eyes. "You're not unlovable, Pru. God knows, it is not easy to love you, even when I'm in the best of health. But you're not unlovable."

"So, what the hell, Rudy?"

He sighed. "Look, it's hard to explain. It's just where I was with Andrea, and therapy, and all that. And then I got sick . . ."

"Who is Andrea?"

He opened his eyes, in surprise. "Andrea Schwaiger. Dr. Schwaiger."

Suddenly, she understood. "You were sleeping with her? With your *shrink*?"

"It was kind of crazy," he said. "I kept thinking you were going to get suspicious—you know, all those sessions. But I didn't sleep with her until after you and I split."

She'd never met Dr. Schwaiger: in fact, she hadn't even realized that she was of sleeping-together age. She'd imagined Rudy's shrink, in fact, to be something like Angela Lansbury, crisp and stern. She now had the rather wild image of Angela Lansbury in black lingerie, a whip in one hand.

"Andrea said I was only cheating on you to get your attention, anyway. Not that I *cheated* on you, technically. I mean, we fooled around, but we never . . ."

She stopped him. "Rudy, I don't care what you did with Andrea Schwaiger, or when you did it."

"All right, I just want it on the record: I didn't cheat on you."

"Fine. You weren't a cheater. Duly noted."

She stroked Whoop's fur and thought about all the times she might have picked up on the fact that Rudy and Andrea Schwaiger were involved. She wasn't about to get into the fine points with Rudy about what constituted "cheating" and what didn't. But it made her feel stupid. How could she have not known?

He fell asleep on her couch while she sat thinking about everything and stroking the cat. Something about the way he looked in sleep, vulnerable and slow, always made her a little resentful. She watched him sleeping, and remembered driving to his aunt's summer home in Pennsylvania. Rudy had fallen asleep next to her while she drove. His mouth was open a little, and he looked like a little boy. They'd just survived a horrendous visit by his vicious parents, and Pru, who wasn't used to such behavior, was still reeling. She'd felt very sorry for Rudy in that moment, and determined to show him something better.

After a while, Rudy stirred on the couch, then sat up. He drank a little more water from his special cup, then said he was ready to leave.

"Can we see each other sometime?" he said, putting on his coat.

"I don't know," Pru said. "Why?"

"You know, to be friends. I'd like to stay friends with at least one of my exes."

"Sure," she said. "We can do that." She was pretty sure he'd never call.

"Great," he said. He stopped, outside her door. "Hey, are you going to the Fresh Fields on P Street anytime soon?"

"I wasn't planning on it. Why?"

Rudy shrugged. "I could just use some things, from time to time. It's hard for me to get out as often as I need to."

She began to laugh. "You really are something, Rudy."

He looked at her, a little uncertainly. "I'll give you money," he said. "It's not like I'm expecting you to pay for my groceries."

"I'll let you know, the next time I go," she said, pushing him out the door.

"That'd be great," came his voice, as she closed the door between them.

She found Whoop waiting for her in bed. He blinked at her silently, and she said, "Don't worry, buddy, mean old crazy Rudy isn't taking you anywhere." As if relieved, he settled down and began to groom himself.

They were like two old people, in bed together. Whoop licked himself while she rubbed moisturizer into her hands and feet. She read for a while, then turned out the light. Whoop had taken to resting his chin on her nose while she slept. If he didn't do it, she picked him up and made him reposition himself until he remembered: chin on nose.

You, we get. You, we get.

Twelve

"Come on in," Edie said. She climbed down from a ladder where she'd been cleaning the track lights and came over to kiss Pru on the cheek.

Edie was big and surprisingly unkempt, for one of the town's few fashionistas. Her lipstick was never quite right, but her taste in clothing was beyond question. In Pru's opinion, her boutique, just past Dupont Circle on Connecticut, was one of the few places in town where you could find clothes that actually made you hold your breath. She hadn't been here since she'd been fired.

But now, she finally had a bit of money. The writing job for a foundation, which she'd landed after meeting the Mortensens, thanks to Kate, had turned out to be a huge amount of work. There were hundreds of pages to be read and absorbed, and major revising to be done on three different grants, all of which came due on the same day. The foundation's work had to do with medical compliance laws in developing countries, not an easy thing to wrap her mind around. For weeks, she was up and at her desk first thing in the morning, staying up well past her usual bedtime to scour the pages. She couldn't believe it when she'd gotten paid two days after she'd e-mailed the final drafts. Having replenished her dwindling checking account, she found herself drawn irresistibly to Edie's on Connecticut. It had been ages since she'd bought anything for herself.

"I was starting to think you were seeing another boutique," Edie said, as Pru gazed around. There were body-hugging skirts, pointy-toed heels, a whole rack of slinky evening gowns. She hardly knew where to start.

"I've been too poor to shop," she said, fingering a silk Pucci print blouse with a plunging neckline.

Edie made a sound with her tongue. "Tell me about it," she said. "I can't afford a damn thing in my own store. I was just in a cleaning frenzy. You take your time."

Pru was either a terrible shopper or a very good one. She was attracted to clothes the way arsonists were attracted to fire, but she took forever making up her mind. Typically, she would try on absolutely everything and buy almost nothing. She had to touch every piece in the store, feel the fabrics next to her skin. There was nothing as satisfying as a dress settling over your body in just the right way. Unless it was a pair of great-looking shoes that didn't make you feel like a wounded racehorse begging to be shot and put out of your misery at the end of a workday.

She knew that other people's childhood memories consisted of vacations, favorite teachers, and perhaps the odd humiliating moment or two. Pru remembered what she wore. At seven years old, when she fell and got her first stitches, she'd been wearing a patchwork jumper made by her grandmother, brown tights, and brown oxfords. When, at twelve, she got her first period, she was wearing a blue bandanna on her head, like Laverne and Shirley on the line at the bottling plant. She wore a seven-tiered white Gunny Sack dress that made her look like a wedding cake for the junior prom. For her first date with Rudy, truly fine, buttoned sailor pants (he'd said, "Ahoy there, matey!" when he came to pick her up), and for the breakup, of course, the now destroyed vintage sweater.

There wasn't anyone else in Edie's store. Pru felt like she'd been sprung from jail. She spent an hour trying on various outfits. There were things that hadn't been in, the last time she was shopping—peasant blouses and asymmetrical skirts. Edie sat in a chair outside her dressing room, eating from a cup of noodles with chopsticks. Every now and then Pru came out to show her something, so Edie could make pronouncements. They were like Annali with her Barbies, Pru thought. When she saw the Pucci print blouse with a pair of Capri pants and Pru's blue Keds sneakers, Edie said, "*Oooooh.* I never would have put those things together, ever, in a million years." The tag on the blouse said that it was almost three hundred dollars. Despite what McKay remarked about her extravagance with clothes, Pru actually *did* bat an eye at this. A few months ago, she reflected, she wouldn't have.

"You look fabulous," Edie declared, around a mouthful of noodles.

"This is not my life," Pru said. "When would I ever wear this?" She stood on a little box in front of a three-way mirror. She had to admit, she looked impossibly glamorous. Even in the Keds.

Edie waved the chopsticks at her. "Try something else."

Pru was still considering the blouse and chatting with Edie by six o'clock, when two women came in. They were obviously heading home from their jobs as, perhaps, cultural attachés, from the look of them. They were slim and well-dressed in that funky/elegant style of Edie's shop. Clearly, they had money. "Lucia and Ramona," Edie said, getting up to kiss them, too.

"Oooh, a dress-up party," one of them said, and headed right back out to the liquor store across the street. Lucia wanted to try on the blouse and Capris that Pru was wearing, so Edie helped her find the size twos. Ramona returned with two bottles of champagne in a paper bag. After Edie went to the back room and found some plastic glasses left over from the store's opening, she kept bringing Lucia and Ramona things to try on, while Pru poured champagne and suggested accessories. Lucia liked a two-hundred-dollar beaded evening bag that Pru found; Ramona, three-hundred-dollar chandelier earrings. By the time Edie opened a second bottle of champagne, Lucia and Ramona had spent almost a thousand bucks.

"That was fun," Pru said, after the two women had gone tottering tipsily down the street together, shopping bags clattering on their looped arms. "You should make champagne a regular thing." She hung the three-hundred-dollar Pucci print blouse back on its wooden hanger. Maybe it was because she'd just worked so hard for the modest income she'd made, but suddenly, three hundred dollars seemed like a ridiculous amount of money for a blouse. It was almost her entire grocery bill for the month.

"I never thought of getting my clients drunk before."

"You could advertise it," Pru suggested. "Champagne Night at Edie's. Come in for a free glass of champagne and see the new stuff. It'd be the most stylish event in the District. Of course," she added, "a sale at the Gap could be considered the most stylish event in the District."

Edie nodded, thoughtfully. "It's not a bad idea. You were great with them, by the way. You were born for retail sales."

Pru didn't think so. She associated "sales" with desperation and the kind of faked enthusiasm that meant you were about two seconds from a serious suicide attempt. To be very honest, she thought it a little beneath her. But later, Edie called and said that if she would help out on the first official Champagne Night at Edie's, she could wear anything she wanted from the store. Pru found her fabric lust outweighing her pride, and agreed.

An hour before the party was supposed to start, Pru stood before the three-way mirror in a bronze satin movie-star gown, cut on the bias. It had come in only the day before. The plunging neckline and the diagonal swoop of satin made her body look amazing. She blushed to see herself in the mirror. Edie had purchased ten bottles of a good, cheap champagne, and at six o'clock on the nose women began streaming in, filling the shop with the sound of their throaty, reedy voices.

Pru spent the evening running around with her arms full of clothes. Many women came just to chat and drink champagne, but others were grateful to be told what to wear. They were the ones, she found out by talking to them, with the big jobs and busy lives and the tired everything: tired hair, tired eyes, tired shoes. They would be total bitches at work, you could tell. Pru rustled around in the satin gown, bringing them soft flats with butterflies on the toes, mohair sweaters in impossibly delicate colors, hydrangea-print pouf skirts that hit just below the knee. The women's eyes softened and their lips parted when they saw her coming, as if her arms held exotic flowers. Edie went around filling everyone's champagne glasses and ringing up purchases. Her little helper guy patiently folded everything into lavender tissue paper and popped them into brown bags adorned with the purple EDIE's stickers. After two hours the attitude became pretty loopy, with half-dressed customers parading around in front of the windows overlooking busy Connecticut Avenue.

Pru felt as though she'd discovered a secret gift. She seemed to know what to bring in to the dressing room. She didn't have to schmooze the customers. She found that if you just concentrated on the best feature of each one, you could make her look like Gwyneth Paltrow. She'd even come up with her own mantra: "If you love it, buy it. Don't worry about the cost." Edie wanted her to persuade the customers not to rely on their wardrobes at home to complete the outfit, in order to sell more. But usually she didn't even have to go that far, to sell them two pieces instead of one. She merely showed them how the cut of the pants actually enhanced the slenderizing effect of the jacket, or whatever. "Look," she'd say, "how the leg of these trousers balances your hips." Pru didn't know how she knew any of this. By the end of the evening, she was so familiar with Edie's collection that she could dress each woman in her mind as they walked in the door. "Wait!" she kept yelling. "I have the perfect thing for that," or "You," she called out, grabbing someone's wrist, "would look *amazing* in this."

The only women who left without buying anything, she noticed, were the size twelve-and-ups. Which was surprising, given that Edie herself wore sixteens. It might be true that Edie couldn't afford anything in her own shop, Pru thought, as another woman struggled to button the largest-sized blouse she'd been able to find. But it was also true that she couldn't fit into any of it. There were plenty of non-single-digit-sized women in the city who worked hard, who had money, who appreciated style. Didn't they deserve such beauty, too?

"YOU'RE, LIKE, GLOWING," JOHN SAID, THE FOLLOWING day. Pru was sitting at a table she liked because someone had carved AG + SW?? into the top, and darkened it with pencil. She liked to think about who would do such a thing, and whether the question marks had been added afterward, or if they were the whole point? She thought of it as the table of yearning.

John was wearing an apron tied in the back, and listened patiently as she babbled on about the event, the pleasure she'd taken in making the women feel beautiful. It was good to have something positive going on. She felt like he'd only ever seen her whining, or making a fool out of herself.

"A woman spent almost fifteen hundred dollars on *one* outfit that I put together for her," Pru said, pressing her finger into the sugar left on her plate. "I hate to say it but, man, it felt good."

"I know what you mean," John said. "Last week I sold a hundred and twenty cups of coffee."

She wrinkled her nose, and did the math. "That doesn't sound like it's going to keep you in business long."

"It won't. I'm not sure what I'm going to do, but I can't keep doing this."

"Maybe you have too many freeloaders here. Like me. We just hang around all day and never buy anything." She meant it lightly, but her heart sank. She'd come to rely on John's company in the mornings. What would happen if he closed the Korner?

"Maybe I should start offering women's fashions," he said. "Listen, I think you're on to something."

"I know," she said. "Three months of freelance, and nothing *near* the jolt I got last night. But, retail?"

"Why not?"

"I'll be honest. I have snobby feelings about it. At least in non-profit, you know, you can feel like you're doing *some* good in the world."

"Not to hear you talk about it. I don't know, but I think you ought to listen to this feeling."

She drank her coffee, thinking. Edie had said that she'd hire her, anytime. She wouldn't make much, of course. In fact, the money she'd gotten from the one writing job was more than she'd make at Edie's in a month. But Edie had also offered to let her keep a percentage of her sales, so Pru had told her she'd think about it.

She dragged herself homeward, slowly. Despite Whoop's recently improved behavior, she still dreaded going back to the aloneness of her apartment. The other night she'd found a blue sock of Annali's shoved behind a door, and felt a heave in her chest. It had been almost a month since she'd seen her. Patsy and Fiona were always complaining about how kids weigh you down. But what, she wondered, was she staying light for? To be available to bring Rudy organic trout from Fresh Fields?

Her cell phone rang just as she was about to open the front door. It was McKay wanting to know if she'd had dinner. It seemed that Bill was out of town and McKay had finally consumed the last edible thing in the house. Her spirits lifted considerably as she agreed to meet him for tapas and cocktails, and she turned and sprinted gaily down the rest of the steps.

Okay, she thought, so being single and childless had its merits. For dang sure.

"WE'RE THINKING OF MOVING," MCKAY ANNOUNCED, when the waiter had brought their drinks.

Pru looked up in alarm. McKay and Bill, not right next door? "What do you mean? Where? When?"

"Just in town. Don't worry. We're just looking to buy something, that's all. We're getting tired of renting. And our place is a little small. We're not going to adopt now, but you know, Bill does keep going on about it . . ."

Her heart rate had shot up at his words. "But—but—"

"We'll still be nearby. Don't worry! We'll try to stay in Adams-Morgan."

She shook her head. First John, talking about selling the café, then McKay and Bill, possibly leaving the neighborhood. And becoming daddies, without her! She was going to be left behind, she could feel it. "You'll end up out in the suburbs, I know you will. No one can afford to buy here anymore. I'll have to take a train out to see you, and it'll be too much of a hassle, and you'll make new friends. Before you know it, we'll never see each other anymore."

"That's a cheerful thought. Thanks for that."

"But you're leaving me!"

"We're not leaving you! I promise."

"No one's doing what I want them to do. You're going, Patsy's coming . . ."

"Is she really?"

"Oh, yes."

"When?"

Pru sighed. "They want to do Thanksgiving at the beach house. They're flying lobsters in from Chad, or something fabulous like that. At least, that's what Patsy said, the last time I talked to her. No word on whether or not she and Jacob are actually still seeing each other, or what. I swear, I worry about her mental health. It's like she's living in la-la land."

She hadn't gotten more than two minutes with Patsy on the phone. Her mother kept telling her that everything was fine. Pru worked on ignoring the ominous voice in her head, the one that said something had changed with Jacob and that another shoe was looking to drop.

They walked past the Kozy Korner on the way home. She sneaked a glance in the window, but John wasn't anywhere in sight.

"You want to stop in?" McKay suggested.

She sighed. "No."

"What's going on with you two, anyway?"

"I don't know. Nothing. Do you remember that scene in *Airplane!* where the guy with the flags is waving a jet into its gate, then someone asks him where the bathrooms are, so he begins gesturing in the other direction?"

"So the jet crashes into the airport. Yes."

"That's how it is, with him. I think I'm getting these signals, you know, and it turns out he's just looking for the toilet."

THE MORNING THAT PATSY AND ANNALI WERE TO LEAVE for Rehoboth, Pru was at her usual seat in the café, watching John do the morning puzzle, when her cell phone rang.

They were already halfway through Pennsylvania. Patsy talked so fast that Pru was having a hard time understanding her, but finally understood that she wanted help unloading the U-Haul. She wasn't "completely sure" when Jacob would be there. When Pru pressed her, Patsy admitted that she hadn't spoken to him "in a couple of days."

"Just turn around," Pru said immediately. "Go back home."

"Honey," said Patsy, "I don't have a home to drive back to. To the ocean, right, Annali?"

"You can stay at Mom's. She's got room, until you find a new place."

"Honestly," Patsy said. "He's just busy at the hospital, is all."

"Busy at the hospital? So busy he can't call you, right when you're supposed to be moving?" John looked up from his crossword.

"Listen, I'm not saying that everything's perfect," said Patsy.

"Maybe he did get cold feet. But trust me, okay? I know him." Pru could hear Annali singing along to the soundtrack to *Grease* in the background. *We made out, under the docks!* "Anyway, can you come up? I might need help getting the trailer unloaded, if I can't reach him tonight. I'm supposed to have it back in the morning, or pay something like a thousand bucks on it. I can come and pick you up."

"No," said Pru, "you don't want to drive that thing into the city. Just get to Rehoboth. I'll meet you there."

"What happened?" said John, when she'd hung up.

"Patsy," said Pru. "She's moving here, with a U-Haul full of their stuff. And now Jacob's not showing up to help, and she just told me it's been days since she's even talked to him." Her mind was racing. She had to get to the bus stop, to check the schedule . . . no, she would rent a car. There was a Hertz on Fourteenth . . .

"Jacob's the guy she's been seeing, right? The doctor?"

She shook her head. "This is bad. I don't know what to do."

"I can drive you up there," he said. "Ludmilla can handle things here until dinner. I'd have to be back then. But we can get the big stuff unloaded, don't you think?"

Normally, she would have found a dozen different reasons not to accept the favor. It was always easier for her to offer help than to accept it. But she was so grateful that she wanted to throw her arms around him.

In the van, they didn't talk, but listened to the public radio station. Pru found herself looking at all the cars on the BWI Parkway, hoping to see a look-at-me blue convertible going in the same direction.

John turned off the radio. "Where's Annali's father, in all this?" he said.

"Jimmy Roy? My mother says they haven't heard from him in

a while. I guess he's kind of a burnout. I always liked him, though. I think he means well."

"Were he and Patsy married?"

"No. They were part of this big circle of friends, and the plan was they'd all raise Patsy's baby together."

This was one of her sister's more dubious schemes. Pru had met the friends, left-of-center hippie types, who had read Proust and *On the Road* and could talk about Cocteau's *Orpheus* and often had to pool their money to buy a twelve-pack. They would jump in a car and head down to New Orleans for Mardi Gras. Jimmy Roy was the one with the most responsible job, working in the automotive department of Sears. Pru liked them well enough, but she was certain that Patsy's vision of a communal life was doomed.

Sure enough, the friends kept partying while Patsy took child-birth classes and scoured tag sales for a secondhand stroller. With a month left in her pregnancy, she began to understand that she was going to be not the biological mother of a child raised by a family of parent-friends, but left to feed and educate and worry over a child all on her own. Pru flew to Columbus to help her pack up her few things and drive home to their mother's house, two hours away. Within a week, Patsy had found a house down the street to rent, and later, when Annali was six weeks old, a job teaching language arts at a private school for girls in Akron. The very house and job she'd just given up, to be with Jacob, who was currently nowhere to be found.

"The father should be there," John said, with so much vehemence that it surprised her. "Jimmy Roy. They need him."

"He was, in the beginning. All the time," Pru said. "He'd come up to my mother's at least every weekend. But then he had an accident on his motorcycle. He was in bad shape. He ended up having all these surgeries, and living in his mother's basement. The next thing we know, he's in the Antarctic, on a research boat. I know they hear from him, but I doubt that Patsy would welcome him with open arms, at this point."

"Well," he said, "they should work something out. It's not fair to Patsy or to Annali, this arrangement."

"Patsy doesn't want anything that looks like a conventional marriage. Frankly, I don't entirely understand it. Our parents had a great marriage. But . . . I don't know. It just freaks her out, for some reason. Or it *used* to, before Jacob, anyway."

They pulled up in front of the beach house, just ahead of Patsy and Annali, who came roaring up in Patsy's old Honda, pulling behind it the U-Haul trailer. Patsy hopped out, full of happy smiles. She wore a polka-dotted chiffon scarf over her hair and big sunglasses, and laughed while she ran up the steps to the house. Pru found it impossible to join in her enthusiasm. She unbuckled Annali from the backseat of the car, then gathered her up in her arms. Oh, how she'd been missing that warmth, those tight arms around her neck! Annali was in one of her self-made outfits: leotard and tights, ladybug rain boots, and a shiny red Wonder Woman cape. It would have been twenty degrees cooler, in Ohio, where she'd gotten dressed. Pru admired her cape and thought, *Only a mother like Patsy would let her go out like that in the middle of November.*

All afternoon, while they unpacked, Pru watched her sister's every move. Patsy seemed perfectly unfazed that Jacob was not showing up, or giving any sign at all that he *would* show up. Pru did catch her checking her cell phone several times, but she never seemed in the least bit dissatisfied. John and Pru, passing on the stairs, exchanged an uneasy look.

"This is just so weird," Pru said, under her breath.

They got the queen-size mattress and box spring up the rickety stairs, two dressers, and carton after carton of clothes, books, teaching materials, and toys. Although it was a cool day, they were all bathed in sweat. At three o'clock, when it was time to go, Pru tried to persuade Patsy to let her stay and help get them settled. But Patsy, who was seized with the notion that Pru and John should be alone together, absolutely refused.

"Get out of here," she said, as if they were a couple of kids, and she the old married lady. "Go have your fun. We'll be so close now, we'll see each other all the time!"

When they were in the van and heading south, John said, "So, what's the deal with this guy? Jacob? You think he's cutting out on them?"

"I'm almost positive." She repeated what Jacob had said in the car, about "explaining it" to Annali.

He frowned. "It doesn't sound good. What did Patsy say?"

Pru shook her head. "She didn't take it seriously."

"Maybe you should try again?"

"I don't know," she said doubtfully. "Would you have listened, if someone had told you that your marriage was in trouble? Is that the kind of thing that can come from anyone else?"

"I guess not." He quickly sank into silence. Pru had seen this from him before, this sudden mood change, usually at the mention of his marriage. One minute he would be attentive and animated and she would start to have hopes. The next, a sad look came into his eyes, he looked a million miles away, and nothing she said could shake him out of it. She turned and watched the passing scenery out of her window.

She felt very irritated with John Owen. What did he want from her? What was he doing with her, what were they doing with each other? What about his girlfriend and his not-yet ex-wife?

In-betweenness, how she hated it. She wanted to be at home now, with Whoop, who was probably thinking that she had finally abandoned him, too.

They pulled onto New York Avenue, a major thoroughfare made narrow on both sides with construction blocks and orange cones. It was an ugly strip, banked by cheap motels, and peopled by the usual transient window-washers who approached with their squeegees as soon as the car slowed. Pru hated this entry to the city. You just couldn't believe the road could possibly lead to anything worthwhile.

Pru said, "Hey, I'm sorry, if I said the wrong thing, there." She'd tried, but there was nothing friendly in her tone.

"That's all right," he said, just as flatly. "It's not your fault."

WHEN SHE GOT HOME, BEFORE SHE EVEN TOOK OFF HER coat, she sat down on the couch, and dialed the number for the beach house. Her head was still buzzing from the six hours' round trip she'd spent in John's van.

"You don't have to tell me everything," she said, when Patsy picked up. "But at least tell me why you're not freaking out about Jacob. I care about you, and I care about Annali, and I don't understand what you're doing here. I mean," she said helplessly, "I'm glad you're nearby. I really am. But I don't understand you and Jacob. I just don't understand what's going on. Patsy, what's going on?"

Patsy was silent a moment. Then she said, "It's not what you think."

"Well, what is it?"

"I don't want to tell you. I know how you'll react."

"What's that supposed to mean?"

"You'll get all judgmental."

The word made her stiffen. Patsy could always stop her dead in her tracks with that word. Anything she didn't want to hear was instantly "judgmental," and Pru could never think of a rebuttal. She was discerning, not judgmental. There was a difference. Wasn't there?

"It's just that, well, Jacob's wife must have come back from wherever she was. He told me it might be harder to get together." She paused. "Don't say anything," she said.

Pru didn't say anything. She was surprised, but not surprised. Jacob had a wife. It made perfect sense—all the weekends in Rehoboth, the way Patsy would look at him, sometimes, when he disappeared to take a phone call . . . In a way, it was a relief. It took the whole problem out of Pru's hands. It was like she'd been trying to help Patsy pack for a trip to France, and it turned out she was headed to Malaysia. Or Jupiter.

Pru didn't have much experience with affairs with married men. She knew such things went on. Her friend Kate had had one—more than one—so she at least knew the routine. It seemed to consist mostly of keeping your expectations to a sub-minimum. But to get this far involved . . . to move across the country, with a child, to be near someone who was *married* . . . Pru sat there, in her coat, the only light coming from over the stove.

"So," she said, "what happens now? Do you just stop seeing each other. Or what?"

"I don't know."

"Is this all okay with her? The wife, I mean?"

"Well, they have some kind of an understanding. But we haven't talked about it."

"Why not?"

"Why are you getting so angry?"

"I'm not angry."

"Then why are you shouting at me?"

"I'm not shouting, I just want to know if the guy who my niece calls *Daddy* . . ."

"Just shut up," Patsy said.

"Fine."

For a while, neither one of them said anything. She began unbuttoning her coat. Whoop came out of the bedroom to twine himself between her legs, purring.

"He's not the Great Pumpkin, honey," she said, at last. "He's not going to disappear just because you want a little clarity. Is that so wrong, to want to know if he's on board with all of this, or not? Why don't you wait to unpack the rest of your things, until you can talk to him? You know, maybe you should call the school, see if they've found a replacement—"

"I have to go," Patsy interrupted. "I'm exhausted, and so is Annali. You just have to trust me on this, Pru. It's what my gut is telling me to do. It's what my *whole body* says to do."

Great, Pru thought, hanging up the phone. Her niece's entire well-being depended on a hundred twenty pounds of inert, unthinking, Jacob-obsessed flesh.

Thirteen

For days she kept trying Patsy's cell phone, and the number at the beach house. Patsy never answered, never responded to any of Pru's messages urging her to call as soon as she could.

Pru wanted to be not shocked and saddened by this development, this Jacob-was-married thing. She hated thinking of herself as she suspected she really was, *prudish*. She was old enough to know that marriages were like children. They had lives of their own and didn't necessarily act the way you thought they should. And that the rules were different for each one.

But she *was* shocked, and saddened. She liked Jacob. She liked Jacob because Patsy liked Jacob, and Patsy never liked anybody, for very long. Pru could almost understand her sister's actions, but Jacob's? Did he have to get Annali to fall in love with him, too? It didn't seem fair to say that Patsy had made her own bed and now must lie in it. She'd had plenty of encouragement to make that bed. Pru had seen it herself.

It wasn't that she had such puritanical positions on monogamy. Okay, maybe *some* of them were puritanical. Maybe her basic position—that monogamy was a good thing, and rather inflexible—was puritanical. But she wasn't unevolved on the subject. Weren't there worse things than being cheated on, weren't there other ways of being disloyal? Of being unloving? Of betraying?

She doubted that Jacob's wife was completely in the dark about his affairs. (Affairs, plural? More than one? Probably so.) When Pru looked back at the past few months, she couldn't see a lot of sneaky, suspicious behavior. There seemed to have been no limits on Patsy's access to him. They talked on the phone every night, well into the night, according to Patsy. Of course, they'd never spent any time at his apartment in the city. Always the beach house. Perhaps that was part of the wife's requirements, that he not conduct his extramaritals in their home. Pru wondered if they had one of those "open marriages." She pictured an open marriage like a Venus flytrap, waiting to snap closed on some unsuspecting victim.

Almost a week after Patsy's move, Pru still couldn't reach her. She was growing frantic. She went mechanically through her day with her head full of questions: When had Patsy found out that he was married? That first night, out on Pru's stoop? Had he told her that the marriage was ending? Did she have hopes that it would? Patsy had to think that being nearby would change things. Pru simply couldn't believe otherwise. Even for the love of her life, Patsy would never do something like that to Annali.

She kept remembering the day they walked around Rehoboth with the puppy. Jacob showing off his "daughter." There was a picture on her refrigerator that represented that day, drawn in crayon. Annali had asked her to draw it. It didn't look any different from what it would have looked like if Pru had drawn it thirty years earlier, so lame were her artistic skills: Stick mommy, stick boyfriend, stick little girl, stick dog. Stick auntie. The crudeness of it made her sad now. Annali deserved so much better.

She'd give Patsy one more day to call, Pru decided, before renting a car and driving up to Rehoboth herself. She was just about to turn off her computer and go to bed, when someone buzzed from downstairs. It was Patsy, her voice ragged and raspy, over the security speaker.

"Let us up," she said.

She came in carrying Annali, who was fast asleep. Pru could see right away that Patsy had been crying. Her nose and eyes were red, and she was nervously chewing the inside of her bottom lip, as she always did when she was upset.

Pru pulled back the covers on her bed, and Patsy lowered Annali carefully, until she was lying on her back. She smoothed Annali's cap of curls from her forehead and kissed her. Patsy's shoulders began to shake. Pru reached out and took her arm and said, "Come."

Patsy followed her out to the other room, and then she began talking.

She'd just come from GW Hospital. She'd found Jacob's car in the hospital garage and waited there until his shift ended. When he finally came out, she'd confronted him. Where had he been? Why hadn't he called her back? Didn't he care that they'd come all this way?

It was like talking to a robot, she said. He told her that he was sorry to have given her the impression that he could ever be a serious part of their lives.

"'Serious part of your lives,'" Patsy said again, contemptuously. "Was he kidding?"

He apologized if he'd led her to believe that he'd ever leave his

wife for her. He hadn't meant to, but if he had, he was pro-
foundly sorry. "Led me to believe?" Patsy cried. "We only talked
about it constantly. How he couldn't wait for her to come back,
so he could start the divorce proceedings . . . How he was hiring
a lawyer, to look into adopting Annali . . . How we'd give her
some brothers and sisters to grow up with—" At this, Patsy's
voice broke and she buried her face in her hands again, sobbing
violently.

Pru was crying now, too. At first she'd been relieved to hear
that Patsy hadn't actually been as deluded as she'd feared—but
how reprehensible! To promise such a life, such sweet relief for
two souls who had suffered so much—

"Oh!" Patsy's head snapped up. "You know what he said? 'I
love my life.'"

"Oh, honey," Pru said.

"Not 'my wife,'" Patsy fumed, now pacing the apartment.
"'My *life*.' 'I love my life.' You want to know why he said that?
I'll tell you why—because her father's in charge of handing out
research grants, that's why. That is the only reason he's with her,
and not me." She turned around to face Pru. She looked as
shocked as she had when Leonard had shown them the little cat
bones, in the basement. "How could he say no to us? I mean,
how?"

Pru had no idea her sister could be so gullible. She wanted to
gather Patsy up in her arms, and she wanted to shake her, too.

"I don't know, honey. I guess there are other things that he
wants more than love."

Patsy paced back and forth. One minute she thought he might
still come back to them; another, she wished him dead. She cried
and cried, and she drank most of a bottle of wine Pru had found
in the refrigerator. Finally, Pru persuaded her to go to bed. She

led her into the bedroom, and got her to lie down next to Annali. Annali rolled over in her sleep and put an arm around her mother's neck. Patsy closed her eyes and her mouth turned down, then her face relaxed as she fell into sleep.

Pru curled up in the bay window and looked out at the city. People were going to the movies, parents were putting their children to bed. Suddenly, she feared for them all. She remembered, as she did from time to time, that everyone was going to die. Plane crashes, heart attacks, the slow erosion of bones. How did we manage to forget this, she wondered, and get through our daily lives? It was astonishing to her. Everybody was going to die, but still they did the laundry, watered the plants, dug out the scum around the taps in the bathroom. They let themselves love others, who were also going to die. They created little beings, who they also loved, and who will, one day, cease to exist. What did it matter how love ended? So it ended for Patsy with Jacob returning to his wife, instead of with his death. Did it really matter so much? She thought of something her mother used to say, a warning she gave whenever they'd begun to fight over some precious object or another: "It's going to end in tears, girls! It *always* ends in tears."

For a long time, she'd thought the whole problem was about finding love. She'd thought that, once she'd found it, she'd basically be done. Set. Good to go. Funny, how until just now, she hadn't put it all together: All love ended, somehow. One way, or another.

It was *all* going to end in tears, wasn't it?

THE NEXT DAY, PRU DROVE THEM BACK TO THE BEACH house in Patsy's old hatchback. Patsy had left the puppy alone in the house. She didn't even know anyone in the neighborhood well enough to call and check on her. The arcade in Rehoboth was closed up, as were most of the tourist shops. It was the week before Thanksgiving, and the beach town felt desolate, abandoned. Low, dark clouds hung over the ocean.

They could hear the puppy, Jenny, howling plaintively as they came up the stairs. She'd been alone for the past day and night. She came bounding outside and back in again, racing around in circles, nipping at their hands.

Unpacked boxes were everywhere. The place reeked of neglected pet.

"Oh God," moaned Patsy, sinking to the couch. "I can't face this."

"Patsy," said Pru, "why don't you just come back with me? You don't have to deal with this right now. Just for a few days, until you've got your feet back under you."

Patsy looked at her, uncertain and relieved. "Are you sure?"

Pru shrugged. As crazy as the night before had been, she didn't feel ready to let it end yet. There was something comforting about the three of them being in the apartment together. She'd forgotten all about the dog . . . but, well, she'd worry about that later.

"Of course. It'll be nice to have you guys around."

Patsy found a carton and began stuffing it with clothes for her and Annali. Pru cleaned up the various messes the dog had made, and found its leash, food, and bowl. She wondered if Whoop would start pissing everywhere again when he saw the dog. Patsy locked the front door, and they headed back out of town. Jenny was in her crate on the backseat, next to Annali, who spaced out stroking her hat-lovey, until she fell asleep. Patsy, who had started crying again, leaned her head against the window and fell asleep, too. Pru drove the rest of the way home, listening to the news on the radio and the sounds of Jenny gnawing on her rawhide bone.

THE HAIR ON WHOOP'S BACK STOOD UP WHEN THE puppy came running in. He flew to his former place under the couch, and Jenny raced after him. The dog's nails on her parquet floors made Pru cringe. Jenny stopped suddenly, and made a puddle on the floor. *Here we go again,* thought Pru, reaching for the paper towels. Whoop let out a low, threatening yowl from under the couch, where Patsy had flopped, and Annali began running after the puppy.

Patsy camped out in the living room, where she took to falling asleep in front of the television Pru had finally bought, following the last weekend she'd had Annali. Annali and Pru took the bed. The first few nights, she woke up to the sound of Patsy's crying in the living room; after a few awkward, early attempts to soothe her, Pru began rolling over and pulling a pillow over her head to block the sound.

There wasn't much going on that gave shape to their lives. Pru felt as if they were all waiting for something to happen. In the morning, Annali played with her toys or carried her hat around, looking bored. Patsy watched TV, and Pru continued to look for work. The money she'd recently earned hadn't gone far, even though she'd been careful with it, and she was getting dangerously near the end of her severance. After that, she'd have only her father's inheritance, which she figured she'd better save for the nursing home, without a husband or kids to foot that bill.

One day, after much nagging from Pru to get up off the couch and at least go outside, Patsy finally went out while Annali took a nap. She came back looking even worse than when she'd left. Her eyes were red, her hair in a tangle, and she seemed uncharacteristically slow and heavy. It was as though she was inhabiting a different body altogether. Pru imagined her sitting in the park, weeping, dead leaves and trash swirling around her feet.

For days Patsy didn't shower, phone anyone, or do anything besides sit in front of the TV and take her afternoon walks. Sometimes Pru tried to talk to her, but Patsy gave only the briefest of replies to her questions. Compared with what Patsy was going through, Pru's grieving for Rudy seemed like some harmless sandbox dust-up. Patsy wasn't just missing the life she thought she'd have, like Pru had done—the phantom children, the beautiful house in Cleveland Park—she was missing all that *plus* a person. Pru missed Rudy in the way you miss the electricity when it goes out. You think, Okay, I can't check my e-mail, I'll watch TV instead—*damn it!* It was annoying, persistent, and pretty much everywhere you turned, for a while, but then the lights came back on. Patsy missed Jacob the way you'd miss your hands, if they fell off.

Pru hated to say it, but if Patsy didn't have Annali to think about, would she have held out for Jacob a little longer? Would faithful persistence have made any difference? Her slide downhill was, in the long term, very fast, but for those living with her, a day seemed like a whole lifetime. One minute, she'd be walking around the apartment like a stoned zombie; the next, she couldn't stop crying. Increasingly, Pru found herself in charge of Annali.

"Are you sick, Mommy?" Annali would say, hovering nearby. "Does your tummy hurt?" Or, "Are you mad, Mommy?" Patsy tried to play with her, but after a few minutes she would turn away, back to watching *Oprah,* or staring out the bay window at the view over the rooftops. She couldn't get lost in her thoughts, or wherever it was she was trying to go, with Annali pulling at her legs. Pru did what she could to distract Annali, whose eyes never left Patsy for more than a few minutes, before she'd go over and touch her and the questions began again: *Does your tummy hurt? Are you mad?* The harder Annali tried to bring her mommy back, the farther away Patsy wanted to go.

Pru wondered how long she could live this way without losing her mind completely. She wanted to hide under the couch with Whoop, waiting for the strangers to go back to wherever it was they'd come from.

ON THE FIFTH MORNING AFTER THEY CAME TO STAY, PRU took Annali to the café for breakfast. She had to get away from Patsy for an hour or two, or she'd go mad. She knew enough this time to pack some crayons and a few toys, and to give her niece several stern warnings as well as the promise of chocolate chip pancakes, if she behaved herself. This was what she'd been reduced to, she thought, walking down the street with Annali: out-and-out bribery.

It was a busy morning at the café. John waved from behind the counter. They slid into a booth by the window. When Ludmilla came over to take their order, Annali carefully and politely asked for pancakes and milk. Pru watched John nervously out of the corner of her eye while they waited. She hadn't talked to him since the drive home from Rehoboth and she wondered what kind of footing they were on. But he stayed behind the counter, talking to the other regulars and serving to-go orders. She couldn't even count on Annali to lure him over with one of her spectacular tantrums. Her niece sat quietly coloring in her coloring book, for a change.

"Hey," she said, elbowing Annali in the ribs gently. "Don't you want to have a fit?"

"No, thank you," Annali said, pleasantly, not even looking up from her crayons.

They finished their breakfast, Pru paid the bill, and they gathered their things to leave. Then Annali said she wanted to spin on one of the stools at the counter, and Pru consented. It would waste time, she reflected, and put them in proximity of John.

He came over to stand near them while Annali clambered up on the stool. "Who's this?" John said, pointing to Dipsy.

"PBSKids," Annali muttered, clutching the Teletubby closer to her. She climbed up on the stool. "Dot org," she added. Pru gave the stool a good push and Annali shrieked with laughter.

"How's everything going?" John said.

"Crazy, actually." While Annali spun herself around on the stool, Pru explained in a low voice what had happened.

"Married, huh?" John said, when Annali left the stool to check out a basket of toys on the floor. "What the hell was he thinking?"

"I don't know," Pru said. "I'm worried about Patsy. I've never seen her like this before. She's always been moody, but this is pretty extreme."

"You've got everyone staying at your place?" John said.

Pru nodded, grimacing. "It's very cozy."

"I'll bet," he said. "It's like Aunt Pru's home for lost souls, over there. Good for you, though. You're doing a fine thing. She's lucky to have you."

LATER THAT DAY, PRU DECIDED TO GO SWIMMING. HER absence that morning hadn't seemed to affect Patsy one way or another. John was right; she'd been taking care of everybody for days, and she needed a break.

"Will you be okay?" she said to Patsy, sitting, as ever, in the bay window.

Patsy nodded, not moving her eyes from the scene below the window. "Of course," she said, dully.

"Okay," said Pru. "I'll be home before dinner. Is there anything special you want? Should I pick something up?"

"Anything," said Patsy, without any interest.

The front desk at the Hilton on P Street had been giving her funny looks, so she decided to try the R Street Radisson. She did hard laps that left her limbs burning and sore, and afterward she floated gently on her back, letting the water turn her this way and that. The Radisson's pool was very pleasant, and the staff had smiled at her kindly. She left feeling more optimistic. That was what everyone needed, she decided—a little sunlight, some firm, cheerful direction. Enough moping.

She trudged slowly up Sixteenth, bleary-eyed and spent from the water. She thought of what awaited her at home. The cat would need attention. The dog would need a walk. Annali would need dinner and a bath. Patsy would need . . . something she didn't have. Turning onto Columbia, she tried to work up the kind of brisk energy she'd need to get everyone settled in for the night.

She walked into a quiet apartment. Whoop sat in the middle of the room, washing himself. The TV was silent for the first time in forever. She was slightly alarmed at first, but then she relaxed. No doubt her absence had forced Patsy finally to take action. Perhaps she'd actually gotten Annali out to the swings, or to the park across the street.

She sighed, looking around. Without the distraction of human bodies, the place looked like it had been trashed in a police raid. A pile of Patsy's dirty clothes occupied one corner of the room, Annali's toys another. The coffee table was strewn with toiletries, magazines, and dirty plates. There were cat toys scattered all over the floor, and the smell of curdled milk persisted in the air, from when the puppy knocked over Annali's cereal bowl yesterday morning. Jenny was leaving Whoop in peace, for the moment, sleeping on the bed in the other room. But soon, she knew, they would be chasing each other through the rooms, tearing up the hardwood floor and upsetting pieces of furniture.

She'd started to pick up Annali's Legos, which were scattered all over the floor, when she heard the sound of water dripping into the bathtub. It was an ominous, forlorn sound, and made Pru shudder.

She pushed open the bathroom door, to see Annali, naked, about to back into a glowing red space heater. It was the old-fashioned kind with exposed heating coils. "Whoa!" Pru said, and grabbed Annali before she burned herself, hoisting her onto a hip.

Patsy was sitting in the bathtub. She was motionless, her arms wrapped around her body, and she was staring at some spot on the wall above the taps. Pru was shocked to see how thin she'd gotten. Her hair hung in damp ropes around delicate collarbones. Her skin looked almost blue, under the water. Her lips were purple.

"Pats?" Pru said. Patsy grunted in response, but didn't take her eyes from the spot on the bathroom tiles where she was staring. Pru put a hand in the bath water. "Patsy, that water is freezing!" Patsy was starting to shiver. She seemed to be in some kind of waking coma. Pru eased Annali off her hip.

"Okay, silly," she said, forcing a light tone. "Let's get out now."

She slipped her hands under Patsy's armpits and helped her sister stand. Patsy didn't resist.

Patsy's teeth were chattering now, and she shivered even more as soon as she was out of the water. Pru grabbed a towel from the bar and wrapped it around her. "I'll be right back," she said. "Stay here, okay?" Patsy didn't say anything but looked down at her toes, curled on the bathmat.

Pru quickly got Annali dressed and found a thick, wool blanket in her closet. In the bathroom, Patsy was shaking, staring at the bathmat. She was completely naked. The towel had fallen to the floor, and she hadn't even bothered to pick it up. Pru got the blanket around her and began rubbing her arms.

"How long were you in there?" Pru said. She was still trying to act like nothing was wrong. "You'll be lucky if you don't get pneumonia. You better not have pneumonia, missy. Mom'll kill me!" She led her to the couch in the living room. The blankets Patsy had been using at night were on the floor. Pru picked them all up and piled them as best she could around her sister. Annali, who had been trailing after them, looking worried, had started to cry. Pru brought her over to the table, and let her eat out of a carton of ice cream with a spoon.

"I'm sorry," Patsy finally said, her teeth clattering. "I'm sorry." Pru was so relieved that she was talking that she almost cried. Now that she was warmer, Patsy seemed basically fine. Except, of course, that she was clearly having a nervous breakdown. But she hadn't taken pills, or cut herself, or done any of the other things Pru had been fearing. There was no sign she'd done anything intentionally self-harming. The color was coming back into her lips.

"I can't leave you alone for a minute," Pru said, smoothing back her wet hair. She had to work to keep her tone neutral so that Annali, who had come wandering over, wouldn't know that her mother was scaring the crap out of her aunt. "*Such* a drama queen, you are." She rubbed Patsy's arms, still shaking under the blanket. They felt like sticks. The skin around the diamond in her nose was greenish, and peeling.

Annali had her hat-lovey in one hand and a pickle she'd found somewhere in the other. She came climbing up between them. "What's wrong with Mommy?" she said.

"Mommy is a little sad, honey. That's all."

"Why is Mommy sad?"

"Sometimes people just get sad."

Annali put her hands on either side of Patsy's face, stroking it. "There, there, Mommy," she said. "Shhhhh." Pru smelled pickle juice and baby shampoo. It was all she could do not to put her head down and weep.

Patsy turned her head to kiss the inside of Annali's hand, then closed her eyes. "You are my sweet peach," she said.

"Let's give her some Tylenol," Annali said.

"That's a good idea," Pru said.

"And a beer!" shouted Annali, jumping up. "Mommies drink beer when they feel bad."

"Oh, that's just great," muttered Patsy, from under her blanket. "She's really learning some life skills this week, isn't she?"

AFTER ANNALI WAS IN BED AND PATSY WAS IN FRONT OF the television, dressed and no longer shivering but not having eaten, Pru sat down at her computer to write an e-mail to her mother.

She didn't know where to begin. Nadine knew almost nothing of what had been going on. Pru hadn't been able to talk to her privately, with Patsy and Annali always around. After a while, she decided to say only that Patsy and Jacob had broken up, they were now at Pru's, and Patsy seemed "a little depressed." The four lines took Pru twenty minutes to compose. She certainly didn't mention wives, subzero baths, or walking comas.

Just before she was about to sign off and go to bed, a reply came from her mother. Nadine didn't use e-mail the regular way, like chatting back and forth. She still thought of it as a sort of telegram service, where you paid by the word. Her e-mail said: "Help on the way. Coming day after tomorrow. Arrive National, 6 pm." You could practically hear the "Stop" after each sentence.

It was the first time all week Pru could remember smiling.

TWO DAYS LATER, NADINE CAME OFF THE AIRPLANE AT National holding a Styrofoam carry-on cooler. She wore stretch slacks and a flowered shirt, lemons and oranges on a blue background, and her tennis shoes.

Following behind her, holding two suitcases and grinning from ear to ear, was Annali's father, Jimmy Roy.

Fourteen

Jimmy Roy still looked like what he was, a former local-circuit rock star, dressed in black jeans and boots and a Sex Pistols T-shirt. He could also pass for a pirate. The guitar slung across his back could have been a scabbard. His eyes were satiny and almost navy, just like Annali's, and he had the same expressive, almost feminine mouth. He wore several thick, silver rings and bracelets on both wrists. He and Nadine, in her two-piece Stein Mart stretch rayon outfit, made a hopelessly incongruous pair, but Pru couldn't think of anyone she'd rather see at the moment.

"Hey," Jimmy Roy said, coming over to kiss Pru on both cheeks.

"Now, this makes me happy," Pru said. "Annali will go nuts."

"Ah," said Jimmy Roy, "but how about her mother?"

Pru had no idea how to answer, so she pointed to the cooler her mother held. "What's in that thing?"

"Turkey," Nadine said, as if Pru was a little slow. "We always have turkey at Thanksgiving."

Pru wanted to point out that the grocery stores in D.C. carried turkeys, too. But she was too glad for the reinforcements, and instead lifted the cooler out of her mother's arms and hugged her hard.

ANNALI CAME SKIDDERING OUT OF THE BEDROOM, SHOUT-ing "Grandma!" She'd been furious that she'd been made to stay behind and take a nap, and had clearly been lying in bed all after-noon, fully awake and alert.

As soon as Nadine put down her bag and opened her arms, Annali shrieked and ran into them. "Oh, my pumpkin butter, how I've missed you!"

Over her grandmother's shoulder Annali saw Jimmy Roy, who'd been hanging back, outside the door. Patsy saw him at the same moment. Her mouth turned down as if she'd bitten into something unpleasant.

For a moment, Annali hesitated, uncertain. "Do you know who that is?" Nadine asked her, quietly. Annali nodded, then scrambled out of Nadine's arms.

"Daddy!"

Jimmy Roy crouched and Annali came flying at him. As she slammed into him, his face flooded with relief. She'd only just learned to talk, the last time he'd seen her, he'd told Pru in the cab.

Jimmy Roy let Annali knock him clean to the ground, his motorcycle boots flying up in the air. "How big you are, Peach!" he said.

Pru's mother was beaming, acting as though she didn't notice Patsy glaring at her. "Isn't this nice," she said in her gentle voice, wiping her eyes. "Everybody together again."

Pru had to agree. Already it felt less desperate, and although maybe not festive, at least things were looking up.

She opened the cooler to look at the turkey her mother brought from Ohio. It wasn't about to fit in her oven.

ANNALI WANTED CHOCOLATE CHIP PANCAKES AT THE Korner. Patsy stayed behind, saying she had a headache. She'd barely exchanged two words with Jimmy Roy, who seemed to be taking her coolness in his stride.

Her mother shook hands with John, smiling at him warmly. John showed them to a table by the window, took their jackets, and brought over the box of toys for Annali. Was he being particularly solicitous of her mother? Pru wondered. Maybe. Unless she was just imagining it. There she was, spiraling into weird. *Stop,* she told herself. *Just stop it.* Then John brought their food, too, Pru noticed, even though Ludmilla was hanging around doing nothing.

Jimmy Roy and Annali were pretending to be deposed royalty from another country, which Annali called "Acobia."

"Patsy did the same thing when she was little," Nadine was saying. "Some kids had imaginary friends, Patsy had imaginary resorts."

Annali was, of course, the Princess of Acobia, and Jimmy Roy was her bodyguard, both of them disguised as ordinary American tourists. Annali and Jimmy Roy jabbered at each other in a nonsense language that nobody but them understood. It sounded eerily convincing.

When John gave them the check, Nadine and Pru were still talking about the problem of the turkey.

"Why don't you eat here?" he said. "It'll be closed, you'll have it all to yourselves. I have a six-burner Viking," he added. "The oven is huge."

"My mother had one of those!" said Nadine. Before Pru knew what was happening, her mother had accepted the invitation to use the diner and had made John promise that he'd eat with them. Before Pru could calculate whether this was a good idea or a disaster waiting to happen, John said that he'd love to.

Annali didn't want to let go of Jimmy Roy when it came time for him to leave for the night. He and Nadine had gotten rooms at a little hotel in Dupont Circle, as Pru's apartment was so over-occupied that it probably violated fire and safety regulations.

"I'll come back later, Peach," Jimmy Roy said, kneeling to kiss her. "Don't worry, we have a lot of time together. I'm here for a long time."

"Daddy will come back," Patsy said, holding out Annali's hat and her sippy cup of milk. "Bedtime for you."

"I want Daddy to put me to bed!" Annali shrieked, clinging to him.

Jimmy Roy looked at Patsy, who said, blandly, "Of course, Daddy can put you to bed. I think I've done it enough these past two and a half years."

"To Acobia!" Annali shouted, charging off to the bedroom. She could be Wendy, Pru thought, flying away in her white nightgown.

After Annali had fallen asleep, Pru walked her mother and Jimmy Roy to the hotel. It had been renovated in sort of a faux art-deco style, with reproductions on the wall of vintage ocean liners and the Empire State Building. Jimmy Roy and Pru saw Nadine to her room, then went for a drink in the hotel's bar. It was dark, lit by blue neon lights.

"You were so great with Annali," she said. "Your timing couldn't be better."

"She's great," said Jimmy Roy. "Patsy looks like hell. What's going on?"

"Jimmy Roy, you'll have to ask her. I really don't know what she'd want you to know."

He nodded, drinking his beer. "I get the picture."

"But, tell me about you, Jimmy Roy. You look good."

"Thank you, Pru." He said this so seriously and politely that she had to hide her smile in her beer. "As a matter of fact, I've been on a campaign of self-improvement." He looked her in the eye and said, "I'm sure Patsy told you I was an addict."

She shook her head. Worthless, loser, burnout, yes. Addict, which implied needles and desperation and dangerous friends, no.

"I could say that it was just because of the painkillers, after the accident. But that wouldn't be totally truthful. The painkillers just happened to be in my hand at the time. I'd take anything anybody wanted to give me. I didn't care. So, when I was in the hospital and they gave me those pills, it just seemed natural to want more. It could have been anything, though. Anything that made me feel better than I was feeling at that moment. I'm not saying it's not what most people do. It is what most people do. But for me, you know, getting stoned or watching TV, taking a few pills or going shopping—it was all on the same order."

He took a long sip of his beer, then said, "I was living in my mother's basement. I wake up one morning, and realize it's January the fourth."

"Annali's birthday," said Pru.

He nodded. "I hadn't sent a present. I didn't even have the money for gas, so I could drive up and see her. I called and sang 'Happy Birthday' to her on the phone, then I hung up and flushed all the pills and my last dime bags down the toilet."

Pru listened, fascinated. She'd always wondered what it would be like to completely give in to something like that, some impulse that took you over. She wanted another beer, but it seemed a little odd to order one. She was relieved when Jimmy Roy ordered another one for her, and a soda for himself.

"One's my limit," he said to her. "I'm allowed to feel a little better, then I have to go back to feeling whatever I didn't want to feel in the first place again. It's not much, you know. It's not like I had some traumatic childhood. Just regular old boredom."

The father of one of his former band-mates was piloting a research boat to the Antarctic, Jimmy Roy explained, so he had offered himself as a crew member. His mother loaned him the air-fare to Argentina and he signed on as an assistant cook. For weeks and weeks the boat made him sick, and his injured back gave him constant pain. He saw penguins and elephant seals and jagged mountains of green ice. He thought about his place in the universe, the stray speck of time that was his allotment in life. He calculated how many hours of it had been passed nearly comatose in the dark basement of his mother's house. When he returned, just two weeks ago, he came with the understanding that he had been given three great gifts: his mother, Annali, and Patsy.

He rolled the label off the bottle of beer he'd drunk while he talked. Pru watched the bar's neon blue light play in the rings he wore on every finger. "The whole time I was on that boat, I kept thinking about being in the hospital with her. Watching her give birth. How her body knew what to do, even after all those hours in labor—I mean, it was amazing. And I started to think about how God was right there, in Patsy's body. If God isn't there, then where?" He looked up at her with his liquid, satiny eyes. "You know what I mean?"

Pru remembered Jimmy Roy the night after Patsy gave birth. Pru had flown in for the birth, and had been standing next to

Jimmy Roy when the baby came out. There weren't any complications, and Patsy had even gotten up and walked around. All day, she nursed the baby, made phone calls, and in general enjoyed herself. Then, for reasons nobody could figure out, she'd started bleeding, a full twelve hours after Annali was born. Jimmy Roy was helping her to the bathroom when the first blood clot slid right out of her. They all stared at it as it trembled on the floor like a jellyfish. Then Patsy moaned, and went as white as a sheet. Pru ran out into the hall and called for a nurse, who followed her in, took one look at the clot quivering on the floor, and ran to call another nurse.

Jimmy Roy didn't leave her side all night. They had to put in another IV and change the thick pads under her almost constantly. Each time a clot passed, Patsy turned deathly white and shuddered to the tips of her fingers. They ran a line into her arm and gave her Pitocin, to control the postnatal hemorrhage. She missed one nursing, then another. Finally, the medication contracted her uterus and slowed the bleeding, and color slowly returned to her face. Pru and Jimmy Roy both fell asleep in chairs on either side of the bed.

"Pru," Patsy whispered the following morning, as soon as Pru had opened her eyes. "Was that as bad as I thought it was?"

Pru went over and took her hand. "Oh, I don't know," she said lightly. Patsy's eyes were already closing again. "Not compared to, say, the prom scene from *Carrie*." And Patsy had smiled as she drifted back off to sleep.

Jimmy Roy stayed in her room at the hospital for days. He fed the baby with an eyedropper so that Patsy could sleep. He wouldn't let the nurses give the baby any more bottles, knowing that Patsy would be crushed if she couldn't get the baby to nurse.

Now Jimmy Roy said, "You know what else I realized? The

day that Annali was born was the happiest day of my life. And not just because it was the day she came into the world. But because it was profound. *Profound,* Pru. Everything after that was just anticlimactic. Even Antarctica. I want to live a profound life, you know? That was the day that I found my purpose."

Pru nodded. "Being Annali's father."

"Yes. Absolutely. And a nurse-midwife," he added.

"Oh," she said, practically yelping. She breathed deeply, hoping he couldn't see how desperately she wanted to laugh. He was, she could see, completely serious. "Wow. Ah. Okay. Gee, a midwife."

"I want to deliver babies," he said. "I want my hands to be the first thing they touch in this world. *My hands.* Can you imagine anything more profound than that?"

Jimmy Roy's hands were nice enough hands—she'd been admiring them as he played with the label on his beer—but they did hang on the ends of heavily tattooed arms. She had a little trouble seeing them, say, at Fiona's knees.

She decided to focus on the process. "So, how does one become a midwife?"

"*Nurse*-midwife. I'll have to go to nursing school. I've already started the application process." He took a drink of his soda. "I thought I'd check out University of Maryland and Johns Hopkins while I'm here," he added. "Just in case Patsy stays in this area."

"Oh," Pru said again. "Hm."

"I know what that means," Jimmy Roy said. "That means, don't get your hopes up."

"Listen, you have a right to be in Annali's life. But Patsy's in a terrible place right now. It's not the right time to spring this on her. Just wait awhile before you say anything. That's my totally unsolicited advice."

He looked sad, but nodded. "I know I have a lot of amending

to do," he said. In her mind, Pru crossed out "amending" and wrote in "making up."

"I'm glad you're here," she said as they hugged good night. She really meant it. "I'm really glad, Jimmy Roy."

WHEN SHE OPENED THE DOOR TO HER APARTMENT, Patsy's head popped up from the other side of the couch, where she was, as usual, watching TV. Pru saw the opening credits for *Beverly Hills 90210.*

"He's not here, is he?" Patsy said.

"Jimmy Roy? No." She stooped to pick up Big Whoop, who stood to put his front paws on her shoulders. It was a new trick they'd been working on.

"Lord," Patsy yawned dramatically. "What did I ever see in him? Be careful who you have a baby with, Pru. You're stuck with them for life."

"I like Jimmy Roy." She puckered her lips and Whoop touched his nose to them. She smiled, thinking of McKay seeing her do that.

"How did such a perfect kid come from that guy?" Patsy shook her head. "I'll never know."

"She must have gotten your genes," Pru said dryly. She stood up with Whoop now cradled in her arms. "I'm going to bed. Are you staying up much later?"

"I have to see if Dylan picks Kelly or Brenda, don't I?" Patsy said, stretching out on the couch.

Pru crawled, utterly exhausted, into bed. On one side of her, Annali turned and threw a leg over her, and Whoop settled himself on the other. Then Jenny nosed open the door and scrambled up on the bed, curling herself at Pru's feet.

Thank God she'd gotten the queen-size bed. It wasn't exactly the activity she'd imagined for it, she thought ruefully, shifting her leg to reclaim an extra half-inch of space. But she liked having all the breathing things around her.

She thought again of Jimmy Roy as a nurse-midwife. She smiled in the dark. Maybe that was exactly what Patsy needed right now: a steady pair of hands to ease her passage back into the world. She knew she was watching the worst suffering her sister had ever known. But it was also true that Annali had saved Patsy. If it hadn't been for her, Pru was certain, Patsy would have shut herself up in that beach house, and never come out again.

THE NEXT DAY WAS THANKSGIVING. AS EVERYBODY GATH-ered around the large table John had put in the middle of the Korner, Annali counted out loud the number of chairs. Jimmy Roy, delighted, said, "Peachy, you can count to six? I didn't know that."

"She can count to *twelve,*" Patsy said. "Where the fuck have you been?"

Nobody said anything. They all froze, rather ridiculously, thought Pru, in various stages of seating themselves.

"I was wondering when we would get to that," said Jimmy Roy. He was wearing a belt with silver studs all the way around it, his hair pulled in a topknot that made him look like a samurai.

"It's a fair question," said Patsy, buckling Annali into her booster seat.

Pru's mother was the first to recover, and as she eased herself into her chair, she turned to John and asked, "Have you lived in D.C. long?"

"Seven years," John said.

Where the fuck have you *been?* Pru wanted to add. She was in oddly high spirits. The past two weeks had been depressing, despite her efforts to keep everybody cheerful. Sometimes she felt like shoving Patsy and Annali out the door and curling up under the covers. But having her mother and Jimmy Roy there had buoyed her. Even if Nadine seemed content to watch the proceedings with a detached air, as though she were thinking of happier times. Or perhaps she knew something Pru didn't. Perhaps she had seen enough to know that all you had to do was sit back and wait for everyone to come to their senses. Pru hoped very much this was the case.

"I'm here now, aren't I?" Jimmy Roy said, to Patsy. Pru's heart sank. *Dumb move,* she thought, as Patsy rolled her head dramatically.

"Oh, you're *here,*" Patsy cried, mockingly. "Okay, it's *your* turn! Here's the kid. I'll see you in a couple of years!"

"And where did you grow up, John?" Nadine turned her smooth face in his direction.

"New England. Maine, actually."

"Is your family there?"

"I have two sisters, both in New Jersey. My parents died years ago."

"Mommy," said Annali, nervously, "where are you going?"

"I don't know, honey. Maybe the North fucking Pole?"

Nadine issued a soft "*Patsy.*" As if in response, Annali's mouth turned down and she began to cry.

Patsy threw down her fork. "Annali, hush. Jesus, I can't even be *ironic* anymore."

"I don't want you to be ionic!" Annali sobbed.

Jimmy Roy pushed his chair away from the table. "Thanks for

dinner," he said, addressing John. "But this isn't good. I think I should just go."

At his words, Annali let out a howl. She began kicking and yelling. "No!" she cried. "No!" Instinctively, Jimmy Roy turned and reached for her.

"Don't you touch her!" Patsy cried. Her voice was steely, but underneath there were unmistakable notes of panic and fear. Instantly, Annali stopped crying.

Patsy was holding Jimmy Roy with her gaze; Jimmy Roy had his hands under Annali's armpits. He was only going to comfort Annali, but the panic in Patsy's voice had startled everybody. Suddenly Pru realized what Patsy was afraid of, what they were *all* afraid of: There was very little to stop Jimmy Roy from picking up Annali and running out of the café with her. And like *that*, they'd be in a whole new world, a world where "state lines" and "court order" and "kidnapping" and "suspect" were part of the everyday language. Of course, Patsy could do the same. Pru saw, in that moment, what a narrow channel they had to navigate. Rocky shoals stood on either side. It would be nothing, her absolute gut instinct told her, for Patsy or Jimmy Roy to try to turn Annali against the other. Annali was the little wishbone in their Thanksgiving turkey, how easily she could snap; and how much provocation would it take to reach out and start pulling? In Annali, Patsy and Jimmy Roy had the perfect tool with which to torment each other for the rest of their lives.

Pru closed her eyes. Her bright mood vanished. How had this happened? One step further, she thought, and we'll be throwing chairs at one another on a cable television show.

Even Annali understood that something very serious was up. She gave a loud hiccup.

Pru opened her eyes to see Jimmy Roy sitting back down. It felt like he was lowering a gun he'd been pointing at their heads.

"You're the boss," he said easily. "Don't be scared, sweet girl."

"It's over, everybody," Patsy said, reaching for the platter of turkey. "Let's go back to feeling awkward for other reasons."

Pru looked up and saw John watching her. They exchanged weak, uneasy smiles.

Nadine touched John's arm. "That looks like a lovely wine. Let's have some. Let's all drink a toast to Daddy."

Suddenly, Pru was overcome with a longing for her father. Leonard, sitting coolly at the kitchen table with his long legs crossed, his fingers steepled, while she and Patsy tore the house apart, looking for some lost piece of jewelry or library book. Steering the car with one knee in heavy summer beach traffic while doing a crossword puzzle that he'd rested on the wheel. Waving his metal detector along the sand, patiently digging until he came up with a quarter. None of this would be happening if Leonard were still here. The last, unshakable stake in the family tent, or so it seemed to Pru.

"To Leonard," Nadine said.

They drank. Then John said, "Women do get weary, wearing the same shabby dress."

Nadine brightened. "So, when she's weary—"

"Try another shabby dress," finished Pru.

They were smiling now. Except for Patsy, who muttered, "Idiots."

AFTER DINNER, PRU CLEARED THE TABLE AND WATCHED Patsy and Jimmy Roy out of the corner of her eye. The rest of the meal had passed in relative peace, with the two of them hardly speaking to each other and Nadine, John, and Pru assuming the conversational responsibilities.

Now, as Pru watched, Jimmy Roy walked up to her sister, who was standing at the counter. He had his hands behind his back. Hearing him come up, she turned, irritated. It was clear that he was waiting for her to choose a hand. At first she didn't want to, but finally she gave in and pointed to his right side. Pru could see that whatever he was holding behind his back had been in his left hand, but he passed it smoothly to the right, so that Patsy didn't notice. He brought the hand forward and opened it, palm up. Pru could see that he held a peach. Patsy's face softened, and she gave him a sort of begrudging half-smile.

Peach, their nickname for Annali. When Patsy was in labor, she wasn't supposed to eat anything, but Jimmy Roy snuck her a bite of peach, just after she'd gotten the epidural. Pru was collapsed in a chair at the time, exhausted from watching Patsy screaming for the drugs, which she'd refused earlier, and swearing to herself that if she ever had a baby, she'd begin asking for the drugs in about the eighth month. They finally administered the epidural, and as it kicked in, Patsy took the first bite of the peach that she wasn't supposed to have but Jimmy Roy gave her anyway. Another huge contraction came crawling up on the monitor's screen, but Patsy seemed unaware of it. She closed her eyes and grinned, fear and tension sliding from her face. Jimmy Roy kissed her forehead, already slick with sweat. As the needle on the monitor continued to chart another one of those killer contractions, Patsy sighed contentedly and said, around the fruit in her mouth, juice dripping down her chin, "Oh my God, that *peach*."

Pru brought a stack of dishes into the kitchen, where John was washing up. "Pretty exciting stuff, huh?" she said.

"I've seen much worse," he said. "You should see my sister Emily's husband's family. It's like some kind of bad social experiment. Like they've been forced to live in one of those environmental bubbles together and can't get out. Made me and Lila look pretty good, by comparison."

Pru smiled. "Were you very sad today?"

"Well, I sure thought about how it was probably a good thing we never had kids. Me and Lila," he added, hastily.

"And Patsy thinks it's a good thing they never got married," Pru said. "But it hasn't made this any easier, has it?"

"I like your family," he said. "They explain a lot about you."

"Like what about me?" she said, trying not to seem as eager as she felt to hear what exactly about her he'd noticed.

He shrugged, scraping turkey bones into the trash. "I knew your sense of humor came from your dad. But now I see where your sweetness comes from—your mother. And you're the one they count on to keep her head." He slid a stack of dishes into the soapy water in the sink.

"I'm not *that* sweet."

"Yes, you are. I bet you were the kind of kid who went around saving baby birds."

"Not sweet." She tapped her head. "Stupid."

"That's right. You're a softie. I've got your number, Whistler. You rock."

He was so sincere that Pru was embarrassed.

"I do," she said. "I rock and roll."

ON NADINE AND JIMMY ROY'S LAST DAY IN D.C., PRU looked out the bay window to see Patsy, Annali, and Jimmy Roy walking together down Columbia Road.

They looked like members of the same combat unit, with the matching flyer caps Nadine had knitted for them over the weekend, chin straps flapping on either side. Annali swung between her parents, who at least seemed to be carrying on some kind of conversation.

"I can't tell if it's good or bad," Pru said, when her mother came to the window to look, too.

"It doesn't matter, as long as they're talking," her mother said. "I have hopes for them," she added. "Jimmy Roy has changed. He's grown. He was determined to come here, even if it was to find her with someone else. I told him, point blank, 'There's someone new, Jimmy Roy. And he's really got her. You don't have much of a chance.' But he came anyway."

"Well, for Annali."

Her mother shook her head. "Not just for Annali. Jimmy Roy has qualities, indeed he does. I think Patsy's sold him a little short."

"What happened between them, anyway? After Annali was born? The next thing I knew, we couldn't even mention his name around her."

"I'm not sure. I think Jimmy Roy disappointed her by going along with everything she wanted. He didn't fight hard enough for her. She's like me in that way. Unless you make a big show of it, she doesn't believe it. That's why she got lured in by that Jacob. All flash, that one."

Nadine had been apprised of the Jacob situation just that morning, by Patsy. Pru remembered how it wasn't so long ago that her mother, too, had been taken by "that" Jacob, but she didn't say anything.

"Call it what you will," Nadine said, turning from the window. "It was no accident that Jimmy Roy showed up right when he did." She sighed and sat down with her knitting. "Your father would have liked that. Oh, it's so sad he never got to know Annali. He would have been so smitten with her." She shook her head, sadly.

"I miss Daddy," Pru said.

"Of course you do," she returned. "He was your father."

Fifteen

Nadine cried at airports. Usually she began on the ride over. It was wordless crying, almost soundless, something that happened incidentally, like breathing. Pru would look over and there would be two rivulets working down each side of her nose.

Nadine held Annali and talked to her quietly. "You'll see Grandma soon," she said, holding Annali's face in her soft hands. Pru saw how tall and erect her mother still stood, her broad face split by a smile, as she turned to wave from beyond the security gate. But when Pru glanced again, Nadine was bent low over her suitcase, with a hand to her chest, as if she couldn't catch her breath. It scared Pru, and she almost reached for Patsy's hand; but then Jimmy Roy lifted the heavy bag from Nadine's shoulder and transferred it to his own. Nadine straightened up then, wiped her face, and they moved on, down the concourse.

. . .

DESPITE THE FACT THAT IT STILL HOUSED TWO WOMEN, a child, and two animals, the apartment seemed quiet and empty without Nadine and Jimmy Roy. Pru realized that it was the absence of her mother's sounds, with which she was intimately familiar. She knew the exact rhythm of her mother's footsteps, how her heels brushed the floor slightly as she walked. She knew the intonation and duration of her inhale, that very slight whistle as breath moved through her nose and past her vocal chords. If she couldn't see Nadine, she could always find her just by listening for her to clear her throat. She wondered if she would ever be on such familiar terms with any human again.

Patsy went back to her moping, but it didn't seem to display the same vigor she brought to it before. For one thing, Pru made a new rule forbidding the TV to be turned on while she was trying to work, and Patsy got bored pretty quickly without it. For another, Annali had started preschool.

One of Nadine's big accomplishments of the week had been to get Annali enrolled in a school up the street, where Fiona sent her little boy, Sean. It meant that, at least twice a day, Patsy had to leave the apartment to escort her daughter to school.

This foray into the preschool world brought with it new demands of play dates and school-related activities. Fiona and Sean welcomed Patsy and Annali into their circle of mom-preschooler couples. It also seemed to cement Patsy and Annali's stay in the neighborhood. Pru wasn't sure how she felt about that, but she didn't say anything. Patsy never spoke of returning to Rehoboth, and the truth was, Pru liked having them around, even though, more and more often, Pru found herself alone in the apartment.

One day in early December, it began snowing. Pru looked up from her computer to see white flakes swirling against a gray sky. It took her a minute to figure out what they were. When Patsy and Annali came home that afternoon, they reported that the schools were closing early.

Storms always took D.C. by surprise. Back in Ohio, the traffic kept moving in the worst snow. But here in the mid-Atlantic states, at the first sign of snowfall people pulled their cars off to the sides of roads and left them there. By nightfall, Columbia Road was filled up and down on either side with abandoned cars, even in the no-parking zones.

Patsy turned on the local news channel and they watched the storm come in on the radar. There were warnings not to leave the house unless it was absolutely necessary. News footage showed people buying out all the available milk and batteries from a grocery store, where the shelves were already almost bare. Pru went out to scrounge what food was left at the Safeway, where she waited in the checkout line for forty-five minutes. She stopped at the video store on the way home, and Phan helped her choose what seemed like enough movies to entertain Annali for weeks. As the snow swirled around outside, they baked cookies and watched TV. Annali sat in the bay window, watching the snow as if it were the first time she'd ever seen it.

It snowed while they slept, and all the next day. They stayed indoors and kept watching the snow from the bay window. By the following morning, the snowfall had finally wound down to a gentle flurry. They were dying to get out, so they bundled up and trudged outside. Where two days ago there were dirty streets, now white, brilliant snow sparkled. There were huge drifts and giant hills where the snow had buried the abandoned cars. Columbia

Road looked like a long white cake edged with gloppy white marshmallows.

Regular life was suspended. There was a festive, magical air. Nothing moved. All the shops and restaurants were closed. There were no buses rattling by, no airplanes overhead. The massive, noise-absorbing snowbanks had turned the city into a giant sound studio. Pru had never heard it so quiet. They could hear people talking a block away. Were it not for the presence of Patsy, frowning at everything from behind her huge black sunglasses, a glamorous wreck, they could be in a Hans Christian Andersen tale, Pru thought.

John was out in front of the Korner, shoveling a path in the sidewalk. He looked up and smiled and her heart lurched. They talked about the snow, and he told Annali about his new hot-chocolate machine. Then Pru, Annali, and Patsy moved on and he returned to his shoveling, apparently determined the neighborhood should have one place that was open, despite the conditions.

They hunkered down to wait for the city's snowplows to make it to Adams-Morgan. Everyone said that it would take days for the city to dig itself out. The District's few plows were old and known to break down frequently. Capitol Hill and the financial district would be first, of course, before the residential neighborhoods, which would be plowed in order of income. Adams-Morgan would be farther down on the list, well after Chevy Chase, Cleveland Park, and Dupont Circle. Pru was glad for the food she'd purchased at the beginning of the storm. If she hadn't stocked up on bananas, oatmeal, and pickles, Annali never would have survived.

Pru was figuring out, little by little, how to handle her. She was getting better at anticipating where Annali was headed. On one occasion, when she saw that the child was on the verge of throwing a huge tantrum, Pru suddenly fell to the floor. She rolled around on the floor, gagging. Finally, with a final shudder, she groaned and lay still, dead. Annali stopped the tantrum and cracked up. "Aunt Pruuuu!" she cried, jumping on top of her. Pru felt quite proud of herself. It seemed like an enormous victory—she had figured out something essential about living with a child. For some reason, she thought of Dr. Bond, the vet. She felt he might approve of how she was doing, these days.

Three times each day, Pru made everyone get dressed and go outside with the puppy. She felt like the commander of the *Intrepid,* making the troops play football while waiting for the great ice to melt. Every day they saw John, working to keep the diner open. His staff and suppliers couldn't get through, but he did his best, and some of the customers even pitched in and helped. It was always packed. People read books and drank coffee, and played Parcheesi and Chinese checkers. No one seemed to be in any rush to go back to work. John walked around beaming, thrilled at the café's being, for a change, full up almost every minute of the day.

"This is just what I'd envisioned," he told Pru, happily, as he swept by with a tray loaded with cups. "Like the old corner store, or something."

"He's just the kind of guy you'd fall for," Patsy said one day. They had just left the diner and were walking home. "So utterly *decent,* so *regular.* So *boring.*" There was a note of such bitter contempt in her voice that Pru stopped in her tracks, stung.

Patsy kept walking, then stopped. She circled back to where Pru stood. "I'm such a bitch," she said. Pru could see, under the sunglasses, that she'd started crying. "I'm sorry. I'm sorry. I'm really sorry." Her voice was high, and tight in her chest.

"It's okay," Pru said.

"He's a nice guy, Pru. I just said it because I wanted to hurt somebody. That's all." She swallowed. She still looked as small as a bird, to Pru, in her mottled fake-fur jacket, her nesty hair. Her nose was red and running. "I really like John," she said. "I want things to work out for you, I really do."

Pru nodded. "Okay."

"You do like him, though, don't you?"

"Let's not talk about it now."

Patsy nodded. "Okay," she said, and they moved on.

BY THE NEXT MORNING, FIVE DAYS AFTER THE STORM had hit, Annali's patience was wearing thin. She missed her school, her routine, her new friends. She'd watched enough Disney princess videos "to choke a horse," as Patsy put it. Pru still hadn't shook off the bad mood that had settled on her since Patsy's crack about John. Patsy was making an effort to be happier, but she was working with limited resources. By dinnertime, Pru had lifted the ban on eating in front of the TV, and they were dining on canned soup and watching *Mulan*—the least sexist or saccharine entry in what Pru referred to as the Disney Princess oeuvre.

In this oeuvre, all the princesses have fabulous hair and little animal friends to help them. They sing and dance and are brave and kind. They teach others how to care. They are rewarded for their suffering with men—brave, kind, stand-up guys, all of them. Captain John Smith stares at Pocahontas as she appears before him, like a big-eyed doe, through the mist. Her face is caressed by the velvet curtains of her hair. All the princesses have a sort of pouty collagen-lipped look, and heinous personalities.

Snow White is stupid and so sweet you want to strangle her. Pocahontas has a great body, and she is silent and mysterious, the perfect woman. Ariel is supposed to be sixteen but she has huge breasts, and Belle is supposed to be a more acceptable heroine to modern moms because she reads books, though in the end she watches the action as helplessly as that twit White. Only Mulan knows how to fight, and her boyfriend is the hottest, in Pru's opinion. He goes shirtless through most of the film. He's brave and daring, and his body looks to be carved of stone.

An hour into the movie, Pru couldn't take it anymore. She put on her long, warm camel-hair coat and went out into the night.

The streets were busy. No doubt she wasn't the only one bored and restless and entirely sick of the other co-captives at home. Columbia Road still hadn't been plowed. There were even people out cross-country skiing. She walked along quickly in the cold air. She couldn't believe it, but Mulan's boyfriend had done something to her. She was—could it be true?—actually *aroused*. She hadn't felt this way in a long, long time. She began walking faster.

She passed under the Cluck-U Chicken sign, dark for the time being, its arrogant fowl hidden under snow. Without the lurid glare of its neon lights, the street looked serene, classic, even charming. Although it was late in the evening, she could see light coming from the Korner's big plate-glass window. She peeked inside. She meant to take only a quick look and continue walking by, but she saw that John was there, looking right out the window at her. He had closed up for the night, and sat alone, with his feet up on a chair. She was about to pull back from the window, when something—perhaps her sudden, furtive movements—drew his attention. He smiled at her and jumped out of his chair. When he opened the door for her, the most beautiful music poured out into the cold night air. Pru recognized it as a Duke Ellington suite—languid, lush, sensual. The music and the way he pulled her indoors and wrapped his arms around her left her discombobulated.

"I was looking for you," he said into her hair. "And look, here you are."

"Oh?" she said. She still hadn't recovered.

She closed her eyes. She felt the knot of worry that had been lodged at the base of her neck loosening. She felt their legs pressing together, his hands slipping inside her coat, the camel-hair with the robin's-egg-blue silk lining. Ellington swirled around them, making her knees buckle. She felt as though she'd just walked in the door to a Moroccan brothel.

"You smell clean and neat," John said, brushing his nose against her temple.

She smiled into his shirt. "A person can't smell neat," she said.

"Well, you can. Neat as a pin."

His shirt was soft, and he had another shirt, a thermal one, on underneath it. For some reason, Pru was touched that he thought to layer two shirts together. He smelled like a wood fire, and of soap.

He kissed her then. It was their first kiss, and it might as well have been her first kiss ever. No: She was glad it was not her first kiss ever. Because if she hadn't been kissed before, she might have thought that this was how it always felt.

"John." They were moving to the area with the couches, near the back.

"What?"

"Are you seeing that girl? Gaia?"

"Gaia?" he said, as if it were a name from a distant past. "Not really."

"Not really, or no?"

"No."

"*Were* you seeing her?"

"Yes," he said, as if pleased to be able to answer something in the affirmative.

It knocked the wind out of her sails for a minute. She wanted him to have been pining for her. Why hadn't he been pining? An ex-wife, first, to contend with, and then another lover? It was too much. She sat up and put on her glasses, which she'd removed when he'd started kissing her.

"Listen," he said, raising himself up on one elbow. "You don't just decide one day you're going to run a marathon, right? You have to do some training first."

"Aren't you being a little glib about this?"

He sighed. "I am. I'm sorry. I'm embarrassed, I guess. I don't want you to feel bad."

His hands slid around her, inside her sweater, touching her naked back.

Everything in her wanted to melt. Oh, just let it go, she told herself. "Am I the marathon?"

He smiled and nodded. "The New York Marathon."

"The Boston is harder," she muttered.

"Okay, you're the Boston, then."

"And what was she? Just a little warm-up?"

"She was like a 5K," he said, so near her ear that she got goose bumps. "Well . . . maybe a 10K."

He was nuzzling her ear, and shivers went up and down her arms. She could hear the end of "Thunder Road" in her head, the wordless part, the part with bells and exploding riffs. She wanted to laugh—it was the same make-out song she always heard inside her head. But the something pissy inside continued to gnaw at her. She wished she could be the kind of girl who could just let something go. It bothered her, the idea that he had slept with someone else so recently, while wanting to sleep with her. That wasn't how she'd imagined this going. When was the last time? How had it ended? What did it all mean?

Then she realized something, as they found each other again: All she had to do, to be the kind of girl who lets something like that go, was to let it go. *Let it go, let it go, let it go, let it go.* Maybe she'd have to let it go a thousand times. But she'd just do it, over and over. As often as she needed to.

So she did. She just let go. She all but shoved it away from her, with both hands.

Sixteen

She had forgotten what it was like to be so into another person, under a warm coat and entwined together on a junky couch, that nothing else outside of you could possibly exist.

You forget you have to get up and go home. You forget that people are waiting for you, wondering where you are. You forget that, at any moment and for no apparent reason, the cops could bust down the door and drag you, naked, through the streets. Well, that might be a stretch, she thought, watching John sleep. But they *could*. There was misery lurking just outside the camel-hair coat that covered them, in its many unhappy forms.

She managed to slip out of the café before the first customers came, before even the sun was up. She'd never really fallen into deep sleep, as two people who are in the process of discovering each other on a ratty old coffee house couch never really can. Rather, one minute she was drifting off, and the next she was walking down Columbia Road, practically buttoning up as she hurried home. John had kissed her and said they would talk later. Suddenly, two big lights, then four, came around the corner at Connecticut and down Columbia, shining right in her face. They were accompanied by a mechanical roar that seemed deafening, in the silent morning. The plows. They had finally made it to Adams-Morgan, and their headlights came creeping toward her like a slow-moving search party.

SHE WOKE UP FROM THE FEW HOURS' SLEEP SHE'D GOT-ten to feelings of bliss, followed closely by feelings of remorse. She *really* had let herself go. She wanted to laugh, and she wanted to cry. She stayed in her bedroom as long as she could, until hunger forced her to emerge, around noon, to find something to eat. Patsy watched her, suspiciously, but didn't ask any questions. Pru wondered if it had even registered that she'd spent the night out of the apartment, somewhere, with a someone.

John called that afternoon, just to tell her that he was thinking about her. His voice was warm and close, immediately erasing Pru's feelings of remorse. Patsy had Fiona's little boy, Sean, over for a play date, so Fiona and Noah could get ready for their annual holiday party. At the moment, Annali and Sean were engaged in a particularly rambunctious game of wrestling on the furniture, so Pru moved into the bedroom and shut the door.

"What are you doing tonight?" he said.

"Fiona and Noah's Christmas party. They decided to go ahead and have it, now that the streets are getting cleared. It'll be a bunch of NPR people, and moms. My plan is to wander around feeling awkward and ill-informed."

"Lucky NPR people, and moms," he said. "I miss you."

"I miss you, too," she said. Her toes curled.

"Can we see each other later?"

A thrill went through her. *Plans for later.* She loved plans for later. "I might could do," she said.

"Good. Call me when you get home. Don't meet anybody at the party."

THAT EVENING SHE WORE THE BROWN FLORAL MARC Jacobs dress, with her knee-high lug-soled Frankenstein boots, and trudged through snow to the town house where Fiona and Noah lived. She'd met Fiona when they were both new to D.C. It seemed it was about two minutes later that Fiona had married Noah, quit her job, and started having babies.

She found Fiona in the kitchen, mixing up sangria. She wore a simple aqua halter top and jeans and she looked fabulous. Fiona had that touch—she could slap a picture she'd torn from a magazine on the living-room wall, and it looked like something from *Metropolitan Home.* Pru stood with her for a while, listening to the stay-at-home-mom lingo. It was like being in a foreign country.

"Seven hundred dollars for a Bugaboo!" Fiona was exclaiming. "It better freakin' nurse the kid at the same time."

"I love my Emmalunga."

"I have an Inglesina."

"I just use the Björn. That's how I dropped all the baby weight."

These were not, Pru realized, the names of Australian tennis stars of the 1970s, but baby transport devices. Nobody mentioned a Peg Perego. Evidently it was no longer the Rolls-Royce of strollers.

Ferberizing, they said. "I am always, always, *always* Ferberizing that baby!" "Oh, Gahd, if I have to Ferberize Lucrezia one more time, I'll *kill* myself," cried a sweet-faced woman with frizzy hair.

"Where do you take them to have them Ferberized?" Pru said to the mom who wore a Nirvana T-shirt and a white belt and looked like she might have a sense of humor. "Is it a drive-through, like Speedy Muffler?"

"We didn't have to Ferberize Ezra. Ezra *never* cried!" exclaimed a statuesque brunette in an orange pashmina. *"Never!"*

"Jonah never *stops* crying," chimed in another, throwing out her bony chest. *"Never!"*

Boys' names clearly tended toward old Biblical names, among Fiona and Noah's highly educated set. Pru thought maybe she should invent a baby of her own. Baby Nebuchadnezzar. "We had to take Nebuchadnezzar down to the Ferberizing station, in his Emmalunga," she might say.

"Yasmina licked my breast today," said the woman in the Nirvana T-shirt. She had a flat, adenoidal voice. "She's four," she added. "And then Henry can't understand why I won't have sex with him."

That's the dad, right? Pru wanted to say. But she didn't. She could see why Patsy had never joined a group of moms. She remembered that, at the only community playgroup Patsy ever went to, the group leader asked if they had any requests, after "Itsy Bitsy Spider." When Patsy shouted out, "Free Bird!" only one other mom laughed.

Fiona gripped her arm and said, "Come upstairs with me."

Fiona pushed open the door to each of her kids' rooms and peeked in, to make sure they were asleep. At the landing at the top of the stairs, she stopped and sat down.

"I'm fucking pregnant again."

"Oh." Pru sat down next to her. "Great, right? Great?"

"Cecily is only one year old. I'm still *breastfeeding.* Three kids under the age of five? What the hell am I going to do?"

"You'll get help. Don't you have a babysitter already?"

"It's not just that. It's everything else." Fiona sighed and put her head in her hands.

"You know, I lose two years of my life with every baby. *Two years.* I feel like we were just getting to a normal life again. You know, we could actually go out to dinner without agonizing about a baby the whole time, or me running home to nurse. I was going to get certified to teach yoga. I was starting to paint again. Forget all that, now."

"You'll just do it, Fi. There's lots of time to teach yoga." Pru started to touch her back. Then she remembered that Fiona didn't like to be touched, especially while she was still nursing a baby. Which *was* pretty much all the time, in recent memory, Pru had to admit. She floated her hand to rest on the floor, as if that was what she'd meant to do all along.

"You'll just do it. You'll be fine. Two years isn't that long."

"I will be forty-one," Fiona said, mournfully.

"But you know," Pru said, bracingly. "A *baby.*"

"*Three* babies. You just can't imagine what that means. It would be nice if even one of them could, you know, tie their own friggin' shoes. Imagine, getting the two oldest ready for school while I'm still nursing the third . . ."

"Can't you not nurse this one?"

"Oh sure." Fiona rolled her eyes. "I'll just tell him when he grows up that I nursed the first two, and not him. Maybe I'll have the other two baptized and leave them trust funds, while I'm at it."

"Well," Pru said, delicately, "have you thought of, *you know . . .*"

There was one thing that hadn't changed in twenty years, she thought: *"You know,"* the universal euphemism for abortion.

Fiona closed her eyes and sighed. "I don't know if I could. It's not just mine to do with whatever I want anymore, you know? I mean, before, when I didn't have *any* children, that was one thing. But now, I don't know. It'd be weird. I already know the date this one is due, you know? I've already pictured telling the kids. But thanks for asking. These moms, you know"—she gestured downstairs, toward the kitchen—"I feel like if they knew I was even considering it, they'd have me forcibly sterilized."

"I know what," Pru said, brightening. "I'll be your nanny. It's not like I have anything better to do."

"Still no work?"

She lifted up her empty hands, shrugging. "I think soon I may qualify for Meals on Wheels."

She wanted to tell her about John, and last night, but it didn't seem like the right moment to spring fresh, hot new love on Fiona. They went back downstairs and Pru moseyed into the living room, the other conversational black hole. The talk among the NPR people was all snow-removal budgets, federal funding for the arts, and digital versus analog tape.

Noah was talking to one of the better-known on-air personalities, and clearly flirting with her. Fiona knew that he had a big crush on the personality. When Pru had asked her if this didn't bother her, Fiona had shrugged and said, without a smidgen of doubt, *No, it's cute.* Pru secretly coveted Fiona's relationship with Noah. It was a tacit understanding between them that she did. A husband like Noah would love his wife so much that it'd be okay for him to flirt with other women. Fiona, however, coveted the time Pru had for manicures and movies. At least, Pru hoped it was a tacit understanding. The problem with tacit understandings was that they might all be in your head.

Pru pictured herself and John here, in Fiona and Noah's fashionable row house. That was her in the kitchen, putting more lemon in the hummus and complaining about the cost of preschool. That was her husband, John, flirting with the NPR personality. Well, maybe not flirting but talking with her in his amiable, friendly way. It was their baby upstairs, in her crib. Her stomach lurched. What if she was pregnant? It seemed unlikely, but it was possible, of course. It was the first time she hadn't been flash-frozen with fear from the inside out, thinking of that possibility. Maybe the timing wasn't ideal, but they could handle it. Just like being stranded out at Shenandoah, they'd make the best of it. They'd learned that much about each other during that night in the woods. It was something they'd always have going for them—no matter what happened, they could count on each other to try to make the best of things. It wasn't such a small thing, either. With Rudy, she'd believed in her own abilities to make things work. With John, she trusted him, too. Trusted him absolutely.

The sole other person at the party who seemed to be unattached was an unpublished novelist named Elliott Barstow. She met him while he was anchored at the buffet table, mowing through Fiona's baba ghanoush. He was a stocky, hairy man, and Pru had never heard of him. She asked him what he wrote, and he said he was working on a series of detective novels based on "The Twelve Days of Christmas."

"You have to have a gimmick like that," he said, gesturing with a triangle of pita bread. "Stand out from the crowd. The letters of the alphabet, numbers, the cardinal virtues—already taken. But no one's done the Twelve Days yet."

He'd said it as though that was what everyone called it, the Twelve Days. She wanted to remember that, to tell McKay.

"Will you hold my drink?" Elliott said. "I've got carpal tunnel, so it's hard for me. From all the typing, you know."

He handed Pru his drink and she stood there, holding both his drink and her own.

"It's an automatic twelve-book deal, see?" Elliott continued. "It can't lose."

"Are you starting at a partridge in a pear tree? Or—what's number twelve?"

"Drummers drumming. Yes, from twelve to one, to mimic the song. Each holiday season, see, I come out with another. Oh, and I have the TV ad already worked out. Can't you just hear it? *Clink clunk.* That prison-door closing sound. *Clink clunk.* A quiet band camp in a sleepy upstate hamlet is ripped apart by a series of mysterious teen murders. *Clink clunk. Twelve Drummers Drumming.* The latest Sydney Pearson murder mystery, from crime writer Elliott Barstow."

He took his glass from her hand and drank. "Available this Christmas at fine bookstores everywhere," he added thoughtfully.

She spent half an hour listening to the plot outlines of Elliott's books. Although *Five Golden Rings,* about brutal murders in the porn industry, was certainly titillating, her personal favorite was *Ten Lords A-Leaping.* "Why are members of the British Parliament committing suicide by jumping off London Bridge? Detective Sydney Pearson investigates," Elliott recited, in a low voice.

"Clink clunk," Pru added.

She danced with Elliott when Noah put on some music, then called it a day and walked home by herself. She felt charmed by everything, Elliott and his funny ways, the moms, who'd gotten quite loud and drunk, the Christmas lights and the snow-peaked houses. Her apartment was dark and quiet when she let herself in. Whoop and Jenny both padded over quietly to greet her. She called John's cell and left him a message that she was home. She had to struggle to stay awake. She hadn't gotten any sleep the night before, and had had a little too much sangria at Fiona's. John must have been having a busy night, she thought. It was after midnight, and she still hadn't heard from him. Had she missed him? Was he expecting her to call earlier? She was just mulling over the options when the phone in her hand rang. She picked it up quickly.

"It's me," said John. "Can you talk?"

"Hold on," she said. Patsy was asleep on the couch, so she took the phone out to the hall.

"I've been thinking of you all day," he said. "I really want you to know how much last night meant to me. How great it was. You know, I forgot about everything. About the fact that, well, I can't just do anything I want to." He stopped talking. Pru sat down. She felt this could not be going in a good direction. The elevator doors opened and some people stepped out, their noses red from the cold. Pru pulled her feet back as they walked past.

"I just hung up with Lila," John said. "I have to tell you something."

"Okay," said Pru, trying to keep her voice neutral.

It seemed that Lila was unhappy. She claimed that she had made a terrible mistake leaving him. Being alone in the snowstorm forced her to do some thinking. She'd broken off her other relationship. She wanted John's forgiveness. She wanted to fix their marriage. She was willing to do whatever it took. She had left him only because she couldn't handle losing the baby. But now she realized she needed him. That they needed each other.

John's voice was sad, and quiet. Pru listened quietly. She didn't say anything.

"Hello?" he said, after a long pause.

"I'm here." She could hear the sounds of a TV on her floor. Someone was watching *Seinfeld*. She wondered if she could figure out which episode it was. She thought maybe the one with man hands. She tried to parse the voices on the laugh track, decide what each of the laughers would look like, if they were real people.

"Are you still there, Pru? Will you talk to me?" he said. It was heartbreaking, the way he said it.

"I'm still here." Her throat was dry and the words stuck in her throat. "Here," she said again. *Googly googly googly,* she thought, would be a tall man with adult acne.

"Will you say something?" he said again.

There was that familiar heaviness, like someone sitting on her head. It was so heavy that she forgot everything else. Suddenly, the cracks in the plaster on the wall fascinated her.

"This has nothing to do with me," she said. "I have to go. I have to get back inside."

"Pru," he said, then stopped.

"What?"

"I don't know. Can you just . . . can you slow down for a minute?"

"What do you want? Permission? Forgiveness? *Advice?*"

"Listen, I don't have it all figured out. All I know is, I had to talk to you. Tell you everything. Isn't that right?"

"John," she said, "we were together for one night. You don't owe me anything."

"What would you have me do?"

"That's just not relevant," she said.

"It is, to me."

"Then," she said, "I'd say, you have to try again with Lila. You'll never know, if you don't. And no matter who you love after that, you'll always wonder whether you did the right thing."

"And us?"

"There's no 'us.' There's a last night. That's all." She bit her lip, waiting for him to tell her she was wrong. That, of course, there was an us, and that he didn't want Lila or Gaia or anybody else. That he wanted her, only her. But he didn't. He didn't say anything.

"John, I have to go. Annali's awake," she lied. "The phone must have woken her up."

"All right," he said. He sounded tired. "Pru, I'm so sorry. You know I didn't mean to hurt you, right? Especially so soon after—"

"John, it's fine. I'm fine, really. I don't have any expectations of you. You're not my boyfriend, we just fooled around. That's all."

"Pru—"

"I've gotta go," she said. "I hope everything works out."

THE NEXT DAY SHE WENT TO EDIE'S AND TOLD HER SHE'D work for her during the holiday season. Then she went with McKay to see a house in Cleveland Park.

It was a huge old three-story on a good street, in beautiful condition. She wondered how McKay and Bill could afford it. They sat on the couch in the sun room, facing the blank television, for a while. Then the agent, a friend of McKay's, took them into the master bedroom suite. The suite's bathroom featured a huge, black whirlpool tub.

McKay and Pru climbed in the tub, to see if they could both fit. They sat facing each other, and the tub was so big their feet didn't even touch. The agent went off to take a phone call, and McKay called after him, "Bring us cocktails!"

"I think I did something stupid," Pru said, when they were alone.

"Uh-oh. Did we wander off the subject of you for a moment?" Then he saw her face and said, "Oh, sweetie. What happened?"

"I slept with John Owen," said Pru.

McKay blinked a few times. "Okay," he said. "So far that sounds like a good thing. A *great* thing."

"And I think I'm in love with him."

"Well, that *is* stupid, I must say. Sex with someone you love—*yuck*."

"And now his wife wants him back."

"Oh. And?"

"And I told him he should go back to her."

"You didn't."

"I practically sent him off with my blessing."

"Did you tell him you were in love with him?"

"No. But I'm sure he must know."

"Bad assumption," he said. "Why didn't you tell him?"

"Listen, if he's not sure he wants me, then I don't want him."

"Don't lie to me, Pru. I know you too well."

"I mean, I don't want him to do anything on account of me. He needs to figure out where he is with Lila. And if he wants to be with her, he should be with her. And if he doesn't, well, he needs to say so."

"You didn't give the guy a thing, did you? You just threw him back to the sharks, with no escape route?"

"I thought this notion of dating as a game was outmoded."

"You thought wrong, sweetheart. And it's not a game, it's a war. Winner take all."

"Thank you, Joan Collins."

"Anyway, I'm not saying play a game. I'm saying give the guy something to hold on to. He's floundering out there, and you throw him a stone. I mean, what if this guy is your destiny? Are you going to give up on your destiny so easily? On your whole future? On your *children's* future?"

"What if I'm not up to my own destiny?" she said. "What if I'm the wrong girl for my destiny?"

The real estate agent came back into the bathroom. "What do you think?" he said, brightly. Of course he was from McKay's vast network of gay professionals and friends. On the ride over to the house in his BMW, Pru saw a plastic Playskool phone, the kind with the smiley face on the dial. While they were driving, he'd snatched up the receiver and said, *Hold all calls, Joyce!* Gay men, she had noticed, were in fact an extraordinarily happy bunch. Maybe there was something in all that sleeping around and staying friends, spending their disposable income on toys and cars.

McKay scootched over in the bathtub. "Let's see if you can get in here, too," he said to the agent.

JUST BEFORE MCKAY DROPPED HER OFF AT HOME, HE said, "Listen, we're really getting married. In the spring, in Provincetown. Put it in your planner."

Pru looked at him in surprise. "Really? That's exciting."

"I don't know. I'm worried that this is all because we've gotten to be a boring old couple, and we need to do something for excitement. Do you think that's why?"

"I don't think Bill finds you boring," said Pru. "I think you guys are crazy about each other."

"Well, he's stuck with me," said McKay. "Anyway, we were hoping you'd be in the wedding."

"You know I will. Always the bridesmaid."

"I hope it was okay to tell you. I know it's a little weird."

"No, it's okay," Pru said. "I guess I better get used to it. Even my gay friends are getting married before I do. And it's not even legal in forty-nine states."

Seventeen

Nadine liked to say, among other things, "When a door closes, a window opens."

This had never seemed like a particularly good deal to Pru. What was a window, after all, compared to a door? A window was smaller and not always where you could reach it. It wasn't intended to get you out of the house, in case of a fire. In fact, it had probably been painted shut by the previous owners. She had to guess that her mother's point was: In a real pinch, it'll do.

Edie was happy to let Pru help out at the shop over the Christmas rush and then stay on after the holidays. Her father was ill and she was having a hard time taking care of him while working at the store. She taught Pru how to handle the merchandising, and how to use her financial software. Pru was glad to have even a little more money, so that she didn't have to draw on the inheritance she'd received when Leonard died. Christmas and Annali's birthday had pretty much wiped out her severance. She bought extravagant presents for everyone, hoping to fill up the big empty holes in their lives.

Working at the shop gave her a reason to get dressed and out of the house. Patsy had signed on with one of the temp agencies in town, and most days they had something for her. She would get calls to report to the downtown law offices, where she typed up documents and did filing. She learned not to let on that she could probably fix the copy machine, whenever it broke. The lawyers she worked with liked flirting with her. With her jumble of hair and her nose ring, and her utter lack of interest in the partners, she stood out like an exotic bird next to the grimly hardworking, black-suited women of the firm. A couple of the partners had even asked her out, but she always said no. Patsy found lawyers reprehensible.

Patsy left first in the morning, so she could take Annali to preschool before heading downtown for her current assignment. Pru had a nice hour or so alone to herself, to read the paper, walk the puppy, and drink coffee. Then she walked down Connecticut to Edie's, where she'd help the few customers who'd wander in, or work on organizing the stockroom or Edie's hopelessly tangled finances. Edie came in sometime in the early afternoon, after settling her father down for his nap. Pru was glad to have coworkers again. There was the little guy, Paco, who folded the clothes, and Edie, and the stylists at the hair salon across the street, and the Vietnamese women in the nail salon upstairs. "Good morning, sweetie," they said to each other, and "Pretty," touching each other's clothes, and, yawning, "*Lord,* I'm tired." It seemed to Pru that they spent a *lot* of time walking around, yawning, touching things, and saying, "*Lord,* I'm tired." They made excursions for coffee and lunches. Mai came down looking for an aspirin. Pru ran over to the hair salon when she needed change.

She even had her own regular customer. Her name was Lola, and she was about ninety years old. She told Pru that she used to be Eleanor Roosevelt's press secretary. Her ankles were swollen, but she liked to try on the highest pumps she could find. She was barely able to stand in them. Pru had to hold her arms and help her up from the chair. Lola would stand for a few seconds in front of the mirror, and then sigh deeply. "I used to have the most gorgeously turned ankle," she said. She had Pru bring her clothes that she could never wear in public, long, revealing columns of silk that exposed her leathery décolletage, her liver-spotted arms. She looked like a dried moth in a butterfly's wardrobe. She spent a long time looking at herself in the mirror, then asked Pru or Paco to get her a cab. Lola always gave them five dollars for performing this service, which they would accept, and use to buy chocolate from the gourmet chocolatier around the corner.

At four o'clock Pru would walk home, back up Connecticut Avenue. She stopped to pick up Annali from preschool, then they'd take the puppy to the playground, where sometimes they'd find Fiona and her kids. Fiona wasn't showing yet, but she looked pale, nauseous, and exhausted. They passed the time by pushing the kids on the swings and trying out baby names: Delia. Cornelius. Cady. Lionel. Then it was home to make dinner, listen to Patsy complain about the capitalist swine she worked for, and perform the extensive, rather exhausting ritual that was Annali's bedtime routine. If she was lucky, she could fit in a swim there somewhere. If she was really lucky, she didn't go through her whole day thinking constantly about John Owen.

ONE NIGHT WHEN SHE WAS HIDING IN THE BATHROOM, crying, she had a realization.

She hid in the bathroom to cry because she was still trying to keep it together in front of Patsy, who was just getting *herself* together. She'd always had the idea, as far back as she could remember, that she had to set an example for Patsy. She didn't want Patsy to hear her cry, because she didn't want her sister to start indulging her grief all over again, and because she didn't want to have to answer any questions. The walls of the apartment were paper-thin. In the bathroom she clenched and unclenched her hands, and when it seemed unbearable, as though she was going to burst from not crying, she watched the girl inside her cry. Pru made her double over, hands over her eyes, going hell for leather with the weeping. Always in a gray belted dress, her hair in a forties-style up-do, a handkerchief clutched in her hands. She looked like she was crying for a dead soldier. Pru would watch her cry, and afterward come out to Annali and Patsy, who never seemed to notice anything strange about these extended bathroom retreats.

She missed John. She missed talking to him and seeing him every day. He never called her again, after that last phone call, asking her what he should do. She tormented herself, wondering whether McKay had been right. Maybe she should have let him glimpse her heartbreak. Maybe she should have yelled at him, scolded him for what he'd done to her. Since she hadn't heard from him, she had to assume that he'd gotten back with Lila. But she couldn't bear knowing, right now. She avoided his corner of Adams-Morgan, orienting her daily life in the other direction, westward, toward Dupont Circle. She even began shopping at the other Safeway, the smaller one, and took her clothes to a different dry cleaner, one that didn't, unfortunately, take such good care with the buttons.

But one night, as she was staring into the bathtub, which had begun to crack around the drain, she had the realization that this was not what John would have chosen, if he could have chosen. If he *felt* he could have chosen. After all, what kind of life was he returning to? With Lila there had been abandonment. Sleeping with other people. The unhappiness that led to the separation in the first place. The yellow half-painted room. They still had to deal with all that. She'd been imagining them mostly in bed, or having breakfast together, smiling and happy. She imagined running into them at the movies, their arms comfortably around each other. But, in reality, maybe it wasn't like that.

By the end of January she was able to walk past the café on her way home from swimming. Normally she would cross to the other side, the "safe" side. As she hurried by, she was torn between peeking into the big window and keeping her head ducked low, so he wouldn't see her. She ended up keeping her eyes on the ground in front of her, but it was a start. When she got home, she went straight into the bathroom and sat on the lid of the toilet. She waited for the choking pressure in her chest to come and the tears to start, but nothing happened, so she went back out and started making dinner for Patsy and Annali.

The next time she passed the café, she forced herself to walk slowly, and then to glance inside. She returned to visiting Phan at the video store, and began using her favorite cleaners again. She risked seeing him. Them.

She was getting over it. She could feel it. Maybe she would never entirely be over him, but she thought she was beginning to see that a fairly normal future could be hers again.

She needed to see him, to make sure.

WHEN JOHN UNLOCKED THE DOORS EARLY ONE MORNING in late winter, she was standing there, waiting for him.

"Hi," she said. He was surprised to see her, and jumped a little.

But of course, it was still dark outside, so perhaps he'd mistaken her for a mugger.

Before he could say anything else, she said, "This is rehearsed, okay? Okay. So. Here goes." Her heart was beating fast and she had to take a deep breath. "I'm really sorry for the way I acted. I was a jerk. It was just . . . a little overwhelming, everything happening all in the same day, and I guess I kind of shut down." It was freezing out on the sidewalk, and her words came out in wisps of vapor from her mouth, like a steam engine. The Little Engine That Could! She tried to smile at him. "Can I come in?"

"Of course," he said, pushing open the door.

She sat at the counter and he poured her coffee, the same as always. "I've missed you," he said, putting the cup in front of her.

"I've missed you, too."

"Pru, I'm so sorry . . ."

She stopped him with a hand and a wince. "Apology accepted. But, really, it's over. I'm fine now. And I want us to be friends."

"Why can't I say I'm sorry?"

"I don't know why not, but I just can't stand to hear that. It has something to do with what remains of my pride."

"No," he said, shaking his head. He brought his bartender's stool over to sit across from her. He put his hands awkwardly on the counter in front of him, then in his lap. "You did nothing wrong. Nothing. It was me. I forgot myself. I forgot what I was doing—"

"I think it's right, what you're doing now. With your marriage. Not easy, but right."

"You do?"

"Absolutely."

"Thanks," he said, uncertainly. They were clumsy with each

other. This wasn't exactly how she'd rehearsed it. Maybe it would take some time, after all.

"So," she said briskly. "I had this idea we could go back to being friends."

He looked at her for a long time. Then he said, "Can we just do that?"

"Why not? It's what we were doing, you know . . . before. Gay men do it all the time," she added.

He looked at her, amused. "They do?"

"Oh, yeah. They just sleep with any old body, no hard feelings."

"That might be a little bit of a generalization, don't you think? Anyway, I didn't think of what happened between us as exactly 'sleeping with any old body.' Did you?"

She shook her head, lost for words.

Some customers came in and he went over to take their orders. She tried to breathe deeply. Just that one tiny shake of her head had cost her something, to admit that. She drank her coffee, glad that it was all over. She'd really gotten hurt, she knew that. But she'd ridden it out, had her cry, and it was over. All over, now.

"Friends, huh?" he said, coming over to refill her coffee.

"Friends."

"So, how do we do that?"

"Just like we used to. We tell each other things. We talk about what's happening in our lives."

"Like what?"

"Well, what's happening in *your* life? With . . . Lila?" She had to push his wife's name out of her mouth, like a seed or a pit. She tried pretending she was just one of his buddies, asking. Buddies! Pals! *Friends.*

He winced a little. "It's so weird talking about this with you. You sure you want to?"

She gave him a gesture that said: *Bring it on!*

"Okay. Well, we're in counseling. Obviously. We're living apart, for the time being. And we're supposed to have dates. Like, real dates. You know, with each other. And, of course, stay monogamous."

She wanted to give him another gesture that would say, *Take it away again!* But she forced herself to nod understandingly, and respond, "I can see that. Make it special again. Something you have to plan for, instead of something you do by rote."

"I'm supposed to call her up and ask her out. Can you imagine? After sleeping with her every night for seven years . . ." Suddenly, his voice broke off and he swatted the counter with his towel. He said, rather irritably, "I'm not *talking* about this with you, anymore."

He turned away and she let out a long exhale, as though he'd been holding her by the throat.

When he turned back toward her, he said, "Let's talk about you."

"I'm working at Edie's. I'm an official retail hack."

He put on his apron and began tying it, in the back. "But you love it," he said, smiling, "so who cares?"

SHE DID LOVE WORKING AT EDIE'S. IT WAS TRUE. SHE loved being around the clothes. She loved her twenty-five-percent discount. She loved listening to Edie talk about fashion. On the subject of fabric alone, Edie could talk for hours. Pru loved how she referred to everything in the singular. The pant. The shoe.

Edie referred to the construction of a piece of clothing as if it were a model airplane or a skyscraper. She showed Pru how you could judge the quality of a garment by the way it was finished. She taught her about drape and slubbing and warp. How some fabrics provided a crisp hand, some a smooth hand. Absorbency, temperature sensitivity, wrinkle recovery. Pru learned to feel a fabric's pile, judge its luster, listen to its rustle. She learned there were two types of rayon, viscose and cuprammonium, and the differences between those fabrics made from animal-hair fibers— camel, alpaca, llama, vicuña—and those made of cellulose or wood pulp. Twist, luster, open weave, tight weave, filling. The types of satin: slipper satin, crepe-back satin, faille satin, bridal satin, moleskin, and royal satin.

And the rules! How Pru loved rules! It wasn't so much that she liked following rules, but knowing what they were gave her a sense of order, and peace. She felt safer knowing that if she broke one, there would be repercussions.

Happily, fashion was full of rules. There were rules governing fabric and color combinations. Rules for fit and body type. Leg openings no smaller than the hip. Deep V's for short necks. Square toes on tall women, only. Then there were the mysterious, fluid rules of taste and style. Rules that broke the rules. It was a world she could figure out. Learn the rules, and you're good. Or you'll look good, anyway, and maybe that was half the battle.

She tried to give her customers a few minutes of browsing time before pouncing on them with the perfect dress. Or pant. She loved saying, This is a great pant for your body. They trusted her. They took what she offered, and emerged from the curtained dressing room shyly pleased. These were the same women who had clawed their way to the tops of their fields, and screamed abuse at their interns. But here at Edie's they were heavy thighs, wide hips, crooked ears. Every woman had some part of her that she couldn't forgive. *Forgive,* the clothes said to them. *Forget it, and move on, love.*

All in all, Pru felt, it didn't seem like a grown-up life—living with her sister, trying to get over John, and working retail. It was like being in college again, except with a little more money. Grown-up life didn't involve so much hanging around, being called "sweetie," talking about what kind of chocolate to try, and whether the nail polish color "Cherries in the Snow" was a truer red than "Redcoat Red." Grown-up life was the thing that would resume, once this phase of Pru's life was over. This was just the intermission. Circling the airport. The little voice in the back of her mind, when it wasn't taunting her about John Owen, liked to bark, *This is your life? This is why you've had a job since you were sixteen years old, and got a graduate degree in nineteenth-century British literature, which took you ten years to pay off? So you could become a lowly . . . shopgirl?!*

ONE DAY, EDIE WALKED INTO THE SHOP AND AN-nounced that they were going on a buying trip to New York. They would be given private tours of designers' new lines, and make purchases for the store. She wanted Pru with her. Pru agreed to go along, mostly to make sure they'd bring back more double-digit sizes. The twos and fours looked great on the mannequins, but she was still seeing too many average-sized women leave the store, empty-handed and discouraged, because Edie failed to stock twelves or fourteens.

Also, it was a chance to see her friend Kate, who could always be counted on for solace after a good heartbreak. Kate was frequently going through heartbreak herself, in one form or another. But when she called, later that night, Kate said, "Listen, I've been meaning to tell you. I'm seeing a doctor."

For years, Kate had been talking about her nonexistent throat cancer. Every cold, every cough, every catch in the throat was carefully scrutinized for possible malignant causes. It all started when she was twenty-nine, and realized she had been a smoker for more years of her life than she had *not*. At least it had gotten her to quit.

"Good," Pru said. "It's about time you sought medical attention."

"No, I mean, *dating* a doctor," Kate said. "I met him at the gym."

"Wow. Well, will he be able to administer your chemo?"

"I asked him to feel my throat!" she laughed.

"It seems so grown-up," Pru said. "A doctor."

"I know," she said. "He's a nice, stable, normal guy. Can you believe it?"

Pru felt a little twinge of jealousy. Kate was drawn, as if by a force beyond herself, to the unavailable ones. The married, the phobic, the plain lazy or narcissistic. Poets. Priests. That kind of guy. Pru was the one who was supposed to be dating some nice, stable, normal guy. That was the way it was always, always, always supposed to have been.

Eighteen

A few hours before she was supposed to leave for New York, she was still unpacked, and instant-messaging with Kate about where to meet that night, when Patsy burst through the front door, breathless.

The door's bursting open upset Whoop, and he jumped up, which triggered the puppy Jenny to jump up, too, and go sprinting after him. If they owned anything like a Ming vase, Pru thought, it would be crashing to the ground right about now. Except, of course, they didn't.

Patsy rolled Annali's stroller over Pru's foot, in her excitement. "Tell her, honey," she said to Annali.

"We found a new 'partment!" Annali announced. Her cheeks were flushed, as were Patsy's.

"I found us an apartment," Patsy said, nodding. She was flushed and out of breath.

"Three bedrooms, a deck, and a dining room. Oh my God, hardwoods, and you won't believe the price."

Us? thought Pru, pushing the stroller off her foot.

"You'll love it. I mean, we can't keep living here!"

Pru realized she hadn't given their situation as much thought as perhaps she ought. They were living together day to day, but she hadn't really considered making it permanent. But Patsy was so happy and excited that she didn't want to say anything that would ruin her mood.

"Even better, it's just around the corner," Patsy added, all in a rush. "Moving will be a snap!"

"Why does everyone say that?" said Pru, closing up her laptop and rolling up the cord. "You still have to pack up your stuff, put it on a truck, take it off a truck, and put it all away. The driving it a thousand miles across the country is the easy part."

"It's rent-controlled," Patsy said, turning the stroller around, "so it's not going to last. Noah tipped me off about it, at drop-off this morning. It's practically right next door to them! The kids can play together all the time! So, come on, stop sitting there looking reluctant and get your coat. You have to come see it now. *Right now.*"

"I have to go to New York," Pru said. "I can't go look at an apartment now. I haven't even packed."

"Throw your stuff in a bag. Grab a cab and have it wait for you. We'll go and sit on it, so no one else takes it."

Pru started to laugh. "It's not a parking space, Pats!"

"Please," said Patsy. "This place reeks of despair. We have to get out of here."

"It does not reek of despair," said Pru. "*We* reek of despair."

"Just come and see it. If you don't love it, then what have you lost? A few minutes of your time. Come on."

Twenty minutes later, she was standing outside the address Patsy had scribbled on a sticky note for her. It was indeed only a few blocks away from her apartment on Columbia Road, but it had a very different feel. Where her street was clearly "city," this was what she'd call "suburban-urban": strollers and tricycles on front porches on a tree-lined street. The building itself was a white four-story brick structure separated by a courtyard from another building, its mirror image. The linoleum floor in the foyer was dirty and ripped up around the edges. All the names on the mailbox cards were written in different inks, by different hands, and most of them had been scratched out so many times there was no room to write the current occupants' names. Pru looked at the dirty linoleum, the lack of a chandelier. Her first thought was, *No.* Absolutely not.

But when she stepped inside the apartment, she drew in a breath. There were big windows overlooking the courtyard and the building on the other side, just like in Jimmy Stewart's apartment in *Rear Window.* The view was crisscrossed by the fire escape, which gave it a soundly urban look. There were hardwood floors, high ceilings, crown molding. Two huge rooms upon entering—the living room giving way via pocket doors to a formal dining room.

The kitchen was small, as with all city kitchens, but it had an additional, walk-in pantry with built-in shelves. Patsy had followed her into the kitchen, and gestured to the dark, ornate handles on the kitchen cupboards, saying, "As you see, the kitchen is decorated in 'early conquistador.'"

Pru ventured farther down the long hallway: yes, three bedrooms, unbelievably, for only a hundred dollars a month more than she was paying now for her one. True, one of the bedrooms was little more than a closet. But it was perfect for a child. Annali, who loved small spaces, had already claimed the little room as hers, and was twirling around in it, her arms thrown open wide.

As soon as she stepped out on the deck, she knew it was hers. Rather, theirs. It wasn't much to look at now, in the winter. The deck was only big enough for a table and a few chairs, but it was clear that the building's residents did most of their living outside. The other balconies were decorated with potted plants and twinkly strands of lights. Pru imagined sitting on the deck on summer mornings, drinking her coffee. Having dinners with tea lights lit all around the railings. It was worth giving up her beloved bird's-eye view of the city, her bay window seat, her immaculate parquet floors, for a little bit of outside space in the middle of the city. She thought of her hike in the woods with John, that quiet, that fresh air. After that, she'd intended to become more outdoorsy. "The indoorsy type," that's what John had said about her. She still smiled, thinking of it.

"And they'll let us have the pets," Patsy was saying, standing at her elbow. "As long as they're small. They didn't say anything about bad behavior."

SHE GAVE A CHECK TO PATSY TO SECURE THE APART-ment, then dashed to Union Station for her train. She was pushing through the cars of the crowded Metroliner, looking for a seat, when she ran into Elliott Barstow, mystery crime novelist (*clink clunk*). He moved over and she took the seat next to him. A major publisher was interested in the series and he was going to New York to talk about a contract. His suit was rumpled, and when he looked at her, it was through glasses that were smeary. Pru wanted to take them off his face and wipe them with the square of silk that she carried in her purse for her own glasses.

"I can't believe it," he said, clutching a dirty, torn envelope with a coffee ring on it. "I've been working on this for so long.

You know, I haven't had a meal out in six years." He was trembling with excitement.

Pru dug in her briefcase and found a blue plastic sleeve she'd brought along for her travel receipts. She gave it to Elliott, who discarded the soiled envelope and slipped the pages of his manuscript inside.

"Thanks," he said, twisting the string closed around the circular clasp. "Do you think it'll help?"

"It can't hurt," she said. "You're going to be great, you know."

"You're so nice, Pru. Will you have dinner with me, after we get back? My treat," he added.

"I'd love to," she said. A year ago, she would have seen a good fixer-upper in Elliott Barstow. Replace the glasses, get him to the gym, read his books and tell him how great they were—but after thinking about it for a moment she said, "Is it okay if it's not a date?"

"Sure," he said. "But don't expect me to sleep with you."

"Okay," she said, laughing.

PRU WAS TELLING KATE ABOUT RUDY FISCH, AND KATE was laughing so hard that she couldn't breathe. Kate had pale blond hair in a sort of Tuesday Weld up-do and a slight lisp, which Pru adored. She wore one of what she called her "party frocks," a little yellow swirly number from the fifties. Whenever they were together they instantly became twelve years old again. Kate was easy to set off, and watching Kate laugh always made Pru laugh, too. In high school they annoyed their other friends when they got this way, giddy and boisterous and falling all over each other. Pru was now telling Kate how, in addition to his weekly Fresh Fields order, Rudy had recently gotten into the habit of asking Pru to stop at the health food store on Columbia Road for things like stevia and amino acid spray.

"What can I say to the poor guy?" Pru had said to Kate. "I mean, he stays home all day, grinding his own nut butter." And for whatever reason, because she'd known Pru forever and because she was happy to see her, Kate almost fell off her chair laughing, drawing looks from the other diners.

"So," Pru said, after they'd given the waiter their orders. "Tell me about your doctor."

Kate brought her hands to her face, hiding behind them. "Shit," she said.

"Uh-oh," said Pru.

Kate peeked out between her fingers. "I'm in love, doll. I want to spend the rest of my life with this man. Like, shackled to his side."

"You are? You do?" Pru leaned forward. "This is going to sound weird, but—how do you know?"

Kate tipped her head to the side, thinking. "You know how you're at a party and you pick up the wrong beer, and you know after one sip that it's not yours? But then, when you find the right one, you know it right away? Why? What is it? The temperature, or the taste of your own spit that you somehow recognize? Or the weight and moistness of the can? Or maybe everything, all together. But it's all so subtle and complex you can't explain it. If someone asked, How do you know that's your beer? well, you wouldn't know what to say. You just *know*." And that was the great thing about Kate. There she was, in her delicate party dress and with her lisp, talking about how true love was like a beer. And she'd gotten it exactly right, too.

"That's how I feel about my friend John," Pru was surprised to hear herself saying. "He's married, and something was going on with us, but now it's not. I'm so ready, and he's so what I want, but it's not going to happen." Her eyes filled with tears. "Oh, Katie, I was so hard on you, wasn't I, when you were seeing your married guy. I'm so sorry. I was just stupid. I didn't know anything about anything."

"Stop it," Kate said. She'd gotten tearful, too. "You totally know I was over it as soon as it happened. Anyway, you were right. He was a shitbag."

"He wasn't your beer. Oh, Kate, I'm nobody's beer," Pru said, laughing and wiping her eyes. "Some drunk kid is going to pick me up and drink me, and my real owner is never going to find me."

"No, no," Kate said. "He's out there. He's just still looking for you, that's all."

"Or he's upstairs in the bathroom, throwing up. Let's talk about your beer."

Kate straightened up. "We can meet him after dinner, if you want. He wants to meet you."

"He does?" Whoever this guy was, Pru liked him right away, for no other reason than because he wanted to meet her. Kate said he was waiting for them at the bar around the corner from her place. He was already there, sitting at a little table, when they came in. He had a copy of *Spin* magazine and a medical journal. He was quiet and rumpled, friendly and distracted. He drank his drink and let Pru and Kate continue squawking at each other. When Kate mentioned her ex-lovers—she was still in touch seemingly with everyone she'd ever dated—he didn't even bat an eye. Pru wondered exactly how many of them she'd told him about. He paid for their drinks and hailed a cab. He opened Pru's door for her and gave her a big hug, and when he said "we" he meant himself and Kate. He looked at Kate with dreamy eyes. He was what Kate never in her life seemed interested in: a really nice guy with no visible hang-ups.

Pru was happy for her. When she got home, she would send Kate a card to tell her how happy she was for her. She gave the cab driver the address of her hotel and then asked him if he had any children. She found that cab drivers loved to discuss their children. She sat back in her seat and listened to the man talk about how his youngest daughter was doing better at school now that she was learning karate. It was giving her discipline, he said, and self-respect. She'd have to remember to tell that to Patsy. Annali would look adorable in a those little white pajamas and an obi. She wondered how they were doing back at home. She hoped Patsy had gotten the check to secure the apartment. *God,* she thought, *thirty-six, single, and living with her sister, like a couple of spinsters out of a Victorian novel.* It certainly had never been part of her five-year plan. But neither had been becoming a shopgirl, and she and Edie had had a blast, earlier in the day, looking at clothes. So maybe plans were overrated. They never worked out as you thought they would, anyway.

STILL, SHE FELT COMPELLED TO MAKE A FEW NOTES, with regard to the upcoming move. After all, she had less than a month to figure it all out.

It seemed an interminably long time to wait. It was becoming harder and harder to spend another day in the apartment on Columbia Road. The two rooms (three, counting the bathroom) felt claustrophobic and cramped. There was constantly someone underfoot, and although Pru did practically nothing but start cleaning the minute she got home from work, the place was always a wreck. Patsy's and Annali's clothes were spread out everywhere, there were toys in every corner of the place, and it seemed she could hardly cross the room without startling an animal.

A bedroom, all to herself! She couldn't wait. It seemed a lifetime since she'd slept alone, or just with Whoop. Not sharing a bed with at least two, sometimes three, other living creatures— she could barely remember what that was like.

She pulled out her Daytimer again and quickly filled it with move-related tasks and errands. She spent her day off from Edie's at her table of yearning at the Korner, the one with AG + SW?? carved into it, making calls on her cell. She loved the feeling of crossing off the items as they were completed. The café was much busier now, so there wasn't as much hanging out and talking with John. Her heart still lurched in her chest whenever she saw him. She thought that sensation would have gone away by now, but maybe it was one of those learned, Pavlovian responses. They smiled and waved to each other. She kept thinking she'd see him with Lila, but if she was there Pru couldn't identify her. She thought John was looking tired and unhappy. Unless of course it was just her own wishful thinking.

Then, very suddenly, Edie arrived one morning and announced that she was closing up the shop. She had decided that her father needed a private-duty nurse, and the only way she could pay for that was to go back to practicing law, and her old firm was willing to hire her again.

Pru was working only part-time—in theory to supplement her nonexistent grant-writing income—but the news threw her. She was happy at Edie's. She knew it wasn't her whole life, of course, but she'd been enjoying the restful interlude.

After work, instead of going home, she went to the Korner. She wanted to sit and think about what to do next, and the one thing she could no longer do at her apartment was sit and think.

To her surprise, she found McKay and Patsy sitting together at a table.

"Great," she said, joining them. "Are you two plotting my death?"

"Relax," said Patsy. "We just ran into each other. I have to go get Annali, anyway. But I'll see you in the morning, right?" she said, to McKay.

"I'm just taking her to meet our human resources person," McKay said, when Patsy was gone. "Don't be so suspicious."

"Oh, honey, that's nice. Thank you for doing that. Just don't like her better than me. That is *not* allowed."

When she told him about Edie, McKay said, "Why don't you just buy her out?"

"Buy her out? What, and run the store myself?" She felt her skin prickle a little, and, sure enough, here came John.

"Sure. Why not? John, don't you think Pru should buy Edie's?" McKay said smoothly, when he was near.

"Better yet," said John, seating himself at the table. "Buy her inventory, and open your shop here."

"In Adams-Morgan?"

"Absolutely. I bet Edie's spending a fortune to rent that space. You'd do better here, anyway. I'm telling you, another year from now, you won't be able to buy your way into this neighborhood. Hey, the Chinese bakery is moving. It'd be perfect for a dress shop."

"But I don't know the first thing about running a business," Pru said.

"I'm sure Edie would help you. And you'd have me. I didn't know anything, either, when I bought this place."

"But I don't have that kind of money."

"So, you take out a loan. Find investors. Do you have any savings?"

"Of course. But that's what it is—*savings.* Besides . . . retail. It's not exactly what I envisioned doing with my master's degree."

"What did you envision?"

A good question. "I don't know. Read?"

She had to admit, she was intrigued with the idea. Afterward, instead of going straight home, she and McKay turned and went up Eighteenth to look at the Chinese bakery. It was an appealing site, an Adams–Morgan landmark that she'd always loved. The building was situated where Eighteenth curved around, so the building itself was actually rounded, too. It stood between an Ethiopian restaurant and a tiny electronics store, the kind where everything was all mumble-jumble and, one suspected, hot.

From the outside, it looked perfect for a small boutique. A dress shop, that's what John had called it. There was a tall, narrow display window that, for the six years she'd lived in the neighborhood, had held the same giant, many-tiered plastic wedding cake. The window, she realized, had great visibility from three of the four corners of Eighteenth and Columbia, the busiest intersection in the neighborhood. Right away, she imagined replacing the cake with an artsy display of boots and shoes hanging from invisible strings. Already, she could see the sign: THE DRESS SHOP. Or PRU'S FROCKS. ALFRED J. PRU'S FROCKS, as a nod to her master's in literature. No, that was goofy. Still, she felt a surge of excitement, as she headed home. She didn't feel quite so annoyed when she got home to see the usual accumulation of daily mess, while Patsy sat on the couch with Annali, watching something on PBS and not making dinner.

IT TURNED OUT THAT JOHN KNEW THE OWNER OF THE bakery, Mr. Yao, from the neighborhood business association. He was able to get them in to see the space the next day. That morning, Pru stood in the middle of the store, watching the sunlight come through the tall front windows.

Mr. Yao and John chatted amiably while Pru looked around. Pru was embarrassed that she couldn't understand much of what Mr. Yao was saying. John repeated what he'd said in a low whisper: the bakery had done so well on Columbia Road that they had bought a building on U Street, a part of town where Danish-modern furniture stores and bistros were beginning to replace the pawnshops and check-cashing places. Pru would be taking over the lease on a storefront that had already proved itself successful. Of course, John pointed out, she'd pay more for that.

But when Mr. Yao told John what the rent was, and John told Pru, she was shocked. It didn't matter that Edie paid at least twice that for her shop on Connecticut. How many dresses would she have to unload to make that back? she wondered. Back at the Korner, John began running the numbers. He showed her how to make a cash-flow estimate. Their heads were bent together over the calculator as he punched in the numbers. She tried not to notice how close their noses were. He gave her the number of a loan officer at a downtown bank, who'd given John his start-up loan.

"Are you actually thinking seriously about this?" Patsy said later, as they ate Indian take-out at the kitchen table, surrounded by half-packed boxes. Patsy had spent the whole day getting ready for the move. They had less than two weeks now, and while Pru was wondering how on earth they would pull it off, Patsy was packing up boxes. She'd even thought to reserve a moving truck for the date of the move. Jenny and Whoop had figured out by now that something strange was happening in their habitat, and zipped frenetically between the jumbled-up rooms.

"I don't know," Pru said. "It's so risky. I'd have to use everything Dad left me *and* get a loan. For something I've never done in my life. But the timing is lucky. Edie already ordered the fall inventory, and her current stock I could sell in my sleep. So, I don't know. It's tempting."

To her surprise, Patsy said, "Well, I have money."

"You do?"

"Of course. Dad loved me, too, you know."

"But . . . is this what you'd want to do with it?"

"I've been looking for a good investment opportunity," Patsy said.

"You *have*?" Since when did Patsy, who once spent four hundred dollars on a serpent-shaped wrist cuff, look for investment opportunities?

"Do you know how much a college education is going to cost in sixteen years?" Patsy said, sopping up the curry on her plate with a piece of garlic naan.

"No."

"Forty thousand dollars."

"So? That's about what it cost us."

"A *year*, my dear. For *one* year."

"Jesus. Can't she go to a public university?"

Patsy popped the naan into her mouth. "That *is* public. Private school is twice as much."

"Can't she go to secretarial school?"

"We can only hope."

"What about Jimmy Roy? How much do nurse-midwives make?"

Patsy snorted and cast Pru a doleful look. "Please. You know this is not going to happen. He's always talking about the things he's *going* to do. I've never once known him to actually complete anything. I'm totally serious, by the way. If anyone could make this work, it's you."

Pru looked at her sister, feeling overcome with gratitude and affection. She was touched that Patsy would make such a commitment to her, to help with something that she cared about. She had never really regarded her sister as someone who could help her. It was always Pru—the older, wiser one—who helped Patsy. But that was before, when she thought that bad things happened to only certain *types* of good people. This was now, when practically everything she seemed to touch had fallen to pieces. Maybe she did need some help. Maybe it wasn't such a bad idea, after all.

"So, okay," Pru said. "Let's do it."

"Really? Wow, that was easy."

"You got me in a weak moment," Pru said. "But you know, I think I want to do this. I really think I want to."

"I'm your backer," Patsy said. "Your sugar daddy. This is going to be *fun*."

Nineteen

Both John and Patsy accompanied Pru to the closing of the loan, for moral support. Pru took the pen the loan officer handed her, and with trembling hands, as Patsy whispered *"Breathe!"* in her ear, signed away her entire life in exchange for sixty thousand dollars, due with interest in seven years. Her hand wrote out her name, then was seized and pumped by the loan officer. John popped the cork on a bottle of champagne he'd brought along, and that was it.

The loan took up its place in Pru's life. It was like another new housemate, sitting on the couch all day long, unchanging and unmoving, using up most of the air in the room and asserting its massive presence. It dwarfed the little student loans she'd struggled to pay off after college. It was dismaying to think she'd be going back to those days, eating cheap food at home, getting her shopping fixes at secondhand stores and flea markets.

John and Edie, true to their words, were with her every step of the way. They made sure she made the right decisions, gave her encouragement, and more advice—often conflicting—than she could handle. John had the names of painters, plumbers, and contractors, all of them dolefully taciturn and usurious. The amount of things she bought from Edie, and had yet to buy, was staggering, yet thrilling. The clothes, of course, and mannequins. Wooden hangers, mirrors, display racks. A glass jewelry case. A sound system. All manner of hooks and washers and screws and bolts and nuts. And incandescent lights, and floor lamps, and a bazillion lightbulbs—she absolutely refused to torment her customers with bad lighting. She also added some things that Edie didn't have in her shop: pretty antique soap dishes and vanity trays, high-end hairbrushes and French milled soaps. Girly things. In the future, she wanted to add more accessories, and makeup, for when customers didn't feel like trying on clothes. She wanted to have vintage items, too, and made up a little sign for the counter that read: NOW ACCEPTING CONSIGNMENTS. At night, she and Big Whoop sat together in her new, private bedroom, on a bed littered with paint chips, flooring chips, linoleum chips, and her ever-present Daytimer, stuffed to bursting with pages and pages of lists and plans.

THE NIGHT BEFORE THE SHOP'S GRAND OPENING, PRU jumped off a ladder, where she was hanging a display of purses, and sliced open her foot.

It happened during a fight with Patsy. They were still in the shop after midnight, trying to finish up the billion little things that weren't yet done. Pru was in a rotten mood. It suddenly seemed like lunacy, the whole idea of the shop. She couldn't imagine what she'd been thinking. They hadn't even finished moving into the new apartment. Every morning, she pulled something to wear out of a cardboard box, sniffing it for wearability. For the past six weeks, it seemed that she'd done little else besides plan, fret, pack and unpack, and fret some more.

The day before the opening, she was in a panic. Patsy opted out of one of her temp assignments to come and help. "These aren't even last-minute things," Pru complained, throwing down the manual for the new, complex, digital cash register she'd been foolish enough to buy on eBay. "These are first-minute things. We can't possibly open tomorrow. Not *possibly.*"

"We'll be fine," Patsy said, stepping back to admire her work. She'd dressed three "Brazilian butt" half-mannequins Pru had gotten from eBay in hundred-dollar jeans and hung them in the front display window. From where Pru stood, they looked like very pert, recently executed bodies swaying in the breeze.

"Are you going to put up nooses and cheering peasants, too?"

"You don't like it? I thought it was kind of funny."

"No, I don't," Pru said. "Take it down, please."

"Fine," Patsy grumbled. "Testy Testerson."

They'd been working since early morning. Annali was at Fiona's for the night. At dinnertime, John showed up with sandwiches and coffee. After he left, Pru climbed back up the ladder, barefoot, to finish the display of evening bags, which had already taken way too long. She was so nervous that she accidentally ripped the lining of a very expensive evening bag, and in frustration she threw the purse across the room. Its long, heavy shoulder chain flew out and wrapped itself like a whip around a glass vase full of blue pebbles, some mystical thing of Patsy's which was supposed to bestow good luck. The glass vase wobbled, then fell to the floor and shattered.

Patsy put her hands on her hips and said, "God, Pru, you are such a moody fucking nightmare lately."

"Just shut up," Pru said, from the top of the ladder.

"What is with you?" Patsy said, going to the closet for the broom and dustpan. "Is it all really just the store? Or is there something else going on?"

"Isn't the store enough?" Pru said. "I mean, look at this place. It's a disaster." And of course, she'd just made it worse, breaking the damn vase. Why did Patsy have to bring such a ridiculous thing into the shop, to begin with?

"I think it's that John Owen," Patsy said, beginning to sweep up the glass. "Every time you see him, I swear, you go absolutely haywire. He sure is around often enough, too. Why don't the two of you just get it over with, and fuck?" She said it absently, as she worked. She even looked up at Pru and grinned.

"I'm not the one who fucks married men," Pru said, before she could stop herself.

Patsy stopped grinning. A look of pain crossed her face. Pru felt as if she'd slapped a small child.

"No, you're not that stupid, are you?" Patsy said tightly. "I didn't know John was married," she added. "You could have said something. Ever."

That was when Pru jumped off the ladder. She jumped because she was so angry with herself. She couldn't believe she'd been so awful. She meant to go to Patsy and say she was sorry, but she didn't look before she jumped, and her bare feet landed on the pile of glass shards Patsy had just made.

As she hit the ground, a white-hot pain seared the bottom of one foot. She tried to stand on the other foot, but fell. The bottom of her right foot had been split open. Patsy came over and looked at the gash. She pulled a length of paper towels from a roll, and wrapped up Pru's foot in it. Soon it was soaked in blood.

"You have to go to the hospital," Patsy said, firmly. "No—don't even argue with me."

Patsy grabbed her purse and the roll of paper towels. They hobbled outside and flagged down a passing cab. Pru's foot throbbed and bled through the second paper towel. Patsy said, "The nearest hospital, please," and the driver hit the accelerator. When they arrived, Patsy threw a twenty at him, and helped Pru inside. While they were in the waiting room, someone came with more gauze, to hold her until she could be seen by one of the doctors.

The waiting room was packed with people, many of them much worse off than Pru. One guy held a wad of gauze over an eye, and Pru was afraid there was nothing behind it. Everyone looked up at the TV screen, which was showing old reruns. Patsy went to find the cafeteria. Pru watched an episode of *Three's Company.* God, that Furley was a creep. She tried not to think about all the things that needed to be done at the shop before the opening. Her foot throbbed, but she couldn't bring herself to look at it. Her threshold for pain, as with fear, was down around dirt level.

As the program ended, Patsy came back with two cups of herbal tea. She handed one to Pru, who said, "I'm sorry, Patsy. I shouldn't have said that. And I don't think you're stupid."

"Gee, thanks."

"I guess John Owen is a sore spot. I mean, you were right. Well, you were wrong. We've already . . . had sex." She couldn't bring herself to say "fucked."

The truth was, she still felt like they were sleeping together, behind his wife's back. She felt every bit as if she were having an affair. It was all done without any physical contact, of course, but they found reasons to see each other every day. It was because of the shop—always, ostensibly, because of the shop. It was too easy for Pru to pop around the corner, to see if he had any spackle. Or he would stop by, with another idea for her. Each day, she felt more and more guilty and confused, on account of the way they'd looked at each other. It was almost worse than if they were merely sleeping together. Were it just sex, at least she'd know how to define it. But what was this? Was she preventing him from working on his marriage? She worried that it was true.

Pru took a sip of her tea, and suddenly realized that she wanted to tell Patsy everything. She told her about the night they spent out at Shenandoah, then sleeping together, and the night Lila asked him to come back. She tried to emphasize the noble aspects, how she believed that John was doing the right thing. How, in fact, she'd encouraged him to, because it was the only honorable way . . .

"I can't believe this," Patsy interrupted. "This was all going on while we were living together? While I was right there, in the same apartment?" Her eyes filled with tears. "That makes me feel like absolute shit," she said. "We're going through the exact same thing, and you don't once mention it?"

"I wouldn't call it the exact same thing," said Pru. She was annoyed with Patsy for interrupting her when she was trying to make a point. And could they for once have one little conversation about Pru, not about her?

"Excuse me, but we were both in love with guys who happened to be married to someone else. How is that not the same?"

Pru didn't want to say how, so she said, "I'm not in love with him."

"Stop that," Patsy said. "The question is, does he know that you are, or not?"

Pru opened her mouth, then closed it again. "Do you really think I need to spell it out for him?"

"In my experience, you usually do. And I do mean *you* you. I mean, I didn't really think you were even that into him, until you reacted that way, back in the shop."

"Really? I feel like every time I look at him, there are goofy little hearts twirling around my head."

"Nope. I wouldn't have said what I did if I had thought that, you know. About fucking him." Overhearing them, the man with the one eye looked over at them.

"Keep your voice down, Patsy, honestly." She noticed that the ankle she'd fallen on was beginning to swell up. "Anyway, I don't see what good it would do."

"Try not to think of it in those terms," Patsy said. "Maybe it's not supposed to *do* anything." Before Pru could ask her what the hell that meant, a nurse came through the swinging doors and called her name.

The nurse helped her down the long hall and into one of the examining "rooms," essentially a bed and some machines separated from other "rooms" by a white curtain on a U-shaped track. Pru sat on the paper-covered table, and listened to the moaning of an elderly woman nearby. "Ma'am!" the woman cried out, every five seconds. "Ma'am!"

Pru's curtain was being pulled aside and the doctor came in. He was bent over her chart, reading, but Pru recognized him immediately. She almost jumped off the table. It was Jacob, looking not nearly as surprised to see Pru as she was to see him.

"Hello, Prudence Whistler, foot trauma," he said, pleasantly. He squinted at her chart. "Is this right? You can't be thirty-six!"

"Can't I see someone else?" she said, almost desperately.

"This isn't a restaurant, Pru," he said, tossing the chart aside. He spoke with a doctor's assertiveness. "Lie back, please, so I can look at your foot."

The gauze bandage she'd been given was almost entirely soaked with blood. She thought of the crowd out in the waiting room, and lay back on the bed. She felt as stiff as a plank. Jacob unwound the bandage. She could feel him carefully pry open the wound with his fingers. She felt it all the way up inside her belly.

"What'd you do here?"

"I fell on some glass."

"Yep. I see it, right there. It's in pretty deep."

"Can you get it out?"

"Well, of course I can, silly. I'm a doctor!" He put his fingers on her ankle and the pain that shot through made her gasp. "Sprained, but not broken," he said, after some probing.

He put his face right up against her foot, to peer inside the wound, and she found herself wondering if she'd showered lately. "First, though, you have to tell me how they're doing," he said softly.

She was so astonished that, for a moment, she couldn't speak. When she collected her thoughts, she said, "You're bribing me? Can't I sue you for that?"

"Probably," he said.

"You can't be serious."

"I've got an eighty-three-year-old woman who no doubt has many long stories to tell me, waiting in the next cubicle," he said. There was no trace of a smile behind his words. "I could go do that first, or I could just get this little guy out in about two seconds, and you'd be on your way home."

"They're fine," she said, tightly.

"Did Annali ever learn to swim?" He was talking conversationally, as if they were old family friends who happened to bump into each other in the produce section.

"This isn't funny," Pru said. "Just take it out and let me go."

He held up the tweezers, showing her the piece of glass he'd removed from her foot. "Silly," he said, "I took it out five minutes ago."

She crossed her arms over her chest, awkwardly. It all seemed so absurd that she was wondering if he was actually licensed. Could she complain to someone? The head of the hospital, or someone?

"I'll need to stitch you up," he said. "You really gashed yourself. Here's a little something for the pain."

The "little something" stabbed, then burned. Tears came into her eyes. Jacob worked quietly for a while, then said, in a more serious voice, "Does she ever ask about me? Annali?"

"No."

"Okay, what about your sister, then? Patsy," he said, and Pru was surprised to hear something in his voice that sounded like regret.

"No. Not really. Both of them got over you pretty quickly."

He clipped the thread. The sight of it obviously still attached to the bottom of her foot made her stomach tighten. "You sure know how to hurt a guy," he said.

"You hurt yourself."

"Very true," he said, standing up and taking off his gloves. "I will miss them every day of my life. Please tell her that. I'll get them to discharge you soon." And with that he was gone. She could hear his voice in the next cubicle: "Mrs. Lambert! You can't be eighty-three!"

Patsy was asleep in the waiting room when she came out. Pru poked her with one of the crutches the orderly had given her when she was discharged. The orderly had said, "Boy, you must rate. The doc gave you some good drugs. And I never knew him to do his own stitching."

"I saw Jacob," she whispered to Patsy.

Patsy sat up, her eyes wide. "My Jacob?"

Pru nodded, and wincing, eased into the seat next to her. "He stitched me up. He wouldn't do it until I told him how you were. And if Annali had learned to swim."

Patsy's eyes darted past her, scanning the corridors behind them. "You're kidding. What did you say?"

"I said you were fine."

"That's it?"

"That's it."

Patsy stared at her for a minute. "Tell me the whole thing," she said.

Pru told her, word for word, as much as she could remember.

"Weird," Patsy said, at last.

"I think he was actually in love with you, Pats," Pru said.

"Yes," Patsy said. "That's what I've been trying to tell you."

"Sorry."

"Prudence," Patsy said, looking at the clock above her head. "We open in six hours."

Twenty

The alarm went off at six o'clock, a mere two hours after they got home from the hospital. Pru hit the clock and groaned. Her ankle throbbed, and the bottom of her right foot felt tight and raw. She didn't think she'd be able to get out of bed. Then she remembered the piece that was supposed to run in today's *Post,* and forced herself up. She was hoping it would generate some interest in the opening. And she wanted to see how she looked in the picture.

When she and Patsy arrived at the shop, it was still dark outside. There was so much to be done, she couldn't see how they could possibly open the doors by ten. She wasn't used to the crutches and her foot throbbed constantly, despite the Percocet. She wondered whether Jacob really knew what he was talking about. He'd said that her ankle was only sprained, but it certainly felt worse than that.

They pulled the protective paper off the sign above the door, before going in. The sign looked exactly as she'd hoped, with the

store's name, "peach," styled in rounded lowercase letters, feminine and hopeful. Inside, they went around turning on the lights.
McKay had had the walls painted a soft gray with a slightly blue
cast, cool and soothing, and he himself had hand-stenciled a
chocolate-brown ribbon around the top, to look as if it were
threaded through the walls. A neat, squarish bow faced you as you
entered the store. That, at least, was perfect. *Absolutely* perfect.

The air was still permeated with the faint scent of Chinese
meat buns, despite all the fig-scented candles Patsy kept lighting.
There were cartons of clothes to unpack, steam, price, and hang.
They got to work sweeping up the glass still scattered on the floor
after last night's accident. Pru got a call that the shipment of
spring dresses she'd been really excited about had been held up;
the girl she'd hired to help out was late; the toilet kept running.
Then there were all the things that only Pru could see. The price
tags, which she'd insisted on doing by hand, looked sloppy and
hurried, not homey and cute, as she'd hoped. And there was the
matter of her still-throbbing foot. At nine she took another Percocet, and kept going.

She tried to breathe through these things, or accept them into
her karma, or whatever it was you were supposed to do in order
not to completely lose your cool. It had all sounded so simple:
rent a place, buy some clothes, come up with a cute name. Then
you find out that there are all these obstacles and problems. You
keep thinking: Once I solve this, it's smooth sailing. But then a
leak pops open, as soon as you've plugged the previous one.
Before you know it, you've run out of fingers and the dam is still
threatening to burst everywhere.

It was Patsy, oddly enough, who was the calm eye of the
storm. They were still writing the tags when the first customers
showed up; Pru hadn't wanted to unlock the door, but Patsy

strode over and let them in, practically pushing Pru out of the way. When Patsy realized that the girl Pru had hired was not going to show up, Patsy stepped in, welcoming customers, continuing to pull things out of boxes, ringing up sales. Any minute, Pru thought, someone was going to figure out that she didn't know what the hell she was doing. She hopped around on her crutches clumsily, saying what she was sure were nonsensical things. Her mother and Jimmy Roy showed up in the early afternoon, having driven all morning from Ohio. "Oh!" Nadine said, when she walked in. "I love it! I absolutely love it!" When the cash register's computer went down, Patsy started writing out each sales receipt by hand. Jimmy Roy fixed the running toilet, and Nadine helped by cleaning out the dressing rooms. By five o'clock, the little shop was crowded with people and noise, things were actually sold, and Pru moved as if in a trance through a swirl of questions, problems, friends, fabric, and Percocet.

And women. Women, women, women, of all shapes and sizes, needs and demands. Some she recognized as former customers of Edie's. They all seemed to know Pru, probably from the picture of her in the *Post,* a shot of her from below which made her look, she'd said to Patsy, like Bea Arthur. She'd previewed peach's inventory for the newspaper's fashion editor last week, who'd gone mental over it. "Style *(at last!)* Comes to Adams-Morgan," read the headline, above the towering photo of Pru.

Patsy had had the brilliant idea to take private appointments—a brilliant idea she'd stolen from Nordstrom's—and by the end of the day the appointments calendar was booked for the next three weeks. The idea was that you'd come in, after work or at lunchtime, and there'd already be a roomful of clothes in your size waiting for you, chosen by the shop's stylish proprietor. Patsy suggested that the private-appointment customers should get a pot of *kukicha* tea and a foot massage, too, but Pru wasn't ready to go that far. Or maybe just the tea—that wasn't a bad idea. Still, she was happy with the three weeks' worth of bookings—she hadn't expected half that many.

At six-thirty she hung out the official CLOSED sign on the door, and Edie started opening champagne. That was when things for Pru started to get fuzzy. She remembered that everyone was there: John, with his friends Ralph and Rona, who made the trip down from New York especially for the opening. Rudy Fisch came, and Pru overheard her mother clucking sympathetically as he ran through his list of symptoms. McKay, who made Pru sit down, and Bill, who was prying the plastic casing off the cash register to have a look at the computer inside. Fiona, who showed everybody the ultrasound pictures of her embryonic girl. And Jimmy Roy, who'd made a bunch of compilation CDs for the shop, and who whistled appreciatively when Pru showed him the Bose sound system. Even Phan from the video store, along with his girlfriend, whose name really was Chuckie, and whom Pru hired on the spot when she offered to replace the girl who didn't show up; and Lola, her elderly regular from Edie's, who immediately pointed out that she'd tried on all these shoes, already. Edie kept opening bottle after bottle of champagne, and someone spilled a glass on a lilac satin skirt, and after that it was all pretty much a happy haze of kisses, laughter, Burt Bacharach, and the Sex Pistols.

THREE WEEKS LATER, SHE WAS HURRYING ACROSS THE Mall toward the Hirshhorn Museum, where she was supposed to meet Rona at lunchtime. She winced a little as she jumped up on the curb and landed on her sprained ankle. It still hurt occasionally, but at least the stitches in the bottom of her foot were gone and she could walk without the crutches.

Rona wore the same windbreaker she'd been wearing the first time Pru had met her, the one that matched Ralph's. Although Pru had seen her only three or four times, she always felt like they were old, old friends. Rona was the kind of woman who took her friendships very seriously. She sent Pru an e-mail at least once a week, chatting about this and that. She made Pru feel carefully vetted and chosen, and as though the fact that Pru liked her, too, was some favor to her.

They exchanged fond hugs and kisses and made their way into the main galleries. The Hirshhorn is a circular building, and as you make your way through it, it gives you the sense of being perpetually around the bend from something great. They circled the galleries, around and around, up and up. Rona chatted about the art, and as she knew something about it her comments weren't uninteresting, but Pru was having a hard time following her. After half an hour, she was practically crawling out of her skin with curiosity. Why had Rona summoned her? She'd only ever seen her in John's company, and felt it would be rude to ask if she had some purpose in calling Pru, out of the blue, for lunch. But she couldn't help thinking that Rona did have an agenda. She wondered if it had to do with John. She hadn't seen much of him in the past few weeks, she'd been so busy with the shop. There was still no end of things to be done: the toilet refused to run properly, the electrical outlet behind the counter kept shocking her whenever she plugged something in, and she couldn't for the life of her decipher the assembly instructions for the new Bjärnum/ Järpen shelving units she'd bought at Ikea. She was struggling to stay on top of the marketing and advertising, inventory control, property maintenance. She'd had to come up with a return policy. And, of course, run the shop.

In a way, it was a relief not to see so much of John. The struggle to maintain friendly feelings had taken its toll on her. Sometimes she felt lonelier in his presence than when she was actually alone. She had to watch herself when he was around. Ever since Patsy had confronted her about her feelings for him, she worked harder to tamp them down. Sometimes she could barely speak for fear of revealing her feelings. She felt her personality was slipping away as she tried to remain Miss Neutral Pal. She never could bring herself to ask about Lila, after that first time. And he never volunteered anything, either. Once or twice she'd caught him looking at her, about to say . . . *something*. He would clear his throat and take a deep, announcing breath. But then what he said was always something silly like, Did you remember to check on your building permits?

Finally, Rona decided she'd had enough art, and they headed to the Air and Space Museum for lunch, because that was where everybody went for lunch.

There weren't many people outdoors, as they made their way across the Mall. It felt lonely and desolate in the glare of the early-spring sun. Pru preferred the winter's clean, white snow to this, acres of dead grass mashed into dirt. More in-betweens: late afternoon, early spring, adolescence, falling in love. She hated the in-betweens. Always, she just wanted to get where she was going—to be there already. She was almost paralyzed by in-betweenness. She didn't know how she was supposed to behave.

They sat near the big windows of the cafeteria and ate their salads. Rona's father had just died. He had been very old, in his nineties. Rona had been with him, holding his hand, when he went. "For the first time in my life," she said, "I felt absolutely and utterly in the right place at the right time. Death has a way of focusing everything like that." She gave Pru a sidelong look. "Like love. It fixes you, if you know what I mean. You have to be absolutely in that time and that place."

"You and Ralph seem like you've known each other forever."

"We were lucky. There aren't many who've survived as long as we have."

"So what's your secret?" Pru said, smiling.

"I don't know," Rona said, spearing a cherry tomato that looked a bit yellow. "It just works. We just can't shut up, is the truth. Even when we're mad at each other, you know, neither one of us can walk out on an argument." She laughed her warm, rough laugh. "Ralph tried to, once. It was when we first got together. We were involved in a terrible fight, and he slammed out of the apartment. He made it about five blocks before he stopped to call and yell at me from a pay phone. He had a terrible temper in those days. We talked for so long that there was a line for the phone, people shouting for him to hurry and hang up, so he comes and yells at me under my window for a while, and when it gets too cold he comes back upstairs to continue. And here we are, forty years later, and we're still talking."

"What was the fight about?"

"He was supposed to marry someone else. I knew her, too. A dancer. I liked her."

"Wow. That sounds awful."

"Falling in love is always awful, isn't it?"

"So what happened?"

"He dumped her and married me. We'd only known each other six weeks."

"And the dancer?"

Rona waved the yellowing tomato on the fork. "She married someone else. An architect in the city, lots of money, a lovely man. Not bad, huh? We're still good friends with them." She paused significantly. "I have to say," she ventured, "we don't know what on earth Johnny is doing. We've spent hours talking to him, and it just doesn't make sense."

"You mean, with Lila?"

"She's all wrong for him." Rona scowled, looking like a little girl.

"I think he's trying to honor his wedding vows."

"Vows, shmows. That's not a marriage. That's a prison sentence." Rona popped the tomato in her mouth. "He should be with someone like you," she said, from around the tomato. "Or, you know, *you*."

Pru could feel her face going red. "Oh, I don't know—" she started to say, but Rona interrupted.

"I told him the first time we met you, and I told you, and I'll keep telling you both: *You*, we get." She made a dismissive wave with her hand. "*Her*, not so much."

"Well, it's not up to us, I'm afraid." Pru smiled at her. "I wish it were, believe me."

"Have you tried?"

"Tried what?"

"To get him to leave her for you!"

"No," Pru said, laughing. "Of course not."

"Why not?"

"Self-respect? Respect for John and his wife? Pride?"

"Oh, yeah," Rona said, waving her hand again and looking pained. "Pride. I remember that."

"Yeah, the thing that goeth before a fall."

"I never knew what that meant," Rona said. "Does that mean

if you lose your pride you're going to fall? Or when you're already falling the last thing to go is your pride, which you've foolishly been holding on to?"

"I think it amounts to the same thing. But the point is, look, I can't do anything while he's married. It would be wrong. It just would. And you know it."

"Can I just tell Johnny you like him?" Rona said, with a seventh-grade smile.

"No. Besides, I really do think it's beside the point."

"I suppose it is. I just keep thinking that if he knew . . ." She sighed, turning more serious. "Ralph and I love to fight. It's not really Johnny's nature, though. He and Lila bring out the worst in each other. There's no other way to explain it. Like, early on, they found each other's buttons, and can't stop pressing them. I guess Ralph and I do that, too. But Johnny doesn't like it. It's not his nature," she said again.

PRU ENTERED THE DINGY FOYER OF THE NEW APARTMENT building and started up the stairs. Then she heard Patsy yelling, and started running. She ran up three flights and pushed open the door, breathlessly.

"Shut up!" Patsy was yelling into the phone. "Shut up, shut up, *shut up!*"

Pru gave her the universal hand signal for, *you* shut up! She still hadn't gotten over thinking they were about to be evicted, for reasons she couldn't quite understand.

"You are *seriously* fucking with my serenity!" Patsy shouted, then slammed down the phone, and burst into tears.

Jacob, Pru thought. She knew that having seen him in the ER was a bad sign. He *had* to make sure Patsy still loved him, didn't he? What else could have sent her into such a tailspin, especially when she'd been doing so well?

"What is it?" Pru said, going to her. "What happened?"

"Jimmy Roy," she sputtered at last. "He says he's still in love with me. That *fucker!*" she said, throwing herself onto the couch and weeping loudly.

Pru dropped her purse on the floor. *Thank God,* she thought.

"Yeah," she agreed. "He's got some nerve."

"You don't understand," said Patsy. "He only said that because of . . . because of Annali. He thinks she needs a father. That's all."

"Patsy, that's crazy."

"Children just fuck up everything," Patsy said. "Oh, stop looking at me that way. She's not here. She's having a play date at Fiona's."

"Listen, Patsy, if you don't love Jimmy Roy, then just say it. But quit blaming the fact that you have a kid for everything that happens to you. It's just ridiculous to think that's why he says he loves you. And quit looking for every excuse under the sun why you can't be together. You can, if you want. And if you don't want to be with him, then don't. But it's not worth all this . . . *drama.*"

Patsy looked at her, resentfully. "Thank you, Voice of Reason," she said.

"You're welcome," said Pru, and left the room.

Twenty-one

A few days later, she was sitting behind the counter at peach. The morning sun was coming in the tall front window of the shop, making the blue-gray walls glow like deep ocean water, and she was watching John fix a giant hole she'd made while trying to screw in a wall anchor with her new most prized possession, an eighteen-volt Black & Decker FireStorm cordless drill.

It was the first time he'd been there since the opening. She'd run into him at the café that morning, where she'd stopped for a coffee before work. It had been a foolish impulse. She had come to the conclusion that the only thing she could do now was to avoid seeing him altogether. She wasn't any closer to controlling her feelings now than she'd been five months ago, the night they'd spent together. It was also foolish to agree to let him come back with her and look around the shop, but she hadn't been able to think of any kind of rational reason why he couldn't.

She was gazing at him absently, admiring the way men seemed to know how to fix all sorts of little problems, when his shirt came untucked from the waistband of his jeans to expose the tiniest little grab of skin. Pru's breath caught in her throat. It wasn't what you'd call a roll, in any way, but it was the kind of extra flesh forty-year-old men get, even those who spend most of the day on their feet and don't shy away from physical labor. The sight of this skin—warm, she was sure—made her palms itchy. She remembered running her hands there. Before she knew what she was doing, her mouth opened and she said, "John."

He turned around and came down off the ladder, concern instantly splashed across his face. "What is it? What's wrong?" She must have sounded as if she was having a heart attack and, really, it almost felt that way.

She wanted to say, "Nothing," but she knew this was a moment that might never come again. Here she'd introduced the possibility of something serious. If Jimmy Roy can do it, she thought, so can I. She heard Patsy's voice in her ear saying: "Breathe!"

She looked at her hands. They were as familiar and as reassuring as anything in the world.

"I think I'm in love with you."

It was as if she'd opened her mouth and a hundred birds had flown out. She was shocked, and so was he. It wasn't exactly what she'd intended to say. Rather, it *was* exactly what she'd intended to say. She just hoped it would have come out a shade more nuanced. She squeezed her eyes shut. No matter what he said, she figured, it had to be better than shlumping around, pretending everything was just fine. Fine! Great! *Friends.* Inside there was a huge sense of relief; indeed, she had been holding a hundred birds there for the last six months. She was about to laugh, she felt so good.

Then she opened her eyes, and saw his face. He looked stern

and unhappy. He was looking at his feet, frowning. She didn't know what to say. She couldn't take it back. She didn't want to. She certainly hadn't chosen to fall in love with him. Out of nowhere, she thought of Big Whoop. She wished she could go home, scoop him up, and bury her nose in his fur.

Then John said out loud, "I don't know what to say." He looked furious, suddenly, and embarrassed.

The door opened and Annali came dashing in with Jenny on her leash, followed by Patsy. As soon as they saw Pru and John, they came to a stop, their laughter dying away.

"Oopsie," said Patsy, looking from John to Pru and back again. Annali was about to run to her, but Patsy held her by the shoulders.

"Come on, honey, let's take the dog around the block again."

"No, Mommy, I want to stay with Prudy . . ."

"Annali."

"It's okay," Pru said. "We're done."

John turned and, nodding absently at Patsy, strode straight out the door.

"Hello and good-bye," Patsy said, looking at Pru. "What the hell happened?"

She couldn't speak. She only shook her head, and looked up at the ceiling, blinking.

The door opened again and a young woman poked her head inside. "Hi," she said, "you open yet?"

"Yes," Pru said. "Come on in."

"Did you—" Patsy hissed, clutching her arm.

"Not now."

"Just tell me—"

"*Later.*"

. . .

BUT LATER, IT WAS MCKAY AND BILL SHE TOLD, HAVING accepted a strong Billtini but passing on the cookies. They were in their customary seats, around the TV in the living room. Bill and McKay had decided to postpone buying a place until after the wedding. *Thank God,* she thought. She wanted them never to move, never to change.

"The funny thing is," she said, "I don't feel as humiliated as I thought I would. Being dumped by Rudy was a hell of a lot worse, somehow."

Bill had put down his computer magazine, and McKay had gone so far as to mute the TV. Even Oxo came in and sat quietly at her feet, as if she were listening, too.

"Look," said McKay. "Good for you."

"I agree," said Bill.

"What's his kink anyway, that he stays with her?" said McKay. "Okay, so he wants to be a good guy—isn't this going a little far, to prove it?"

"I don't think he's trying to prove anything," Pru said. "She had a miscarriage, just before they broke up. I think that had a lot to do with it. I think it's one of the reasons she left, and why he felt like he had to give the marriage another chance."

"Fine," McKay said, "but enough already. They've been back together, what, since Christmas? And I just saw you two mooning over each other at the opening. He certainly didn't seem like a man in love with his wife."

She changed her mind about the cookies and reached for one. "He was mooning? John was? Can you describe the mooning, in great detail?"

"We were all mooning over you that night," McKay said. "Laced up on your Percocet."

Pru groaned. "Don't remind me. Was I a complete idiot?"

"Not at all," said Bill. "You were cute."

"Let's talk about your wedding," Pru said. "Something happy."

"Okay," said Bill. "First thing is, we want you to be our maid of honor."

"Oh!" she exclaimed, happily. "Of course! You guys, I'm so . . . I'm so touched!"

"There's one hitch," added Bill.

"Hold on," said McKay. "I think we need another round first."

Bill disappeared into the kitchen, then emerged with a fresh pitcher of Billtinis. He refilled their glasses, and Pru saw them exchange another look.

"Oh, no," she said. "What now? Just tell me."

"We should tell you," McKay said. "John's bringing her to our wedding."

Pru groaned. "Oh, no," she said. "You have to be kidding me."

"I didn't know what to say," Bill said. "Apparently she's really pushing for it. I'm so sorry, Pru."

"Oh, whatever," Pru said. "It's fine. I'll be glad to get a chance to see them together. Maybe it'll knock some sense into my head."

When she returned home, Patsy was busy arranging things on a shelf in the living room. Pru noticed that the moving boxes were all gone, and the furniture was arranged in each of the rooms. She'd been so busy at the shop that she hadn't so much as unpacked a box.

"Hey," she said. "This looks great. We'd never have gotten through this move without you."

"We wouldn't have the new apartment without me."

"We wouldn't need it without you." She saw that Patsy had a drink going, and took a sip. Sadly, it was only ginger ale.

"Speaking of 'without me,'" Patsy said, sitting on the floor, "there's something I've been meaning to tell you. You know the day you found me in the bath? I never would . . . you know . . . kill myself. I mean, I thought about it, but . . ." She sighed, and drank her ginger ale. "I guess I must think Annali's better off with half a mommy than no mommy at all."

Pru pushed her sister's foot with her own. "You're more than half a mommy. You're at least three-quarters of a mommy."

"Wah wah *waaaah*," Patsy said, like a rueful trumpet.

"You are a wonderful mother," Pru said.

"Really? Am I?"

"You are. I don't think I could have done what you did. I never realized how rough it must have been for you. I don't feel like I did much to help."

"Oh," Patsy said. "Well. That's all right. She wasn't your mistake . . . I mean, blessed child."

Pru's mouth was still buzzing from the Billtini. She remembered John's face when she'd told him she was in love with him. She could still summon his exact expression. "What did you decide about Jimmy Roy?" she said. "Are you going to give the guy another chance?"

"Oh, Jimmy Roy."

"He cleans up good, you have to admit."

"He cleans up okay."

"He is clean, right?"

Patsy shrugged. "Says he is. And one thing Jimmy Roy isn't, is a liar."

"Jacob was the liar," Pru said, yawning. "Wasn't that a book?"

"Jacob never lied, either," Patsy corrected her.

"Jacob the bigamist? Jacob the weak?"

Patsy was quiet, looking off into space. Then she said, "Well, Jacob the something, anyway."

Twenty-two

Pru found herself alone in the new apartment for the first time ever.

Patsy was away at a yoga retreat in the Berkshires—a thirty-third-birthday present from Jimmy Roy, Pru, and their mother. Jimmy Roy had shown up earlier in the week to pick up Annali. They were going to stay at the beach house while Patsy was away. Pru had decided to give more hours to Phan's girlfriend, Chuckie, to work at peach, so that she could have some time to herself.

It was full-on spring in D.C., now. The tourists were arriving, to see the cherry blossoms. As Pru stepped out onto the balcony, her neighbors waved from their respective decks. Whoop was still a little freaked-out, but before the move Pru had gone to see Dr. Bond, who told her how to minimize the trauma. *Trauma.* She still had a hard time assigning words usually associated with Vietnam vets or burn victims to a being whose biggest challenge was which spot of sun to lie in. But she did what Dr. Bond suggested, and both Whoop and Jenny seemed minimally "traumatized." Anyway, they weren't tooling around the neighborhood in little wheelchairs, swearing at everyone.

She spent her day off arranging her bedroom, putting her clothes away, and unpacking the boxes that had been sitting there for weeks. When she was done, she fell asleep on the couch, next to an open window, where she could hear the neighborhood kids calling to one another. She woke up late and famished, and decided she'd just pop into the café for a sandwich. John had finally taken some of Lila's ideas about the menu to heart, and, although she'd hoped to be disappointed, Pru had become somewhat addicted to a particularly satisfying arugula sandwich.

She'd been avoiding John since telling him she was in love with him. She knew he usually left the café before nine, so she assumed it was safe. The girl behind the counter, who was new to Pru, was just handing her the bag that contained her sandwich when Ludmilla pushed through the swinging door to the kitchen, and she saw them. There, in front of the six-burner industrial-grade Viking stove, stood John, embracing a woman she knew instantly was Lila. Because it was her job to size up women's bodies, it registered that Lila was a luscious, curvy size ten, possibly even a twelve. She was wearing a stretchy top that showed off her curves, and a flowy skirt and sandals. She had fabulous curling hair that cascaded down her back. *Enviable* hair. The overall impression was of a salsa dancer. If she had come into Pru's shop, Pru would have reached for the red silk strapless with the black roses on it, hands down.

Lila held John's head in her hands as their foreheads pressed together. As Pru watched, the door reached the full extension of its swing, making a heartbeat-like sound, and started to swing shut. John looked up and, in the narrowing gap, their eyes met. The noise of the café fell away.

It was a fantastically timed moment. She could almost hear the sound of the door pushing the air as it moved. Like Elliott the crime novelist's prison-door sound: *Clink clunk.* A woman's chest opens up and her heart falls out. *Clink clunk.* Coming this summer, to a floor near you. Pru felt the wind leave her body in a rush.

"Hello?" the girl in front of her was saying. "Six twenty-five?" Clearly, it was her third or fourth repetition.

"Okay," Pru said, digging in her shoulder bag for her wallet. She still couldn't breathe. There was no little circular window in the swinging door to the kitchen, like such doors usually had, so she couldn't see them anymore. She pushed a ten at the girl and left without the change.

She stepped outside into a gorgeous spring night. Everyone was out, enjoying the weather. Her feet turned and took her in the direction of Malcolm X Park.

She tossed the arugula sandwich into the first trash can she came to, and although she wasn't wearing the right shoes for it, she began jogging. As she hit the park, she broke into a full run, and sprinted across the entire length of the grassy field to the stone wall where the park begins to slope down dramatically in a series of stone steps. She stood against the wall, panting. She'd come here with John, once, after they'd been dumped by their respective exes. That day had been a nine on the loneliness scale for both of them. *When do you think it'll end?* he'd said. And here she was, again. Without any kind of a scale that could register what she was feeling now.

She stood in front of the statue of Saint Joan of Arc for a while, hoping to gather courage from her. Joan was on horseback, and the statue's arm that would have been thrust in front of her was missing. Pru stood there, looking at the statue; then she sat down on a bench to cry. Except . . . nothing happened. She tried again to conjure up the image of John and his wife. Then she tried to imagine seeing them together at McKay and Bill's wedding, dancing, Lila's fabulous hair spilling out everywhere, while Pru stood against the wall, her own hair pulled tightly back in its unforgiving knot. Still, nothing, no tears, not even a sniffle. What was wrong with her? She was certainly miserable, sad, lonely. Brokenhearted. For longer than she ever had been in her life, and *not* getting used to it, either, like everybody kept promising. The tears simply wouldn't come. Had she lost her ability to cry? Well, maybe that wasn't so bad. She was sick to death of it, anyway. She stood up and walked home. She didn't cross to the other side of Columbia, but walked straight by the Korner. She'd thrown out her sandwich and still needed to eat. The souvlaki place was closed, but the Cluck-U was all lit up, outside and in. She hesitated for a second, looking at the garish bantam rooster, then pushed open the front door.

The inside was lit by strange yellow lighting, and an Indian man stood behind the counter, eager to take her order. She walked up to him, staring at the menu above his head. She could hear the sounds of bubbling oil coming from the kitchen. The only other person there was a woman in a bright turquoise sari with a baby on her lap. The baby's ears were pierced, and she wore a frilly headband. They both had incredibly sweet, open faces, and smiled at Pru as she placed her order.

While she was waiting for her "Clucker on a Bun," the woman with the baby and the man behind the counter began talking quietly. The man came around and picked up the baby and held her up in the air. His wife and child, Pru realized. The woman said something to him in a low tone. The man looked at Pru, shyly. They had probably put every cent they owned into the Cluck-U. To Pru, the establishment had been nothing more than an embarrassment, an affront to her satisfaction and well-being. The eyesore of her otherwise clean, upscale-tending street. To this couple, though, the Cluck-U was their entire future, the happiness and security of their child. It was her college tuition, the down payment for her house. They probably didn't even realize that its name was a crude pun. Maybe they thought of it as a happy name, childlike, funny. Maybe, in the country they were from, cigar-chomping roosters were considered sacred.

When her sandwich was ready the man put it in a paper bag. He folded the top of the bag over neatly and handed it to her, saying, "You are owner of the peach?" Pru nodded and smiled. There were some slips of paper on the counter and the man motioned for her to take them—coupons, she saw, for a free Coke with the purchase of a "Cheese Mutha Clucker." They looked as if he'd made them on a computer. She pictured him cutting each coupon out by hand.

"For the store," he said, then again, "For the peach." Then she understood. He wanted her to give out his coupons at her store. "Yes," she said, nodding and smiling, and she took the grease-splattered coupons. "Yes, yes, of course." The man's wife beamed at her, from behind the baby.

She felt sorry that she had wanted to throw rocks at the sign. Once a week, she promised herself, she would come and buy something, even if she ended up tossing it in the trash. Which, she thought, seeing the pool of grease on the bottom of the bag, wouldn't be a bad idea.

. . .

SHE DIDN'T CRY AT BILL AND MCKAY'S WEDDING, either. Her tasks as maid of honor and event coordinator kept her too busy for tears. As they spoke their vows in front of each other and the assembled group of friends and family, she kept her eyes on their faces, wanting to remember every second of this moment. They were at a B&B in Provincetown owned by three Finnish brothers, at least two of whom, Pru thought, were gay, though she couldn't really tell them apart. The Unitarian minister performed the service in the back parlor of the house. They were going to do it outside, in the garden, but the weather had turned cloudy and cool at the last minute. Bradley Bond, the pet therapist, was there. He sang "The Wedding Song" in a man's suit, and, later that evening, "Dim All the Lights, Sweet Darlin'" in a lovely, shimmering white dress. Somehow he looked perfectly right, both times, as at home in his linen trousers as in the three-inch platform heels.

It helped a great deal that John and Lila were no-shows. McKay, when they had a moment alone together, said that no explanation had been offered, but Pru knew why. John had decided to spare her. It gave her a bittersweet feeling, to think that he'd felt the need to protect her feelings. She still wasn't used to them being so entirely on display.

She came home from the weekend to an in-box full of chatty, descriptive e-mails from Patsy, still at her yoga retreat. She'd found an Internet café in town that enabled her to talk to Annali via webcam. She was having what she called a "life-changing" experience. She sounded so bubbly that, if Pru didn't know better, she'd say Patsy was getting more than her chakras realigned. If she didn't know better, and if McKay had been around to say that to.

But he was heading off with Bill for their two-week honeymoon in Italy.

Sitting at her desk, now in the new living room, Pru read the most recent e-mail from Patsy. Suddenly, an Instant Message window popped open. She saw the name on the screen: jowen32. Who is Jowen? she thought. Then her hands froze above the keyboard. Her computer pinged softly, as he sent each line of text:

The screen door slams
Mary's dress waves
Like a vision she dances across the porch
As the radio plays . . .

She couldn't breathe. The heat was rising in her face, her blood pounded in her ears. The next lines, she knew, were "Roy Orbison singing for the lonely, Hey that's me and I want you only."

My friend, he wrote, *where did you go?* Okay, so it wasn't going in that direction, then. She felt the heat drain from her face, and her heart rate stabilized.

Whoop, who hadn't been more than a yard away from her since she'd gotten back, jumped up and pushed his head under her hand for a scratching. John wasn't lonely, and he didn't want her only. With the memory of McKay and Bill standing up in front of God and the world to declare their love for each other fresh in her mind, Pru knew what she wanted. And it wasn't half-quoted Springsteen lyrics. She sat there for a minute longer, then closed the messaging window and turned off the machine.

Twenty-three

A week later, Patsy came home. She was, indeed, transformed. She was mellow, glowing, flexible, serene, contemplative. Blissed out. And, she announced, holding up the margarita Pru had just poured for her, she was pregnant.

They were sitting on the balcony, at a little green table Pru had purchased at the flea market in Georgetown. It was their first night out on the deck. To celebrate, Pru had made melted cheese tortillas and the pitcher of margaritas, pretty much the full extent of her culinary expertise.

Pru had brought up her glass in preparation for a toast. It froze there, stopped cold by Patsy's news. "You're *what*?"

"I know," Patsy said, smiling happily and leaning across the table to clink Pru's glass. "Are we fertile or what?"

"Who's we . . . Jimmy *Roy*?"

"I know, it's crazy. We just can't keep our hands off each other." She shrugged. "I guess it's a sign. He's a sexy little bastard, that's for sure."

"But . . . when did you even see him?"

"The night of the opening. Just the once, can you believe it? Oh, no, wait. Three times, technically—"

"Patsy!"

"I guess it must be some kind of biological imperative. You have to admit, we make amazing kids."

"You've been sleeping with him? And you didn't tell me?"

"Yeah, well, I thought it was just a sex thing. Besides, who's seen you to tell you anything?"

Patsy drank a huge mouthful of her margarita, and so did Pru. "Oh, that was good," Patsy sighed. "My last mouthful of alcohol for the next eight months."

"So, this is good?" Pru said, when she could talk again. "It's not just a sex thing? You're happy?"

"Yeah," Patsy said. "I can't tell you what it was like, finding out I was pregnant, then doing all that yoga. I was fucking blissed out, I'll tell you that."

"Annali's going to have a little sister! Or, I guess it could be a brother. Oh, she'll love it, don't you think?" Annali loved seeing the babies at the playground. She'd pat their heads and coo, "Oh, you cute li'l fella!"

Patsy smiled. "Let's hope for a sister," she said.

Pru was mentally scanning the apartment they'd just moved into, a month ago. "Oh my God, we've already outgrown this place!"

"And then there's Jimmy Roy," Patsy said, half closing her eyes.

"Him, too?"

"Yeah. We're going to see how it goes living together. He got into one of those midwifing programs he applied to. He can live here and commute. If it's okay with you, that is."

"Patsy, of course." Everything was moving so quickly. Everything except for her, rooted at the center of it all, unmoving, unchanging. Good ole Pru.

From somewhere inside Patsy's jeans came soft male voices intoning *"Om."* It turned out to be her cell phone, which she pulled from a pocket. "Hi, baby," she said into the phone, like the happy, sexy, pregnant woman that she was. "Yeah, I just told her." Her eyes flicked up to Pru's. "I miss you guys," she said. "When will you get here?" She stood up and went inside the apartment.

The leaves in the trees overhead made a dappled pattern of shadows on the table in front of her. A new baby! Already, she was making plans. They could move Annali into Pru's room, to make room for the nursery. She pictured billowy curtains, a tinkly mobile of stuffed animals, maybe an original Pooh theme. She imagined the baby's soft, newborn smell. Large, moist, alien eyes, blinking quietly in the morning sun. She saw it reaching up to grab her nose as she changed its diaper.

She drank her margarita. Did their mother already know? She would probably want to move in with them, too. Well, why not? Pru thought. She could get her to finally sell that house, and it would be so good for the girls to have her around. She finished Patsy's margarita, too, as Whoop came leaping through the door, followed by Jenny. Whoop took off and landed in Pru's lap, leaving the puppy to almost skitter off the edge of the deck.

She could feel her heart pound in her chest. She thought it had dropped out of her chest and onto the floor of John's café, but no. Here it was, pounding away to beat the band, threatening to leap out of her mouth and dance around the deck, with wild abandon and glee.

. . .

SHE WAS LOOKING UP LISTS OF BABY NAMES ON THE IN-
ternet (she was liking Hero, for a girl, and Gabriel, if it was a boy)
when the phone rang.

She picked it up and was surprised to hear John's voice. "I'm
downstairs, outside your apartment. Can I come up?"

She was wearing cheap jeans, a stretched-out T-shirt, and
underpants that rode up above the waistband of the jeans. Her
glasses, of course, and she'd just taken off all her makeup. If possible, Pru looked worse than she had the first night she met him,
in her bathrobe and slippers. Again, she remembered the exuber-
ant, oversexed hair of his wife. Well, what did it matter? "Sure,"
she said, and buzzed him in. She knew she couldn't go on avoiding him forever.

As she waited for him to walk up the three flights of stairs,
Patsy came out of her room.

"Was that Jimmy Roy?" she said, sleepily.

"No, John Owen. He's on his way up."

Patsy looked at her, suddenly wide awake. "Oh my God," she
said. "Pru."

Suddenly, Pru felt like there was a whole farmyard inside of
her body. Chickens, roosters, pigs, cows, and sheep, all braying
and jostling each other, trying to find room between her liver and
kidneys. She realized that her hands were shaking. For Pete's sake,
she told herself sternly, get it together!

"You don't have to say anything," Patsy was saying. "Just
breathe. That's all you have to do. Be in the moment, and breathe.
Think of your feet. They're rooting down into the earth. If you
don't know what to say, just think of your feet."

"What the fuck are you talking about?" Pru said.

Someone tapped lightly on the front door. Patsy said, "All right, then just go for a walk with him, or something."

Pru opened the door, and there he was. His smile was the first thing she saw. It was that big, shy, excited smile, the one that made her want to smile back. He was wearing a jacket over his T-shirt and jeans. He was holding an armful of flowers, a small, blue book—poems?—and a bottle of wine.

She backed away from the door, as if she'd opened it to a king cobra poised to strike.

"I waited a week," he said. "I hope that was long enough."

"I can't be your friend," Pru said, all in a rush. "I'm sorry, but I just *can't.*"

"No," said John, apparently confused. "I know."

"You do?"

Patsy had started laughing. "Pru!" she said. "Don't be so dense! Look in his *arms.*"

He gestured with the flowers, as if to say: For you. She opened her mouth to say something. And instead, she burst into tears.

"Oops," he said. "Uh-oh."

Her body shook with sobs so badly she couldn't see. Then she heard Patsy say, "Oh, for heaven's sake. John. Come on in."

Pru felt a chair against the back of her legs, and Patsy said, *"Sit."*

She sat. She just could not stop crying. It was insane. She was like Annali having a meltdown. She was feeling all the misery of the past few months, and—oh God, what *was* that? *Happy,* she thought. *Happy, happy.*

"I don't really want to be your friend, either," John said. He crouched down in front of her. She looked up at him, a hand covering her mouth and nose, which insisted on still crying. "It was really cool of you to try, though."

"Really?" she gasped, in this awful, shaky voice. "Not friends?"

"Not just friends," he said. "Not *just* friends."

"Oh," she said. "Thank God."

He smiled at her. Then he began to laugh. He tried to take her hands.

"Don't look at me," she said. "I'm a mess."

"Come on," he said at last. "Let's go for a walk."

AT THE FAR END OF MALCOLM X PARK, YOU CAN SEE ALL the city lights from the top of the stairs built into the side of a sloping hill. You can see all the way down to the Potomac, and beyond. It was the same view from her old apartment. John Owen reached over and took her hand.

They walked down the hill, stopping to sit on a stone bench that was set back inside a little hedge.

"I've missed you," he said.

"I've missed you, too."

"I hope I didn't wait too long. But I didn't want you to feel like I ran from her to you." He gave her a sheepish look. "I made myself wait a week. One whole, horrible week."

"What was with that IM? The 'Thunder Road' stuff?"

"My lame attempt at romancing you. I should have stuck to Dylan. Or Leonard Cohen."

"Did I break up your marriage?"

He shook his head. "No. Lila and I didn't need any help doing that."

"Are you sad?"

He nodded. "I'm sad. I'm happy, too. And excited. Is that okay?"

"Yeah, it's okay." Sad. She could work with that. She'd been sad before, too.

Suddenly there was so much to say, things she'd been wanting to tell him for so long that it didn't seem possible to get them all out fast enough.

"Patsy's pregnant," she said. "And that plumber whose number you gave me ripped me off. Oh, and do I need a certificate of occupancy?"

"No. Did you tell Carl I gave you his number?"

"It wasn't Carl. It was Ray."

He shook his head. "Ray's no good. You have to see Carl. It's not Jacob's, is it? Patsy's baby."

"Jimmy Roy's. They slept together the night of the opening, apparently. Carl's in Antibes."

He whistled. "You're kidding."

"Antibes?"

"Jimmy Roy."

"Did you notice? She's walking around like Eartha Kitt. All slinky and sexy. She's practically purring. She's happy, though. I can see it, she's really happy."

It was growing dark. *I'm scared,* she thought. "Hey," she said, pointing. "Is that the North Star?"

"Um . . . no. You have to look over there, toward the north. Did you ask to talk to Carl?"

"You didn't say I had to talk to Carl."

"I most certainly did."

"Are we dating now?"

"Well, I think we're just together. Is that okay? If we just be together?"

In response, she squeezed his hand.

"How is she? Lila?"

"Good. Okay. We got it all figured out. I'll have to buy her out of the business, but she's actually being very cool about it.

And listen, I want you to know—it was me who asked for the divorce."

Pru nodded. "I'm glad to know that. Oh! I was going to tell you about these weird-but-good cookies one of our customers makes. Chocolate chip–oatmeal, but get this—*salty*. She brought some in for us to try one day. You should think about selling them."

They talked about the new display she was planning for the front window, and what John would have in the pastry case tomorrow morning, and whether or not the water cooler she ordered would finally arrive. While they talked, softly, in the dusk, she thought about how, soon, they would walk back toward Columbia Road holding hands, and she wondered where they would spend the night. She thought about Kate and her new love, and if their new loves would like each other. The dark settled in around them, and she thought about Patsy's new baby, and Fiona's new baby, and all the new babies yet to come. Nadine *had* to come and live with them, now. A little shiver passed through her, and John pulled her closer to him, wrapping her arm around his back.

She couldn't wait to see what would happen next.

Acknowledgments

Thanks first and foremost to my beloved husband, Andrew, for defying all reason and common sense and believing in me every step of the way. Thanks to my families, of origin and in-lawism, for their love and encouragement and for being such damn funny people: Jim, Eileen, Paul, Leslie, Stephie, Gerry, and Lisa. I thank my faithful, whip-smart readers: Jamie, Reetie, Paulette, Anita, and Dana; the Worth Our Salt writing group, in Washington, D.C.: Eliza, Carollyne, Paula, and Anne; and the short-lived writing group in my living room: Marc, Frank, Aaron, and Cynthia, who were there to welcome Pru and Whoop into the world. My writing teachers, Lee K. Abbott, Rosellen Brown, and Jim Robison. Thanks to Art Silverman, Larry Massett, and Barrett Golding for getting my work on NPR. Thanks to the inestimable Gail Hochman, and to the patient, lovely, wise Sarah McGrath, and Sarah Stein, inestimable in her own right, at Riverhead. A hearty, caffeine-fueled thanks to Larry, April, and the rest of the crew at my refuge, the Arcadian Shop. Thanks to the best e-mail support group ever: Blobby, Morty, Jon San, and Ditto. Thanks to Dave and Lori for dinners and cheerleading, and to Cristina and Alisa, for taking over the love and care of my spawn in my absence; and thanks to the darling spawn themselves, the Peach and the Plum, for sharing their mommy with complete, fictitious strangers during their earliest, most formative years.

Without Gil, none of this would have happened.